Praise for the novels of Michelle Sagara

"First-rate fantasy.... Sagara's complex characterizations and rich world-building lift her above the crowd."
—#1 *New York Times* bestselling author Kelley Armstrong on The Chronicles of Elantra

"No one provides an emotional payoff like Michelle Sagara. Combine that with a fast-paced police procedural, deadly magics, five very different races and a wickedly dry sense of humor—well, it doesn't get any better than this."
—Bestselling author Tanya Huff on The Chronicles of Elantra

"Well-crafted... Readers will appreciate the complex plot and many returning faces in the vast cast of characters. This magical thrill-ride is a treat."
—*Publishers Weekly* on *Cast in Wisdom*

"Full to the brim of magic...beautiful and intricate...a breathtaking read."
—*Word of the Nerd* on *Cast in Wisdom*

"Extremely fun...[a] fast, entertaining ride full of snark and banter and excellent characters."
—*Tor.com* on *Cast in Flight*

"This is a fast, fun novel, delightfully enjoyable in the best tradition of Sagara's work. While it may be light and entertaining, it's got some serious questions at its core. I'm already looking forward to the next book in the series."
—*Locus* magazine on *Cast in Oblivion*

"Sagara writes with her usual fine attention to detail, tension, and character."

Also from Michelle Sagara and MIRA

The Chronicles of Elantra

Look for Michelle Sagara's next novel
available soon from MIRA.

THE EMPEROR'S WOLVES

MICHELLE SAGARA

mira

ISBN-13: 978-0-7783-0991-8

The Emperor's Wolves

Copyright © 2020 by Michelle Sagara

This edition published by arrangement with Harlequin Books S.A.

For questions and comments about the quality of this book, please contact us at
CustomerService@Harlequin.com.

Mira
22 Adelaide St. West, 40th Floor
Toronto, Ontario M5H 4E3, Canada
BookClubbish.com

Printed in U.S.A.

With thanks to Karina Sumner-Smith,
for daily check-ins and a high tolerance for
the unfortunate whining that sometimes accompanies them.

CHAPTER ONE

ELLUVIAN OF DANARRE DID NOT LIKE THRONE rooms.

For much of his life, throne rooms and audience chambers had been a grueling exercise in humiliation; humiliation was always the outcome when one had no power. His presence in a throne room was meant to emphasize that utter lack of power. He was called. He came. He stood—or knelt—at the foot of the platform that led to the raised throne.

There he had remained, while the disappointment of his lord made itself known.

There were significant differences between this throne room, this audience chamber, and the throne room of his youth. An act of war had given him a freedom he had never before possessed.

And the actor in that action occupied the current throne as a force of nature, uneasily caged by masks of civility and mundane governance. Elluvian had been announced; he had been given permission—or an order—to approach the Imperial Presence. His steps across the runner that covered worked stone were as loud as his breathing.

Before him sat the Eternal Emperor, Dariandaros of the Ebon Flight. Neither name had been used by any of the Emperor's subjects for centuries. Elluvian, however, remembered. The only freedom he had ever known had occurred because of war. At the end of the third war, the Dragon Emperor had demanded oaths of allegiance from each and every Barrani adult who had survived it and intended to live within the boundaries of the Empire.

Elluvian had offered his willingly. He had offered it without reservation. Had the Emperor demanded Elluvian swear a blood oath, a binding oath, he would have done so without hesitation. The Emperor did not demand his True Name. Anything else, he could live with. Nonbinding oaths were just words.

He knelt.

"Rise," the Emperor said. The undercurrents of his voice filled the vaulted ceilings above with a distinctly draconic rumble. Elluvian obeyed, meeting the Emperor's gaze for the first time; the Dragon's eyes were orange, but the orange was tinged with gold.

No discussion between Emperor and subject was private. The Imperial guard and the Imperial aides were omnipresent; an Imperial secretary or three were positioned by the throne to take notes where notes were necessary.

"Approach the throne."

Elluvian was aware that of all the Barrani—each forced to offer an oath of allegiance to the Emperor directly—only a handful were allowed to approach the throne. It was not considered, by most of his kin, an honor. Were any of those disapproving kin to be present, they would have obeyed regardless. Just as Elluvian did.

The Imperial guards stepped back.

"You look peaked, old friend," the Emperor said, when the guards were standing as far from the Emperor as they were willing to go.

"You did not summon me here to discuss my health."

"Ah, no. But I have been informed that I lack certain social graces, and it seems incumbent on me to practice."

Elluvian raised a brow. His eyes were blue; Barrani blue denoted many things. At the moment, he was annoyed. Annoyed and tired.

"Very well. The Halls of Law seem to be having some minor difficulty." When Elluvian failed to reply, the Emperor continued. "In particular, and of interest to you, the difficulty involves the Wolves." Of course it did. The Halls of Law were divided into three distinct divisions: the Hawks, the Swords, and the Wolves. The only division of relevance to Elluvian was the Wolves.

Elluvian exhaled. "Again."

"Indeed." The Emperor's eyes remained orange; the orange, however, did not darken toward red, the color of Dragon anger.

Elluvian bowed his head for one long moment. His eyes, he knew, were now the blue of anger and frustration. In a life considered, by the youthful Barrani and Dragon kin, long, failure was not the worst thing to happen to him. But consistent failure remained humiliating—and no Barrani wished their failures dissected by Dragons. He struggled to contain emotion, to submerge it.

In this, too, he failed.

"I have never understood why you wish to create this division of *mortal* Wolves. We have power structures developed over a longer stretch of time, and we have not descended to barbarism or savagery. Those who have power rule those who do not."

"That is what the animals do. Those with power rule those with less. We are not animals."

Elluvian's mood was dark enough, the sting of failure dragging it down in a spiral that had no good end. Humans, who comprised the vast majority of mortals within the Empire, were one step up from animals, with their unchanging, fixed eye colors, their ability to propagate, their short, inconsequential lives.

"I do not understand the Empire you are attempting to build. I have never understood it, and the centuries I have spent observing it have not surrendered answers." The admission of ignorance was costly.

For a man who professed not to want to rule by power, his form of communication was questionable. He commanded, and those who had survived the wars and sworn personal loyalty to the Emperor—most Barrani, given the sparsity of Dragons by that time—obeyed.

Elluvian had been summoned. The summons was, in theory, an invitation, but Elluvian was not naive. The oath of service had weight and meaning to both the Emperor who had demanded it and the man who had offered that vow.

Mortals were not a threat to either the Barrani or the Dragons, but many of the Imperial systems of governance—the Emperor's word—were most concerned with those very mortals. The Emperor had created the Halls of Law, with Swords and Hawks to police the mortals who vastly outnumbered those who rose above time and age. He had also created the Wolves.

"No," the Emperor replied, his eyes no more orange than

they had been when Elluvian had approached the throne at his command.

"Why did you want to create a division of men and women as assassins?"

"As executioners, Elluvian." A warning, there. "I am Emperor. My word is law. My judgment is therefore also law. They do not operate in secret; they are part of the Halls of Law."

"I do not understand your law, as you call it."

"No," the Emperor replied again, gracing Elluvian with a rare smile.

"You tasked me—notably not mortal—to find those suitable to serve as your Wolves. I have done this for decades. For longer."

"Yes."

"I have long believed that you have no sense of humor whatsoever."

"I do not find one useful or pragmatic."

"But clearly, you must—if a very black one. Why did you devolve this duty to me? Why do you continue to do so? I have clearly failed and failed again." There seemed to be no end to the probable failures; they stretched out into eternity in a grim, bleak act of humiliation.

"You are one of the few Barrani I have met in my long existence that I am willing—barely, and cautiously—to trust."

"Then let me be your Wolf; you need no other."

"Perhaps the word 'cautious' does not mean the same thing between our peoples. Am I using the Barrani incorrectly?"

Elluvian's snort did not contain smoke, as the Emperor's often did. "We do not, and have never, seen eye to eye in any discussion that involves your Halls of Law or the mortals it is meant to both employ and protect. I feel that you are merely changing the paradigm of power, of who has power, among the mortals. I cannot see this change affecting the rest of us at all.

"Should you merely send me—or someone like me—"

"There is no one like you among your kin."

Elluvian did not wince. "If you send me, I will kill *at your order*. I understand that you consider these mortals part of your hoard; I will not harm your hoard, except as you command. But I would be vastly more efficient than your fledgling mortal Wolves. When you—or one of your kin—sneezes, mortals die. That will not happen to me. If you wish my death, the outcome is not in question—but it would take real effort on your part."

"All of this is true."

"You have always been both humorless and pragmatic."

That dredged a brief grimace from the Emperor. "Not one of my kin would consider my ambitions here to be pragmatic."

"A fair assessment. I withdraw my comment. But surely within this plan of yours, there is room for some pragmatism?"

The Emperor had bowed his head—not to Elluvian, but rather, to thought. It was a thought that Elluvian did not fully understand, although he had once been told that he was capable of it, with time and effort. "This will be their world, this Empire of mine."

Elluvian had his doubts.

"They will labor and build the lives that they will live; there is no other way."

"Then let *them* choose."

"I have not forced mortals to become a Wolf; no more have I forced them to become Swords or Hawks. They have a choice, and the choice will not be coerced. If they decline, they are free to walk out of the Halls of Law.

"But choosing who is offered the duties of a Wolf, as you have learned, is…complex. Wolves will be asked to kill, yes.

To kill at my command, yes—but to kill. Such a death does not bypass the judicial system—I *am* the judicial system. My word *is* law.

"It cannot have escaped your notice that among your kin there are those who enjoy the exercise of power."

Elluvian nodded.

"There are, among your kin, those who enjoy, if not killing, then the slow death of their enemies. Ah, no, their victims."

Silence.

"There will surely always be such proclivities among the mortals as well. It is imperative that such people not become Wolves, or the entire project will be a failure."

"As it has been."

"It has not all been failure," the Emperor replied.

"If every passing day does not result in failure, failure is the end state. The latest difficulty is a telling example."

"Yet before yesterday, the Wolves were exactly what they should be."

"Clearly, the difficulty was greater than a simple *yesterday*."

The Emperor nodded. "Failure does not generally please me," he finally said. "We have built the Wolves, and they have served their function."

"Until yesterday."

"Or forty years ago. Or seventy. Or just over a hundred. One day, no matter how disastrous, does not destroy the years in between." The Emperor raised a hand as Elluvian opened his mouth. "I will not release you from this duty."

"I do not even fully understand this duty. It has been *centuries*, your majesty, and I am possessed of no better understanding than I was on the first day you made this my duty."

"And you believe this is why you have failed? You believe that a different person could create Wolves that would never fail, never falter?"

Silence.

"You are wrong. And among the Barrani I have met, you are one of the few I believe might eventually understand what I wish this Empire to become."

"The Wolves are individuals; they are not politicians. They are not powers. What lesson of value do you expect me to learn?"

The Emperor shook his head.

"You desire me to continue to recruit your Wolves."

"It is what I desire, yes. It is also what I command."

Elluvian bowed.

"Even for you, Helmat, this is in poor taste."

Helmat Marlin, the Lord of Wolves, looked up from his paperwork to see the Barrani man lounging against the frame of what had once been an office door. The large splinters and chunks of wood that had constituted that door had been mostly cleared. The door had not, however, been replaced. Given the Wolflord's mood, replacement would not take long.

It was not the lack of door—or its attendant frame—that was in poor taste. Helmat didn't require a door to keep his various underlings away when privacy was mandatory. No, it was the head—absent the rest of a body—that occupied a prominent position on the desk at which he was working.

The Wolflord, as he was colloquially called by the various people who served in the Halls of Law, was a large man. He was possessed of one striking, almost defining visible scar, and a host of lesser scars; the former cut a line across his face, broken by the thrust of his jaw. It had paled to near-white with age.

"If you'd prefer, you can be the one to file the paperwork and meet with the Emperor to explain the difficulties of the past few days."

Elluvian motioned to the desk. "It's my duty to find replacements for the two Wolves we've lost. Seeing the head of one of them on display in your office is not likely to encourage anyone to join."

Helmat shrugged. "It's enchanted. It doesn't smell."

"The blood does."

"Is that metaphorical?"

"Only if you have a mortal sense of smell. At the least, get your door replaced. I do not want to have to remove splinters every time I pass through what remains of it."

Helmat snorted. "You're Barrani," he said, as if that explained everything.

"What happened?"

Helmat had never been particularly good with words. He glanced, once, at Elluvian, but did not hold his gaze. "I didn't die. He did." The words were accompanied by a grimace more suited to a discussion of mosquitoes rather than people.

"I assume Renzo was attempting to ensure that things went the other way."

"I didn't ask."

"The door?"

"Was closed." *Closed*, in the Wolflord's office, had a different weight, a different meaning.

"Was he on the inside or the outside of that closed door?"

"Inside. En—is this necessary?"

"He was my student, just as you were. It pains me to see his head used as a paperweight."

"Does it?"

Elluvian smiled. It was a Barrani expression; sharp, cold. "What do you think?"

"I think one day you'll tell me why you ever agreed to serve the Eternal Emperor. How is Rosen?"

"I do not believe she will be engaged in ground hunts in the near—or far—future."

Helmat did not curse; he seldom did when Elluvian's appraisal matched his own. "We're down a Wolf." Renzo was clearly no longer considered a Wolf.

They were down two, but Elluvian did not correct Helmat. In his current mood it would be highly unprofitable.

"Who do you have for me?"

Elluvian had, three times in the past centuries, attempted to change the recruitment procedures of the Wolves. He had failed each of those times. Elluvian did not technically or legally command the Wolves, but he found them. Scouted them. Often trained them. Helmat Marlin, current Lord of Wolves, had final say; not all of those Elluvian brought into the office had been accepted into the pack.

But all of them had had, in Elluvian's opinion, the raw ability to become Wolves and to survive it.

"One possible candidate."

"Bring them in."

This was, of course, easier said than done. Helmat was a Wolf of several decades; he understood what *possible* meant in this context.

Elluvian did not generally seek Wolves from the comfortable strata of human society. There were always exceptions; the current Wolflord had come from an older—for mortals—family, and his father was what passed for nobility. Had Elluvian been aware of his family and parentage when he had first approached the younger Helmat, he would never have offered him the job. And that would have been a mistake. He could see that clearly now—but decades had passed, and he had seen Helmat's full measure in the interim.

The Emperor wanted soldiers.

The Wolves, however, were not soldiers. The Emperor's nomenclature preference aside, the Wolves in general were considered assassins by much of the populace.

In the view of the Barrani, the differences between the two, soldier and assassin, were slight and would be considered negligible. One killed on command. The other also killed on command. The difference would be in the small details: the soldiers congregated; the assassins did not. Where an army might be met with the forces of another army, the assassin was free to come and go as competence and strategic planning allowed.

Mortals seldom considered the two to be the same. Helmat, in spite of his experience and knowledge, did not. But Helmat appeared to understand what the Emperor desired of the Wolves—an understanding that continued to elude Elluvian.

The bare bones of it, however, were clear.

Find someone who might be molded into a soldier who could—and did—kill on command. Ah, no, not soldier—executioner. The Eternal Emperor had those: men who saw that death sentences were carried out, both cleanly and quickly. The Emperor did not call the Wolves his assassins; he called them his executioners. His mobile executioners.

There was no shortage of mortals who could, and did, kill. No shortage of Barrani who could, and did, either. But the Emperor had decided, for reasons that made sense to none of the Immortals of Elluvian's acquaintance, that the general formation of the power structure that Immortals understood was not allowed to occur within his Empire naturally.

In the Emperor's Empire, power was not to be the sole measure of worth. There was right, there was wrong, and laws laid out which action belonged in which category. They seemed arbitrary to Elluvian, an echo of the systems around which the Dragons and the Barrani built their societies. Right and wrong simply meant: angers the Emperor or does not anger the Emperor—the person in power.

The Emperor, however, denied that this was the intent.

Elluvian was angry. He had felt low-level irritation—a mixture of resignation and anger—since he had entered the Imperial presence; it had grown steadily as he had reached the offices the Wolves occupied in the Halls of Law.

To see the head of Renzo displayed on the desk of the Wolflord had been something of a surprise, and not a pleasant one. Displaying the dead was not something the Barrani themselves were above—but in general, the display was more tasteful, less immediately raw. There were better ways to make a point.

Renzo's failure was not unexpected. If Helmat was Wolflord, he was not an open book; he could be both jovial and deadly as the occasion demanded, and his ability to deal with emotional fragility was almost nonexistent. No, what frustrated Elluvian was Renzo's decision. Observed pragmatically, Renzo had nothing at all to gain by Helmat's death. He would not become Wolflord.

Those who served as Wolves required two things: loyalty to the Emperor and his Wolves, and a complete lack of attachments outside of that. No children, no family. Where secondary attachments existed, blackmail and extortion also existed. Some men and women could accept threats to family as the consequence of their duty. Most, however, could not. In the end, if forced to endure it by that sense of duty, something in them broke.

Elluvian wondered what had broken Renzo—assuming that anything had.

He was dead. No answers would, therefore, be forthcoming, which was the second reason that Elluvian was angry. He could not gather that information in any efficient way;

he must investigate as if he were a Hawk, which did not suit him in any fashion. Helmat was unlikely to seek the Hawks or their aid; the death was an internal matter.

Rosen's injuries had all but ensured she would never hunt at the Emperor's pleasure again; she was willing to work in the office and willing to train those who could. That left the ranks all but unmanned. Mellianne was, in Elluvian's opinion, skilled but not yet fully come into the wisdom that might allow her to survive particularly difficult encounters. Jaren was the only functional Wolf because Helmat did not hunt.

The Wolflord never did.

This had not always been the case, but trial and error had made clear to Elluvian that the presence of the Wolflord in the office was a necessity. Hunts were, by their very nature, long and often complex affairs; it was not simply a matter of assigning a death and a "reasonable" completion time.

Mellianne was not yet ready, and even were she, she disliked Jaren. She disliked Elluvian as well, but he expected that; affection of any kind was barely part of her functionality at this point. She was, however, good at what she did, and it did not seem to change her markedly. If she hated or despised people as deeply as she sometimes professed, she could nonetheless *do something* about the worst of them. That was the lever that could be pushed: she was no longer helpless.

But her contempt for the helpless was a counterpressure that he had not fully been able to dislodge. Power, and the desire for power, were the province of the living. Even the beasts sought power and supremacy. The balance between feeling powerful and feeling powerless was a gray area. The path from powerless to powerful defined a mortal. Elluvian did not understand the inner workings of most such journeys.

His experience, much of it bitter, had taught him that it was the journey itself that created an Imperial Wolf. Those who stepped on the wrong path, traveled the wrong byway, ended up as a head on the desk of the Lord of Wolves. He had not lied; he found the presence of the head there distasteful. It was, in its entirety, an accusation of failure.

Jaren was older now; younger than Helmat, but older than Mellianne and Rosen. Rosen's injuries, Rosen's lack of suitability, were a fact of life. But she had been an excellent Wolf. The life expectancy of the Wolves was short. Her injuries had probably extended hers into the foreseeable future. She would be bound to a desk. Jaren would train her to take on the tasks of organization and reporting, and Jaren would probably return to the hunt.

This, too, was not to Elluvian's liking. Jaren had once been his hawk. Helmat had been his merlin. Rosen had been his eagle. Hunting birds, all.

And perhaps because that was his personal metaphor, it was natural that they should fly, and natural that one or two, tasting the freedom of the sky and the imperative of that hunt, not return. Perhaps that was why the Emperor had called them Wolves and not birds of prey.

Elluvian could not understand why the name Hawks had been given to the division that was largely investigative; that would not have been his choice of name. Swords, though, he considered apt. It was, however, the tabard of the Hawks he now searched for as he walked through the streets of Elantra.

Ah, he thought. There.

CHAPTER TWO

AN'TEELA WAS A LEGEND IN THE BARRANI HIGH
Court. As with all such legends, gossip and myth had conspired
to obscure fact. Elluvian could not transcribe every word he
had heard about her unless he had a mortal month or more
and an endless supply of both ink and paper. What he believed
of what he had heard would be shorter.

He could, however, attest to the truth of one of the more
scandalous rumors: An'Teela walked the streets of the mortal
city wearing the tabard of the Imperial Hawk. By her side,
likewise attired, strode a man Elluvian had little cause to recognize; Tain of Korrin was not a Lord of the High Court.

He had been drawn to investigate An'Teela because he did
not understand the game she now played. There had been little bad blood between Elluvian and An'Teela, but not none;
it was impossible to be a member of the High Court without
giving offense, however subtle, to someone. An'Teela could
be extremely subtle. It was not, however, required.

He saw that she did not wield *Kariannos* in the city streets.

She did not, in fact, carry a sword at all. The Barrani who served the Halls of Law had been given the wooden clubs that characterized the Hawks, and she carried that, along with the tabard. It was not a risk that Elluvian had expected her to take. He understood that *Kariannos* was not a weapon meant for keeping peace. It had one purpose.

In Barrani terms, she was newly come to the Hawks. In mortal terms, she was not. If her intrusion into the Halls of Law had caused political difficulty—and no doubt it had, for An'Teela—she was nonetheless here, and content, or so it appeared, to abide by the mortal hierarchy that the Eternal Emperor had created.

A game, he thought. Or perhaps she was simply bored. Boredom would carry the day for a time—perhaps a decade. Elluvian himself might have considered it novel to be a Hawk for a small time. He found it vexing to be a Wolf, but he had been part of the Halls of Law for far longer than boredom would otherwise justify.

Boredom, however, remained a problem, and to alleviate it, he often spied on An'Teela. The information—should any useful information arise—would be of value, and he might trade it for information he required in turn.

He had been unprepared for the sight of An'Teela with a mortal child.

The girl was younger than Mellianne had been when he had first caught sight of her and younger than Mellianne was now, but in some fashion, there was a spark of similarity between the two. He might have approached that child in a handful of years, might have offered her what he had offered Mellianne.

But the girl was clearly under An'Teela's figurative wing, which Elluvian found fascinating in and of itself. While she remained ensconced there, Elluvian would not approach her. He would not dare.

Records in the Halls of Law existed for each Hawk, Sword, and Wolf. Access to the Records of the Wolves was restricted to the Wolves, specifically three of the Wolves. The Emperor, of course, had access to everything should he desire it; to Elluvian's knowledge, that was never.

Access to the Hawks and the Swords consisted of access to the reports they had personally lodged, and the reports that referenced them. There were no logs for the child that accompanied An'Teela; no references to her in the Records reports that An'Teela had either made or had been referenced in. The sergeant in charge of the branch of Hawks she served, however, was notoriously slow at such logging. He would have a word with the Emperor about this dereliction of duty.

Though there was one thing of wonder about the child. An'Teela was taking interest in a mortal.

"Why are you interested in the Barrani Hawks? Worried that you won't be special?" Helmat had asked, a half grin robbing the words of obvious challenge.

"No. It is a child's desire to be special, and I have—unlike many of my kin—survived childhood and escaped it."

"There are many men and women who would find that observation offensive."

"There are many who find the weather offensive."

Helmat uttered three words, and the mirror display—technically Elluvian's mirror—showed the Wolflord the whole of Elluvian's current research. His posture and tone changed. "That is not under the Wolves' jurisdiction."

"No. It wouldn't be. The Wolves wouldn't understand the significance."

"En."

Elluvian turned from the mirror toward the titular Lord

of Wolves. Helmat stood his ground; no one else would have dared. "I was against the hiring of Barrani Hawks."

Helmat nodded. "The decision was not yours to make. They're not Wolves."

Elluvian was surprised by the information he had unearthed: the girl had the marks of the Chosen. He better understood An'Teela's almost shocking attachment.

The girl did not appear to understand the significance of those marks. The Emperor did. The Dragon Court did. And An'Teela had come to court to lay claim—of kinship, of friendship—to the child. As had several of the Hawks, although the girl was far too young to be employed as a Hawk.

The Emperor had wanted her dead.

He was Emperor; he was ruler. The girl should be dead. She was demonstrably still breathing, and she remained under the protection of the intimidating and ferociously competent An'Teela—a woman who had killed the head of her line, her own father, and then refused to take that line's name, rejecting the whole of the life she had been expected to lead. Teela was the name of her new line. She had not offered to take the name of her mother's family. To do so, she would have had to push out the current head of that family. Clearly she felt more respect for her mother's kin than her father's.

Teela had always been a mystery to Elluvian—and dangerous mysteries were best kept at a safe distance while one observed, noting weaknesses that might, if necessary, come into play.

He knew the child's name: Kaylin Neya. He knew nothing else, and the name itself had come to him only because he had perfectly functional ears. The girl had a temper. She was prickly. She was, however, trying to *fit in* with An'Teela— whom she called Teela.

Ah, but he knew this one. She did not want to disappoint

An'Teela. She was, conversely, certain that she would be nothing but a disappointment. He had seen this behavior often enough that he was surprised he had not immediately recognized it for what it was. But he associated it with training. The child was too young—by law—to be a Hawk. Yet she was clearly involved in Hawk business. She was a curiosity.

It was his natural curiosity, then, that led him to the boy.

If Elluvian had noticed An'Teela—and the girl—first, it had taken some time to notice the boy. That both intrigued and annoyed him; he was a Barrani tracker. He should have been aware of the boy instantly, for the boy was intent in some fashion on the same quarry Elluvian himself was. He was tracking An'Teela.

Elluvian might have excused his lack of observation; might have said it arose because the streets were full of mortals in all shapes, all sizes. Mortals were trivial; he might just as easily fail to notice one rabbit in a colony of rabbits. But that would have been a lie; his pride was pricked. As none but he was aware of this minor failure, he did not attempt to justify it.

He had overlooked the young man.

The young man's clothing was the clothing of a subsistence thief. It was poor, but some elements were in better repair than others; he had boots, although they had seen better years. His hair was unkempt; some effort had been made, but it was wild and snarled in the back. It would be much better cut and tended, but most things that grew were. His appearance would have been both masterful and impressive had any of it been a deliberate choice. Elluvian was certain it was not.

How long had the boy followed An'Teela? Why had he taken that risk?

He might have told the boy that this was not in the best interests of survival, but the young man appeared to understand this. He kept a good distance. He tracked An'Teela during the hours of city daylight in which the streets would be busy enough that An'Teela would feel constrained by the tabard she wore.

He did so frequently.

Given his clothing and his demeanor, he did not appear to belong to one of the gangs in the warrens, but there was a sense of desperation about him.

Elluvian had time, and time unfolded, but this boy, over the two months that Elluvian had paid attention, did nothing. If he had sold the information he had received simply by observing An'Teela, it had not altered his circumstances.

To Elluvian's surprise—which annoyed him, because surprise implied a lack of knowledge, a failure to anticipate—the boy who followed An'Teela at a safe distance did not look, often, at An'Teela. No. It took some weeks for Elluvian to be certain that the young man's target was not the Barrani Lord or even her attendant, but her adopted fledgling.

Elluvian watched the young man, but the young man made no effort at all to speak with the girl; he made no effort to communicate. Doing so in An'Teela's presence would be exceedingly unwise, of course; the young man was not a fool. But the young man made no attempt to contact the girl at all. And she was not always by An'Teela's side.

He appeared to watch out of concern; he seemed to relax, marginally, after he had been tailing them for a while, as if he desired the simple sight of An'Teela's young companion. It was An'Teela he didn't trust. But Elluvian understood, watching the unpredictable Lord of the High Court, that she meant Kaylin no harm. Would allow no harm to be done to her.

The boy's understanding of that truth appeared to take longer, but it did settle. He followed less frequently, but he would appear in the crowded flow of mortals from time to time.

Today was no different.

Ah, no. Today would *be* different. The Wolves had need of a recruit, and the youth had shown skill at both eluding detection and following his quarry, sight unseen. Certainly, on a different field, he would not have escaped An'Teela's notice, but he was one of a dozen mortals—or more—in the immediate vicinity.

In his condition, age was hard to estimate; he might be younger and worn by life on the streets, or older. He had some basic skills that Mellianne had once lacked, but the rest? Elluvian was uncertain. Eight decades past, he might have been irked to be forced, yet again, to start over, but he was now resigned to it. Even had he been completely successful in his choices those decades past, he would still be required to start over. And over. And over. Mortals did not last.

He was drawn from his thoughts and deliberations by a mortal shout; it was not the type of cry that surprise or panic raised. Inebriation, yes. The poor fool appeared to be attempting to pick a fight with the Hawks. The streets did not empty, but the flow of traffic changed almost instantly: passersby both slowed and moved to the sides of the street. The drunk man did not appear to notice.

Ah, no, he had. "What are you looking at? Hey!"

His belligerence caused the people observing to compress further, but they did not feel threatened. Hawks were in the street. There was only so much damage this angry, drunk man could do before the Hawks intervened. And given that the Hawks appeared to be his target, they felt safe enough watching the drama unfold, as if it were a play performed for their entertainment. If they were wrong, they would pay; Elluvian did not feel any responsibility for the consequence of their choices.

What drew his attention was An'Teela. She ordered Kaylin, by name, to *stay out of it*. The girl had apparently managed not to hear the words—and it was possible, given her expression, that this was genuine, if appalling. An'Teela, however, did something extraordinary.

She dropped the flat of her palm across the top of the mortal girl's head. An'Teela's companion moved in to deal with the fool who wished to aggravate the Hawks, as if their tabard gave the drunkard immunity to Barrani.

Elluvian turned his attention to the young man he had been observing. A knife flashed in the youth's hand; the whole of his body tensed as he bent into his knees. His eyes scanned the crowd, flicking from side to side; they returned, always, to the girl.

Elluvian managed to reach the youth's side before the boy could—as it appeared he intended—move toward the mortal girl currently restrained by the Barrani Hawk. It was not as simple as it should have been; the boy was quick—he made use of any possible opening in a crowd through which a certain stillness had expanded, like rings in liquid will when a stone is dropped through its surface. He did not pause or stop but looked now for the advantage that the crowd might give.

Elluvian caught the boy's knife wrist, but in order to do so, he had to step into, step through, the shadows cast by the unfortunately high sun. The tiny, tiny ripple of magic its use caused would have been beneath the notice of most of his kin. Most of his kin, however, were not An'Teela, and she froze instantly.

"Kaylin."

Something in her tone—the word was softer and shorn entirely of expression—finally caused the girl to freeze. An'Teela lifted the hand that held the girl more or less in place and turned to scan the crowd while her partner dealt with the much noisier, much uglier mortal foolish enough—or drunk enough—to tangle with Barrani.

Elluvian held his position, but his grip around the young man's knife wrist tightened. He was not terribly surprised to see a second knife join the first—the second knife, now wielded in the free hand. "Unwise, boy. I am unarmed, and you now carry two knives. Should you attempt to use one to injure me, you will—of course—fail to do so. In order to preserve your life, I will be forced to break one, or both, of your arms. It will, given the presence of two weapons, both yours, be entirely legal.

"I wish to speak with you. If you attempt to stab me and flee, I will break one of your legs. Anger me further, and I will break it in such a way that your future mobility is not guaranteed. Do you understand?"

The young man sheathed the left-hand dagger without apparent effort. But his eyes flicked, once again, to the mortal and her two Barrani companions.

"You are concerned about the mortal girl that An'Teela calls Kaylin?"

The boy's arm tensed once again.

He did not answer. Would not, Elluvian thought. This was a different type of rebellion. Against his better judgment, he found himself saying, "You do not understand what you have seen. That Hawk is An'Teela. Your mortal quarry ignored the first command An'Teela uttered—and among our kin, there would be no second command. If An'Teela not only accepted insubordination, but also condescended to touch—without intent to harm—the mortal girl, that girl is safe. She is safe from anything that would be incapable of *quickly* killing An'Teela and her companion.

"And boy, An'Teela is among our best. There is very, very little that could threaten that child at the moment. And you, with your mortal dagger, are not among those things. Who is that girl to you?"

He again failed to answer; merely looked down the bridge of his nose to the place where their two arms were joined. "I wish to speak with you," Elluvian said again.

"About?"

"I have no interest in the child. It was not the girl I was following."

"It wasn't the Hawks, either."

"You are observant. Good. The Hawks, at the moment, are irrelevant to me. The girl would have been beneath notice."

"What do you want?" The young man waited.

Elluvian smiled. He released the young man's wrist. The young man remained stationary; he met, and held, Elluvian's gaze. The altercation that had caused the Hawks to pause had apparently ended; foot traffic once again resumed. So, too, the more cumbersome traffic of wagons, carts, carriages.

"I am considering offering you employ. I am, however, undecided."

"Not interested."

"No? A pity." He smiled. Nothing about the smile was friendly; it was not meant to comfort.

The young man shrugged. He was not so sanguine that his gaze did not flicker, briefly, to the backs of the Hawks. He made no attempt to follow them or otherwise draw their attention to his possible predicament. Interesting.

"Who *is* the girl to you?"

The young man shrugged again, as if the shrug was more eloquent than he could otherwise be. And then, before Elluvian could continue, the boy vaulted backward—and onto the edge of a wagon. Given the condition of the road, it was unlikely the driver would notice the momentary weight.

Elluvian smiled; his smile had edges. He did not immediately pursue—there was no challenge, no test, in that. He merely folded his arms and waited as the boy disappeared from the wagon, melting into an alley. *Run, boy. Run. If you can evade me for an hour, we will talk.*

CHAPTER THREE

IN THE END, TO ELLUVIAN'S SURPRISE, THE BOY evaded capture for almost two. He had given the boy a sporting chance, a decent head start; the boy had, of course, taken it and made the most of it. But his most and the "most" of the majority of citizens in this sprawling, messy city were not the same.

When the youth finally came to a resigned stop, he was not wielding weapons. His hands were empty, his arms by his sides. He didn't appear to be exhausted. He had more flight in him; he had chosen to preserve the energy necessary to face what had become clear to him was inevitable.

"Were you trained," Elluvian told his quarry, "you might have lost me."

"You gave me a head start."

Ah. "Yes. Yes, I did."

"So this is a game to you."

"I am Barrani. Most of what we do is a game of one sort or another."

The boy's nod was curt but decisive. "You're not a Hawk."

"No."

The young man's expression shifted. "You weren't following them."

Ah. "I was curious about An'Teela. Among the Lords of the High Court she is…unusual. I assumed you had been paid to follow her and to report on her activities. But you weren't. You weren't following An'Teela at all. You were following the child that she keeps by her side."

Silence.

"You understand that those Barrani *are* Hawks, and even if they were to detain the girl, they would be extremely unlikely to harm her?"

More silence, but this one was heavily saturated in skepticism.

"Regardless, your ability to interfere while wielding two pathetic short daggers of questionable manufacture is less than zero. Ah, no. Your ability to *productively* interfere. In the best possible case for you, they would simply break your arm. In the worst case, they would break your arm and deposit you in jail."

He shrugged.

"Neither of these outcomes would be of any aid to that child should she require aid."

Silence, but the texture of that silence shifted. "Maybe," he said, "they'd just kill me. I think—I think that would make her happy. Maybe it would free her."

Elluvian stared at the young man's bent head. His hair was dark and unruly; his skin was likewise a shade of gray that implied his living conditions involved the outdoors. There were those who made a home near the various bridges that crossed the Ablayne, but it was not a safe abode for the mortal.

His own safety, however, did not appear to be his primary concern. Or perhaps his concern at all. "Who is she, boy?"

Silence. But the young man closed his eyes, shook his head. There was a subtle shift in the line of his shoulders; they bent in, as if at the gravity of a memory or a history he would not put into words.

Elluvian said, once again, "I wish to offer you employ."

"I don't need it."

"Don't you? Most mortals need food, and you live in Elantra, not the forests or the villages beyond its borders. Here, everything is owned and claimed; there, you might forage and feed yourself. You are, if I am not mistaken, a petty thief. But you are whole, healthy. Do you spend time in the warrens?"

"No."

"May I ask why?"

"Can't stop you."

"No." Elluvian exhaled. "What I ask of you would not, in any sense of the word, be illegal. I do not require petty thugs; did I, I would hunt in the warrens. Mortal petty thugs are all but irrelevant to me, to my kin."

"What job?" The youth asked, after a significant pause.

Yes, Elluvian thought. There were trials and tests that the boy would have to overcome. "How much do you know about the Halls of Law?"

The silence was different. The young man could shutter his expression, control it, force the lines of his face to give nothing away. The lines of his body, however, he had not yet mastered; the drop and rise of shoulders, the tightening of arms, of hands, the shift of stance, the slight bend of knee.

"You want me to work in the Halls of Law."

"You would need to submit to a more extensive interview, but yes."

"What kind of interview?"

Clever boy. Elluvian smiled. "You won't like it."

His shrug implied that there was nothing on this earth he expected to enjoy.

"Tell me, what do you know of the Wolves?"

★ ★ ★

"Have I ever been mistaken?"

"Define *mistake*." Helmat's glare fell, rather more pointedly than necessary, upon his new desk ornament. That, Elluvian thought, would have to go. On the other hand, Helmat was still angry. The Wolflord folded his arms and now leaned into them, placing more of his weight and his imposing presence— for a mortal, of course—onto the desk, rather than away from it.

"He was a competent Wolf. The Emperor approved of his ability to carry out the executions demanded by Imperial writ. In the history of the Wolves, he is not the only opera- tive who decided that he could, perhaps, be more effective than the current lord."

"Murder is still illegal. Unless there's a secret writ of execu- tion given to my operatives, my death would disqualify him from ever holding that position. Was there?"

"Was there what?"

"A writ."

"I wish you would not waste my time, Helmat."

Helmat's grin broadened. It remained both cold and sharp. "That's not the way it would work, is it?"

Elluvian lifted his gaze to the ceiling, as if beseeching a nonexistent god for patience. "What did I say?"

"I can't remember. However, it seems germane to point out that we do not always get what we want. I certainly did not want a very competent operative to destroy my door, kill one of his comrades and injure another, forcing her retirement from active duty. There are very few who serve the Wolves who die of happy old age.

"I do not expect to be one of them. But I would prefer— vastly prefer—that the figurative blade that ends my life be wielded by outsiders."

"Or me, Helmat?"

"Or you. That's generally how we retire, isn't it?" The Wolflord's grin was sharp; his eyes were bright. Too bright for a mortal.

"I would be Wolflord in your stead—in all of your steads— had the Emperor ever allowed it." It wasn't an answer. But Helmat had been one of the most successful of Elluvian's students. "You understand why he does not."

Helmat did. He didn't, at the moment, care.

"I do not understand your continuing anger."

"The Barrani expect betrayal."

"Indeed. Where we are not powerful enough, not knowledgeable enough, not cautious enough, we will be betrayed. It is not generally considered a personal slight. If it engenders anger, the anger is pointed inward. We gave our enemies the opening that they then exploited."

"I have some of that anger as well."

"Yes, but that anger does not drive you to put someone's head on your desk as a paperweight, and I do not believe it will help in our recruitment. We are, as you have pointed out, dangerously short on functional operatives at the moment, and I believe this one—even in your current mood—is likely to meet with your approval."

"Why?"

"Instinct."

Helmat relaxed both his arms and his position. He did not speak. The same instinct had, of course, found Renzo. It had, as Helmat had implied, found every Wolf, every Wolflord, including those who had died by Elluvian's hands. That he had found far more, in the past few decades, who did not break Imperial Law, was irrelevant to Helmat at the moment. One mistake, this new, was too many.

"Betrayal is only possible if you are unwise. I have told you this. Trust is folly." When Helmat continued in silence, Elluvian exhaled. "There are Barrani who feel as you feel—and some have spent centuries planning their revenge. Some have even survived it. Betrayal is met with death, where death can possibly be achieved.

"But when they achieve that death—and clearly, you have already done so—it is done. It remains a dire lesson, a warning against foolishness, but it no longer engenders bitter rage. You were meant to die. You survived. Your enemy did not. It is unlikely that your enemy had supporters among your Wolves, or things would have played out in a different fashion."

"I don't understand why he did this," Helmat said. He was now staring at the magically preserved head, as if by doing so, he could demand answers and receive them. "If I understood why and how, I would be better prepared should it happen again. Tell me, En, if I fall foul of the Emperor, will you kill me?"

"I would execute you, yes. And frankly, it would do far less damage to the Halls of Law, or at least this office, than Renzo's attempt."

Helmat's laugh was bitter, dark, harsh—but there was genuine amusement in it. "Have any of your students survived?"

"I fail to understand the question. If you are asking me if I have failed to fulfill the Emperor's commands, the answer should be obvious."

"Oh?"

"I am standing before you with a patience that is decreasing by the syllable. You are my students. You are not my masters. I do not teach you everything I know; it would be, even if I desired to do so, impossible. You have scant decades in which you can fulfill Imperial mandate, and you would be old and doddering long before I had finished."

"And if we were, like you, Immortal?"

"You would not be Wolves. The Emperor has made that clear, time and again. I find it frustrating," he added. "But there is some method to his madness. If we are mistaken, we only have to deal with that mistake for a few decades. If you were Immortal?" He shook his head. "But you waste time."

"You have all the time in the world."

"I do, yes. The possible recruit, however, is mortal. And if I have time, my supply of patience is dwindling rapidly."

"Tell me about your prodigy."

Elluvian was annoyed and did not scruple to hide it. "I have not claimed the recruit as a prodigy; you are aware of my feelings on the subject of prodigies."

Helmat chuckled; he was both aware of it and in agreement. "Is he another young thug?"

"By appearance, yes. But to me, they all are."

"You might select among those who actually apply for the position."

"Why do you insist on wasting both of our time?"

The Wolflord frowned. He kept his words to himself for a long breath, perhaps two, assessing Elluvian. "What is it you want from this one?"

Elluvian hesitated and then, exhaling, said, "He managed to elude me for two hours."

Helmat whistled.

"He had no interest in employ."

"Not when offered by you? Is he from the fiefs?"

"Possibly. I was not searching in the fiefs when I found him. It is irrelevant. He showed no interest until I mentioned that the job would involve the Halls of Law. I believe he was tailing Barrani Hawks."

"Then he's already employed."

"I do not believe so, and yes, that is unusual. That, and the two hours, makes him a promising candidate." He did not mention the drawn daggers. Nor did he mention the mortal girl.

"You're not telling me everything."

"When do I ever tell you everything? Everything would constitute a much larger percentage of your mortal tally than you would care to give."

"Fine. Bring him in."

"The paperweight?"

"I am not yet ready to part with it, and its presence will no doubt be instructive."

"Helmat."

"I don't believe the head itself will be the largest deterrent, as you are well aware." His glance flicked to the side of his desk; a nascent mirror sat in the corner, apparently gathering dust. "Have you described in any detail the interview process?"

"Consider the process a test of his mettle."

"Very well." Helmat waved a calloused palm in front of the mirror, and the flat, silvered surface began to swirl.

The young man surrendered his name when he agreed to be interviewed.

"Severn Handred." Neither of the two names were familiar to the Wolves—or, more relevant, their Records. Neither were familiar to Elluvian, which he considered more important.

It was too much to be hoped that Severn was linguistically skilled; he spoke Elantran, the tongue of merchants and trade. He claimed to understand a smattering of Barrani and a handful of mortal languages; to no one's surprise that smattering generally involved curse words, and would not otherwise be useful to the Halls of Law.

He did not bristle at the questions involving education; nor did he appear to be concerned with the opinion, good or bad, of the two men who conducted the interview. Ah, no, perhaps that was not true; in as much as opinion led to intent, and intent was a danger, he was wary. There was, however, no rage at perceived condescension. He might, or might not, assume they thought themselves his betters—a particular weakness of Mellianne's—but if he made that assumption, he accepted the judgment; in any pragmatic sense, they were.

This was far more intriguing, far more promising, than Elluvian had expected. If Severn noticed Renzo's head, he made no comment; he did not flinch at all. Decapitated heads might have appeared at random in the streets for all of his life. Helmat had asked about the fiefs, and Elluvian understood why.

Helmat was brusque; he had always been brusque. Today, however, he was deliberately unkind; the questions verged, at times, on insult.

Elluvian occupied a space beside the nearest convenient wall, letting that wall support half of his weight as he folded his arms and leaned back. He watched the young man through half-lidded eyes, ticking off Helmat's questions without a flicker of reaction.

Regardless, the boy—he would not be considered a boy among his own kind—paid only a bare attention to Helmat, the man theoretically in charge. Helmat was, in all ways, the boy's superior: weight, strength, experience, knowledge. He was, and had been, a dangerous man, and—for a mortal—an almost worthy opponent. He understood power. Elluvian, dressed casually, and standing well away from the desk, exuded neither power nor authority. It was, however, the Barrani the boy was tracking; it was Elluvian he considered the threat.

He was not naive enough, in Elluvian's assessment, to believe the fables and stories told to the young and the cozened about the Barrani. Elluvian moved away from the wall and came to stand to the right of the Wolflord.

"Which fief?" he demanded, before Helmat could continue his questioning.

"Nightshade." The boy answered without hesitation; his

jaw tightened before he released the word, but he made no attempt to hide his origins.

"For how long?"

Severn shrugged. "Probably born there."

"And you crossed the Ablayne when?"

He shrugged again. "A month ago. Maybe a bit less, maybe a bit more."

"Are you being hunted?"

This earned Elluvian—who had taken the reins of the interview without asking permission—the first of Severn's almost disapproving expressions; his brows folded in toward each other and his forehead creased. Youth wiped those creases clear as the expression faded.

"I will take that as a no."

"Why would the fieflord hunt me?"

"You might be a thief. You might have absconded with something of value to him."

"Have you seen Castle Nightshade?"

Elluvian laughed. The hint of that amusement remained in the corners of his eyes and mouth. Helmat's glare intensified, as if there could only be so much amusement or good humor in his office, and Elluvian had just grabbed all of it. "Yes, I have. It was a ridiculous question, but you will discover that there are often ridiculous questions that nonetheless must be asked. Especially when events become somewhat political.

"Do you understand what the Wolves do?"

Severn shrugged; the shrug was fluid. It was not, however, a dismissal, an attempt to hide ignorance, or a gesture of annoyance. Elluvian waited, and the youth finally said, "No."

"But you've heard stories?"

"Yes."

"Tell me what, among those stories, struck you as accurate."

This caused more discomfort, but Severn's discomfort was

contained. "You're the Emperor's Wolves. You hunt the people who run."

"People who run?"

Severn's impatience was a glimmer in the eye, but he mastered it. "Most criminals aren't going to stand around, waiting to be arrested. They run. I imagine they run a lot—but most aren't very good at it."

Helmat's glare was gone, but his stare was intent.

Elluvian chuckled. "No, they aren't. You, in your two hours, were far better than most. The majority are apprehended by the Hawks or the Swords. The rest, by us. That is all you've heard?"

"No."

"And the rest?"

"The Wolves are the Emperor's assassins. He sends them to kill." He met, and held, Elluvian's gaze. There was defiance in him, but it was difficult to pinpoint—not a problem with most mortals of his age. Elluvian glanced at Helmat.

Helmat said, "They are sent to kill, yes. It is not, however, assassination. The crimes committed have been investigated, and the weight of evidence is considered great enough that the Emperor's jurors, and the Emperor himself, acknowledge a severe breach of Imperial Law." He paused to allow Severn to speak, but Severn was not a talker. He waited, Helmat having—at last—grasped the whole of his attention.

"Do the Wolves always kill?"

"No. In all but a handful of cases, they apprehend the criminal, who then graces our prisons until some suitable punishment for the crime itself is decided."

"Do you want me to kill?" He straightened as he asked the question; the nervous watchfulness fell away, as if he himself were a dagger that had, at last, been drawn from its sheath. "Is that the job you're offering?"

The answer was no. Helmat, however, did not give it. "Is that the job you want?"

"No. If that's the job on offer, I'm sorry for wasting your time." The boy bowed.

Elluvian laughed, then. Helmat smiled—if that grim turn of half his mouth could be called a smile. "You've killed, boy."

Severn did not deny it. "In the fiefs."

"Yes. You don't want to do it again."

"No."

"Who gave the orders?"

"Orders?"

"Who did you kill for?"

"No one. It was my choice, beginning to end."

"Ah. Why did you make that choice?"

"To save a life," he replied.

"Your own?"

He considered that for longer than strictly necessary. "It wasn't self-defense," he finally said.

Helmat was not a kind man; one did not become the Lord of Wolves through a surplus of kindness. Nor was he a stranger to death—causing it, commanding it. But he was possessed, in the end, of a particular perception, an instinct that occasionally moved him; it was an instinct that had evaded Elluvian for the entire duration of his service to the Emperor. Elluvian recognized it in him now.

"I understand that you have no wish to speak about it. To expose it. Understand, however, that if you are to work as a Wolf—as one of *my* Wolves—that information is necessary. The door is behind you. You need only walk out. If you are lost, someone will tell you how to reach the exit; you may rejoin the masses of mortals in Elantra having wasted only a few hours of your time.

"I do not offer you peace. Nor do I offer safety. But what I said, I believe. We are not assassins. We are Imperial Executioners. I could—and will, should you be accepted—list those executions, the reasons for them, and the evidence upon which the Emperor made his decision. Regardless, you will come to understand just how *little* peace or safety becoming a Wolf offers. These executions are not to be spoken of to any but the Wolves.

"You are cautious. You are constantly aware of En—Elluvian, if we're being formal. Trust those instincts. En is the most dangerous man in our ranks. And he is necessary; some of the Imperial Executions we carry out involve the Barrani. The Barrani generally take care of their own criminals; they don't want them judged by the Emperor. The Barrani we hunt are therefore those that are considered too dangerous for the Barrani to deal with." He waited to allow that to sink in.

"I don't want to kill," Severn said again, squaring his shoulders. He did not, however, turn toward the closed doors.

"No. And sadly, Severn, it is that preference that indicates that you might possibly—possibly—be what we want or require of the Wolves who operate in shadow. It is not trivial, the act of execution. It is not commonplace. Most of the men and women you will meet in your travels have not killed, and will never kill anything other than livestock. You are not a soldier, and will not be a soldier should you join the Wolves.

"Being a soldier is not, in the end, being an executioner. Understand that. In the cleanest of cases, you will not stand face-to-face and toe-to-toe with the enemy; you will not be fighting in self-defense. If you can, in safety, kill your target, you will be expected to do so—when he's sleeping, when he's eating, when he's otherwise helpless.

"Your path will cross city streets, city buildings; there will be civilians on your battlefield and you will be considered a murderer should you kill them in pursuit of your goal. Battlefields define soldiers."

Severn listened. After a pause that had grown too long, he said, "How many of your Wolves strike out on their own?" His gaze fell to Renzo's head.

Helmat's smile deepened; there was approval in it. And ice. "That," the Wolflord said, "is a very perceptive question. You understand why choosing the right candidates is vital to an organization such as ours."

"I'm not the right candidate."

"In your opinion, who would be?"

Severn glanced at Elluvian.

"There are many reasons to kill," the Wolflord continued when Severn did not answer. "Rage. Greed. Fear. Such crimes, however, are the responsibility of the Hawks. Most of these deaths occur between family members or people who know each other. They are not, and will not, be your concern. Crimes of passion do not need Wolves. Let us assume, then, that most murders in this city are irrelevant to the Wolves."

The youth could not see the direction Helmat was attempting to steer what was barely a conversation.

"When people think of killers, they think in odd specifics. They think of battles in the warrens. They think of the deaths in the fiefs. They romanticize, for a value of the word; they are telling themselves stories. There are horrific murders that occur within the city proper, and those loom large in the minds of our citizens. There might be one such grisly death, or one such murderer in a decade—but that is the one that people will remember."

"And that murderer," Severn said softly, "is not someone you want as a Wolf."

"Indeed, no. And perhaps I wander, but we have some time yet. Would you care to tell me what you think I *would* look for in a killer?"

"Someone who doesn't want to kill."

"Yes. But most people do not want to kill. And most people would not make good Wolves. En, tell the boy why you would make a good Wolf."

"Given how often you've derided my attempts to carry out my duties, I find the request almost shocking."

"It wasn't a request."

"Very well. I would make a good Wolf for two reasons. The first, to which Lord Marlin has already alluded, is power. I am Barrani, and even among my kin, I am not considered inconsequential. Were I, I would be dead." His smile was slender and almost warm. "The second: I would be willing to accept Lord Marlin as my commander. He is mortal, I am not, but his authority is absolute."

Helmat snorted. Loudly.

"I obviously care more about the respect due his office than he himself."

"It is not the respect due the office," Helmat snapped. "And your second point is almost entirely irrelevant."

"It is not."

"It is. There are many who might consider suborning themselves to the merely mortal. There are Barrani Hawks."

"That, as you are aware, is an unusual case—"

"More than a dozen 'unusual' cases. I would take none of them, regardless."

"Ah. Perhaps my Barrani outlook prevents me from understanding your mortal requirements." The boy's gaze bounced between the two men, following their barbs. It settled, in the end, on Elluvian. "I do not enjoy killing. I do not decry it. It is, like sleep, a very occasional fact of life."

"The Barrani don't require sleep," Helmat said.

"When severely injured, Lord Marlin, even the Barrani require rest. Perhaps, in the end, you do wish to explain? The choice is going to be yours, not mine."

Helmat flicked impatient fingers in Elluvian's direction.

"Killing livestock is not, in the end, more of a burden than killing a man. I take little pride in the act; it is a necessity, not more and not less. I am entirely neutral."

"Why do you do it?" The young man surprised him by asking.

"That is a complicated question. Ah, no, it is a simple question; the answer is complicated. Let me say, simply, that I do it because I want to."

One dark brow rose.

"That is hardly complicated," Helmat said.

"I am famously lazy. Why did you agree to this interview?"

Severn said nothing for one long beat. Two. And then he said, "Because I wanted to."

Helmat laughed. "En is being difficult. You will come to expect that, if you remain with the Wolves. You have killed. You have no desire to do so again. Tell me, boy, would you make the same choices that led you to kill the first time?"

"Yes." He answered without hesitation.

"Even knowing what you now know?"

"Yes." The word was defiant, and given his apparent age, this was not unexpected. But beneath it, Elluvian heard a depth of sorrow, of exhaustion. He wished, not for the first time, that human eyes, like the eyes of any of the rest of the known races, shifted color with mood or emotion. They did not. Various experts over the centuries had attempted to find reasons for this stubborn persistence of color, some going so far as to suggest that humans were simply slightly more intelligent livestock—which had not gone over well.

"Belief," Helmat said softly, "is a dangerous game. En follows the laws because he has chosen to serve the Emperor; he does not feel any personal loyalty to them. Nothing is personal to En."

"That is untrue."

"Nothing to do with the Wolves is personal. En has offered the Emperor his oaths of allegiance, and the Emperor has accepted them. But En has seen the rise and fall of many things in his time, and he oft feels that laws such as ours are merely waiting to become the detritus of yet another mortal civilization."

"The Eternal Emperor isn't mortal."

"That, of course, is the rejoinder to his philosophy. I have dedicated my life to the Emperor's service. In En's view, my life—the whole of it, from birth to death—is insignificant; it will be irrelevant."

Elluvian grimaced. "It is simple to maintain principles for a handful of decades—even I am capable of that. But to maintain them for centuries as the world shifts and changes? It is far, far more complicated. We who live forever—without the malicious intervention of our foes—oft choose to live in the moment because change is inevitable. For you, that is not necessary.

"To live as a Wolf, you must be true to the principles you have chosen to uphold. Those principles cannot be rocked or shaken by anger, by grief; they cannot be ignored when convenient. The act you commit, you commit for a reason, and that certainty is what holds you above the abyss. The abyss," he added quietly, "that you will live on the edge of while you serve. Helmat?"

The Wolflord nodded. "It is easy, in the end, for all who serve the Imperial Law to feel, viscerally, that what they see, what they make their life's work, is all there is to see. The Hawks deal with petty criminals on a daily basis. Some of those Hawks have come to believe that all citizens are petty criminals; that only petty criminals exist. The Swords deal with frightened or angry crowds—and on occasion, with the mobs those crowds become. It is natural for the Swords to believe that people should not—should never—be allowed to congregate; that people in congregations naturally evolve into something more deadly. In both cases, their fear is based on their experiences—both Hawks and Swords have died in the line of duty, and they wish to prevent future deaths of their comrades.

"It is *work* to fight against the growth of those beliefs, when all of your experience screams the opposite. The consequence of a Hawk or a Sword falling slowly into that bleak, gray cynicism is not large, although it should be guarded against. Imagine the consequence of a Wolf who does so. En is Barrani; he believes we are all irrelevant. He does not prize the lords of the mortal caste courts over the beggars in the streets; to En, we are practically one and the same.

"I am not En. I am mortal, as you are. I have had my fights, my difficulties, my rivalries, and my outrages. I bear the scars of some of them; I have emerged from the gauntlet of that life to lead this one. My experiences on the battlefield, on the city streets, and within the closed ranks of my household, form the foundations of my position as Lord of Wolves. But there is a reason that I no longer hunt. Even when I did, I never stood in the shadows. I am aware of my limitations. And it is my job, Severn—perhaps my most important job—to find those who can do the necessary work without being swallowed whole by the shadows themselves." He stood, pushing his seat back from his desk.

"What is the difference between your hunts?"

"Wolves attempt to retrieve escaped criminals to bring them to trial. Shadow Wolves carry a writ of execution. They are expected to kill those the Emperor has deemed guilty." Helmat was silent for a beat, studying the detritus that adorned his desk. "If you were to be given a job, a task, a duty, and you could choose it for yourself, what would you choose?"

Severn said nothing.

Helmat, however, expected an answer to this particular question. He folded his arms across his desktop, leaning into them, his gaze intent and almost unblinking.

"Do I have to be good at it?" The young man finally asked.

The question surprised Elluvian. It did not, however, appear to surprise Helmat. And this, of course, was the interesting thing about mortals. They gained wisdom at an astonishing rate, and the insight that accrued from that wisdom was unpredictable. They did not view the world the way Elluvian did, although, in theory, the world itself was the same. He had taught Helmat much of what the Lord of Wolves now knew.

But in the interstices of concrete lessons, Helmat had developed some strands of intuition that Elluvian did not possess. His understanding of Lord Marlin, however, made it clear that the boy's question had been, on some level, the right question.

"No. I should not have asked; it is a question meant for daydreams and yearning, no more." Helmat rose like the movement of mountains. "When I was young—younger than you are now—I did not dream of becoming a Wolf. I did not dream of serving the Emperor and protecting the Emperor's Law. I do not remember what I dreamed of then. But I remember when dreams did, finally, arrive. They were not the dreams of a happy child. They might more accurately be called nightmares—but they came to me as daydreams do. Or perhaps I threw myself into them. Bitter as they were, they offered—" He paused then, and turned to Elluvian. "This story will no doubt bore you. You may wait outside."

Elluvian raised a raven brow. "I am not entirely certain I've heard this one," was his mild reply.

"En."

The urge to argue surprised Elluvian. To Severn, he said, "You are free to leave. Remember that. You are not our captive; you are not our debtor; if you have broken laws—and I assume you must have, some laws are so lamentably trivial—we are unaware of them. Lord Marlin may intimidate, but he will not break the law we serve."

The young man nodded.

CHAPTER FOUR

ELLUVIAN STEPPED OUTSIDE, WHICH TOOK HIM into a hallway. It was designed for, and by, mortals of the human variety; the ceilings were not high, and the halls themselves were not wide; one might walk three abreast in them, but two was more comfortable. They were currently empty. Although the hall had not, in theory, been designed to intimidate, it usually had that effect on those summoned into Lord Marlin's presence; there were no doors on either wall, nothing to break its length. When one approached the Wolflord, one did so in isolation; there was no hope of escape.

Helmat had had the door repaired; the wall was sound now, but required paint. Structural integrity was more important than appearance to Helmat.

He wondered what Helmat was telling Severn. But more, he wondered why. Elluvian had seen some potential in the boy but in truth, some of that he derived from the fact that Severn had been tailing An'Teela and her two companions and he had been neither caught nor apparently noted. Helmat, clearly, saw something more.

If Helmat had begun the interview with some reservations, they were gone; his reluctant agreement had, with a few words from an otherwise suspicious young man, become genuine approval. Perhaps he saw something of himself in the young man. If he did, Elluvian had not seen it—and he had known Helmat for all of the Wolf's career in the Halls of Law.

He left the hallway like an incarcerated man leaving his cell; he disliked mortal architecture's suffocating density, and oft felt like a rat trapped in a maze, albeit a familiar one. Beyond the narrow hall, the office opened up, although the ceilings did not. Here there were desks, and those desks occupied a much larger room than the Lord of Wolves did. At the front of that room was a desk that was meant as a choke point.

"En." The single syllable traveled the length of a room that was not entirely empty, as the woman at the desk rose and turned.

"Rosen." He offered her a shallow bow. She was the oldest of the Wolves present, which did not make her old in mortal terms. Injury—her left hand was missing two fingers, and her left leg was not stable without a brace—had sidelined her permanently. Even given those injuries, she could be intimidating. None of the force-of-nature elements of her personality had left her. She disliked her name, and he thought it amusing that she was willing to use Helmat's diminutive when addressing him. Only the very drunk or the very foolish attempted to call her Rose.

"I've a message from Garadin. The Tha'alanari cannot send us an interrogator today. Garadin has suggested we try Draalzyn in Missing Persons."

"Did we?"

"*I* did, yes."

"Your expression implies that he was likewise unavailable."

Rosen did not hide her distaste. "He asked if it was an emergency, while simultaneously making clear it couldn't possibly be."

"To be fair to Draalzyn, it isn't."

"It's none of his business." She folded her arms, her lips compressing.

"No. It's not." Draalzyn and Garadin were Tha'alani. The Tha'alani were natural telepaths. They could bespeak members of their own race with an ease that even the mirror network did not provide. Which was not, of course, why they were feared. They could traverse the thoughts and memories of other races, as well—although that required physical contact.

Every person who served as a Wolf had undergone that examination of thought and memory at least once. The Shadow Wolves, however, were called upon to endure it after the conclusion of each successful mission. Some endured it with a fatalistic stoicism. Rosen had never been one of them.

"Draalzyn would not be in charge of choosing a member of the Tha'alanari for our task. Garadin would be."

"Garadin didn't seem to be in a hurry to be helpful."

Elluvian sighed. "Let me speak to him."

Elluvian swept dust off the surface of his desk, pulled his chair out, and sat in it. It gave a comforting creak as it adjusted to his weight. His mirror had suffered less neglect, and the reflective surface swirled away as he called it from sleep. "Garadin," he said to the mirror. "Now, if he is not otherwise involved in a similar conversation."

The Tha'alani were, in general, far more rational, far less emotional, than other angry mortals. Garadin's face did not look particularly placid or calm, but even had it, his eyes were an almost livid green. The thin set of his lips relaxed as his eyes met Elluvian's. "Is Rosen unaware that we are essentially on call to Imperial Security?"

"She knows."

"And that the Wolves are not part of those services?"

"She is aware of that."

"Then perhaps you need to inform her that we are not required to jump to obedient attention the moment she mirrors us."

"In her defense—"

"Don't bother. I suppose she told you to mirror."

"She informed me that there had been some delays, yes."

Garadin snorted. The antennae on his forehead were almost rigid, which was unusual, even for Garadin.

"What happened?"

The Tha'alani eyes were a dark enough green Elluvian was mildly surprised to see that color deepen. Garadin did not answer. Would not, Elluvian thought. He watched Garadin's expression freeze in place; watched as the stalks on his forehead eased into gradual motion. "Apologies," he said in stiff Barrani.

Elluvian answered in kind, without the stiffness. "None are necessary. It appears that our request arrived at an inopportune time. Our needs are not urgent; we are not in a state of emergency."

"Rosen did not choose to inform us of the reasons for the request." No, of course she hadn't. "Has a Shadow Wolf returned from a hunt?"

"No."

Garadin's eyes became a lighter color of green; had he been Barrani, he would have been as relaxed as Barrani allowed themselves to become. Sadly, green was not a calm color in the Tha'alani race. "We—the Tha'alanari—have encountered some...turbulence."

Elluvian made a mental note.

While the Tha'alani could all, in theory, perform the duties demanded of the Tha'alanari, in practice very, very few were asked to do so. The race itself shared experience and emotion openly. Most of its citizens had no idea whatsoever how not to do so. What they felt—fear, anger, anxiety—they transmitted to their kindred far and wide.

Those who served the Emperor had proved that they could withhold their personal experience from their kin. They could shut themselves out of the Tha'alaan, the group mind in which all racial experience was held. But no Tha'alani could hold themselves above or outside of the Tha'alaan forever; it was to their people that they looked for understanding, prior experience, compassion.

"It is not an emergency," Elluvian repeated. "Not for us."

Garadin exhaled. "I am asked to inform you that Timorri will not be serving the Tha'alanari for the foreseeable future. We do not have a replacement for him at present, and our consequent ability to meet Imperial demands—"

"We understand." Elluvian did not break the connection; he waited. Garadin did not break it either.

After another pause, Garadin said, "Why do you require one of the Tha'alanari?" It was not his question; as far as Garadin was concerned, they were done. But the fact that he asked the question seemed significant.

"We have a possible new recruit."

"An interview cannot possibly be time-sensitive. While we understand the necessity of such an interview for your particular branch of the Halls of Law, it is highly unlikely that we will have an agent available for your use within the next week. Possibly longer."

"It is not my request," Elluvian said softly, "nor even Rosen's. It is Lord Marlin's."

"And this prospective Wolf is *that* impressive?" This question was clearly Garadin's.

"Not to my eye; I considered him a possible candidate, but

I do not quite see what Lord Marlin apparently did in the initial interview. To my eye he is a focused, but oddly desperate, young human. Lord Marlin is still conducting that interview; he asked me to remove myself from the office, but the boy has yet to emerge."

Garadin's brows rose. If the Tha'alanari were capable of withholding information from the mass of their kin, they were not particularly careful with expressions. The forehead stalks began a weaving, staccato dance that implied heavily that Garadin was arguing with someone.

"I have been asked to allow someone else to speak with you," Garadin finally said, voice stiff with disapproval or concern.

"Will they join you, or should I mirror them directly?"

"They will join me," Garadin replied, in a tone that strongly suggested he would far prefer to be left entirely out of it—or as entirely as a telepath could be. "I hear that Rosen managed to offend Draalzyn."

"Which, you must admit, is not difficult."

"It is not difficult for Rosen to offend *anyone*."

Elluvian chuckled.

"I heard that." Rosen's voice drifted into the back of the office. She had always had exceptional hearing, and her injuries had not changed that.

"I am not the person who voiced that opinion," Elluvian said.

"You're not discouraging it, either."

"It is materially true."

He could hear her snort; so could Garadin. Only one of them found it amusing. Time passed. Garadin maintained the connection. Severn remained closeted with Helmat. Rosen took a mirror transmission of her own, and then another.

Eventually, the mirror's view widened to encompass two people. A young woman had joined Garadin. Her hair was the color of pale honey, but her eyes were not green; they were gold. She was not afraid, nor was she worried or angry. "My apologies for forcing you to wait," she said, executing a bow that implied that she was his social inferior. It was a human bow. "I was not in a location to which the mirror network has easy access."

"This," Garadin said, "is Elluvian of Danarre. He serves the Imperial Wolves."

Some hazel clouded the gold of the woman's eyes. She could not, however, be surprised; she had known, before rushing to Garadin's side from wherever it was she had been, who he was.

"And this," Garadin continued, even more stiffly, "is Ybelline. She is a member of the Tha'alanari."

"I do not believe I have encountered her in previous duty rounds."

"I have been admitted to the Imperial Service within the last two years."

"You are new, then?"

Garadin looked offended. Ybelline, however, did not. "No. I have been a part of the Tha'alanari since my coming of age."

"Forgive me, but was that recent?"

She laughed. "By your standards? It could not possibly be anything else. But by our standards, no."

"What are your duties—" He caught Garadin's darkening eyes, and bowed. "Apologies, Ybelline. I have spent so much time with mortals that I occasionally speak my mind."

"It is not customary among your kin," she replied, still smiling, "at least not in my experience."

He wanted to ask her what that experience entailed, but did not. "You have questions about our possible candidate."

"I do."

"Why?"

"Because I have asked permission to fill in the gap in our schedule."

"You have not…"

"No. I have not served the Wolves before. But I *have* served. I understand the risks." She glanced at Garadin and added, "Most of our work involves humans, and I am considered young by their standards."

"And by your own race, surely?"

"Not in the same fashion. Youth frequently lacks authority to you. But it is understood among my kin that I *am* an authority. I do not have to argue or fight for the respect due my abilities; it is granted because it is clear to the Tha'alani that I possess them."

He nodded then. "If you are offering to vet our recruit at a time of…trial to the Tha'alanari, you would have our gratitude, for what that is worth."

Her smile was like bright, unfettered sun—but full of warmth, not scorching heat. "I will make my way to the Halls of Law immediately." She left the mirror's view, and the image once again shifted until it contained only Garadin.

"She is of great import to us," Garadin said. His eyes were almost, but not quite, blue, a color that Tha'alani eyes did not adopt. "I wish you to understand this, Elluvian. She will be, in future, Rabon'alani. She will be our leader, our lord in your terminology. Any harm done her will bring incalculable harm to my people."

"Then why are you allowing her—"

"She will be castelord. The time is coming when 'allow' will no longer apply to her movements."

"And the current castelord?"

Garadin could have said it was caste business, because it was. Instead he said, "We are not Barrani. We are not human. There is no war for succession, and no great power accrues from the leadership itself. She will carry more of the weight of our fears and our hopes than any save our current leader, and he has done all he can to ease her passage into that burden. And no, he is not dying—but he is older, and he is weary. We would take him back into the heart of the people while he still lives; we would give him peace."

"I am almost surprised that you chose to mention this."

"I wish to make certain that there is no doubt whatsoever of her import. If you feel that your recruit is too broken, do not ask her to investigate the depths of his darkness. I will trust you in this."

"You will not."

"I will. You understand the burden we carry better than other mortals understand it. If you feel she will be at risk, mirror again. I will perform in her stead."

"Is she not coming because you cannot?" Silence, then. "You have already lost Timorri."

Garadin's impatience was clear. "As I just said—"

"This loss—was it caused by the discovery of information about the Tha'alani?"

Garadin's eyes were green. Had he been Barrani, they would have been indigo.

"Did Timorri contain his discoveries?"

After a long pause, Garadin exhaled. "I will not play games with you. His discoveries—and the visceral response to them—have been entirely contained within the Tha'alanari. That is our duty."

"I do not believe Lord Marlin will be pleased with your choice of agent. If she is of import, I think it unwise to have you take that risk."

"It was Ybelline who managed to contain Timorri's impressions. Were it not for her intervention, he would be lost to us on two fronts. He cannot serve as Tha'alanari, but he survives to return to our people. I will leave you. I have said either too much or not nearly enough."

★ ★ ★

Helmat left the confines of his safe but intimidating office at the side of the applicant. Severn did not seem to find this unusual, but the office—never loud or boisterous—fell into the silence produced when all of the people in it were straining to hear anything that might be said. In the offices occupied by the Swords, and the less numerous Hawks, silence was never complete; in the lamentable confines of Missing Persons, Helmat was certain that only instant obliteration would achieve that goal.

Not so the Wolves. He could see that Mellianne was now at her desk; that Rosen was standing to one side of her active mirror—standing, which she found tiring in the best of circumstances—and that En was perched, arms folded, on the corner of a desk that was otherwise empty of paperwork. Rosen jabbed En with a pointed glare, and En turned immediately to the Wolflord and Severn.

Severn was possessed of a steady wariness, which was not unusual in young men of his age and upbringing, for want of a better word. That wariness, however, was not rooted in fear. Nor did he attempt to assert his own toughness, as many who were fearful did in order to avoid conflict; his nervous energy—if he possessed it—was contained, controlled, almost silent.

He seemed neither fearful nor angry as he accompanied Helmat.

"How long," the Wolflord asked, glancing at Rosen's mutinous expression, "are we to wait? Is Severn to leave for the day?"

Rosen's jaundiced inspection of the boy continued as she answered. "The Tha'alanari are sending their investigator now."

"Good. We will wait in the conference room."

"We?"

"Severn and I."

En cleared his throat, and Helmat exhaled. "Yes?"

"Timorri has retired from the Tha'alanari."

Helmat's expression and tone shifted instantly into something appropriate for his title. "When?"

"Garadin did not say."

Helmat did not care for the studied neutrality of the response. "Garadin is not the interrogator today."

"No."

"En, I have had a difficult week, and if what you've said about Timorri is true, I am to have a vastly more thorny near future. Who, exactly, have they sent?"

"The investigator is in transit now and will be with us shortly."

"Remind me, have I attempted to stab you recently?"

The Barrani Wolf laughed. "Not recently, no."

"A pity."

"Is it?"

"No. But do, please, keep laughing. And do not leave the office."

The laugh lines still girded the corners of Elluvian's mouth; they left his eyes. "Oh?"

"Intuition. I believe you'll be required." Turning to Severn, he said, "We'll wait in the conference room. You can ask any of the questions you've managed to keep to yourself in relative privacy."

He suffered no great illusion; he did not expect the young man to speak at all.

"…understand that there are several ways one can hide in plain sight. Many feel that lack of visibility is the only choice; this is wrong."

"Disguises?"

"Of course. But disguises are not necessarily about hair

color, skin color, height, or even sex. They are not *about* the clothing, either. They are contingent upon your ability to fully inhabit the role you have chosen. Are you a street sweeper? Are you a cantankerous old woman? Are you—" Helmat broke off at the knock on the closed door.

"Enter." The door faded from view. Severn's brows rose before furrowing. He understood that this was magic. He didn't understand how it worked. Or perhaps why. If he stuck around, he'd figure it out. Helmat almost said as much before words temporarily deserted him.

Abandoning his chair—and the subtle authority of the seated position when one's visitors were to remain standing— the Wolflord crossed the room. He was not a small man, al- though he had learned how to make both the most and the least of the size he possessed. At the moment, he had chosen to make the absolute most of it. He stopped a foot away from the young woman who stood framed in the nonexistent door and glared at her.

"No."

"Good afternoon, Lord Marlin," she replied. Her gaze moved past the bulk of the Wolflord. "And you are?"

"I said no. Not you. You are to return to the Tha'alani quarter immediately. If the Tha'alanari is currently short of investigators, we will wait."

"My name," she continued, as if he had not spoken, "is Ybelline."

Severn had—barely—managed to contain the gawking Hel- mat would have otherwise expected from someone his age. The boy could clearly see the antennae that broke the smooth skin of Ybelline's forehead, but there was no hostility in his expression. Suspicion, yes; no one anticipated the advent of the mindreaders with any great joy.

"Ybelline," Helmat began again.

"Severn," the young man replied. "Severn Handred."

Ybelline could not hold out a hand, human style, while Helmat stood in her way. She could, however, offer Severn a sympathetic smile that somehow implied Helmat was a trial to be endured.

"Perhaps you would care to ask the investigator to step inside before you publicly berate her?" Elluvian said, from behind Ybelline. His eyes were almost green; he was amused.

"I would prefer that she not step inside at all."

"I am not certain," En replied, "that you have that discretion."

Helmat's eyes left Ybelline's. "Records," he said. He didn't invite Ybelline to enter the conference room but ceased to block the door. "Severn, I apologize, but I am going to have to ask you to return on a different day. Rosen will find you lodging and meals should you require them. You are a provisional Wolf, but we take care of our own. I fully intend, if you pass this final stage of the interview, that you will be one of us." He turned toward the wall opposite the door as Ybelline and Elluvian entered the room. The door then became wall again.

"I could swear," Helmat said, in a tone that implied he very much wanted to, "that I apologized to Severn and asked him to leave."

"You did," En replied. "But you must be distracted; you did not hold the door for him. How difficult do you expect the interview to be? You want the boy; on some level you trust him, even now."

Ybelline's smile was soft and warm. "You can, if you desire, send me away, but when an agent is needed, Lord Marlin, I will be coming in the foreseeable future. If it helps in any way, Garadin is in complete agreement with both your opinion and your directive—which I believe might be a first."

"Garadin doesn't want you here."

"No."

"But you are demonstrably here."

"Indeed."

Helmat exhaled a few choice words. "Why?"

"I wish to gain experience of—"

"No, Ybelline, you don't. That explanation might work on Rosen or En. It might work on Severn. They are not the Lord of Wolves; I am. You do not need to prove anything to anyone. You never have. You are here for a reason. You will not proceed until you have explained that reason fully."

Her antennae performed an almost graceful salute. Her face lost warmth, lost any suggestion of softness; steel might have been the color of honey. "Very well, Lord Marlin. But I wish Records to observe that you did ask."

Records flickered to life, sputtering almost fitfully, the sign of an incoming transmission. This transmission occupied the whole of the wall facing the closed door.

Garadin's broad and displeased face filled the wall's surface. "Lord Marlin," he said, glaring past the Wolflord to Ybelline. "I have been directed to inform Ybelline that the information you have demanded is entirely and completely classified."

"I imagine," Lord Marlin said softly, "that it will not remain that way."

"It will. You have asked for an explanation, and while the equivalent of paperwork is being prepared as we speak, the *Emperor* felt it expedient to initiate contact with the Tha'alanari. Ybelline is not, at her own discretion, to bespeak you in the manner of our kin. She is allowed, however, to aid in the interview of your candidate; the Emperor understands that the Wolves are in dire need of people."

Helmat was silent for one long beat. "Understood." And he

did. He turned to Ybelline. "Accept my apologies," he said in an entirely different tone of voice.

"For your suspicion? Or for its accuracy?"

"For the terrible use we force upon you and your kin."

Her smile broke before it reformed; he saw the pain beneath the surface of it, and did not understand, in the moment, the strength it took to smile at all. *You are being a fool*, he told himself, and knew it for truth. *An old, stupid, prejudiced fool.* Ybelline was young; older than Severn, but not, in Helmat's opinion, by enough. It was not the first time the Wolflord had encountered her. Nor was it the first time he had felt the instinctive desire to *protect*. Helmat hoped that this might be the last. If Ybelline was to fulfill Garadin's duties until Garadin was whole enough to do them himself, Severn would be the last interview Helmat would conduct.

"And would you change it? If the decision to do so was yours, and yours alone, would you change it?"

"…No."

"No."

"It is the only way we can arrive at a truth that is not obfuscated."

"Your apology smacks of pity, Lord Marlin. The regret is thin and almost irrelevant." She bowed her head for one long moment; he saw the tremble of her shoulders, the stiffness of her hands. He might have attempted to offer comfort; the Tha'alani had seen, long ago, the worst of what he had been in this life, and he was not that youth anymore. He was not afraid of her.

"And is regret absolute? One thing or the other? You are Tha'alani. You know that that is not the case. Even among your kin—"

She lifted her chin. Her eyes were green. Ybelline. Green. Helmat almost ended the meeting for the day and allowed her to come again tomorrow or the day after, as she had threatened. "Helmat, you regret what *I* suffer. You wish, somehow, to protect *me*. I am the strongest of my kin. You know—intellectually—that my people share experiences. What happens to one is open to all, with very few exceptions. Garadin's pain, you do not regret. Or Draalzyn's. Timorri's. Any of my kin who have been broken, in the end, by the terrible secrecy of the madness of murderers. What you fail to understand is that their pain *is* my pain. I am part of that secrecy.

"Could I, I would do it all myself, and share none of it. You wish to wait for another member of the Tha'alanari. You think that will spare me. It does not, and it *never* will. Do not worry for me," she told him, as if she could read his thoughts without touching his forehead or his skin. "I will find it far easier than Garadin. Had I been allowed to substitute myself for Timorri, we would not have lost him."

"You will not be a good leader," he told her softly, refuting none of her statements, "if you cannot delegate. You will not be a good leader if you cannot accept the losses that come as a natural part of your responsibility."

"Then I will be a terrible leader," she replied. "But that terrible leader is the leader my people need. Be what your people need of you, but keep your concern on the inside of your head, where no one else can hear it, no matter how desperate—" She swallowed.

"Ybelline, I ask you not to do this."

She shook her head.

"You know what Timorri saw."

"I am— Yes. Yes, I saw."

"It was necessary," Garadin said from the wall. "Had she not intervened, we would have lost at least two, maybe three more. You do not understand her strength," he continued. "But perhaps you now better understand my fear."

Helmat ignored Garadin, which was almost second nature. "You contained it."

She nodded again.

"We are not doing this today."

"It will help me," Ybelline said softly. "Unless this young man is a similar monstrosity of fear and rage and pain, unless he is—" She shook her head. "It will help me today."

"Why?"

"Because it will remind me, Helmat, that darkness does not always lead to madness and pain and death. No." She exhaled. "It will remind me that there is a need for what you— for what *we*—do." When Helmat did not budge, she added, "It will anchor me."

The Lord of Wolves moved out of her way. "It is not," he said when she moved past him, "a lie. I regret it, Ybelline. My regret comes in part from my duties, my life choices. I want, and wanted, to protect."

"The weak and helpless," she said, but did not look back.

"And would it be better, then, to have no such desire at all?"

She exhaled. Back to him, she said, "No. Tomorrow, perhaps the day after, we might revisit this. But at the moment, my desire to protect my people is too painful. Were it not for the Imperial Service—" and here she skirted treason "—they would not *require* that protection. What life itself offers—"

"We work for *all* of the citizens of Elantra."

"Helmat—"

"Do you think I don't understand? Ybelline, I command the Shadow Wolves. It is my responsibility to find and train them. How long do you think most of them last?" He was getting old; he couldn't let it go. "Were it not for the Tha'alanari, the Shadow Wolves would not exist. We could not do what we do without the certainty your people give us. We could not keep the Wolves leashed; could not give them the certain knowledge that what they do is for the better. All of our efforts would produce well-trained, deadly assassins, and in the end, too many of them would serve their own interests."

"It is not the same," she replied. "No human is forced to become one of your Wolves. No Barrani, either. The Emperor has not threatened to reduce you, and your home, to ash if the services of such people are not surrendered."

"And are you telling me that the Tha'alanari is created by conscription?"

Garadin, whose face, larger than life and green-eyed, remained upon the wall, said, "She is not. Lord Marlin, today is *not* the day for your games, your political sleight of hand."

"It is not a game to me. It has never been a game." But he stopped.

Severn stepped past Helmat to offer Ybelline his right hand, as if her antennae did not exist and she were a lovely older woman, due a measure of politeness.

Ybelline seemed surprised by this, but it was perhaps the surprise that she needed at the moment, and Helmat could otherwise give her nothing: no aid, no help, no protection. He remained silent but realized belatedly that his hands were clasped behind his back. He corrected this, although En had noticed.

"Do you understand what I am here to do?" Ybelline asked the youth, her head tilted to study their joined hands as if she were translating between a language she had studied and learned and her mother tongue.

"You are here," Severn replied, a tremor gilding the words, "to look at me and my past and to confirm—or deny—the truth."

She nodded. "You've told Lord Marlin the truth?"

"He hasn't actually asked."

En chuckled, fully aware of Helmat's baleful gaze, which was aimed at the side of the Barrani's face.

This time, when Ybelline turned back to the Wolflord, her eyes were almost gold; they were darker, more hazel, but this was natural for Ybelline. "You neglected to ask."

"It wasn't necessary," Helmat replied almost stiffly. "You don't trust me; you don't trust my kin. You don't trust the various Imperial branches of law and security. Nor will I tell you you are wrong, given your context, your experience.

"But Ybelline, I trust the Tha'alanari. It is not to determine the truth of simple statements that you have been summoned. Garadin understands this," he added.

"Garadin," she replied, "is almost shocked to hear you say that." But she smiled as she turned once again to Severn.

"He shouldn't be. It is, in effect, a more complete interrogation. If young Severn cannot handle it at all, he will never be a Wolf. We are, and will be, in your hands."

"Have you explained at least that much?"

"No," Severn said, before Helmat could reply. "I think this was meant to be a test."

"A test?"

"If I run away screaming—silently," he added, "I will have failed. If I'm afraid of my life and my truth—"

"Are you not?"

"I don't want to relive it. Is that what you're asking?" When she failed to reply, he continued, "I believe what I did was necessary. I hate it," he added, voice softer. "But I'd do it again if I had to."

"Are you not afraid to be judged?"

He closed his eyes, which was an answer, but opened them again. "Is that what you're here to do?"

"In a practical sense, yes."

He did not retrieve his hand.

"I require your permission," she continued.

Not everyone who came to Helmat's office passed this test; perhaps a third fled the Halls. One or two of those people made their way to the Swords or the Hawks, but once they crossed the threshold of this office, they were no longer his concern.

"Can I ask a question?" Severn then said, his voice steady.

"Of course."

"What is it that hurts you, when you look at us?" The Tha'alani stiffened. "You don't have to answer, if it's a bad question."

"It is...not a question I am usually asked. Not by applicants, and not by those who grace the Imperial prisons. Why do you ask?"

This time, Severn seemed more nervous, and Helmat realized with chagrin that it was not Ybelline he was wary of, but Helmat himself. But he steeled himself to answer. "I know what you'll see. I *am* me. But I don't know whether or not it will hurt you. Lord Marlin believes it will."

"And if I believe that it will?"

"I won't let you do it. Because I have that choice."

"Even if I don't believe it will?"

"You haven't seen it yet," Severn reasoned. "I think I know what you'll see."

"I do not believe I am allowed to discuss what...hurts us. Hurts me. Helmat?"

"There are no legal guidelines, but the specifics of any given case are, of course, confidential. If Severn were a Wolf, you would have my permission, for what that's worth; he's not."

She looked frustrated; she looked, momentarily, her actual age. "I don't believe, given the question you have asked, you will hurt me. But Severn, if you do, it's a pain I have under-taken willingly."

He shook his head. "You do it to protect your people. You do it because if you don't, someone else will. I'm not stupid. I could pretend I didn't understand a word you—or Lord Marlin—said. But I can't unhear them."

"Then remember the last few words."

"The reminder?"

She nodded.

"That's the problem," he replied, without hesitation. "I'm not sure you'll get the reminder you need. About pain. And madness. And sanity." His smile was lopsided. "And you haven't told me enough that I can make a good guess."

"I am willing to take the risk."

"It's not much of a choice, though. Someone has to do it. You'd rather—" For the first time, the boy's silence felt like slamming shutters.

"I'd rather it was me? Yes. I'm not certain how much you know about Dragons, but I imagine you heard childhood sto-ries. It's unwise to make a Dragon angry. Ever." She waited. It seemed, watching her, that she would wait forever—and un-like Helmat, would not resent the waste of her time.

"If Lord Marlin has rescinded the request, why do you want to do this? It doesn't sound like anything good comes from…that. For you."

"I told Helmat—"

"Yes, but…he doesn't believe you. I don't believe you, ei-ther. I'm sorry," he added. Helmat did not laugh.

"You are difficult," she replied.

Severn shrugged, the motion fluid. In as much as the youth could be, he appeared relaxed. "Most people you mind-read don't have a choice."

"If you wish to become a Wolf, the choice is theoretical."

"I grew up in the fiefs. I survived them. Only people who have power have choices."

"And a street urchin has no power."

"Tell me. What would you do to protect your people?"

"I am doing this. I am seeing—reliving—the visceral desires and thoughts of the murderous. I am taking them into me. I am experiencing their choices *as if they were my own.* Their actions become part of my memories, as real as anything I have ever personally chosen to do. And if Helmat were not here, if the mirror were not Recording, I would tell you what I've done. And done. And done." Her expression, her tone, were serene.

"Would you kill to protect your people?" He continued, almost as if she had not spoken.

"I am unwilling to have the rest of this discussion where any but my kin can hear it. Let us compromise, Severn Handred. I will bespeak you, with your permission, but I will not do more than that until and unless you agree."

He considered this, nodded, and then looked at her forehead, at the antennae. "Should I stand? Or sit? You'll have to—"

"Bend, yes. Or stand on my toes. It is not ideal in either case."

"Should I lie on the table? You can sit."

Ybelline turned, once again, to Helmat, as if to seek his permission. Helmat nodded.

Severn then got up on the conference room's table, and lay across it, on his back. "Just discussion?"

"Until you give me explicit permission, yes."

Severn then closed his eyes.

"Lord Marlin," Ybelline said, as she likewise seated herself, adjusting the position of the chair she had chosen, "I better understand your haste today."

CHAPTER FIVE

IS YOUR NAME REALLY SEVERN?

Is your name really Ybelline?

It is. It is not the entirety of my name, but it is the name I prefer.

Lord Marlin is worried. About you.

Yes. But Lord Marlin is a man who is always worried about something.

This doesn't seem so bad.

She chuckled, both here and out loud, where it might ease the worry of the aforementioned Lord Marlin. *I haven't started yet.*

No? But—

Yes, we're speaking. But we're speaking without moving our lips. Or at least I am. We're having a conversation that would be entirely normal—to you—were it not for the fact we're in physical contact. She paused, and added, *Except this time you're actually speaking.*

She felt his smile. Not a chuckle, not a laugh, but something both warm and reserved.

Helmat—pardon me, Lord Marlin—feels that there is a pressing need to conduct your interview; it's almost as if he's afraid that if he doesn't nail your feet to the floor, you'll slip through his fingers.

Silence. A beat. Two. *I wouldn't slip through Elluvian's.*

You underestimate Helmat, which almost surprises me, given his apparent ferocity. It doesn't happen often.

But I don't overestimate Elluvian.

No. He is Barrani. Be wary of him, if you can.

I know.

There, she thought. Something in the quality of that answer was a thread, a small window, a way in. She had not lied. Severn—unlike so many of the mortals given over to the inspection and ultimate invasion by the Tha'alani agents—had choice. She doubted he understood the nature of that choice although he understood the theory.

Why? Severn's interior voice was soft.

Why?

Why do you think I don't understand?

You did not grow up in the Tha'alaan. You did not grow up surrounded, always, by the thoughts and emotions of your people. Mortals fear judgment, Severn. They fear exposure. They fear to be seen as themselves. But we don't. We see ourselves, and our kin. We see them, always. We see their small fears, but we recognize them for what they are. We do not see weakness and strength as you see it. We do not have to prove ourselves, somehow, to each other. We do not doubt our love, or the love we are given.

She inhaled. *But we don't expect that love to be perfect, either. We see the stress of the day. We see the joy of the day. We hear—* She stopped the rush of words. *If we did not have the Tha'alaan, I fear that we would be like you, for we are mortal as well. The seeds of fear and need would grow in us, shaping who we might become in isolation.*

She was surprised when Severn reached out to hold her hand in his. Not to grasp or steady himself; she saw that. *And we are not one mind. We are not one person. Garadin is, as you perhaps saw, himself. So, too, am I. We disagree, we argue, we make*

*our own choices—but we do so as part of the Tha'alaan. We want
the same things for our people, for ourselves; we don't always agree on
how to achieve them.*

Ybelline.

She quieted, chagrined. *I am trying to justify myself.*

*No. Or maybe. It doesn't matter. You're here because the Wolves
demanded someone be sent. You're here because I might want to be
a Wolf.*

You're not afraid of me.

I am, he said. *But I'm afraid for you, as well. I haven't—*she
thought he would stop; had he been speaking out loud, she
was certain he would have. *I haven't been good at not hurting
people in the past.*

His hands shuddered in hers. The whole of his body shuddered. His grip tightened. He held on as if she were a branch
at cliff's edge, and he had fallen. For a moment, she bore the
whole of his weight. It was a metaphor, and it wasn't perfect,
but as he righted himself again, she felt that it was true regardless.

Severn's reaction to the mention of Barrani was an echo of
the past Helmat wanted unearthed; his flat statement about
hurting people was the heart of it.

I better understand Helmat's interest, Garadin said. He was, like
Ybelline, Tha'alanari. He could see, and had seen, the wild
growth of dangerous insanity in mortals. He had touched the
thoughts and memories, experienced the storm of fear and
rage and fury. He could, and did, contain them.

Ybelline could do so as well. But she was Tha'alani. To
work in constant, unbroken isolation was not possible for any
length of time. Or perhaps at all. To the Tha'alanari, then,
those chosen to bear the burden of privacy and separation, she
remained an open book.

Will you do as Helmat has asked?

Garadin could feel her hesitance, her reluctance. *Severn is human. Humans value privacy, because it is all they have ever known. I don't want to break him.*

Garadin's voice was joined by Scoros's. *You will not break him.*

You are so certain, teacher?

It has been long since I've had anything to teach you, Scoros replied, warmth and disapproval blending perfectly in his tone. *But I see what you see. I hear what you hear. Both before you touched him, and after. I understand your concern—but Ybelline, he is not broken now.*

Humans are fragile.

Some, yes, but is that not true of the people as well? Most of our people are fragile; it is why the Tha'alanari exists. Think of pain and hurt as physical ailments. Our people find healing in each other, and that healing is constant. This boy's people don't have that, but humans do heal.

If a leg is broken, and the injured person tries to walk or run, it worsens the injury.

Yes, yes. Do you think his leg is broken?

I don't know.

You are the only one present who can answer that question, and there is no answer without risk.

I'm worried for him.

Yes. But Ybelline, it is when you cannot be worried for the person you interrogate that you must stop.

The Imperial Service doesn't worry.

No. But they are not Tha'alanari. We are. I will concede, however, that he seems an unusual boy.

He is no longer a boy, Scoros.

You are a mere slip of child, to me. I do not think you will do the harm you fear to do; you have his permission. And permission, child, is everything. Continuing without it is the greatest harm to you, to us, that can be done in the end.

Throughout this, Severn had been silent. *Can I ask a question?*

Clearly, Scoros replied.

I'm worried for her.

We are all *worried for her. Are you worried enough to abandon the possibility of becoming a Wolf?*

Yes, if it comes to that. I've never dreamed of being a Wolf. I wouldn't have come here on my own. Elluvian brought me.

And you want to be a Wolf, do you? Scoros, with as much forbearance as he usually demonstrated, had taken over the conversation.

I want to have a reason to be in the Halls of Law.

Do you understand the Wolves that stand in Shadow?

They're assassins.

Yes, that's exactly what they are. Do not, however, use the word when speaking with Helmat. It annoys him.

Scoros, Ybelline broke in, *that is unfair.*

Helmat believes there's a difference because Helmat has to believe there's a difference. But my jaundiced eyes can't see one.

Assassins kill for money, Severn offered.

Do you think he occupies that office of his for free? Scoros countered.

I don't know.

He doesn't. He's paid, and paid well, for his service.

As are we, Ybelline said. This silenced Scoros. Ybelline did not believe that silence would last for long. *What Scoros meant to say was simply this. If you are a Wolf, you might be called upon to kill. Those who do kill are required to face us every single time. Their jobs are dependent on the reports we then give the Wolflord. And Severn? Unlike today, those sessions are mandatory. You will be a Wolf, and you will be under Helmat's command.*

Will it always be you?

Garadin laughed. Scoros grimaced. Neither of these could

be seen, but both could be felt. Severn was merely embarrassed.

*I can't guarantee that it will always be me. You've seen, from
today, that different members of the Tha'alanari must sometimes retreat from service.*

*Has there ever been a time when you've told Lord Marlin not to
hire someone?*

Yes, Scoros said.

Did he listen?

Garadin laughed again.

*Yes. He wasn't happy about it, but then again, he never is. And
regardless, the appraisal and the recommendation won't be mine. It
will be Ybelline's.*

But...

But we see what she sees?

Severn's nod was a ripple, not a gesture.

*We do not see all that she sees. No more does she know all of what
I see, or all of what Garadin sees. We will have the gist of it, no more.
It is how we function. At the point where we cannot keep our sanity,
cannot keep our internal walls intact, we* must *stop.*

Why are you explaining this to me?

*Because you asked, boy. When we are drowning in darkness and
pain and cruelty, we reach instinctively for our kin. But as with any
drowning person, grip too tightly, grip in the wrong way, and all that
is achieved is two deaths, not one. It is a pity that you are not seeking
to be a Hawk. I believe we would find the experience far less taxing,
were you. Ybelline, decide. The boy is clearly willing.*

Ybelline said yes.

She said it wordlessly. She returned to the silence of her
own thoughts, disentangling herself from the Tha'alanari,
the familiar voices of Garadin, of Scoros, of the others. Here,
in the remaining hush, she was as close as she could come to

a human experience. She felt the isolation keenly, as she always did. But humans experienced this *all the time*. They had no choice.

There was an element of trust in Severn's apprehension, an element missing from those whom the Imperial Service wished to interrogate. Scoros had taught her—taught most of them— that regardless of the emotions of their subjects, the Tha'alanari must be worthy of a trust that would never be offered. They must touch only those things that were relevant, and if they stumbled, if they were sucked, by the vortex of fear and rage, into other memories, other thoughts, they must never, ever speak of the things that were not relevant.

Humans feared the Tha'alani because humans required secrets.

But the Tha'alani feared human secrets almost as much. She wondered, as she sometimes did, what the world would be like if all races, everywhere, could join and live within the confines of the Tha'alaan. She wondered what it would take to create a Tha'alaan in which other races could be at home. In which secrets weren't necessary; in which belonging eased fear and anger.

For she understood, every time she attempted this, that so much of the damage done to humans—by themselves, by the world—was caused by the certainty of their isolation. They were alone. They felt alone. They could not, in despair, reach out for the comfort of their kin, because their kin could not hear or answer them as the Tha'alani could. They felt that they could not reach out to anyone. Eventually, the certainty that no one cared about them at all became inverted: if no one had ever cared for them, why should they care for anyone else?

The inversion took different forms. Sometimes, driven mad by the bitterness of isolation, the lack of external balances, they moved from *why should I care* to *I'll show them all*.

She shuddered but examined her thoughts in the intimidating silence.

You don't have that?

Ah, no, not silence.

I do. But...all children do. All people who feel powerless do. It's not a constant, and as we mature, we feel less and less of it because we understand external contexts better. But it's not the same. Of course, it's not. We can hear the children. We can see what they feel. We can remember—by searching the Tha'alaan, if necessary—when we were that young. Every one of us. We don't judge it because it's part of life. But we open up those memories to those who are in the throes of the anger, and they see it. They see that it's normal, but— I'm sorry. I can't explain it. I've tried but— Can you explain how you breathe?

No. I can't explain how you breathe, either, if that helps.

Are you afraid?

Yes. But this is a minor fear.

She was surprised. He sensed it immediately. He sensed everything immediately; they were entwined now. If she needed secrets, this was not the place to keep them. It was unusual, however; most of the people who were exposed to the Tha'alani were so busy attempting to fortify their defenses and hide their secrets that they didn't look in the other direction. Drawing breath, she said, *Let me show you my life. Let me show you my fears. Let me do this first.*

You don't have to.

I think, if I do, you'll understand.

Some things, it's not safe to know. People kill you if you know too much.

Almost bitterly, she said, *We know. But if you're Tha'alanari, they kill you because there's a possibility that you can. You don't have to do anything. Just exist. Why do you think the Tha'alanari quarter exists behind walls? That almost none of our kin choose to live beyond them?* She had started, and could not now stop. *Even with the walls, we've lost people. And we've lost children to kidnappers, and children to the ambitious who somehow think they can cage those children and use their power* without *alerting—*

His hands tightened. *Something happened today.*

Yes. She swallowed. *Garadin was probably right. I shouldn't have come. But Helmat was right as well, I think. Let me tell you about me.* She was glad, then, of the privacy that humans so prized; she was certain that the Tha'alanari would not have approved. But they weren't here; they couldn't hear or see what she could. They couldn't offer advice, or the strength they felt she needed, couldn't evaluate the choice she had made, and was making.

What she could have forced from Severn, she now offered him, instead.

Helmat saw Severn stiffen; the young man's shoulders curved in, his head bent, as if he were attempting to protect himself from blows he couldn't otherwise avoid. His hands, however, did not tighten around Ybelline's. Ybelline's did; her knuckles were white. The Wolflord moved, and moved again; Ybelline was crying.

Severn was not.

To Helmat's surprise, Severn extracted his hands, although his eyes remained closed. He then shifted his position and his weight, and brought both of his arms around Ybelline, maintaining forehead contact; he pulled her in and held her as if she were a child.

She showed him the first murder she had experienced. The victim had been Tha'alani. She had been six years old, and the whole of the Tha'alaan had shuddered at the death, and the dying. Terror, pain, all of these were etched there permanently—it was as if she herself had died. She, and every person who was part of the Tha'alaan who could hear the dying.

It was how she had discovered the existence of the Tha'alanari. The dying, the *pain* had suddenly ebbed; enough that she could hear her thoughts again. She had run to her mother in primal terror, and her mother had been waiting, as if understanding that every child in the Tha'alaan would be seeking the physical comfort, the physical safety, of their closest protector.

But Ybelline, in the safety of those familiar arms, had stiffened. "He's gone."

Her mother wordlessly told her to hush; she could remember her mother's hands in her hair, across her back.

"He's gone. He's— He *can't go*! He's *alone*!"

"He's not alone," her mother said.

But she couldn't and didn't believe it, and so she had—at six years of age—gone searching. She'd gone searching for a dying, terrified man in the Tha'alaan. No entreaties from her mother could stop her; no entreaties from her aunts or her uncles could stop her either. Because she was searching, because her search grew increasingly desperate, she found the wall. The wall was, of course, metaphorical; it was not a wall in any sense of the word. It was a type of silence, and had she not been looking, she might never have seen it, never have heard it.

But she *did* hear it. And listening, she began to climb that figurative wall. Ybelline, at six years of age, had discovered the Tha'alanari.

Her mother's arms were around her. She was surrounded by a familiar touch and familiar scent, by the safety of home. And because she was, she could climb down the other side of that metaphorical wall. She could hear voices on that side of the wall. Her people.

And she could hear—oh, she could hear—the pain of the

dying man, because his torture, his mutilation, was not yet done, not yet over. The first thing he had lost—to knives, to cudgels—were his antennae. But the Tha'alani did not require them to reach the Tha'alaan. It would have been a mercy to the Tha'alaan, perhaps, if they had—but not the man.

Ybelline was not aware of the men and women whose voices she could hear so clearly; she was not aware of anything but the physical presence of her mother. She was frozen in place by the terror of the man himself—but she was no longer terrified. She understood that his pain was not her pain; that his death was not her death.

And that he was alone and mad with it. She knew what happened to those who lost the Tha'alaan. Every small child did. Every adult, too. It was the fate they most feared.

She could do nothing for this man. She was not as large as her mother, nor as strong as her father. She knew nothing about fighting, nothing about combat. But she knew how to hug someone, how to hold someone.

She passed through the wall of adult voices because they weren't a wall; they were noise now. And she reached for the man. Reached for him, reaching *into* him, reaching into the core of his pain, the injuries he had sustained, the things that would kill him. She hated humans, then. *Hated* them.

But that was not what he needed. Hatred was not comfort. It was not shelter.

Child, no!

Scoros's voice, even then.

Ybelline ignored him. She ignored the other voices that attempted to throw her out, to push her back through the wall. There was only one voice she needed to hear, because there was only one man who *needed* to know that in his final moments, he was not alone.

She could give him that. When he whimpered, she caught

his attention. She demanded it. And she was a Tha'alani child; he turned in the instant of that pain to see her. To understand that she was reaching for him. To turn the whole of his fear toward her, in the process changing its focus.

She wasn't the one who was dying. She wasn't the one who was trapped, who had no way to return home. She did not need or want him to be afraid *for* her.

No, child, Scoros said. *He needs that fear, now. It is the only thread of sanity he has left.* He did not tell her that she should not be here; he'd already tried. Perhaps because she was young, perhaps because she'd had that arrogance of a childhood that had yet to be fully tested, she disagreed. She was certain, however, that she *could* give him what he needed because she had been given exactly that when she had first heard his voice.

She reached for him again, and if Scoros could not be banished, neither could she.

She did not ask for his name, but pulled it quietly from the contact; he tried to push her away. Tried, and just as the Tha'alanari had, if for different reasons, he failed. He wanted what she had wanted and needed when she had run to her mother. How could she not know? How could *any* of them not know?

She threw figurative arms around him, and because they were the arms of her unfolding gift, they fit; they were large enough—more than large enough, they were strong. Stronger than her mother's arms; stronger than her father's; stronger than even Scoros. She accepted the dying man's pain.

And his pain came to her. It became *hers* in its entirety.

She endured it. She endured it, murmuring the same endearments that her mother was even now, in the physical world, murmuring in her ears. She endured it because, as a child, she had believed that love had no bounds, no end to what it could and must endure.

Throughout it all, she held him. And when he wept, in the end, it was not from pain, but relief. Here, in Ybelline, he had found safety, and she cradled him in the figurative arms of her gift until he died.

The Tha'alanari had been upset, of course. Upset and afraid and awed. She was too young to be what they were. She was *too young*. But no one argued that she did not have the power or the strength, because she had, in that one action, proved herself.

They worried for her. It wasn't necessary.

Ah, no.

In the dark of the now, on the edge of Severn Handred, she admitted that they had been right. She had taken the pain into herself, and she had *held it*. She had not shared it with her mother, her father, or even the Tha'alanari themselves—the men and women who endeavored to keep the Tha'alaan sane. She understood, even at that age, that pouring nothing but raw pain, raw rage, raw hurt into the Tha'alaan would help no one. Not the dead man. Not his family. Not her own family.

No one.

But in the absence of the Tha'alaan, in the absence of even her closest kin, the hatred that she had felt in the face of Willan's death sank roots. It grew. She dreamed of finding the men whose faces she could still *see* every time she closed her eyes. She dreamed of cornering them—in their comfortable homes, in an alley, anywhere really—and forcing them to live through *exactly* what Willan had lived through. Except the end.

It was the first time in her life that she experienced what humans—what any other race—experienced daily. She could not speak of his death. Could not share the visions; they remained trapped inside her until they occupied the whole of her. Or so it felt.

Her parents were worried. She understood this. She tried

to take what comfort she could from their kindness and their concern, but in truth, she could not. The memories, the *truth*, became a wall between Ybelline and the comfort and love, the constant warmth, of the Tha'alaan. Shared pain was lessened pain. But she could not share this. Even then.

And why?

Ah, perhaps all children *were* alike. She hated humans. She *hated* them. They had become, in the recesses of her mind, more monstrous than Dragons or Barrani or the monsters that hid under her parents' bed—her own mattress sat on the floor. She did not want her parents, did not want the people who loved her best or most, to see that ugliness blooming within their daughter.

Hatred is normal, Severn said. He had spoken so little, reacted so little, that she had almost forgotten him.

Not for us, was her soft reply.

For anyone who witnessed what you witnessed or experienced what you experienced. It did not make you a terrible child. It does not make you a terrible person. It's not what you feel—it's what you do. *That's the only thing that counts.*

Who told you that?

Silence. He didn't answer with words. But she could see the faded image of a woman—a woman not much older than she was now. Her eyes were dark, her hair dark as well; her skin, except for the smudges across her cheeks, was unblemished.

Your mother?

Not my mother. Her mother.

This time it was Ybelline's arms that tightened. Not yet, she thought.

How did you stop hating us?

Honestly? I hated Scoros instead. For years. There was warmth in the words. Chagrin. *He came to my house. I had hidden as much as I could, but there's a reason the very occasional fugitive doesn't* stay *in the quarter. None of us are* good *at hiding. He spoke to my parents. He worried at them, and they were afraid. For me.*

And then he took me away.

I lived with Scoros for the next several months. And he began to teach me everything I know.

Severn interrupted. *He taught you not to hate?*

Not…exactly. But he taught me not to act on it, ever. He considered it the detritus of terror, of pain—the shadow they cast. And he taught me how to step out from under that shadow, because…it was what he'd had to do. He and every one of his students. He invited me into the Tha'alanari.

And your parents allowed this?

They didn't precisely understand, I think, what it would entail. But Scoros understood what I needed, far better than my parents could. I needed to be among people who had experienced what I experienced. I needed to know that I was not…isolated. I needed to see that there were people who were whole, who had found ways to deal with and contain the hatred that grows from their experiences.

Her smile was closer to a grimace. *We are not good at being alone. We are not good at being human.*

We're not really good at it either, if that helps. But… I think you only see the worst of us. Not just the worst about *us. But the worst* among *us. Maybe it would help if you could…* He trailed off.

Exactly. Even those you consider the "best" among you would not willingly subject themselves to our touch. They wouldn't do what you're doing now.

I'm not the best among us. Once again, an image of the woman—with fewer smudges but darker circles—rose.

She was dead. Whoever she had been, she was dead. But the grief that surrounded this face, this image, was suffused with warmth and regret; there was no lingering rage or hatred in him. Not for her.

She died eight years ago. His grief, while muted, was deep; it was not so deep that it eclipsed the memories that had, in the end, created the path that grief would follow. *We don't share grief. It's a weakness. We don't share weakness.*

Yes, she said. *I know. I don't understand how it is seen as weakness; it is part of life, of daily life.*

Fear was a large part of our daily life. She could feel a shrug, a deflection. He was aware that she could feel it, see it, and she felt him shake himself. His arms loosened, but he did not pull back—he couldn't, unless he wanted to break the contact.

Our?

I lived with Tara, he said. *Tara and her daughter.* As he spoke, she could see them: mother and child. Had they antennae, had they golden eyes, they would have looked no different than the Tha'alani equivalent. Dark-haired, dark-eyed, faces wreathed in exhausted smiles and sleep. The woman looked up. *Severn.*

I scrounged for food. I ran errands. I did what I could to help them. And she kept a roof over my head. In the fiefs, that was not guaranteed. *She gave me a safe place to spend the evenings. Where the Ferals couldn't hunt.* The Ferals loomed large in his memory; they weren't so much creatures of the night as the night itself. Severn's glimpses were imbued with the urgency of fear. Only in the later memories did he see them more objectively.

There were only three of you?

Two, he said. The word was a ripple of pain. *Tara died when her daughter was five. She was ill. She didn't wake up. Without her, we couldn't keep the rooms. We lied,* he added. *And that worked until the money ran out—and there was almost no money to begin with. And then it was hard.*

His words did not convey the enormity of the difficulty; she could see it fly past in memory and fear. He had been, she thought, ten years old—perhaps eleven—a child, attempting in some fashion to protect and care for an even younger one. But he was driven, then. She saw the edge of what Helmat had seen in the boy in that ten-year-old child. At that age, he had accepted—had taken—responsibility for what had become a family of two. A desperate, impoverished family in the poorest part of the fief of Nightshade.

Her own thoughts blended with his. The merge happened without effort on her part, without the strain of bracing herself for the contact. He had not approached her with suspicion or fear, because the power of consent was his own. And he had given it, was giving it, even now; she followed the thoughts that lay beneath the words he offered, the foundation for the experience that words alone could never fully capture.

Or maybe he would never offer the words aloud. Here, the sense of his responsibility, his love, his fear, existed without words. He had no need to communicate them to anyone but the child herself, and she didn't require it. He did not share with others because it was none of their business. He did not want, had never wanted, to draw attention to the child, because almost all attention in the fiefs was dangerous.

He taught her the skills they both needed to survive. Taught her how to find shelter, and when shelter—a roof—was not available, how to climb, how to find places on roofs or balconies of questionable structural integrity, to wait out the night—because even in the warmer weather, the streets were not safe.

Here, at least, it wasn't other people he feared. It was the roving packs of the creatures known as Ferals. To Ybelline's mind, they resembled enormous dogs, but their color and shape were uniform. He feared what the Ferals would do to the child under his protection.

To Elianne.

There was, of course, fear for himself—but so much of it was the fear of what would happen to her if he died; death was the only way he would abandon her. The caution with which he lived this life was due in large part to that fear. He was aware of her fear. He was aware of her nightmares, her broken sleep, the confusion at the absence of her mother. That confusion would become grief over time, but it was not adult grief, and too often the immediate needs—food, shelter—were paramount for both of them.

They survived. There was a quiet, desperate pride in that. They survived. And in time, Elianne's desire to protect not herself, but others—the behavior she had seen and known all her life—had emerged. Severn had had no desire to add to their small family; numbers made everything harder unless one had a stable base of operations, and they didn't.

But into their lives had come children, regardless; Elianne found them. Elianne wanted to help them—just as she had been helped. He could not, had not, said no. Steffi. Jade.

A wall came down.

For someone of Ybelline's training, that wall was porous; it was fragile, thin, easily broken. But she let it fall—or rise, the metaphor was not exact—and waited. On some level, Severn wanted to tell her. He wanted her to see, to understand.

She had not expected that.

She asked no questions. She waited. Time passed, but time was not her concern. This communion was not an emergency to anyone but Helmat, and Helmat could be kept waiting, which might mollify Garadin slightly.

She felt Severn's arms stiffen; he relaxed slowly.

Sorry.

Wordless, she made it clear that no apologies were necessary. What he was willing to share, she accepted without judgment; what he was not willing to share, she would not demand. Here, today, she had that luxury. But she knew, before he began to speak again, that Steffi and Jade were at the heart of the question Helmat wanted resolved.

CHAPTER SIX

STEFFI WAS SEVEN. AN IMAGE ACCOMPANIED THE words, but it was blurred, indistinct. *Elianne decided she was seven, because she wanted Steffi to be younger. To me, they seemed to be the same age. We found her in the winter. We found her in the snow. She was ill. I…didn't want to take her home. Elianne did. Loudly. Angrily.* There was amusement there, but it was swamped by bitter regret. *I thought Steffi would die. I didn't want whatever was killing her to kill us.*

And by *us*, Ybelline thought, he meant Elianne. She could see that dark-haired, dark-eyed child, her skin ruddy with cold. Steffi, however, was pale-skinned, pale-haired; she was slender the way children are, but the gauntness of starvation had not hollowed her cheeks, distended her stomach.

A year later, we found Jade. She was running from a man with a knife. At night. At night in the fiefs.

A child running from a man with a knife—at any time of day—was sensible, to Severn. A man hunting a child at night was the height of suicidal stupidity.

Elianne and Steffi were at home looking out the window when she passed by; they saw her. And Elianne asked if we could save her. It was so hard for me to say no to her. I should have. But—she looked at me as if I could do anything, be anything. I was younger, he added, with a rare trace of self-consciousness. *I didn't want to disappoint her. We left Steffi, but Elianne, I took.*

You risked her? Ybelline asked, surprised.

I had to. Steffi was terrified of me for weeks. And I was pretty sure that Jade wouldn't be much different. I needed Elianne to grab Jade, to keep her quiet. There were Ferals, he added. *Ferals hunting in the streets. You do* not *make noise when the Ferals are out.*

We rescued her. We sacrificed the man hunting her—he was drunk. Loud. We pulled her out of the streets and into shelter while the man drew the attention of the Ferals. And fed them, in the end.

She was *younger than Steffi and Elianne—for real. She was scarred; she was missing the lower half of her left ear. I didn't expect her to trust any of us. She had a foul temper, a foul mouth—everything about her was difficult. Everything but her voice. When she sang, she had the voice of an angel.*

He lowered his head. She felt the motion as if it were her own. *It was hard. There were four of us. But Elianne was happy. They were happy. I was—*he shook his head. *I was worried about feeding us, but in as much as I could be, I was happy too.*

And then it started.

She waited.

The marks started appearing on Elianne's arms and legs.

We were listening to Jade sing parts of a story I was telling. I can't remember who noticed first.

Not consciously, no. But Steffi had noticed. Steffi had shrieked. By nature a quiet child, she had pointed at Elianne's arm. Elianne hadn't noticed herself, too caught up in song and story and the illusion of family she had built.

Her left arm, he continued, speaking the words although he must have known they were no longer necessary. *Jade stopped singing. We watched, as if the marks were a story that ended at Elianne's elbow. I don't remember how old she was.*

Not consciously, but Ybelline could extract that information. Elianne had been ten.

And more marks followed, day by day. Her right arm. Her left leg, her right leg, her back. I went out into the streets. There were people who were sympathetic to us. People who didn't think I was a young, ambitious pimp. People are afraid, he continued, as if this could possibly be news to Ybelline. She agreed, but silently. *I made Elianne hide her marks. She wore long sleeves. In the winter, it didn't matter. Sometimes, in the summer, it looked odd.*

I didn't know what they were. I didn't know what they meant.

But when she had just turned twelve, maybe a month later, she… The words trailed off. The memory did not. Elianne had seen a young boy hit—thrown—by a carriage. She had run to him, not away; she had attempted to lift him. The boy was injured. There was blood, but much of it from the corners of his lips; his eyes were wide with shock. Severn didn't think he'd survive it. No. Severn had been certain he wouldn't.

And yet, somehow, he had.

Elianne told him, with pride and a smidgen of defiance, that she had *helped* that boy. That she had saved him.

Ybelline's surprise caught Severn. She had not recognized the girl's name, but she was suddenly certain she knew who she was—or that the Imperial Service did. *She could heal?*

Wordless, he nodded. *She could heal. I ran tests of my own.* He cut himself multiple times, sometimes deeply. And Elianne had healed them all. *I knew a bit about magic. Nothing I knew explained Elianne. But everything I knew made it clear that if her ability was known—if anyone powerful knew—she'd be taken from the streets and used as a healer until she died.*

She hid her power. But—and this is my fault—she used it any-

way. Because she could. Because it was something she could give to the people around us, who had helped us. Sometimes by turning a blind eye when we stole from them. She always wanted to help. To be useful. To be a good child. The words were bitter.

But Ybelline understood. *You loved that about her.*

I loved that about her mother. But she was a child. I wanted her to be a child, for however long it lasted. I wanted her to be—

Welcoming. Warm.

—who she was. What she was. Desperate people are stupid, and they do stupid, mean things. But there's more than just that in the world, even ours. I wanted her to have that. To be that.

And she was.

He nodded again. Her name was an echo, the three syllables coming and going, the weight of the name a mix of regret and yearning and bitterness, because hope was bitter when there was no possibility that something positive could be achieved.

Benito died, he finally said. But Ybelline could see that, could know that, as well. Benito, the son of one of the men who had allowed them to steal food when things were very bad and allowed them to buy it when things were better. *He died—and his body had been covered in the same marks as Elianne's.*

*Elianne was terrified. Jade was terrified. Steffi—*he shook his head. *It was bad. But she'd kept those marks hidden. No one knew she had them except us. No one could lay blame at her feet.*

No one could lay blame at her feet, regardless, Ybelline said, forgetting, for a moment, to be silent.

You know what fear does. You know it better than most of us *do.*

She fell silent again; he was right.

Benito was only the first death. Tina died next. She was Elianne's age; when Elianne's mother was alive, we saw a lot of Tina. Not so much after. Tina wasn't the last, either. But Tina's body had been covered with marks, and her death—

Elianne was afraid. At first, she thought that the marks had come

to other children in the fief; that she would meet the same horrible end.
It wasn't—she didn't understand, then. I didn't, either. I told her to
stop anything that wasn't normal. I was afraid that she'd be hunted,
that she would be killed. We had no idea who the killers were.

But it wasn't the fieflord. He started to investigate the deaths. He
sent his thugs far and wide. From that, I suspected that those mur-
ders happened only in Nightshade. He didn't care about us. There
were no real laws.

Ybelline wanted to know what they were searching for.

Not sure. I didn't talk to Nightshade's people. No one who wanted
to live—or at least walk or use their arms—did, unless approached,
and even then it was dicey. But I heard them talking about rituals,
ritualists.

He watched Elianne. When at home, he watched her marks.
They had stopped growing, stopped spreading; they covered
no visible parts of her skin—for which he was grateful. But his
fear was strong enough that he remembered, and because he
did, he was the first to notice when the marks began to change.

It was slow; the lines shifted slightly. One thinned. Some of
the straight parts were slowly replaced by curves, curls. They
darkened. He remembered that. They darkened.

He was not allowed to view the bodies. After the seventh
corpse, he no longer tried. Each death caused a drift, a turn, in
the marks that adorned Elianne. He didn't tell her. He didn't
want to scare her. The deaths caused terror enough.

But he was certain, by the seventh death, that the deaths
were connected to her. They occurred in one-quarter of the
fief, and almost nowhere else; the dead were all children of
roughly her age. They had been marked—those marks laid
there by the people who had then proceeded to murder them
slowly, as if the death itself were a sacrifice. No gods who
demanded sacrifices were good news, and Severn knew of

none—but there were a *lot* of gods who received the muttered, desperate prayers of those who lived in Nightshade.

And the deaths kept happening. The presence of Nightshade's thugs became a constant. The fear of the deaths eclipsed even the fear of Lord Nightshade. And the marks continued, death by death, to shift, to change. Elianne was herself—afraid, but unchanged by anything but the shadow of very sensible fear. But he was afraid that she wouldn't remain that way.

He knew nothing.

He knew that he knew nothing. He hated himself for the ignorance that it was almost impossible to relieve. He didn't read much, but even had he, there were no books to read; no experts—on this side of the Ablayne that separated fiefs from the rest of the city—with whom to confer. Even were there, they might demand to see Elianne, and if they did, they might keep her.

In the end, he chose to take the biggest risk he had ever taken in his life—and that life included facing Ferals. He sent a message to Castle Nightshade.

Ybelline could see the spire of that castle; could see the breadth of it, the shadow it cast across the whole of the fief, sunlight notwithstanding. She could see the cages—empty on the night Severn visited—that were meant to display the grisly remains of those who had displeased the fieflord. She could see the gates, and the Barrani who guarded them at all hours of any day. Only when the fieflord chose to venture into the streets of his fiefs did those guards vanish, and their absence was not a good sign for someone like Severn.

The message was verbal. The men to whom it was offered were mortal; mortal thugs, not the Barrani. Against men, Severn was large enough, old enough now, to stand a fighting chance. He had no intention of visiting Castle Nightshade in person; he had seen the use to which those cages were put, and he had no doubt that what was left of him after the fief-lord took offense would fit them nicely.

A scuffle did ensue, and knives had been drawn, but no blood had been shed, and no Barrani had intervened to ruin Severn's day. He offered information to Nightshade about the murders that were even now occurring in the fiefs. A possible lead.

He did not choose to meet Nightshade anywhere near their home—although it would take Nightshade no time to find it, should he choose to do so. But Severn was far more than uneasy now. He was certain that the murders were circling Elianne, terrified that if something wasn't done, she would die.

Or worse.

Severn labored under no illusion. If a nebulous *worse* existed, he was not the man to stop it. He had neither the knowledge nor the power; he had the will, but will was not, had never been, enough. Will alone had not saved Elianne's mother. If anyone could save Elianne, it was Lord Nightshade.

Lord Nightshade chose to meet him. In possible retaliation for the message and Severn's refusal to speak directly with the mortals who served Nightshade—in name at least—he had chosen to meet Severn at night. By the south well. The well itself was relatively safe during the day. Nowhere was safe during the night.

Barrani, however, wandered at will at night; the Ferals did not terrify them. Ferals were cunning but seemed constantly hungry—a feeling with which Severn could identify. They *were* stupid enough to attack Barrani; they weren't—even in a pack—powerful enough to survive their stupidity. It was almost as if they were mortal and not of the shadows across the fief's interior borders.

Severn approached Nightshade. When he was three yards away, he fell to his knees. This allowed him to bow his head, to school his expression.

"Rise," the fieflord said, as if this abasement was both expected and irrelevant. "You are not familiar with the subtleties of court gestures, court language; I will dispense with them for now. For this one evening—and from you—formality is neither required nor desired. You will not be considered lacking in appropriate respect."

Severn rose. He kept his hands loose but by his sides. He had daggers—the guards had not removed them—but they were irrelevant when confronting Barrani. Especially this one. Severn suspected that the lack of inspection was due in large part to that fact: relieving Severn of weapons somehow implied that Severn could be a threat.

He had rehearsed on the way here. He had composed his opening statement, his story, the answers to the questions he thought might be asked. The cold blue of Barrani eyes made remembering any of them difficult. He gave up on them.

"Are these murders happening in any other fief?"

The guards closest to Severn stiffened but didn't cuff the side of his face or force him to his knees; Lord Nightshade had made clear that he would consider very little impertinent.

"That is an interesting question. It is not the one I expected, although I confess I had little in the way of expectation. It was made clear to me that you were both mortal and young."

"And you expected I'd have nothing to offer."

"I considered my presence a reward for your boldness. It is not often that I am...called out of the castle. You are not wealthy; you are not owned; you bear no sign that would indicate you serve one or another of the petty factions that trouble my streets. Even did you, none would have information of interest to me in specific." His smile was gentle. His voice was not. "If you bore me, if you have wasted my time, there is a penalty to be paid."

Severn did not blink.

"Because it is an interesting question, and the answer would not otherwise be difficult to obtain, I will answer. No. These deaths have only occurred within Nightshade."

"What do the marks on the bodies mean?"

Silence, then. Night made the color of Barrani eyes appear darker than they were, or at least that was Severn's hope. "Marks?"

He knew that this was a misstep, then. "There're rumors—"

"Are there? I seldom trouble to listen to rumors. Tonight is a rare exception. I would hear your rumors, boy. In detail."

"The rumors say there are marks on the victims."

"Ah." He glanced to the left, and the Barrani guard standing there detached from his lord's side. He approached Severn slowly. Severn, however, held his ground. His glance flickered once to the guard, but he forced it to return to the fief-lord's cold expression. He had known that there would be a risk; even delivering the message had caused bruises and cuts.

"And do the rumors say much else about these so-called marks?"

He drew a shallow breath before responding. "They're black. They cover the arms and legs of the victim; possibly the back. Some people say they're words, writing."

"Rumor is seldom so accurate."

Severn forced himself not to shrug. While shrugging was a gesture that served in place of many different replies, it would not help him here. He doubted that the fieflord shrugged. Ever.

"Where did you see these marks, boy?"

A pause, then. But not a long pause. "The body of a child in the southern block. Her name was Tina."

"You are lying."

Severn did not deny it. He waited.

"I will ask again while you consider the wisdom of your choices. Where did you see these marks?"

So many choices came down to survival. So many. But for Severn, survival was tied to family, to duty. The simple fact of death did not and had not obliterated the fact of family. Even his own. Silence could protect Elianne, if it was necessary.

"One of my friends," he finally said, "has the same marks."

"I wish to speak with this friend."

"No." Possibly the hardest refusal Severn had ever offered. He knew what his death would to do to Elianne and the girls. He uttered no further words of defiance; he simply waited. The first blow rocked him back; the second doubled him over. He fell to his knees, splaying his hands flat to avoid planting his face into the worn stones that girded the well.

"I wish to speak with this friend."

"No."

There was blood in his mouth. A cracked rib, maybe two. His shoulder was either broken or dislocated. In the distance, as if sensing blood, the Ferals howled.

"Take me to this friend."

This time, Severn remained silent, braced for further blows. Those came, but they were carefully delivered; none broke his legs. It didn't matter. He had been hurt before, and this kind of pain passed, one way or the other. He did not beg, although he considered it; he might have tried if he'd had any sense that humiliation was what the fieflord wanted.

The beating stopped abruptly, although the pain lingered. Severn was hauled to his feet, facing the fieflord.

"Benito," the fieflord said, which surprised him. "Tina— Christina, I believe, if one is being entirely correct. Anali. Do you recognize these names?"

Severn nodded.

"Ah. Amal. Shardan. Lina—again, a diminutive." He continued to speak names, and Severn understood two things: they were the names of all those who had been murdered or sacrificed, and he recognized every single one of them. Some, of course, he'd learned on the street. And those names he almost expected to belong to people he knew—the gossip would barely reach him otherwise. But some of the names? He'd heard nothing.

This, then, was what he feared, and had feared from the beginning. He knew all of the names. He had interacted with all of the dead. And…so had Elianne.

Lord Nightshade watched him for a long moment after the last of the names had faded.

Severn swallowed. "Who is doing this? If you tell me—"

"If it is as I suspect, you will not find him; he might hunt here, but this is not where he dwells. If you managed to find him, you would die. I think you too old to be sacrificed, but it is clear to me that you have a connection with the intended, ultimate victim—and that connection is vital. Let me ask another question. When did these marks appear on your friend?"

"Maybe three years ago. Maybe less."

"You should have come to me sooner."

Severn said nothing. They both knew that this was theoretical. It would never have happened. It would not happen now, not beyond this one meeting.

"Time," the fieflord continued. "These deaths might have started the moment the marks appeared, but it was too early. The risk of being caught was too high. The risk is not small now. I wish to know how they found your friend, but that is not a question you can answer."

Severn wanted to know as well. If he left—if they left— would Elianne be safe? Or would it start again, somewhere else?

"I do not know how much time is left for your friend. Tell

me, boy, have the marks on their skin, the marks with which you are familiar, changed at all since the killings began?"

Severn did not answer for one long beat; it was not an act of defiance. He struggled, for that moment, to breathe. The fieflord's eyes were the color of night, wide and unblinking. He approached Severn, and Severn stood, frozen, until the fieflord's eyes were the only thing he could see.

"The marks on the corpses we have managed to retrieve—and we have not retrieved all of them—are identical. There is no shift or change in the marks made upon those bodies." He paused. "Were you twins—and I assume you are not—I do not believe any of the other deaths would be necessary. Were your friend your child, they would not be, either.

"But you are too old. Neither of these can apply."

"What—what are they trying to do?"

"Do you not already know? Or do you ask simply to confirm your growing suspicion?"

Severn closed his eyes.

"I will not tell you what the marks signify. To you or your friend, they might be simple disfigurements. This magic is not a magic I can easily use, not a magic I would have ever considered. But I will say this: with those marks comes power. It is a power, in its prime, that is almost sorcerous in strength—but perhaps that means little to you.

"The words are the words. Someone attempts to rewrite them. It is not a sympathetic magic, but it is fueled by death. Someone believes that they can rewrite what is written, revising its meaning, reshaping the power inherent in what has been given to your friend. And it is almost time now.

"They have started at the beginning, at what they must feel is the beginning."

"What will happen to—to my friend?"

"If I am correct? Your friend will have power, but that

power will be linked to, and possibly controlled by, those who now complete the sacrifices. If that is the case, boy, I take a risk I should not take—it is arrogance on my part. Or perhaps curiosity. If what your enemies now attempt is successful, your friend will have the power to destroy this fief, and perhaps the city itself. I think it is the fief—or all of the fiefs—at which that power will be aimed."

"All of the fiefs."

"Tell me, do you live alone? Is it only you and your friend? You do not answer. Let me assume that the answer is no. Are the others your age, or the age of your friend?"

Silence.

"They are mortal, and children," Nightshade continued. "And they are the victims your adversary is seeking, even as we speak."

"There are two." The words were strangled, almost inaudible, even to Severn, who uttered them.

"Lord," one of the Barrani guards said.

The fieflord shook his head. "You are too poor to leave this fief, but even were you not, I would not recommend it. The borders will be watched. Unless you attempt to pass between fiefs, or into the heart of *Ravellon*, the shadows that exist at the very heart of the fiefdoms, they will find you. They will find your friend.

"And they will find any others that depend on you. How much have those marks changed?"

He had not answered the previous question, and did not answer this one. "What will happen if they find the others?"

"They will do as they have done. They will sacrifice them. But this time—this time I believe they will have the power necessary to subvert those marks, and the person who bears them, entirely. Your friend will die in any meaningful sense of the word, and that death, that transformation, will be bought at the cost of the lives your friend values most. Tell me where your friends are, and I will confirm my suspicions."

Severn understood. "No."

"They will die anyway, boy. And if they do—"

"No."

"If I kill them, they will not be used against your friend. They cannot be used against your friend. It is the act of dying that defines the sacrifice. And the pain of that dying, the length of it. If you give them to me, the deaths will be swift and painless. If you do not—and we do not find them, cannot follow you—they will be long and torturous. It might happen now. It might happen tomorrow. You are running out of time."

"If they die," he finally said, "if you kill them, will my friend with the marks be safe?"

"From me?" The fieflord smiled.

"From them."

"As I said, I do not understand the magic well—it is, or would have been, a theoretical discussion, a possibility. But if I understand what little information you have been willing to part with, yes. If there are no others, if your friend forms no similar attachments in the fiefs, then yes. For now—and now is all mortals truly have—your friend will be safe. As you can imagine, it is not the fate of your friend that concerns me. It is the fate of my fief.

"Tell me, boy, and I will make certain your friends cannot be made into weapons."

"And the person with the marks?"

"They have shown, by weakness, by vulnerability, that they cannot safely contain the marks bestowed upon them. Yes," he added, to the question that would not leave Severn's lips, "I will execute them. And if you are somehow considering flight from the fiefs, if you believe, somehow, that the law across the bridge will save your friend, you do not understand the threat they pose.

"The Eternal Emperor would no more suffer your friend to live than I. The danger to the Empire is too great. Have you other questions?"

Severn said nothing.

"You want to believe I am lying. You cannot. I will offer another alternative. Bring your friends to the well. To this well. Bring them in the daylight, so they will not be suspicious. I will see to them. Choose for them: swift death, or terrible slow death. They are, by your reckoning, children; they are not capable of making that choice for themselves. They will believe, of course, that they can avoid either death, no matter how terrified they are.

"I have not lied tonight. I believe you understand this. Bring the children here, and I will give them the painless, swift death." When Severn did not speak, the fieflord's voice gentled. "It is clear to me that the marked child is of great import to you. Were they not, you would not have risked both your life and theirs by coming to me.

"You are unwilling to risk their life now. You believe that I will kill your friend. I believe that I *might*, but it is not guaranteed. Even that, however, you will not risk."

"I don't want to lose the others, either."

"No. But Severn, you will. You will." Blue-black eyes narrowed, but even so, they filled his vision. The distant howls of hunting Ferals were harmless in comparison. "Imagine," the fieflord whispered. "Imagine their deaths. You did not see the corpses of the victims. I did. I have. The deaths were slow and painful; they mutilated the children while they lived. Slowly, and slowly, allowing them to inch toward death without achieving the peace of it for some time. I imagine, in the end, death was relief; it was their only escape." And as he spoke, Severn *could* imagine it. He could see it. He could hear it. The screams of the dying. The loss—ah, of eyes, of hearing; the loss of fingers, of toes. Of teeth.

"Imagine it," Lord Nightshade said again. "That is what awaits them. I am not known for mercy, but it is mercy I offer. To you. To them."

Severn closed his eyes, but that did not break the spell—if a spell had even been cast. When he opened them—and he did—the fieflord was no longer directly in front of him.

Lord Nightshade lifted a hand, and his guards once again fell back. "We will go. Do what you know you must, if you are capable of it."

Severn did not wait. The Ferals were too close, and the rains plentiful enough that clinging to the interior walls of the well itself to avoid them wasn't a safe option. Had it been day, he would have remained by the well for a few hours, mingling with the crowd. There was no way the fieflord intended to set him free.

There was no way Elianne would be safe from him. Not now.

Severn sprinted. He was vibrating with anxiety, aware of every movement—every rat, every cockroach, every wind-blown piece of garbage. He could track the progress of Ferals by their distant howls; they weren't hunting yet. They might be, soon. Running when Ferals were close was very, very bad.

Home was fifteen minutes from the well at a brisk walk. Severn returned two hours later. He knew that losing possible tails wasn't the end of it. What the fieflord wanted, he always eventually obtained—but only if they stayed in Nightshade. They couldn't cross the Ablayne without being noticed. But they could cross the Nightshade borders, possibly escape that way.

Elianne was awake when he entered the rooms they shared.

Jade was snoring; Steffi was sleeping. In sleep, Jade's face matched her singing voice, and Steffi had always looked placid and pretty.

"Where were you?" she demanded.

He shrugged. He hadn't prepared an excuse for his absence; should have thought of that before he left. As her brows drew together in Elianne's version of a glare, he said, "Out." When her hands fell, as they sometimes did, to her hips, he grinned. Tweaked her nose. "I wanted to inspect the borders. No, not that one. But Barren or Liatt."

"Why?"

He shrugged again. "We might need to move."

"We can't cross the borders."

"We can."

"They're not safe—"

"They're not worse than Nightshade—and there are no people in the border zones."

"How do you *know* this?"

"I told you—I inspected."

"What if you—"

"This isn't the first time I've been in the border zones." And this, at least, was true. She was angry, but worry ebbed as he spoke, and without worry to drive it, the anger would leave as well. "Look—sleep. You're on water duty tomorrow. And food."

"And you?"

He shrugged himself out of his coat. "I'm beat. I'm sleeping. You can stay awake frowning all night if you want, but water still has to be fetched."

Elianne would die.
Elianne would die.
No, no, that's *not* what the fieflord said. Jade would die.

Steffi would die. The fieflord was hunting for the killers, but even the fieflord—who could find anyone in the fief if his anger was great enough—could not find the murderers in time. Severn did not believe he could do what the fieflord couldn't. And even if he could, what of it? He could send word to the fieflord—if he survived his discovery.

And if these faceless, nameless enemies came now?

Severn would die. Steffi and Jade would—eventually—die. And what would become of Elianne, then? She had survived the loss of her mother because she'd had Severn. What would she have?

Marks, twisted and rewritten, across her body, and murderers as masters.

Power. Nightshade said she'd have power. And if he believed that, he'd be hunting Elianne. He'd *be here* tonight. *Imagine it*, Nightshade said, his voice ever-present, undeniable. Severn could see almost nothing else. Had it not been night, had Elianne not been awake, he might have risked Ferals instead. Their howls weren't as chilling, as terrifying, as sickening, as the vision Nightshade's words had conjured. He was caught in their grip; he thought they would never leave him.

He needed to believe that he could save them.

He *could not* believe it.

"Severn?"

"Sleeping, remember?"

"I can't sleep."

He didn't ask why. He sighed—loudly, obviously—and lifted an arm. Elianne crept across the floor, turned her back toward his chest, caught his arm and wrapped it around her neck and shoulders. "Nightmare?" he asked, throat almost too thick to speak.

She nodded; her chin briefly pressed into the crook of his arm.

He held her. She snored. It had always been like this, even

when her mother had been alive. The rhythm of her breathing was like thread; it bound all of the various years and days
together into one continuous whole. She felt safe. She *was*
safe. She hated to be treated as a child; it was impossible, in
moments like this, to think of her in any other way. He had
kept her safe.

He would keep her safe. He would always keep her safe.
She was the heart of his family, to Severn; she was the heart
of his life, the center of it. What he wanted for her was safety
and whatever happiness could be scraped from the streets of
Nightshade. He did not sleep.

Jade woke, as she often did, from a nightmare. Her eyes
were barely open as she made her way to Elianne's side and
inserted herself between Severn and Elianne. She, too, fell
asleep. He looked at the two of them. The peace shattered.

He could hear Elianne screaming, see her face twisted not in
fury but in terror and pain. And he knew, as the longest night
of his life gave way, almost reluctantly, to dawn, why Nightshade had let him go. Had known before he reached home.

Elianne went out to the well. In the day, it was less of a
risk, although it was unusual to send her alone. She suspected
nothing. She suspected nothing because Severn was home.
Severn stayed with the girls.

He told them a story. He sat against the wall, and Steffi
leaned into him as he spoke. He did not raise his voice. He
fed them and wished he had something that would ease them
into sleep, something that— But no. That was for people with
money.

He had a dagger. Two. He had nothing else to offer them.
He could not shake Nightshade's words, Nightshade's command, and in the end, he didn't try. He believed the fieflord.

Steffi died first, because Steffi was less cautious than Jade;

she had been with them for longer. She trusted Severn be-cause Elianne trusted him. But no. She trusted him with her life because, until today, she could. He had not wanted to bring her home—and he wished, in bitter self-loathing, that he had not. Bringing her home led to this death. To this, or the other death that waited in the shadows.

Jade died less easily, but truthfully, not by much. Both girls had known who their killer was. He thought the pain of that worse, in the end, than the deep cuts to their jugulars. He did not cry, did not weep—not then. But after, hands slick with blood that would not stop flowing, he had been sick in the corner of the room; he could not make it out of the apart-ment in time.

He didn't know what he looked like when Elianne came home. Didn't know what his expression was. He saw hers. Ev-erything that Jade and Steffi felt when they died was there—and worse.

Nothing, not even her mother's death, had hurt her this much. Nothing except Severn *could*.

CHAPTER SEVEN

YBELLINE DID NOT LET GO OF SEVERN. HIS ARMS had long since stiffened and fallen away; hers gained strength. She did not tell him that it was not his fault. He had killed the children. He accepted the guilt, and she did not attempt to pry it from him. Nor did she tell him that he was wrong: what he had done to Elianne on that day had hurt her more than anything possibly could.

But she understood Lord Nightshade's fear far better than Severn did or could.

It would have been better, he said, speaking through the chaos of a past that was always with him, *if they had died at the hands of the killers.*

It wouldn't have been better for them.

It would have been better for Elianne.

What he did not say surprised Ybelline, because he did not feel it either: it would have been better for Severn.

Would it? In the end, would it? You would almost certainly be dead before that happened. Steffi and Jade would die as well. But not cleanly. Your Elianne would have come face-to-face with helplessness and utter despair—and in that state of mind, the transformation of her marks and her essential purpose would be fully formed.

Ybelline brushed hair from his forehead. *In pain, we lash out. In pain, we destroy both ourselves and others. That is the nature of pain. What might she then accomplish with the power she does not understand, when her pain was so deep and so endless?*

She won't come back to me.

I don't know.

Would you?

…It is not a valid question for one such as I. No matter who I am or what I do, I am part of my kin. But you found her. You found her again.

Silence. Walls grew thicker, stronger, and this time Ybelline did not press or touch them at all. She understood what the Wolves wanted of and from her, and she now had the answers that Helmat demanded.

She's here, Severn surprised her by saying. *She's with the Hawks.*

And Elianne did not know Severn was here, with the Wolves—or attempting to join them. *I tried to find her when she ran. But I'm the last person she'll ever want to see. I think—I think she could be happy here. She always dreamed of crossing the bridge. We all did. Ybelline?*

I'm here.

I'm tired. I'm just so tired.

I know. It is safe to sleep here. It is safe, for now.

Helmat did not choose to speak until Ybelline's stalks detached themselves from Severn's forehead. She continued, however, to hold the young man, who appeared to be sleeping. Her arms were slender; shorter and smaller than Severn's in all ways. But there was strength in her, regardless.

"Well?"

Her face was adorned with tears; she had shed them while

in communion, and they had not yet ceased to fall. Helmat was no stranger to Tha'alani tears; they fell often, when the Tha'alani were at work. These tears, however, were different. He knew it. En knew it.

Garadin's enlarged face had long since dissipated from the far wall, the mirror connection severed. Helmat was grateful for the absence. Garadin—and all of his kin—were the most difficult, the most coldly truculent, in the wake of an investigation such as this.

Ybelline, however, was not. Helmat had clasped his hands loosely behind his back; he left them there. Had the decision been his to make, he would have ordered Ybelline back to the Tha'alani compound—ah, no, *quarter*—and canceled the request until someone like Garadin could fulfill it. Seeing her face, her reddened eyes, the tears she did not bother to wipe away, he felt a visceral surge of self-loathing.

He was Lord of Wolves for a reason. None of this conflict now showed. He had, in the end, accepted that she would do the job, and he endured the consequences. "Is Severn sleeping?"

"Yes."

"Will he wake if you let go of him?"

"Probably."

"You don't want to let go of him."

"Not yet."

En moved from the wall against which he was leaning. "What did you find?"

"He killed two children. Girls," she added, aware of Helmat. En didn't often differentiate between victims if they were mortal.

"Ybelline," En said. Helmat was willing to wait for her to gather her thoughts and put them into cogent—and professional—words. Elluvian, however, was not. He had never been particularly patient, a fact Helmat found ironic.

The Barrani were Immortal; they could be killed but absent murder, they had no fundamental lack of time.

Ybelline's glance flickered over En and away. "He was not paid to kill them. They were not assassinations."

"But children."

She nodded. "I think, in his position, you would have done the same."

"Would you?"

She shook her head, but the movement was slow and thoughtful. "I do not think I would have believed that there was no other choice. Even if that were, in the end, proved true. But you? You would have believed it."

Helmat stiffened. "Tell me, then. Tell me everything."

"You are aware that there was some commotion in the Imperial Court recently?"

"There's always a commotion in the Imperial Court."

"The Hawks have adopted a mascot. That was the word that was used. Intelligence documents highlighted it; the person who wrote the report was clearly not a person from whom all sense of humor has been leeched. I would expect you to be peripherally aware of the difficulty; it involved the Halls of Law."

"It didn't involve the Wolves."

Her expression made clear that she was tired of games for the day, but he held his peace for a moment. It was far easier to see anger—even chilly as it was—on her face than pain or grief.

"I am aware of the unusual situation."

"You are aware of the reasons that it became so?"

"Mortals are seldom mascots, but yes, I am aware of the reason the Emperor was against it."

"And against the survival of the child in question."

"And against the survival of the child in question, yes."

"It is my belief that that child, Severn, and the two children he killed are linked."

Helmat regarded the sleeping man in question. The killing of children carried with it a weight of assumptions, evoked a visceral disgust, that the killing of adults of any race did not. Even for Helmat. Perhaps especially for Helmat. Wolves killed, and were killed, in the line of duty. It happened frequently enough that it was not remarkable. It was always regrettable.

Helmat could think of no cases—he would search through Records later—in which those unavoidable and regrettable deaths involved children. The Wolves had hunted children before, it was true—but only in tandem with kidnappers the Emperor had deemed sufficiently dangerous. The Emperor, however, erred on the side of caution when handing down his edicts. Many of those who worked in the Halls of Law felt he was too conservative.

Helmat, oddly enough, was not one of them. He understood that the burden of evidence, the burden of proof, was necessary. Without it, it would be far too easy to pass judgment oneself, and far too easy to turn the Halls of Law into a terrifying, personal fiefdom.

But he was human, same as most of the rest. There were crimes that infuriated him, deaths that made him feel helpless and useless. That feeling drove him to work harder—but it could easily drive him to a merciless rage, and the decisions made from that place might not withstand more rational scrutiny.

Some of the men and women he accepted into the scant ranks of the Wolves had killed before, often in what they had considered self-defense. Helmat tended to agree with their estimation, which was why he accepted their service. But none of those deaths had involved children.

He exhaled. "Ybelline."

"You want me to show you."

"I want you to show me."

En coughed theatrically.

"I will throw you out by the ears," Helmat said, "if you say another word."

En being En immediately proved Helmat a liar. "Are you certain you want to do this? It is not required."

"I do not have the visceral, lasting fear of the Tha'alani that characterizes your people."

"You only have a mortal lifetime to accrue dangerous secrets."

"Your thoughts are appreciated," Helmat replied, in a tone that implied the opposite. "But the decision in its entirety is mine. And children are involved."

En retreated, literally.

Ybelline did not. She approached Helmat, and in spite of his decision, he braced himself for the contact.

Elluvian waited as Helmat stiffened. The Barrani envied the Tha'alani their ability to ferret out truth. It was not something that magic could easily—or perfectly—grant; while magic could be used in a similar fashion, it was prone to damage the target's mind, sometimes irreparably.

But that was an old life, an old series of experiments. He shook himself free of the memories as he watched Ybelline's report of events. Ybelline herself did not speak; she had no need of words now. When she had finished, silence grew. Her antennae left Helmat's forehead. The Wolflord's knuckles were white.

The girl, then. The child he had seen with An'Teela. Severn had been following her, and capably enough that he had not alerted An'Teela to either his presence or his interest. He could now understand An'Teela's interest in the child: she was almost certainly Chosen. A mortal. While it was not unheard of, it was extremely unusual.

"En."

Elluvian turned toward Helmat. Helmat sat heavily in a free chair, hands gripping the armrests. There was about him a look that implied both shock and certainty. Severn, Elluvian thought, would be a Wolf. There was no question of it.

"Tell me," he told the Lord of Wolves. "Ybelline may correct you if you leave out something she considers of relevance."

Ybelline raised a honey-brown brow at the flat statement, but she nodded.

Helmat then spoke of what he had seen and experienced.

Silence followed. Elluvian considered the information Helmat conveyed—hesitantly at first, and then with greater determination as he continued.

"What are you thinking?"

"May I question the interrogator?" Elluvian knew the word annoyed Helmat.

"Please do."

Elluvian then turned to face Ybelline. "Does Severn regret what he did?"

"Yes."

"Would he do it again?"

She hesitated before offering an answer that was far less definitive. "...Yes. Do you understand what these nameless enemies were trying to achieve?"

Technically, Elluvian was not required to answer Ybelline's questions. He had never been an officer to stand on technicalities unless he wished to annoy. "I understand as much as the fieflord did. They failed—but how or why is not entirely clear. Did the girl flee Nightshade?"

"Yes."

"And arrived here."

Ybelline said, "It is not relevant."

"Surely, that is not up to you to decide."

"It is entirely up to me, as you are well aware. What the Wolves require, I have given. If the Wolves require more, they may contact Imperial Intelligence." Which she knew wouldn't happen. Elluvian considered doing so out of simple spite; he would, however, have to convince Helmat it was necessary. To Helmat, she said, "I have a request."

"And that?"

"It's entirely unofficial."

He loosened his hands, gesturing impatiently with the right.

"When—and if—you send him to hunt, I wish to be the agent recalled to examine him after the fact."

"To spare your people?"

"No. His pain would be damaging to my kin, but it will not be damaging in the same way to the Tha'alanari." She grimaced. "Garadin will ask that you not honor my request."

"And you've told him this," Elluvian said, "because his minor desire to spite Garadin might tip the scales in your favor?"

She smiled, then. It was rueful. "We are not all of one mind, although we are connected."

"If you would be so good as to wake our new recruit, I will consider your request with far more favor."

Severn did not wake quickly. In the interstices between sleep and full mental acuity, Helmat asked Rosen to have food sent up from the mess hall. He wasn't entirely certain the youth would eat, and left the babysitting, such as it was, to Rosen, who didn't appreciate it. She did, however, obey. "He could use some weight. You said he was eighteen?"

"I believe he said he was eighteen."

She shook her head. "I'll feed him."

"Do not force-feed him."

She snorted. She wasn't terribly maternal. She was, however, tribal, and if Severn could pass her subtle and unofficial tests, she would accept him as something far more valuable to her than family. Those tests, however, weren't Helmat's current problem. He glanced at En, and En nodded; they retreated once again to Helmat's office.

There, Helmat gestured the mirror into its wakeful state. "Security services, Saidh Mankev. Put me through if he's available." Although mirrors were flat and small, this one now appeared to bristle. Helmat almost groaned. "That was fast."

The head of Imperial Security was a small, tidy man; the set of his shoulders matched the long, narrow width of his face—which seemed to have had any expression leeched out of it permanently. He wasn't a young man, and had probably never been young, even at birth; he had that air about him.

Although he had served as the head of Imperial Security for much of Helmat's tenure, age, like any other sign of humanity, seemed to avoid Saidh. His hair was still jet-black, his back unstooped.

He was respected by the Halls of Law, which balanced the general rage he was almost certain to engender whenever the Halls of Law crossed paths with the Imperial Security services. Saidh could not be bribed. He could barely be reasoned with; he could not be moved by any command that did not come directly from the Emperor himself.

"Lord of Wolves," Saidh now said. "I am delighted to hear from you." His tone and expression conveyed no such delight. Helmat was, however, surprised to hear what might have passed for sarcasm in a different man. "Tha'alani investigation of one crime has led, indirectly, to information involving another—a crime, or a series of crimes, that is now two decades old. The Hawks had given up on the case," he added, in case this wasn't clear to Helmat.

Of course it was clear. Ybelline had come because the Tha'alanari was already in chaos. Whatever Timorri had been charged with investigating, he had been prepared to face. He had therefore faced something unexpected—and damaging.

Helmat shut down that line of thought as unprofitable, because Ybelline was right: he was overprotective because she was a young woman—and they seemed to get younger every passing year. A young woman who would become the leader of her people had to be able to face danger and survive.

"You will have heard, given your earlier request of Garadin, that Timorri has retired from the service."

Helmat nodded, grim now.

"Two other members of the Tha'alanari have requested indeterminate leaves of absence. I have granted both requests."

"You've found our Tha'alani killer."

"Technically, no. We've found one of his mob." There was a weighted pause. "Is Elluvian with you?"

"He is. Is this a case for Elluvian?"

"Yes. Ybelline is with you."

"She is not with us at the moment."

"She has not left the premises."

"By law, Elluvian does not interact with the Tha'alani." As, Helmat thought, with growing frustration, Saidh knew well. "If you believe this job requires Elluvian, you'd better start filing paperwork now. The Emperor is willing to grant exemptions to both the Wolves and the Security services—but the need for those exemptions is to be documented."

"And you are not doing the documentation."

"Not unless it becomes relevant, no. What happened?"

"We asked for the examination of a prisoner in our jails. Timorri was the examiner sent. His search through the specific set of crimes we wished reviewed led to a crime that we were unaware the man had committed. You know that two decades ago, Tha'alani who stepped outside of the Tha'alani quarter—or who lived too close to its less guarded edges—were murdered. The murders were not quick. They were also not committed by a single person; a crowd of mortals engaged in the torture and degradation of their victims."

Helmat nodded.

"The Hawks determined this much. What they did not determine, however, was that the crowd was not composed entirely *of* mortals."

"There was a Barrani present," Helmat said, voice flat.

"There was a Barrani present, yes. This is not proof, of course. But the memories of our criminal made absolutely clear that the Barrani was not simply present; he had engineered both the kidnapping and the creation of the mob that carried out the crime. All of the crimes," he added. "This is one of the few cases of serial murder in which we are absolutely certain we know the names of all of the victims. Not that the perpetrators made any attempt to hide their crimes.

"Our detainee did not provide us with a Barrani name, but we believe Elluvian might at least recognize the target if he is shown what Timorri witnessed."

"Be that as it may, Elluvian does not speak with the Tha'alani in that fashion. If you have issues with that, take them up with the Emperor."

En cleared his throat. Loudly. "Gentlemen. While I find it oddly comforting to listen to the two of you, if your target is Barrani, you waste time we do not have."

Saidh nodded. "We wish to impart information about the target to you in the most efficient fashion possible."

Elluvian's smile was slender. He chose to ignore Saidh's wishes. "Tell me where the bodies were found. Do not force me to make inquiries of the Hawks. It will spoil both my day and theirs."

The location—which Helmat could also easily access—appeared as an overlay in a grid across the image of Saidh in the mirror; the street appeared directly between Saidh's eyes and nose.

"Are we to apprehend?"

"This is an execution, not a standard ground hunt. We have more than enough evidence for the Emperor to make a decision."

"Dragons do not historically require much in the way of evidence," Elluvian pointed out. Helmat snapped his name, and En fell silent. "Very well. Log the date and the time."

"You do not know who you are hunting."

"And that," Elluvian replied, before Helmat could, "is not your problem."

Helmat shut the mirror down, denying Saidh the opportunity to reply.

He then turned to the Barrani Wolf. "There are still forms it's essential to maintain—and criticisms of Dragons are *never* politically wise."

"They are, however, expected."

"From you, yes." Helmat took the seat behind his desk, and once again gestured at the mirror. This time it revealed a very familiar office, at the center of which was an equally suspicious Rosen. "Send Severn in. And send Ybelline in, as well."

"She's no longer in the office."

"She's probably waiting outside the doors."

Ybelline was almost outraged. Almost. She was—as most of her kind would be—exhausted and grief-sick. She required the comfort and safety of her physical home, a reminder that her life was not, and would never be, the life of the person whose thoughts she had briefly but deeply touched.

Instead, she got Rosen's suspicious face, and an invitation to the interior of Helmat's sparse, cold office. And, for good measure, Scoros's and Garadin's simultaneous intrusion through the Tha'alaan, neither of whom were pleased for, or with, her.

Garadin was faintly condescending: *What else did you expect? You wished to go in my stead. And now you will have to deal with the consequences of that decision.* Behind the faint condescension, however, was a mixture of fear and guilt.

The seeds, she knew, of madness.

Scoros was older than Garadin, older by more than Ybelline. He had been part of the Tha'alanari for all of Ybelline's living memory. But the Tha'alaan remembered more, and more deeply.

This is not for you, Ybelline. Understand that. This is not for you. We have seen what Timorri saw.

Timorri was absolutely silent.

Yes, Scoros said quietly. *I am with him, and one other. We will not leave him in the dark alone. But he cannot yet bespeak even the Tha'alanari. It is not safe for us. Do not fear for him. And do not attempt to speak to him yourself. It is not a command, but a request, Ybelline. Consider it a plea.*

The Lord of Wolves has called me.

Yes.

Do you know why?

No, no more than you, but you are not, and have never been, foolish. You have studied the Halls of Law; you understand the Imperial Security Service. You understand what Timorri saw—we all saw it, briefly. Tell me what you think your role will be.

She exhaled. *The criminal is Barrani. In most cases, where the criminal is Barrani, there is no role for us. No role for mortals, either.*

The Barrani deal with criminals who break Imperial Laws if those laws cross racial boundaries. And clearly this has.

The Barrani do deal with criminals when the crime itself is considered petty. But even the Barrani hesitate to risk their own lives when the criminal is powerful. You know this, he added, with a hint of gentle reproach.

Ah, Scoros was tired. Exhausted. She reached out to him gently, enveloped him in the Tha'alani version of a hug; it required no arms, no physical presence, simply the warmth that might accompany the gesture. But it was not simple, and it could be all-encompassing. Ybelline was powerful.

Scoros did not even tell her that it wasn't necessary.

I will speak with the Lord of Wolves, she told him gently, forcing all apprehension from her interior voice. But she was determined, as she headed toward the office door, that Helmat would be allowed *nothing* that further hurt the Tha'alani at this critical time.

She was not surprised to see Severn standing to one side of Helmat's desk. She was, however, surprised to see Elluvian. The Barrani were exempt—even as criminals—from the Tha'alani investigative procedures otherwise employed; it was a matter of the caste court and its demands. While she understood the resentment this immunity engendered in those who were not exempt, she, and the rest of the Tha'alanari, were grateful.

"Apologies, Ybelline. The Imperial office requests your services." Helmat knew she knew this; she did not always understand why the obvious had to be stated. But she accepted that it did, and offered Helmat a weary smile.

She now understood what her role here was. She did not like it. At all.

"I realize that this is not your fault." Turning to Severn, she said, "Do you understand what your role is to be?"

He nodded.

She forced her hands to loosen. "Helmat, this is highly unusual."

"How so? If the hunt involves a Barrani of indeterminate name, this is standard procedure."

"Severn is not yet a Wolf. This duty—"

"He is on the Imperial roster as of five minutes ago. Mellianne is occupied, and even were she not, she is not the ideal partner for Elluvian. Rosen was, at one point, but she's no longer physically capable. And I believe Severn has some idea of what the hunt entails." He did not openly accuse Ybelline of revealing information the young Wolf should not have.

Ybelline flushed. Her antennae were practically vibrating; she had learned to school her expression, had learned to adjust body position, but had not yet mastered that stillness of the one racial feature humans most feared.

Severn said, "I'm on probation." He smiled at her.

"This is not the duty given to someone who is on probation, as you call it."

"Lord Marlin decides what duties are given to the men and women under his command," was Severn's reasonable—and accurate—reply. "I am to receive the impressions of our target that exist in the Tha'alanari. I am to confirm his identity, if we manage to track the target down. Without my confirmation—"

"Yes, yes, she knows," Elluvian interjected.

"I believe he is attempting to demonstrate to Ybelline that *he* knows," Helmat said. "Perhaps you would care to wait outside."

"I do not care to wait, as you put it, at all."

"Unfortunate, then. Continue, Private."

"Without my confirmation," Severn said, obeying the Lord of Wolves, "the target cannot be legally executed."

Ybelline nodded.

"However," Severn continued, "should Elluvian decide not to wait for my confirmation, as long as the only people killed by Elluvian are Barrani, it's unlikely to come under Imperial oversight or review. It would be considered entirely a matter for the Barrani Caste Court, which means officially no murder has been committed."

Ybelline said nothing for one long beat. Yes, she thought as she approached Severn, she was *very* grateful that the minds of the Barrani were closed, locked, and barred.

"Those exemptions don't apply for the rest of us," Severn added, as he waited for Ybelline to make contact. "In as much as possible, I'm to stop anyone else from getting injured."

"The Barrani have a way of making that far, far more difficult than it sounds."

He knew.

Helmat watched them. Severn stiffened; Ybelline did not.

"You want the boy," En said.

"You're the one who brought him in."

"I thought he showed promise."

"He does."

"The Tha'alani is not wrong. This is highly unusual. He has not even had the benefit of your deplorably lax and inadequate training."

The Wolves received good training; they had to, by Imperial dictate. Very little of that good training had ever met with Elluvian's approval. Elluvian's approval, however, would have cost lives in the earlier stages. "You've often said the best training is experience."

"Ah. And so this is somehow my fault?"

"It is an example of the consequences of following your hectoring advice, yes."

En chuckled. "You *do* want this one."

"For however long we can keep him, yes."

"Very well."

"Do you have a clear idea of who we're hunting?"

En didn't answer.

"How long have you harbored suspicions?"

"I am by natural inclination suspicious. It saves both time and—in mortal terms—heartache. I am not a Hawk," he continued, when Helmat failed to respond. "Investigations of a certain nature are not my responsibility."

His tone implied that they were beneath him. This annoyed Helmat, but only mildly; he was aware that En considered most of life—much of it Barrani—beneath him. En understood the chain of command; he was willing to obey orders. Where Barrani were concerned, this was not a given, and was, in fact, unusual; Barrani generally considered orders optional suggestions, if they could be safely ignored.

En had been part of the Wolves since their founding, which was before Helmat's time entirely. He had been responsible for the selective training of many of the Wolves that had been Helmat's seniors, and responsible for at least three of their deaths. In this, Helmat also trusted the Barrani Wolf.

"We will be hunting Barrani," En said, as Ybelline broke contact. Severn's knees locked; to Helmat's eye, it was almost necessary.

"You understand," Ybelline said softly, to Severn. "What hurts us most is the insanity of the hatred and the malice."

"The criminal from whom this information was received was mortal." Severn surprised Helmat; he spoke steadily, although his color had shaded to gray.

"Yes. The pattern of behavior seems to involve humans in

large enough groups that they're malleable. The man that you will be hunting does not—in all of the incidents the human criminal participated in—appear to lift a hand himself."

"Which is irrelevant," Helmat interjected, stepping in to take control of the conversation. "The Emperor has made his decision, and rendered judgment. All that is left is to find and apprehend the criminal. En."

Elluvian nodded.

CHAPTER EIGHT

"YOU ARE NOT FAMILIAR ENOUGH WITH THE streets of Elantra," Elluvian told the Wolf candidate two long days later. Severn's knowledge of the city streets seemed confined to the streets An'Teela and her partner patrolled. This was not their destination.

Ybelline had communicated, to the probationary Wolf, the locations involved in the decades-old crimes. She lived in Elantra; she was aware of how little in the way of evidence might remain.

Severn privately thought "little" and "none whatsoever" were the same, but Elluvian insisted on examining those locations.

In each, Severn had been instructed to stand back and observe.

He did. Elluvian attracted attention; he was Barrani. Here, in the less wealthy parts of town, that mattered. Children were pulled back by grandparents, as if Elluvian's shadow was cast, invisibly, over the people who occupied the streets. He looked, now, for surprise—for a type of fear that hinted at echoes of past violence. He looked for something like recognition. He watched as unheard words passed between adults.

Most of their attention was watchful—the attention Elluvian would have garnered had he been in the streets of the fief of Nightshade. Nothing implied knowledge of what had happened here, in the open, before Severn was born.

Three times, Severn stood in different streets, observing. He wanted to see something that might somehow provide answers, or at least better questions. He wanted to help Ybelline and her people.

But nothing helpful was likely to come from this. He was almost certain Elluvian knew that as well.

"Have you ever experienced difficulty while in pursuit of An'Teela?"

The Hawks had a regular route. They patrolled the city streets with the intent to be seen; their presence was a statement. It was not, given the patrol was primarily Barrani, particularly subtle. And it was not, again given the composition of that patrol, an entirely safe beat. Barrani Hawks were given patrol beats that had caused difficulty for their mortal counterparts.

The young man shrugged. "Nothing I couldn't handle," he finally said, when it became clear Elluvian desired more than a shrug as a response.

Severn's knowledge of their current destination had been given to him by Ybelline—a woman who did not leave the Tha'alani quarter except for need. Imperial need.

The young Wolf was marginally more reasonably dressed. He wore newer clothing, but more significant, shoes that fit. He did not, however, wear a tabard. Nothing about the clothing itself was meant to make a public statement.

Elluvian was not interested in being unseen today.

"You will need to learn Barrani," Elluvian said, stopping to allow a small wagon procession to pass.

Severn shrugged. "I know some."

"You will need to learn to read it. Or to read in general if you lack that skill. It is remarkably useful. Were you taught to read?"

The second shrug was stiffer than the first.

"You have a place to stay?"

Severn nodded.

"I will not ask how you came by it, or how you afford it. But those questions will become very relevant, very quickly, as a Wolf. The people who serve the Imperial Law are expected to uphold it; it sets a poor example otherwise, in the Emperor's opinion." His grin was bitter but genuinely amused. The Emperor's opinion carried more weight with Elluvian than the laws themselves. "You will have access to rudimentary Records once Helmat completes his cursed paperwork.

"At that point, you are to study maps. In the interim, walk the streets of the city itself. Seeing maps—or mortal maps—in Records is not a substitute for experience. Were you to serve the Swords or the Hawks, you would focus the entirety of those studies on the city streets. Most of your work will be done within the city. But not all."

"Do you know where we're going?" His expression was neutral. Good. He appeared to understand that Elluvian had taken a detour from the route Ybelline had offered Severn.

"Yes, in fact. At the moment, we are going to visit a man on Elani street."

"He's an informant?"

Elluvian chuckled. "No. And I suggest, if you do not wish a permanent and indelible mark on your record, you refrain from *ever* asking that question again."

When the door to what appeared to be a fixed storefront opened, Severn noted that the man behind it was old. He moved slowly, his shoulders bent; his face was lined with a network of wrinkles that made it impossible to guess his age. Those wrinkles were folded around the corners of his eyes and mouth in a way that suggested a permanent frown.

"I should have known," he said, glaring at Elluvian. "I've half a mind to shut the door in your face."

Elluvian wasn't offended, which made clear to Severn, if nothing else had, that Elantra was not the fief of Nightshade. No one in Nightshade, no matter how important they were, spoke to the Barrani this way.

"It wouldn't be the first time."

"Why are you here?"

"I've come to introduce a new recruit."

The old man snorted but allowed his gaze to drift to the left and back. "If you've any other options, boy," he said, and his age was great enough that *boy* seemed neither condescending nor diminishing, "take them. Elluvian isn't known for his gentle treatment of so-called recruits."

"My duties do not involve coddling the hopeless."

"No, of course they don't. What do you want?" Severn noted that while the door was open, the old man had not stepped back to allow them entry.

"A word with you, of course."

"Have several." He continued to study Severn, and after a moment exhaled heavily. "You'd best bring him in."

"It is not my apprentice I wish to discuss."

"Of course not." He glanced at Severn before he turned. "But you only bring apprentices when you want to make certain I don't slam the door in your face."

The old man's name was Evanton. Severn introduced himself, as Elluvian didn't seem concerned about something as insignificant as a mortal name. "You're new to Elantra."

Severn nodded.

"And you've joined the Wolves."

He nodded again.

"You've met the Tha'alani." At this, Severn glanced at Elluvian. Elluvian's face was shuttered.

"Yes."

"It wasn't a question. Why did Elluvian bring you to meet me?" When Severn failed to answer, he added, "*That* was a question."

Severn said, "Apologies, but I don't know."

"Evanton—"

The old man held up a gnarled hand. It was, however, entirely steady. "When I want your answer, I'll ask you."

"He has the only useful answer," Severn said. He was not defending Elluvian; nor was he defending his own ignorance.

"You would be amazed at how often that is untrue. It has been some little while since he has brought an associate into my store."

Severn now glanced at the Barrani Wolf. Even by mortal standards, it hadn't been that long since Elluvian had last had a mortal partner.

Elluvian said nothing.

"Come, why are you here? My time is of some value. Who are you hunting?" Evanton now asked, folding his arms and gaining a few inches of height as he straightened the line of his shoulders.

Elluvian appeared to find the question boring, but the Barrani Wolf appeared to find everything boring. His eyes were blue, but the shade didn't darken. He didn't, however, look away from the old man.

Severn accepted that this was some kind of test. "We don't know."

"And you think *I* will?"

"I don't," Severn said, almost apologetically. "Will you?"

The old man's eyes narrowed into slits. He couldn't physically look down at Severn, but nonetheless managed to suggest that he was. "Elluvian, perhaps you would care to enlighten me? It appears clear that the boy feels there are some things he can't discuss."

"You're not a Wolf," Elluvian replied. "But truthfully, we do not know."

"And you've money in your coffers to bribe me?"

"To *pay* for services rendered, yes, if it comes to that. You may mirror Lord Marlin if you doubt me, but you would do that only if you wished to waste my time."

"You think nothing of wasting mine," Evanton snapped. He looked at Severn again.

"I am not wasting your time. For reasons I do not wish to discuss in the open, I believe you will find this particular hunt of great value to your garden."

Evanton stilled. It was an odd way to describe the lack of motion, as the old man hadn't been particularly active to begin with. He seemed to gain the entire weight of his age as he examined Elluvian. To Severn's surprise, it was not to Elluvian he spoke. "You might take a look around my store. Pardon the dust; I'm not as young as I once was, and to those who know what they seek, a little bit of dust is not an impediment. Elluvian and I must discuss something of a sensitive nature, and I would spare you that discussion."

"I would not," Elluvian began.

"Then the discussion will not occur. You are not in your domain now, but mine, and you will obey my rules, or you will leave." There was no doubt in the old man's voice.

Severn wondered if he was bluffing, and decided—uneasily—against. He knew little about the Halls of Law—this was his third day on the job—but bullying harmless old men didn't seem to be any part of his stated duties.

"I offer you the opportunity to be of aid to the Halls of Law."

Evanton clearly didn't think much of the opportunity. Severn moved away from the two men—the two *old* men—and began to examine the store itself. Evanton's "bit" of dust seemed mountainous; Severn was certain that whatever lay beneath it hadn't been moved in decades. Or ever.

He leaped to the side, rolled into cobwebs, gained his feet, and touched the hilt of his long knife as the store itself was illuminated in a harsh blue light. Thunder temporarily deafened him, but he rose slowly. He could see the old man's back; he could see Elluvian; it was the Wolf that was surrounded by a crackling glow of light.

This was magic. It was not the first time Severn had encountered magic, but magic was never safe for the merely mortal. He wasn't certain if he was meant to come to Elluvian's aid; the Barrani Wolf didn't draw his weapon. Elluvian didn't seem to be injured, and this *was* the old man's space. He didn't imagine that Lord Marlin had intended that he somehow assassinate an old man.

Severn cleared his throat. "When you say a *bit* of dust, you didn't mean this room, right?"

The crackle of blue light faded. Evanton didn't turn, but said, "Of course I meant this room. If you've the cheek to criticize, do something useful about it instead." He gestured, and a bucket appeared in the corner of the room. Given its age, it hadn't been created by magic. Given the room, it might never have been used.

"You should find a different partner," Evanton said. "Or a different vocation."

"You should leave the testing of Wolves to the Wolves,"

Elluvian told the old man. His eyes were a much darker shade of blue.

"I find your tests to be suboptimal, given how often Wolves go rogue."

"And when we desire optimal testing, we'll come to you and request it."

"Ah? I am not afraid of the Tha'alaan or the Tha'alani. You are. Were you more courageous, you would not be here at all."

"I'm not afraid of the Tha'alani," Severn said quietly.

This time, the old man turned to face him. "I can almost believe that, when you say it. And that is unusual. But if that is the case, anything you require you have already taken. And anything Elluvian requires, he has not. No," he added, "I would never subject the Tha'alani to the interior of a Barrani mind. I feel there is a reason we all have minds of our own. As I said, you may stay and be of use. If you dislike dust, clean. The well is down the road, to the left. There are cloths in the kitchen. The bucket is stronger than it looks."

"It looks like it leaks."

"Do you really think that is my concern at the moment?"

He wasn't the one who'd be carrying the water. Given the presence of angry Barrani, however, Severn shook his head wordlessly and went in search of water.

Severn had time to find the well, to return to the store—Evanton had kindly not locked the door in his absence—and to find cloths; he had time to consider the cobwebs and also time to find a broom. He even had time to, as Evanton had put it, make himself useful; the use had not unearthed any objects of apparent value to the junior Wolf. He doubted that he'd find anything, and even if he did, doubted he could afford it.

When Elluvian returned to the storefront, he returned alone. "Do not give me that look."

"Where's the old man?"

"The old man is lording it over his damn garden. We're to show ourselves out."

"We don't have keys."

"If you think that petty thievery is a concern, you have failed to understand Evanton."

A casual glance around slightly cleaner shelves followed. "What do you expect Evanton to know?"

"It's not what he personally knows that's relevant. It's what he refers to as his garden. We call it the Keeper's Garden, and Evanton, the Keeper. It houses the heart of the elemental forces, and when they are in a reasonable mood, they will condescend to speak with us."

"Only one of the four speaks in a way we can understand."

"You spoke to the one who can."

"Yes." Elluvian sounded annoyed. "And I will owe the Keeper a future favor, or the communication would not have been allowed at all."

Severn thought of the flash of blue light, the crack of thunder, the anger of dark Barrani eyes. He then nodded. Those eyes were, if anything, darker; in the lack of sunlight they looked almost black. "You know who we're hunting."

"There are complications."

Severn nodded. Where Barrani were involved, the bigger surprise would be lack of complication. As he rinsed his hands in water that was now almost the color of Elluvian's eyes, he said, "Hostages or rank?"

"You *have* been talking to Helmat."

"Rosen, actually."

"At the moment? Rank. The one thing you will understand before you graduate: the Barrani do not take hostages."

"Rosen said—"

"Rosen fails to appreciate what a hostage is. If mortals were hunting the Barrani, they might take hostages, because they could believe that the mortal in question could be swayed to stay their hand. I am not mortal. There are very, very few who could be used as hostages against me—and frankly, if my quarry were foolish enough to even make that attempt, there would be nothing left of him for us to hunt; what is important enough to me is important to a great many powerful Lords of the High Court."

"Where are we going?"

"We are not going anywhere. You, however, will return to the Halls of Law."

"Have you ever heard the phrase 'don't kill the messenger'?" Rosen asked, as Severn lingered by her desk.

"Not in those exact words."

"Well, I advise you to repeat those exact words. Helmat is not going to be happy. Did En say where he was going?"

Severn shook his head.

"Helmat's orders to En were that you were to tag along with him. You heard the orders?"

Severn nodded.

"If you're here, you're not tagging along with him. I expect you're going to get very specific orders once Helmat clears a bit of hostility." At Severn's expression, she added, "Swears his head off."

"You want me—me, new, on probation—to tell Elluvian—Immortal, Barrani, probably a mage—what to do?"

"I can see how that might be a problem for you," Rosen said, with reluctant sympathy. "To be fair, no. But Helmat will. There are orders. There are requests. En chose to confuse the two, and he can deal with the fallout of that. You, however—on probation, as you pointed out—don't have that option. He's going to make it clear that his orders are *not* guidelines."

"Will he dismiss me?"

"What? For this? Not likely. Anyone who gets assigned to Barrani—well, to En, if we're being technical, because he *is* our entire Barrani division—makes this mistake at least once. He won't be angry with you. Ah, no, he *will be*. But most of his ire will be directed at En."

"Who isn't here."

"Remember: don't kill the messenger."

Severn didn't open with Rosen's saying. Lord Marlin didn't open with cursing, either. He was rigid, and his jaw was set in a way that implied he was only barely holding on to his temper. He asked where the investigation had taken them.

For two days, it had taken them nowhere. Ah, no. It had taken them to the areas of three different murders from twenty years ago. All of the victims had been Tha'alani. But the trail had been cold for long enough, it was impossible to call it a trail anymore.

At the end of today, however, they had gone to Evanton.

Helmat frowned at the name. "Old man, dusty store, looks like nothing has been moved or sold, ever?"

Severn nodded.

"Where did you go after speaking with Evanton?"

"Elluvian spoke with Evanton."

"You weren't present for the discussion."

"Not all of it; some of it occurred in a garden, apparently."

Lord Marlin cursed. Liberally. Some of the words, Severn didn't understand, but tone alone made clear what their content probably was. "And after this garden party?"

"I came here, as ordered."

"Where did Elluvian go?"

"I'm sorry; he didn't say."

"Didn't, or wouldn't?"

"Wouldn't. I did ask."

The Wolflord was no longer seated; he paced. No, Severn thought, he prowled. "Understand that Elluvian is not your commanding officer. *I am.* When executing the duties of a Wolf, you obey *my* orders, not his. I will make clear to him that you are not a page or a servant. You are, in this hunt, his partner."

Severn said nothing. He had no doubt that this had already been made clear to Elluvian.

The Wolflord exhaled and finally returned to his chair. "Very well. There are lessons you must learn. You can, I assume, handle that knife."

Severn nodded again.

"Competently?"

Competently enough that he was alive. Severn nodded.

"While we wait for Elluvian to return, I will attempt to discern what lessons are the most urgent."

Severn cleared his throat.

"Yes?"

"If I understand what's happened, the only reason I was assigned to Elluvian is because Elluvian won't—or can't—speak to the Tha'alani. What the Tha'alani could give *me* was a picture of the man Elluvian is now hunting. They couldn't give him that because he won't allow it.

"Evanton clearly somehow gave him that picture—which means, as far as Elluvian's concerned, I'm now useless. My presence is unnecessary."

"And if Elluvian were Wolflord, that would be relevant. He's not. I am."

"Mortals hunting Barrani are—"

"At a large disadvantage, yes. And if I want to hear En's

words, I'll listen to them from his own mouth. I have my reasons. You are *ordered* to accompany him. I don't particularly care if you accompany him to the High bloody Halls. Have I made myself clear?"

Something about Severn's expression caused another round of cursing, but it was softer. "Let me give you a crash course in Barrani politics and the composition of the caste court as it pertains to the law."

Severn had a great desire to be anywhere that was not the Wolflord's office when it contained both Lord Marlin and Elluvian. Elluvian was angry. Lord Marlin was angry. Nothing Severn could say—or do—would materially affect that. Nor were his words or opinion asked or desired. His presence, however, was.

Lord Marlin opened on the offensive. "Who are we hunting?"

Elluvian said, "I am attempting to determine that now. It is safer for your cub if he does not enter the High Halls." His tone implied that Lord Marlin already understood this, and that the question was a waste of time.

"Save your lies for the Imperial Service. You know who we want. Give me a name."

"You have no way of ascertaining the veracity of any name I choose to place on your desk. The criminal subject to the Imperial Tha'alani did not possess a name. Or rather, they did—but it was not a name by which the Barrani criminal would be recognized by his own kin."

"Barrani recognition is not my concern."

"But it is mine," Elluvian replied. His arms were folded.

Severn stood stiffly to the side of Lord Marlin's desk, nearest the wall; he kept his hands loosely at his sides.

"You went to the High Halls."

"I am a Lord of the High Court; it is my right to do so."

"And yet you seldom exercise that right."

"I exercise it, as you well know, when I am bored. At the moment, I am not bored."

"You are favoring your left leg."

Severn was surprised, but his surprise—or lack—was as irrelevant as the name the Barrani criminal had given to the mortals who had carried out the murder.

"I was perhaps overfocused on my current mission. You understand that I am not well loved at court; I was careless. I survived it."

Severn wondered if the other person had. He didn't ask. Nor did Lord Marlin.

"Given the nature of my welcome, I feel it would be an act of negligence on your part to insist that the private accompany me in the future."

"You do not."

Elluvian shrugged.

"Severn, explain to En why he is lying."

Severn exhaled. "Lord Marlin feels—" he began.

"Do not speak for me; I can do that for myself, and a damn sight better."

Elluvian had turned only his face in Severn's direction; his eyes were a forbidding martial blue. But Lord Marlin was the boss here. Severn began again. "If I'm with you, and they hurt *me*, it's no longer a matter for the Barrani Caste Court. The laws of exemption won't apply; it won't be a Barrani fight. It will be a cross-racial fight."

"I am going to have Rosen fired."

"You are not," Lord Marlin snapped. "Severn doesn't understand enough of the laws that govern Elantra. She's been explaining them at *my* request. Private, continue."

"If I'm with you, your enemies are far less likely to attack you because it might injure me. If I'm injured or killed, the laws of exemption won't apply. The Halls of Law can charge the Barrani with assault or murder, and the Barrani High Court can't block the charge."

"You would not be the first mortal killed by my kin."

Severn's childhood had been spent in the fief of Nightshade. He knew. But the fiefs weren't subject to Imperial Law.

"I'm a Wolf," Severn replied, testing the words to see if they'd hold. They did. "I'm not just any mortal. I serve the Emperor. Killing a random person in the streets, they might get away with. Killing a Wolf?"

"Helmat."

Lord Marlin nodded at Severn; Severn shut up.

"I don't care what games you play with Barrani on your own time. You are not on your own time now, but mine. You will take Severn with you on any work-related investigation. You will do so without fail." He rose. "You are not a Sword or a Hawk. Your time is not parceled out in the same way. Your mission is an execution, and until you have achieved that—or died in the attempt—you are working for me. Is that clear?"

Elluvian, wordless, nodded. Severn didn't like the color of his eyes. Lord Marlin didn't appear to notice.

"I want a name, En."

"I do not have a name to give you, yet." The Barrani Wolf smiled. "I promise, however, that if I kill a man, you will know who he is after the fact."

Severn lifted his chin. "Do you believe that the man you're hunting was not the man in charge?"

Both of the Wolves in the room now looked to Severn.

"We only have permission to hunt one man," Elluvian said. The words were soft; there was a warning in them.

"You have a question," Lord Marlin added. "Ask it."

"If the Emperor chose to dispose of Elluvian, and Elluvian

was acting under your orders, would he be considered the criminal, or would you?"

"I see you understand the mechanisms of power," the Barrani Wolf replied. "I will answer this question, Helmat, if you have no objections."

"I have a great many objections; I will, however, hold them in abeyance. Answer the boy, if you will."

"It would depend." The Wolflord snorted. Elluvian apparently didn't hear it. "If the Emperor considered Helmat an unpleasant but nonetheless necessary presence, I would be considered the criminal. I would—if it were possible for the Wolves, and I have my doubts—be disposed of as a warning to Helmat that he had exceeded his authority. In that case, I would be considered the criminal. The hunt would involve me and me alone.

"If, however, the crimes committed were severe enough and problematic enough, Helmat would no longer be considered a distasteful necessity. He would be considered a primary threat. In that case, Helmat would be the criminal, and Helmat would be the target. My death—and my death would be required—would be ancillary. Removing me would disarm Helmat; it would be like destroying a weapon. In this case, I would not likely be named as the hunt's target. But in this case," he added, with a sharp, almost predatory smile, "the Wolves would not be hunting. Not even the Emperor would be foolish enough to assume he could order insurrection from within Helmat's ranks."

Severn looked to the Wolflord, who nodded, expression almost completely absent from his face.

"You think the criminal the Tha'alani witnessed was operating under someone else's orders."

Helmat nodded. Elluvian didn't answer Severn's question.

"You are perhaps aware of informants," Helmat said, when Elluvian continued to be silent.

Severn nodded.

"I do not know if you have ever chosen to work in that capacity; it is often the choice of people who are not otherwise a power in their own right."

"I know of them."

"Informants can play both sides of the table if they're careful, ambitious, or stupid."

"Informants didn't kill people."

"No, not generally. En probably thinks the man responsible for the murder you witnessed via Ybelline to be the equivalent of an informer. He is not a man who is highly valued by the court; he is unlikely to technically be a member of the High Court, if I judge En's actions correctly. Lords of the High Court lose some prestige when they deal directly with all but a handful of mortals; they therefore have servants who do so in their stead.

"The men who became a small mob at the encouragement of the Barrani would not be considered among that handful of mortals. It is possible that the criminal in question was operating on his own, out of petty boredom—but En clearly feels that's unlikely."

Severn bowed his head for a long moment. When he lifted it, both men were watching him. "Was the command of execution for the Barrani indirectly witnessed by Ybelline?"

The Wolflord and the Barrani exchanged a brief glance.

"What do you think?" Lord Marlin asked.

Severn shook his head. "It's not what I think that matters. I don't have enough information—"

"I told you," Helmat then said to Elluvian.

Elluvian nodded. Anger—if it had been genuine—left the lines of his face. "The Emperor's writ of execution is not for the underling, although the underling has been charged with conspiracy to commit murder. My goal at the moment is to find that underling before the investigation becomes common knowledge.

"We do not," he continued, at Severn's expression, "have recourse to the Tha'alani; it is not, and has never been, required. The writ of execution itself follows Barrani law in some fashion: it is the man who was responsible for giving the orders to that underling that the Emperor has now condemned."

"You know who he is."

"I have suspicions, yes. They are not certainties—and even if they were, I would not speak of them in this office. Those certainties are covered by the laws of exemption. *Any* action that we take in this case will be covered by those laws."

"Except the execution."

"Even that, Wolf Cub. It is why this is purely a matter for the lone Barrani Wolf the Emperor employs. You do not understand the necessity for this particular political dance because you have never seen the Barrani go to war.

"We have."

"We?"

Elluvian didn't offer any further explanation.

CHAPTER NINE

"I WOULD LIKE TO APOLOGIZE FOR WHAT I AM about to do to you," Elluvian said.

On this fourth day of their partnership, it had been decided that no further murder sites would be examined for now. Severn suspected that Elluvian considered the prior three days—with the exception of a visit to an old man in a shop that saw no custom—a waste of time.

"It was not a waste of time," Elluvian said, when Severn made this clear. "I am forced, by the Wolflord's dictate, to take a mortal partner."

"There are no Barrani Wolves."

"No. I suggested that he might second one of the Barrani Hawks; he did not seem enamored of the idea. While the Halls of Law serve the Emperor—and the Emperor's Law—they are like fractious siblings. Seconding a Hawk implies that the Wolves are incapable."

This made more sense to Severn than it seemed to make to Elluvian. Severn, therefore, said nothing.

"You will not be of particular aid to me dressed as you are; we are therefore remedying that problem." Elluvian nodded at one of the storefronts in this collection of storefronts—all of them fronted by large glass windows and the scent of wealth and power. Such shops didn't exist within the fiefs that Severn knew; he suspected that those with power in the fiefs simply left the fiefs and returned.

"Wealth—" Elluvian said, as he inspected those windows—or what lay behind them, safe from the grubby hands of thieves "—tells a story if one knows how to listen to its cadences. You think of your fiefs as separate kingdoms within the greater city, and this is materially correct. You think of Lord Nightshade as a distant power. To you, this is also wise. But he is a man, no more and no less.

"A very talented, very ruthless man. His wealth, such as it is, must come from somewhere, yes? It is the roots of that somewhere that define him."

"Do you know?" Severn asked, unable to keep the bite of curiosity from his tone.

"I know of some of it, yes. Much would be considered illegal by the Emperor. But the fiefs stand, regardless. Do you understand why?"

"The Towers."

Elluvian's brows rose. "Do they speak of the Towers in your fief?"

"Castle Nightshade," Severn replied, voice low.

"Yes. It is one of six, and it is a necessity. I am not always cognizant of what those without power think of the Towers; do you understand what *Ravellon* is?"

"It's where the Ferals live."

Elluvian was silent for three steps. "It is," he finally said, "where the Ferals live. To you, that is dire enough. To those such as I, the Ferals are as dangerous as a starving wolf pack.

They can, in the right context, present a challenge—but it is a challenge that can be met with simple weapons. Were *Ravellon* to contain only Ferals, the Towers would have been smoke and rubble in the wake of the Emperor's ascension.

"The Ferals are animals. The borders that prevent the escape of far more deadly creatures cannot prevent their passage into the streets of the mortal fiefs. And were those creatures to escape, we would lose not only the city, but the world, in the end." At Severn's raised brow, he added, "It has happened.

"What is now impassible and deadly was once the heart of the world. Not just this world, but many. In ancient times—lost to us with the fall of *Ravellon*—we might enter a door into an entirely different world and learn much from the experience. There was art, music, drama of a kind that will never be seen again."

"Why didn't the Emperor destroy it?"

"Could he, he would have. There is not a man alive who could do that now." Severn said nothing. "It has been tried in the past, and each attempt failed—but the cost of that failure was profound, and it haunts us all." Elluvian's expression, for one brief moment, was the essence of despair. He shook his head, and despair vanished.

"And that is irrelevant at this moment. You are mortal; you have not seen the cost, the things lost. You have seen loss, as all who live must; I do not mean to denigrate the importance of that. But my people have adjusted, and they have, in their fashion, thrived. It is the now of the political machinations that you must consider."

"And this shop?"

"Part of the politics of appearance. If I am to obey the Wolflord, you are to be my human assistant. A servant, of a kind. And no servant of mine dresses in a fashion that evokes the most mundane of mortal streets."

★ ★ ★

If anyone had told Severn that he would spend days being poked, prodded, and *fitted*, he would have laughed. Or, if the person were obviously powerful, acquiesced. Since Elluvian was the latter, he made no complaint—but he had been in Elantra for long enough that the expense of this awkward, invasive procedure was almost impossible to ignore.

During this time, Elluvian spoke of the High Court. He started at the top, with the High Lord—a man whose reign encompassed centuries—and from there moved down to those he considered of import. Severn did what he'd always done: he attempted to alleviate his ignorance. He didn't trust Elluvian, but he seldom wasted trust. Elluvian had knowledge. He required Severn to learn some of it.

What he felt was appropriate for Severn to know was implied by the freedom with which information traveled, and during the days of endless fittings—and at that, for more than one day's worth of clothing—Severn learned. He noted the gaps in information. He noted, more particularly, the gaps that Elluvian would not fill.

It was harder to remember names. Barrani names sounded similar to his ears, and for years, they could be pragmatically interchanged with *avoid at all costs*. Only Nightshade was different; no one avoided Nightshade if he wanted to speak with them—not and survive.

"It will become markedly easier to understand the politics of the court if you see them in action. They are similar to any form of territoriality. I have spent little time in the fiefs, but I've scouted the warrens from time to time. You will see gangs rise and fall in the streets that comprise the warrens, and you will see the posturing of those who have power and wish to maintain it; you will see the maneuvers of those with less power who wish to have more of it.

"There is little subtlety in either: the gangs are not known for delicate words or the small turns of phrase that might be otherwise used at court. In the High Court, lives and their fates are decided with the simplest and politest of words."

"But people still die."

"Yes. The death sentence, however, is given long before the actual sword falls, and the hand that wields the literal sword is seldom the hand that commanded the death."

"Like the Emperor."

"Indeed, very like the Emperor." Elluvian nodded at the man who was in the process of rescuing his clothing from Severn's hands. "Those will do. We will, of course, be back; it is quite likely that my young companion will need a far wider range of clothing in the near future." Elluvian did not offer the man money; the man did not seem to expect it.

Having followed Elianne through the streets of this city, Severn knew that this was not the norm—not for Elianne or her Hawks.

"To be fair," Elluvian said, when they were once again en-closed by the open streets, "the Emperor's reason for having the Wolves is not the same as the reasoning of those Lords of the High Court. If the Emperor is charged with the execu-tion, whole city blocks will perish as he carries it out. Drag-ons can be astonishingly subtle in many ways—but when they descend to dealing death, there is nothing subtle about it. He has us because he wishes to be surgical in the implementation of his decrees. He does not wish the innocent to perish in his pursuit of the guilty."

"And the Lords of the High Court?"

"They wish to maintain the appearance of innocence."

"But you don't believe they are?"

"No, of course not."

"Then they're failing."

Elluvian chuckled. "*Innocence* is the wrong word, my apologies. They wish to remain above the fray, where they are also beyond reproach. We do not expect the Barrani to act as the Emperor desires his subjects to act. We are not a credulous people, and *trust* is a word that only barely exists in my mother tongue. Trust, love—these are the remnants of a childhood that we managed to survive by abandoning either."

Severn said nothing.

Elluvian expected silence, but something in Severn's silence annoyed him, judging by the darkening of his eyes. "You have survived. Did you do so by being trusting?"

"No."

"And love?"

Severn observed his feet as they crossed the cobbled stone. "I survived," he said, voice low, "because I had something I wanted to protect. I don't know what love means to the Barrani. Maybe it means nothing. But everything I've done for most of my adult life—"

"You are hardly adult."

The Wolf on probation didn't dignify that with an objection. Nor did he finish what he'd started to say.

"You know, boy," Elluvian said, when the silence had made clear that no further words would be forthcoming without prodding, "I have the oddest sensation that my opinion in this regard means nothing to you."

Severn continued in silence.

Helmat looked up when Severn entered the office. The Wolflord was not alone; a young woman, near to Severn in age, stood to one side of his desk, her hands behind her back, her expression forbidding.

"No, don't leave. You aren't interrupting anything. Mellianne, this is Severn."

Mellianne's frown was instant, changing the contours of her slender face. She was shorter than Severn, but not by more than a couple of inches; her hair was as dark as his, but straight. Her eyes were a brown that was close to black, her skin sundarkened and even. "You're Severn?"

The Wolflord's face was chiseled in neutral lines.

"A bit fancy for us, don't you think?"

Severn shrugged. "What we think doesn't matter, does it?"

The Wolflord's brows rose slightly before they settled into an almost unbroken line.

"How have you found working with Elluvian?" Lord Marlin asked.

"He's Barrani," Severn replied, the shrug implied in the words.

Mellianne snorted. "You've been dumped on Elluvian?"

Severn's smile was pleasant; it revealed nothing.

She cursed. "You really have, haven't you?"

"You don't like him."

"And you can say you do?"

"He's Barrani," he repeated. This time he did shrug.

"Your funeral. You realize that, right?"

"Mellianne, enough."

"Did you tell him?" Mellianne countered, turned toward their boss. "Did you tell him what happened to the last person partnered with Elluvian?"

"Enough." The word sounded gentle.

Mellianne shut her mouth. Audibly. She didn't wait to be dismissed. She left the desk and the office, the heaviness of her step belying her size.

Silence descended. It took effort to overlook Mellianne's comments—but not much of it. Elluvian was Barrani. If his duties involved the Barrani, normal humans—even those trained as Wolves—didn't stand much of a chance.

"No questions?"

Severn shook his head.

"You don't want to know?"

"I don't need to know. Unless Mellianne's implying that Elluvian killed him."

"Not directly, no."

"You send Elluvian after Barrani."

"The Emperor does, yes. Look at me, boy."

Severn did.

"I don't need—or want—suicidal Wolves. Value your own life; this isn't meant to be a method for throwing it away that absolves you of responsibility for your own survival." These words were harsher.

"I don't intend to die in the line of duty," Severn replied. Then, briefly, "Rosen already gave me the lecture." She'd waited until he was eating, assuming there'd be less chance of interruption. It happened she was right.

The Wolflord grinned. "You'll do. Darrell allowed himself to believe that he was Elluvian's equal."

"And I won't?"

"You understand the advantages the Barrani enjoy. You don't appear to resent them."

"Would it change anything?"

"Resentment is seldom subject to practical considerations of that nature."

"Is it?" Severn bent his head. Lifted it. "I understand wanting to be stronger," he finally said. "I wanted to be stronger. But Elluvian is—the Barrani are—faster, stronger, Immortal. Resenting that I'm not would be like resenting the rain."

"You'd rather find an umbrella?"

"I'd rather find shelter." Umbrellas had been no part of that shelter. Severn didn't feel up to explaining his life to a man who had never lived it.

"Good. I am uncertain that this probationary period is going to be either comfortable or safe."

"For me?"

"For either of you. Elluvian isn't usually this cagey, and when he is, it implies a depth of politics that the Wolves are unsuited to navigate. You will have to take your lead from him—but I see, by your clothing, that you're doing just that."

"Was Darrell hunting Barrani?"

"Yes." The Wolflord exhaled. "He was considered the most promising of the young Wolves; he was quick, clever, focused. There is always a danger when hunting Barrani, but none of us expected his death. Mellianne, as you have seen, has still not forgiven Elluvian for it. She believes that if Elluvian had desired it, Darrell would have survived."

"Do you?"

"He is not the only Wolf we have lost in training." The Wolflord rose from his desk, a signal that this meeting was over. "Not many of the Wolves retire in old age. We are Imperial Executioners—but it is seldom that those who have been condemned accept the Imperial edict with grace."

Mellianne was sitting on the edge of Rosen's desk when Severn left the Wolflord's office. She didn't look friendly, but Severn didn't expect friendliness from strangers; her lack of welcome made him more comfortable, not less.

She pushed herself off the desk, and behind her back, Rosen rolled her eyes. She offered Severn no warning, but her expression—resigned, weary—made it clear that Mellianne was always prickly; there was no surprise in it.

"You always dress like that?" Mellianne asked, giving the clothing Elluvian had purchased a much more thorough once-over.

"Only at work."

"What do you wear when you're on your own time?"

"What you're wearing."

Rosen coughed. Mellianne turned instantly to look at the older woman, but Rosen didn't seem intimidated by the expression Severn couldn't see.

"Where do you call home, then?"

Home? It wasn't a question the Wolflord had asked. Nor was it a question Elluvian or Rosen had asked. Severn shrugged. "I don't."

"You don't have a home?"

"Not anymore."

This seemed to give Mellianne pause. A pause, however, wasn't a full stop. "You lost your family?"

And this was not something Severn wanted to discuss with a stranger. It wasn't something he wanted to discuss with anyone. He offered a fief shrug instead of an answer; it was a closed door.

Mellianne didn't appear to appreciate closed doors, and she didn't let this one stop her. "You an orphan?"

He shut the windows as well. "Unless it's relevant to my duties as a Wolf, I don't see any point in discussing it."

Her brows folded inward. "You understand what we do here, right?"

He nodded.

"Don't give yourself airs. We're assassins. We go where the Emperor tells us to go, and we kill who the Emperor tells us to kill."

Severn's nod was politer. She understood the difference between a fief shrug and a polite nod.

"Did you ask him what happened to Darrell?"

"You told me. He died."

Her eyes narrowed into slightly curved slits. "I'm trying to be helpful here. I'm trying to give you a warning you're obviously too good to need." She followed this with street slang before she stalked away from Rosen's desk, her hands in fists. Severn didn't watch her leave; he'd turned to Rosen. He did hear a door slam.

"She wasn't always like this," Rosen said, when Severn said nothing. Rosen cared for Mellianne.

"Neither were you."

"No—until recently, I wouldn't have been at this desk or in this office; I'd've been given a mission. But I was never a Shadow Wolf," she added. "Neither is Mellianne."

"The difference?"

"We hunt, yes, but we don't have permission to kill, except in self-defense. Most of us are good enough—or were—that it's hard to sell self-defense as a cause. We find kidnappers. We find thieves if the theft is of a 'sensitive nature.' All of our work," she added, "is of a sensitive nature. If it's not, the work goes to the Hawks.

"Mellianne and Darrell came in at around the same time; he was two years older if you believe the age he gave us."

"Given the Tha'alani, is there any reason not to?"

This pulled a reluctant smile from Rosen, a woman who didn't look as if she smiled much. "No." The smile faded. "Darrell was promising—but he was young. Elluvian made his report to Helmat, not to the rest of us. He's refused to discuss it with Mellianne."

"You don't think that was a mistake."

"No."

"And me?"

"I understand why you're his partner. Mellianne doesn't. She thinks it should have been her. She's been here longer than you have, she's fully trained, she understands the ins and outs of Imperial Law. You'll have to do the same," she added. "But in this, Elluvian requires a partner by Imperial decree.

I would have been that partner if not for my injuries; Jaren would be if he weren't absent."

"She'd be happier with Jaren?"

"She'd be happier without Elluvian. Don't trust him." Short of feeding him and supervising him to make sure he ate, this was the most serious he'd seen her.

"He's Barrani," Severn replied.

"I cannot decide," Elluvian said, his voice measured and quiet, "whether to be impressed or appalled."

Severn looked up from the book he was laboriously reading. "Rosen made clear that I'm to read competently."

"Yes—but laws?"

"If I don't know the laws, I won't know when I'm breaking them."

"Use common sense."

"I grew up in the fiefs."

A black brow rose. The Barrani Wolf's eyes were blue, but not the indigo that indicated imminent death. Severn picked the book up and walked it back to the librarian's desk. He also waited while she logged it. Books were of value, and it seemed important not to be considered a thief.

"I am not certain you are ready," Elluvian said, "but we have an appointment at the High Halls this afternoon. I wish to arrive early."

Severn nodded. He didn't ask if Elluvian expected trouble; he understood that Elluvian always expected trouble. The injury he'd taken had never been discussed.

"You don't ask many questions," Elluvian said, as they made their way from the Halls of Law.

Severn shrugged.

"Helmat said you met Mellianne."

He nodded.

"And?"

"She seemed either angry or worried."

Elluvian chuckled without warmth. "Yes, she would. Did she mention Darrell?"

After a pause, Severn said, "Yes."

"And you still have no questions?"

"I'm not Mellianne, and I'm not Darrell."

"No. Tell me, Severn, what do you want from the Wolves?"

"A job?"

"That was a question. You've accepted the contract offered you, and you are on probation in a particularly tricky hunt. You are not a complete fool, and you are not completely impulsive—but had you lacked some of that impulsiveness, I would never have found you. Helmat did not ask; I will. What do you want from the Wolves?"

"A job."

"And what does that mean to you?"

"A roof over my head. Food in my stomach."

"A place to belong?"

Severn shook his head.

"In that case, you will not find the High Halls intimidating. Your ignorance will intimidate you, yes—but you understand power. You merely need to understand the differences in its trappings. Nothing that occurs in the High Halls will be about you, but your desires may cause a lack of objectivity."

"Barrani have little use for mortals."

"Indeed. And you are mortal. Your presence implies much about me, none of it complimentary."

"If it doesn't bother you, I don't see why it should bother me."

"Some people do not take well to condescension or pity when they are the target of either."

"Given your presence, I doubt people will have much time to pity me."

★ ★ ★

Elluvian did not entirely understand Severn. He did not, if he were being fair, understand most mortals, and the understanding he had developed over the passage of decades had been of a practical bent. The boy had presence, but it was difficult to pinpoint the reasons for it. He was slightly taller than average; his skin, with the exception of one scar, youthful; his eyes were a lighter shade than his dark hair implied. He spoke seldom, but he did not appear to resent words; he simply offered few of them.

He did not seem to desire either attention or approval—and approval was something Elluvian understood well. It was a lever that drove many people. He himself, in his distant youth, had been one of them.

Mellianne desired approval. Darrell had been more complicated. Severn, while of an age with both, was like neither of them. He seldom allowed his emotions to dictate his behavior. No subtle attempt to annoy him had apparently succeeded, Elluvian observed. That would have to change, in some small fashion, but Elluvian was content to observe this new recruit in return. It would certainly be a day for such observations.

He regretted the necessity. If Rosen was not at home with the Barrani, she understood both her role and Elluvian's, and she could, without comment, make herself so invisible she became just another nameless servant, even given the handicap of mortality.

He was not yet certain that Severn could do the same.

Certainly, his reaction upon seeing the High Halls was in keeping with Rosen's later reactions; he glanced at the entry, at the larger than life statues that girded the pillars, at the stone steps that seemed immune to the simple passage of time. He did not crane his neck, nor did he otherwise attempt to take in the intimidating architectural splendor; it appeared, to El-luvian's eye, that Severn found the High Halls as important as the shop in which they had procured the clothing he now wore: different, but not awe-inspiring.

No, the boy's eyes seemed to take in movement, people; his gaze focused only when the distance was slight. *You know where they are*, he thought, surprised. He shouldn't have been. Severn had tailed An'Teela for some time without alerting her; he had not caused difficulty in the distant crowd in his attempt to keep the Barrani Hawks in sight.

He meant to remain unseen. Here, that would not be possible.

Elluvian took the stairs that led into the High Halls. Severn followed, to the left and behind, keeping pace at a distance of perhaps a yard. Elluvian recognized most of the men and women within the sparsely populated halls; none were of concern. They noted him, as he had noted them, but chose not to address him or acknowledge him.

In a distant youth, it might have stung. The thought irritated him, coming as it did from nowhere; he glanced once at Severn. No, not nowhere. *Who are you, boy?*

Severn's assumption—that he would be insignificant in comparison to Elluvian—was proved both true and false. Elluvian did garner immediate attention, but Severn, being mortal, came very close. There was an edge to the curiosity, a desire to ascertain whether Severn was somehow important enough to Elluvian that he might make an effective lever, however ephemeral. Elluvian offered no instructions and no subtle warnings. When he wished to break visual contact, he simply continued on his way, forcing his servant to follow.

Only once did this fail to have the desired effect.

Once was more than enough.

★ ★ ★

"Elluvian! I had heard you had returned, briefly, to court, and I hoped it was not a singular event."

Elluvian's smile was glass. He was not outcaste, but was considered a pariah. Only those with enough power could freely interact with him in public. The adoption of the expression hid nothing as he slowed, turning in the direction of the speaker. Severn slowed as well, keeping pace with his supposed master.

"And I see you've brought a guest."

"An'Tellarus," Elluvian replied, surrendering movement and the brief daydream of speedy escape. He offered the woman a deep bow, allowing himself the time to more gracefully smooth his expression. Severn had ceased to walk; the shape of his shadow implied that he had not instantly folded into a similar bow.

He had given the boy instructions about necessary etiquette for servants, and had made clear when to stretch that etiquette and when to follow it as if his life—or both of their lives—depended on it. *I will not, of course, introduce you. Even if your presence is explicitly noted, I will offer a name in your stead. At court, a demand for an introduction is complicated. It would be a slight to me—and may be desired for that reason; a man does not single out and fete his servants.*

If the High Lord asked?

Clever. I would, of course, offer that introduction. I do not believe I have annoyed the High Lord enough that he would publicly humiliate me, but I am not at court much, and I am not part of his interior circle; there are always political alliances, and the ground shifts constantly. It is part of the reason many of my kin seek to be at court at all.

Elluvian had implied that his position was therefore irrelevant, inferior; that while he bore the title Lord of the High

Court, he was akin to a distant country cousin. It was in name only. This might give the impression that the woman who now addressed him, and who commanded the trappings of obedience and respect, was likewise irrelevant.

She did not bid him rise. A rustle of fabric, a slight shift in the shadow she cast, told Elluvian that she had turned.

"And you are?" she asked.

Severn was silent for one long beat, as if evaluating the insult done to his master. "I am Severn Handred, Lord."

"Handred?" The single word was far sharper; the velvet that sheathed claws suddenly torn, frayed. Severn did not answer vocally. "Is that a common mortal name?"

"It is."

"I see. And you have come to the High Halls as Elluvian's companion?"

"I have."

"Do you serve him?"

Again, silence.

Still, she did not bid Elluvian rise. He understood this game; it was one of the earliest of the games he had been taught in his distant youth—a youth he had barely survived.

"Let me give you advice, child," she then said, the warmth once again fronting her words. Her eyes, however, would be a deep, fathomless blue. "It is neither wise nor safe to serve Elluvian in this court. You are young, even for one of your kind. Games are played here that started before—long before—your birth, and they will continue long after your death, should that death be decades hence and you in your dotage. You will not understand all of the subtle currents that inform these games.

"You will not understand Elluvian. Bringing you to court was ill-advised on his part, but should you desire it, I will escort you out and guarantee your safety."

It was not a request.

Elluvian cursed Helmat, silently, in all of the languages he knew.

"You are young and healthy," An'Tellarus continued. "This is not your world. Elluvian should never have brought you here."

The shadows across the ground shifted suddenly; Elluvian closed his eyes. He opened them again when he heard the clang of steel against steel; he lifted his face—although he did not rise—to see Severn, of the line Handred, arms raised, steel daggers glinting in either hand, crossed to prevent the fall of a sword.

Those arms strained, briefly; the boy shifted to the side and the sword fell toward the bright marble flooring without drawing blood. He had moved, was moving, the daggers ready, his knees bent. He had not said a word, but he looked, for a moment, at home.

"Enough."

Beside An'Tellarus was a Barrani man, dressed not as guard but servant; it was his sword that weighed against Severn's daggers. His eyes were a steady blue; no rage drove the attack. An'Tellarus did not gainsay Elluvian's visceral command; nor did she give him permission to rise. It was a challenge; it must be a challenge.

If he could kill her, if he could strike out at her, if he could treat her entirely as an enemy, it would never have been issued.

"I see," she said pleasantly, eyes still upon Severn, "that you have some rudimentary skill. It will not be enough."

Severn nodded.

She lifted a hand; her servant's sword was sheathed almost before she had lowered it again. He had not spoken a word, nor did Elluvian expect it. But the fact remained, silent and heavy, between the four people present: Elluvian had broken discipline first. Elluvian had given an order.

"You are here to speak with Corvallan. I should not keep you. But I have availed myself of the Tellarus rooms. You will come to attend me before you leave the High Halls." There was no honey in the words, no mockery of kindness.

"An'Tellarus."

CHAPTER TEN

ELLUVIAN CONTINUED IN SILENCE. IF THE EN-counter had been noticed—and no doubt it had—no one spoke of it, no one dared to ask. Not even Severn, whose daggers were once again in their almost invisible sheaths. All words spoken in the High Halls were heard. It was expected. One could attempt to limit the audience, but such attempts were also noted.

Privacy, if one desired it, was not obtained in the galleries. Some privacy might be obtained within the chambers occupied by those lords who had the right to inhabit them, but that privacy was in the hands of the host.

"That was well done," Elluvian said softly.

Severn said nothing, his expression remote, his focus on the inhabitants of the hall. He did not seem to value the praise—but he understood it as praise. It was not a common reaction for a young Wolf. There was no anger in him, no visceral denial, no need to declare that he didn't want approval. Would disapproval meet the same fate?

The silence was weighted with Elluvian's expectations, and

sensitive to them, Severn broke it. "If she wanted me dead, I'd be dead."

"Yes. But had you not responded so swiftly, you would be dead regardless. It would have been regrettable, but unavoidable."

"I doubt she would have regretted it."

"Our regret is not your regret," Elluvian replied, agreeing. "And her tests were ever thus: one passed them if one survived." All of this could be said, could be heard, without ill effect in the Halls. "We will meet with Lord Corvallan while I consider what to do with An'Tellarus's invitation."

There was a texture to Severn's silence that implied no consideration was needed. In spite of himself and the situation, Elluvian was almost amused.

Corvallan was of the line Mellarionne, a younger cousin of the current ruler. His wife, for he was married, was of the line Casarre. Tradition demanded that the wife become Mellarionne in name; in the absence of offspring, loyalties were flexible.

Corvallan himself was a Lord of the High Court, but, as Elluvian, a lesser lord. There was room within the Mellarionne hierarchy for the ambitious to rise, to make a name for themselves, but ambition was a double-edged blade. Corvallan was known, but he had not distinguished himself in a way that would be threatening to the current An'Mellarionne. It was not because of his slow and steady rise through the ranks of the line that Elluvian knew him.

Nor did he expect Corvallan to welcome his company. He had, however, agreed to a meeting, the single condition being that it occur within his suite of rooms.

They therefore left the public gallery, with its fall of light, its statues, its paintings, its perfect, gleaming floors. Severn said nothing as the ceilings descended to a mere body's height above their heads. He had once again resumed the position of servant, and his bearing suggested subdued pride at the privilege.

"The Halls are large," Elluvian said. "The personal quarters are placed in order of import. The more powerful you are, the more difficult it is to reach your personal rooms. There will be guards here, as there were at the entrance; they will be aligned far more specifically."

"The guards at the entrance serve the High Lord?"

"Yes." Nominally.

"There's no livery."

"No. At times, there is no armor, either. Armor, like the clothing you currently wear, is decorative. It is an encumbrance. An'Tellarus did not wear armor. Nor did her guard. We found armor of use during the wars; it could be enchanted, it could be created to provide protection against the breath of the Dragon Flights."

"Cloth couldn't?"

"Not as effectively. I am not a smith, and I do not pretend to understand the arts of the artisans. Here, it is an echo of that history. We have sworn our oaths of fealty to the Dragon Emperor—personally. Protection from his wrath is, in theory, unnecessary."

"And the swords?"

"Swords have a different function. Not all of our kind are adept at the use of arts arcane. Those who are are infinitely more dangerous than those who are not. But you understand this."

"Power rules."

"Yes. But power is oft determined by survival. The weapons on the walls to either side have pride of place; they were used by those who did survive the wars."

"The Dragon wars?"

"Yes." Elluvian smiled. "The wars always refer to our battles with Dragonkind. We were not, however, a peaceful people in their absence. Think of our wars as territorial disputes such as those that occur in the warrens; we have better tools, but the intent is similar. The warrens and their various conflicts are not considered significant to most of Elantra.

"Our internal battles, again, are similar. The Dragon Flights were one of the few things that could unite us as a people. It is perhaps the reason we give these weapons places of honor."

"They were meant to damage Dragons?"

Elluvian smiled at the incredulity in the question. "Weapons were made by smiths of old that could, yes. Of those, the most significant do not remain upon the walls here; they are held by those who made use of them during the final war. They are called The Three, and they are named."

"Named?"

"To our people, names have significance. Yes, they are named. If you mean to ask if they are sentient, I cannot answer with any certainty. You would have to ask their wielders. You have been tailing one of them for some time."

"The Hawks?"

"One of them, yes. That is not what she is called within the High Halls unless one wishes to insult her. Ah. I see Corvallan is expecting us."

The hall had narrowed, although the ceilings were, by mortal standards, high. Contained beneath them were eight men, dressed in the armor that Elluvian had disparaged; they held weapons, unsheathed, as if in challenge, and their faces were obscured by helms.

They did not bar passage; they did not demand to know Elluvian's business. Nor did he appear to see them. Severn followed his master's lead, but even his breath had become silent. His steps became almost silent as well, the better to hear movement.

If Corvallan desired their deaths, Severn would likely die here. Elluvian, however, would not—and Severn's death would be costly.

The twin rows of armed guards pointed indirectly to two large doors at the end of the hall; this was their destination. Elluvian considered their presence and what it presaged. In some of the oldest of his kin, these men would be considered a sign of respect. Corvallan was not among their number. He showed respect seldom, where it could be at all avoided.

Such a display of guards might be considered a sign of caution, or its more problematic cousin, fear. Corvallan was not given to displays of fear, either.

No, he thought, wariness sinking roots. Corvallan was not alone.

The doors were opened to allow Elluvian and his servant entry before Elluvian reached them; they rolled to the side in utter silence. Magic, then. Standing in the doorway, dressed in a violet gown that pooled elegantly at her feet, was Corvallan's wife, Cassandre. Her hair, the black of her kin, was drawn up and around her head with gleaming strands trailing amethyst and gold. Her eyes were blue, but the blue was that of caution, not anger or fear, and the gown itself was sleeveless, a summer dress. She tendered Elluvian a deep bow, but did not hold it long.

"We have been asked to allow you to leave in a timely manner," she said, as she rose. "Please, join us. My lord is waiting within." Her expression was gentle and welcoming, which put Elluvian instantly on guard. If Corvallan was not a man to show either respect or fear, his wife was more gracious. Elluvian guessed that the honor guard had been her decision.

"It has been far too long," she said, waiting until Elluvian was forced to offer her his arm. "And I regret the brevity of such a meeting." She did not glance once at Severn. "Has there been difficulty?"

"It is to avoid difficulty that I am here," he replied. "You are correct. It has been too long, Cassandre."

Her eyes lightened, a surprise to Elluvian. It implied that her delight was more than simple facade.

Corvallan had chosen a room in the interior for their meeting, which was unexpected, but not unheard of. When they entered the room, he was standing in its center, his back to the open door, the posture a symbol of the trust he most certainly did not feel.

He turned as they entered the room, looking first to his wife and then to the man whose arm she held. She released that arm, and Corvallan tendered Elluvian a nod. In this environment, a nod was sufficient to meet the demands of Barrani etiquette.

The lift of both brows as Severn entered the room behind Elluvian was not. Corvallan brought his expression under control, but the blue of his eyes darkened; there would be no green in them for the duration of the meeting.

"You spoke with some urgency on your last visit," Corvallan then said. The side doors opened, and refreshments were carried in by a silent man. Elluvian did not recognize him. "I regret that I was otherwise occupied. It may have prevented some difficulty."

"Misunderstandings cause wars," Elluvian replied, smiling.

"And this was a misunderstanding. You must know what you are called at court among those who are not your friends."

Elluvian nodded.

"And you, boy," Corvallan continued. "Do you know?"

Severn's silence would not be acceptable here. Elluvian did not choose to command him to answer. He was curious to see how the boy handled himself.

"I do not," Severn said. "Perhaps it was not considered of sufficient import that I be informed."

Corvallan's eyes narrowed. What he would tolerate from Elluvian he would not, could not, tolerate from a mere servant, and at that, a mortal one.

Severn's expression, however, was diffident; there was no challenge in it. In a different circumstance, it might have seemed apologetic, but absent an actual apology. Unless Corvallan intended to target the boy deliberately, it was hard to find purchase for offense.

As if to underline this, Cassandre chuckled. "It is certainly not of import to your master, and that must, of course, be your primary concern. Loyalty is valued. It is a pity you did not attend Elluvian on his last visit to the High Halls. I would love to know how you came to serve him—but now it is I who am being almost rude. Forgive me."

Severn bowed his head.

This exchange did not appear to amuse Corvallan. His eyes retained their midnight coloration as he turned, somewhat stiffly, to the tray set upon the table. Empty glasses were arranged in a pattern around a decanter of cut glass; the liquid within was the color of honey.

Food was also placed upon the wide sideboard. An expensive array of delicacies from the West March had been far more artfully arranged; it was meant to impress. It was certainly not meant to be eaten by Corvallan or Elluvian.

"You will join me?" Corvallan said, gesturing to the decanter.

"Given the appointment that is to follow this one, I must decline."

"Ah. We had heard that An'Tellarus has chosen to grace the Halls with her presence. It is fortuitous timing. Will your servant join us?" The emphasis on the word *servant* could not be missed. The words, aimed at Severn, demanded an answer.

Severn, however, stepped back, toward a wall, as if he were in truth a helpmate, a public adornment. He did not answer Corvallan, but the tone of the question did not demand a response beyond that; the question had, after all, been indirectly addressed.

The boy was not Darrell, although their early environments had much in common.

Cassandre now took a seat; she also took the drink she was offered and held it in perfectly still hands, her gaze drawn to its surface as if it were a work of art meant to be viewed, not consumed. Elluvian almost regretted his decision to avoid it.

Silence now settled over the gathering. Social skills might have allowed a superficial recovery, but Elluvian did not consider this a social visit. Severn's presence emphasized that. He glanced at Cassandre, who now chose to sip the amber liquid.

"You have come to my husband with concerns," she finally said, taking, as she often had in the past, the lead that no one else desired.

"Yes."

"Elluvian." Her voice was chiding; the husband in question had not said a word.

"Recall that perhaps two decades ago—in the Imperial calendar—a string of Tha'alani kidnappings and murders took place."

"Surely the killers were apprehended, given the nature of their victims?"

"Some, yes. Not all. It was mob violence—mortal mob violence—and the dying memories of the victims were not coherent, given the number of aggressors."

"And this is relevant to us how?" Corvallan said.

Cassandre's eyes narrowed briefly, the color darkening to a shade that more closely matched her husband's.

"Very recently, one of the mob who had remained at large was apprehended for a series of much more mundane crimes. As is the Emperor's desire, the Tha'alani were called to review the details of one of those crimes. I am not at liberty to speak of the nature of the crime itself."

Silence.

"That man, however—mortal, of course—had one item of relevance to the earlier murders: there was a Barrani man present at the time. The man himself was not a participant in all of the mob violence—but the Barrani man appeared to have been at the scene of each death that this particular man participated in."

The silence grew depths as both Corvallan and Cassandre focused on Elluvian.

"The Emperor now desires information."

"Who was the man?" Cassandre's question was casual.

"I do not know. As you are well aware, the Imperial Tha'alani are not required where Barrani are concerned. I did not see the man in question. I spoke with the Tha'alanari, but their description in simple words leaves much to be desired.

"One of the Tha'alani who serves the Halls of Law, however, has drawn the likeness. I have seen that—as, I imagine, have most of the relevant officers in the Halls of Law."

"And you have brought this with you, then?" Cassandre asked, voice far steadier than her hands. She set the drink down gently, her former reverence shattered. "You believe that we may somehow identify this criminal for you?"

"Ah, no. I have some desire to speak with the man myself. I do not wish his body to be deposited near the Halls of Law like the inconvenient detritus it will no doubt become."

"You wish, or the Emperor wishes?" Cassandre asked. It was the first time she failed to contain the edge in her voice.

"The Emperor wishes," was Elluvian's neutral reply.

"You are still the Emperor's Dog," Corvallan snapped. He turned to Severn then. "And you must be one of his dogs as well—hunting dogs, but dogs subordinate to their master."

Severn inclined his chin. His expression was placid, as if Corvallan's words were the expected words, the only possible words, in this situation.

Elluvian did not understand his temporary partner. Had he believed the boy capable of great subterfuge, he might have been impressed at his self-control—but it seemed to Elluvian that no self-control had been necessary. He had just been called an animal, and no twitch of facial muscle implied that this had unnerved or angered him.

No, definitely not Darrell, not Mellianne. Not Rosen, he thought. Not Helmat. Not Jaren. For perhaps the first time, he truly wondered who or what this young man was. And yet, if he asked, the reply he was certain to receive was *Severn Handred*. He did not ask; this was not the time for it—and in the end, it was a question whose answer must be teased out by observation and experience. The words themselves would convey nothing.

"Do you believe that Elluvian will keep you safe, boy?" Corvallan continued. Cassandre's eyes narrowed as she turned in her husband's direction; her husband failed to notice. The failure was not, in Elluvian's opinion, deliberate.

Corvallan was canny; he was a survivor. But this momentary lack of control made clear to Elluvian why he was not, would never be, a master of men; he did not have the necessary mastery of himself.

"I am not his offspring," Severn replied. "Nor am I his dependent."

"You cannot believe you are his equal—you cannot believe you are the equal of even the lowest of my servants."

"No," Severn said, nodding gravely. "But I am, regardless, not his responsibility. If I cannot keep myself safe, I have no useful purpose."

"You would not be the first mortal to die in his service."

"It is not Elluvian, in the end, that I serve; it is not to Elluvian that I have sworn my oaths."

"Boy—"

"You speak excellent Barrani," Cassandre said, before her husband could continue. Her voice continued gentle, but her eyes were now darker than the eyes of Corvallan. Elluvian's had not changed. Severn had spoken little, but it was now clear that he had understood all that had been said. How had he described his knowledge of the Barrani tongue? *Some.*

Severn's gaze shifted to her. Not for the first time did Elluvian regret the consistent color of human eyes. Eyes were called the windows of the soul for a reason, and this particular branch of mortality denied the phrase utterly simply by existing.

"Thank you," Severn said, bowing once again to Cassandre. The bow, Elluvian saw, was an indication that he had no desire to be questioned, or perhaps that he would not answer questions, no matter how gracefully they were phrased.

Cassandre perceived this as well; her eyes lightened in color, although they remained an almost martial blue. "Young man," she said, in the indulgent tone with which one might speak to a beloved pet, "were you of my kin, I would do everything in my power to obtain your service."

This time, he reddened slightly, although his expression didn't otherwise change. Elluvian thought that would be the entirety of his response.

"Even were I," Severn replied, in the excellent Barrani

which Cassandre had praised, "I could not serve you. My oath of service has already been given."

"And if you were released from that oath?"

"How can one be released from oneself?"

Her brows rose. "Definitely everything in my power," she finally replied. "Which is not inconsiderable." Collecting herself, she returned her attention to Elluvian, as if Corvallan were no longer present. "You are aware of the identity of the man behind this series of murders."

Elluvian nodded.

"And you believe my husband to be the person who pulled his strings?"

"Ah, no, you mistake me. I am blunt, Cassandre, but I am not—all courtly criticisms aside—a fool. I have come for two purposes. I desire information, and I wished you to be apprised of my concerns."

"We are grateful for the warning," Cassandre said softly. "Are we not?"

Corvallan's eyes remained indigo. "The man of whom you speak has run errands for me before?"

"He has." Elluvian rose. "It is not to accuse you that I have come. It is merely to gather information about this particular man. You obviously have little love for the Tha'alani—none of us do. But indulging that disgust in such a public fashion serves no purpose for you."

Corvallan accepted a drink from the servant who, unlike Severn, remained nameless. His expression was now schooled in familiar lines. "I would need the name of the person you wish to interrogate."

Cassandre's eyes narrowed again.

"I will give it—but be aware, cousin, that his subsequent immediate death would not be to your advantage. His actions are, of course, not covered by the laws of exemption; mortals were involved in the commission of a crime the Emperor considers serious—two distinct races. The laws of exemption require both perpetrator and victim to be wholly and entirely Barrani."

"He will not survive, regardless, if that is the case. The Barrani are not—are *never*—to be treated as mortal criminals are treated."

"No, of course not."

"You understand our laws, distinct from Imperial Laws."

"Yes. But I—as every other member of the High Court—have sworn personal loyalty to the Emperor. His laws of exemption provide legitimacy to our laws. I do nothing here of which the Emperor would disapprove. Should the man involved directly in facilitating these murders die—and no doubt he will, after we have spoken—the Emperor would consider the death irrelevant."

"And if he dies before you have spoken with him?"

"My investigation will, of necessity, become much broader in scope."

"I am not afraid of you or your petty threats."

"Cooperation does not, of course, imply fear," Cassandre said, her tone once again a living expression of ice, "but a desire for privacy, surely? You must forgive us," she added, speaking once again to Elluvian. "Only give us the name, and we will tender any information we have regarding his activities as it relates to other families, other lines. The list will not be complete; I am certain that your particular skills will in the end unearth more information—but perhaps it will give you a place to start."

"It is more complicated than that," Elluvian told her, voice soft. "The men executed to prevent incursions of the Hawks—or the Emperor they serve—are not usually lords of any of our kin's courts in their own right. Were it a simple matter of servants and those who have not undertaken the Test of Name in the High Court, I would not be here at all. It has not escaped my notice that my company is considered, by many, a blight upon our proud heritage."

Cassandre abandoned her chair, joining her husband. "Two decades past," she whispered, her pallor washed clean of color.

Elluvian nodded. "You understand why the normal method of dealing with infractions is not perhaps available to us."

She did. Corvallan struggled to put meaning to Elluvian's words, and his realization arrived later.

"Does the Emperor know?"

"If the matter is resolved by the Barrani," Elluvian said, evading the question, "it will be irrelevant."

"And if it is not?"

"He will be angry. He does not play at games—not the games of our people—but we have long understood the importance of hoard to Dragonkind. The city, the Empire itself, is his hoard, and the value of the Tha'alani to the Imperial Service cannot be overestimated."

"The name," Cassandre said, her voice thinner, weaker.

"An'Sennarin."

Silence. In its folds, Elluvian waited.

"Impossible," Corvallan finally said. "An'Sennarin would not—has not—lifted a finger in any endeavor that would cause this political turmoil. He has no love of mortals, no love of Dragons, but there would be nothing to gain. He is aware of the exact boundaries of the protections the laws of exemption cover."

"He is."

"Your informant must be mistaken. Mortals have difficulty telling the Barrani apart."

Cassandre was watching Elluvian; her gaze did not move. "Lord Corvallan is correct. An'Sennarin has extensive con-

tacts in the High Court and the lower courts; he has acquain-
tances that belong in neither."

"He became An'Sennarin," Elluvian countered, "two decades ago, rising in prominence from the moment that he
shouldered the line. While he was always considered ambitious, his rise implies genius."

"Or luck."

"Luck is made." Elluvian now rose and turned to Severn.
"We will be late if we linger much longer, and An'Tellarus
does not forgive tardiness, in my experience." He then turned
to Cassandre and Corvallan. "I regret any discomfort this has
caused; think on my words and consider the situation with
care. The Emperor, for reasons known only to himself, has
chosen to place his trust in me, but I am Barrani.

"If An'Sennarin continues unchecked, the Emperor will decide to oversee this investigation in person. He would not send
mortals to deal with the Immortal, and I am not an army."

"And if An'Sennarin is not your criminal?"

Elluvian smiled.

He did not speak to Severn as they left the Corvallan apartments. The guards remained, but no signal from Cassandre—
who saw them out, in the same fashion as she had invited them
in—caused them to become would-be assassins. Severn was
alert, but he did not appear to expect trouble from that quarter.

He had not, however, expected trouble in the wake of
An'Tellarus, either. His reflexes, youthful, were good. Having
experienced An'Tellarus's particular style of testing, there was
some small chance they would both escape with their lives, if
not their dignity, intact.

Elluvian had ceased to consider dignity—in the eyes of
others—of great import. It was a lesson he had learned over
centuries, but a vital one. He did not wish to keep an appoint-

ment that had been made for him without his desire or permission. At any other time, he would have failed to arrive. But if what he had said to Cassandre was not the entirety of the truth, it was true enough that it required careful handling of the High Court. And as An'Tellarus was here, it would require far more caution than was Elluvian's wont.

He wished again that Helmat had not insisted that a partner of any kind was required, because Wolves were mortals. It irked him; Severn might have fast reflexes, but had he been with Elluvian at his most recent visit, the boy would be dead.

Unless he chose not to interfere, of course. If he chose not to interfere at all, the matter would remain within the laws of exemption.

An'Tellarus's apartments did not follow the same halls as Corvallan's; Corvallan was not the head of his line. He was significant enough that he was granted the use of Mellarionne suites, but his suites were a geographic reminder that that significance was lesser. An'Tellarus, being head of her line, was not treated as if she was insignificant. The High Lord respected her, as did the Consort who ruled, like a statue, by his side.

She, in turn, seemed to bear some affection for the High Lord and his Lady, but An'Tellarus's affections were never gentle.

Her quarters were, however, magically protected. No show of guards—armed, armored—graced the halls that led to doors almost the height of the ceilings, and while these ceilings were not the vaulting, multistory ceilings of the public gallery, meant to inspire awe and a sense of open space where none existed, they were nonetheless taller than Corvallan's ceilings had been, and they artfully implied sunlight as they passed beneath them.

No armor, no metal, adorned the wall alcoves here: instead, there were small sculpted trees and artfully arranged flowers—things that implied growth, change, and ephemerality. Severn saw them, just as he had seen the armed men.

"Is there a significance to the colors?" he asked, which surprised Elluvian.

"The colors?"

"The flowers on the left and right alcoves, the third alcoves, are of a kind, but the colors are radiant—and different."

"Different?"

"I haven't seen green flowers before. Leaves, yes—but these are the color of emeralds."

"Cassandre was right," Elluvian replied. "Your Barrani is excellent. All of the Wolves—all members of the Halls of Law—must speak passable Barrani, and more to the point, read it. The use of the word *emerald*, however, is not legal cant. And yes, the colors are significant: emerald and indigo. It is highly unlikely that either plant was cultivated without the use of magic."

"You use magic for plants?"

Elluvian chuckled. "For beauty," he replied. "You will find that all living beings will spend much of their labor and time to acquire or become things of beauty."

"Do you find them beautiful?"

"I? No. They are a statement, of course. You know that green, in the eyes of my kin, denotes happiness, comfort, perhaps joy. Indigo is its opposite. To pass between these flowers is to accept that broad spectrum of Barrani emotion."

"Oh."

"Oh?"

"It seems like more of a warning."

"Ah."

"You might cause the one or the other. Both are possible."

"I almost regret offering you to the Wolves. Yes. The middle path—the path we now walk—is the safe path. It is possible that you might be the bearer of tidings that invoke happiness, contentment—but I have never seen either in An'Tellarus's eyes."

"And the short trees?"

"They are a signal that all beauty, in the end, is a matter of will and design; that one can be both alive and sculpted into something better or more interesting."

"The tapestries?"

"Do not spend time gazing at them. They are meant to draw and hold the eye in an endless way; they imply pattern, but there are inconsistencies in the flow of the design that challenge the viewer. Would you have preferred armed guards?"

Severn shook his head. "But armed guards are far easier to understand."

"They offer an obvious warning, not a subtle one, but they can be seen as a sign of respect for another's power."

"That's not what guards meant where I grew up."

"No? No, perhaps not. But in the warrens, they are not referred to as guards by those who are not residents of those streets."

CHAPTER ELEVEN

ELLUVIAN OFFERED SEVERN NO WARNING AS they reached the tall and forbidding doors—doors meant to imply lack of height and therefore lack of significance of the visitors who approached them. Or so it had always seemed to Elluvian.

Severn did not seem to feel the implied condescension.

Even his interest in the adornments An'Tellarus had chosen, admittedly unique in Elluvian's experience, had been absent the taint of any apprehension; he was curious enough to ask questions, but he did so without fascinated dread. He was willing to own that curiosity openly—something even the youthful Barrani of Elluvian's acquaintance would not have done, for fear of exposing their ignorance. But he understood that the time for questions had passed.

Elluvian waited. The doors did not begin their outward roll. Grimacing, he said, "Do you have any experience with door wards?"

Severn shook his head. No, Elluvian thought, ignorance

for Severn was a simple fact. The denial did not seem to cause him discomfort.

"They are common in the city. They are common within portions of the High Halls."

"They're locks?"

"Of a kind, yes. But locks can easily be picked or broken if they are purely mechanical in nature." Elluvian lifted a hand. Lowered it. "The central element of the pattern carved in the wood of the right door is a ward. If one desires entry, one places one's palm against it, and waits."

"It's a magic that's designed to be touched?"

"Yes." Letting his hand fall to his side, he gestured to Severn.

"Does it matter which hand? It's on the right-hand door, not the left."

"No."

Severn stared intently at the pattern—a spiraling relief of vines and leaves—and then lifted his left hand and placed his palm firmly against the ward.

"Is it that time already?" a disembodied voice asked. "Do step back. I would not want the doors to hit you when they open."

Severn stepped back, as if such voices had been an everyday occurrence in his life. He returned to his position at Elluvian's side and one step behind; the opening doors framed them both. No one was waiting behind the doors that opened into a wide, airy gallery, as if they were a simple barrier in the public halls, and not in private quarters.

No guards, but An'Tellarus did not require them. Lack of guards was its own statement, but context was required to decipher meaning.

Severn waited on Elluvian's lead, as well he should. Elluvian allowed himself no more than a brief hesitation. This visit had nothing to do with the current investigation for which Severn's services had been considered necessary. Had it been possible, Elluvian would have declined the invitation and returned alone. He had considered it, but was now old enough to accept a fate that could not be changed without outward struggle.

Inward struggle was a simple fact of life.

He had instructed Severn about the High Halls, its relevant factions, and the people with whom they had made their appointment; he had not mentioned An'Tellarus at all. No hurried warnings, no information supplied within the Halls themselves were likely to serve Severn well, and even had they, they would have done Elluvian no good. He was almost certain she would hear of the words, their tone, their implications.

But Severn had not once asked, either.

The flowers were a simple matter of curiosity. Their creator was not; he clearly understood the difference.

Stepping into these halls was like stepping into the past; the centuries fell away. Mortals oft envied the days of youth that had passed them by. Barrani seldom did. Age implied wisdom, the ability to survive, the knowledge one accrued if one did. Survival was implied, and the ability to survive considered a sign of strength.

Elluvian had survived. He would survive. It was not his death An'Tellarus sought. Death would have been a form of escape, after all.

Severn's gaze was far less focused here than it had been in Corvallan's apartments. He noted the arches, the open spaces carved into halls that invited inspection. He did not stop; nothing that drew his eye caused him to linger, and if he had questions, he now kept them to himself.

Within the lion's den, Elluvian did not speak of what they passed, although he could have; he was almost certain that Severn's questions mirrored his own in the youth he had no desire to relive. He did not hurry past it; as no doubt intended, he fell into introspection instead. The weapons on the walls in this hall were encased in glass or suspended in the air above them, with no obvious anchors to support their weight. An'Tellarus had always had an eye for symmetry; she found it more pleasing than what she deemed visual chaos.

Some of the weapons displayed were illusory—the equivalent of paintings. These had been lost to war and death and the literal fracture of earth in bygone years. They were remembered down to the small nicks and obvious wear in leather; they would be remembered thus by any who had seen them in life. The ability to romanticize the past was one the Barrani did not possess; where they desired it, they remembered everything. Where they did not, they oft remembered everything as well. The trick to survival of a different sort was not to desire it, not to be trapped by those memories.

But while all of the weapons were significant to the line, there was a gap at the end. Severn appeared to note this but did not ask. He had not spoken a word since they had entered the hall. Elluvian hoped he would not be required to break that silence before they left it.

It was always hope that stung.

They came at last to a set of doors as tall and forbidding as those they had first entered, if not taller. Severn, in silence, studied the double doors; they were smooth, the wood gleaming but otherwise unmarked. No section of door implied door ward, and indeed it would have been unusual to ward one's inner sanctum—but An'Tellarus was not known for her traditional tastes or behaviors.

Elluvian simply waited. The voice that had invited them in, in a manner of speaking, did not emerge from the stillness or silence of that wait. One could infer that she was not pleased with Elluvian as the minutes passed, but again, that would have been the traditional snub.

Severn's head was slightly bowed, as if he were listening.

Elluvian was surprised—completely surprised—when the boy drew both of his daggers and wheeled instantly to face what appeared to be empty air. He heard, again, the clang of mortal steel against blade, but this blade he could not see.

"*Enough.*" The word was Elluvian's; it was a crack of lightning in a thunderstorm. Light, harsh and unmuted, instantly flooded the halls, washing color and substance from the rest of An'Tellarus's enchantments.

Robed in a blue that was almost black, a single long knife in her hands, was their host.

The sudden light, the loss of whatever allowed her to remain invisible, did not discomfit her at all. Her long knife was locked in the intersection of the two daggers Severn wielded, just as the sword of her armsman had been. Elluvian was almost embarrassed; he was also almost enraged. It had been at least a century since she had humiliated him this badly.

But her gaze seemed fixed to Severn, the Wolf cub; her intent lay there, her eyes an odd shade, seldom seen in Barrani. Elluvian could not remember seeing it in hers—not when her gaze fell upon him. Her eyes were brown, a warm color that Barrani of any age did not possess. She approved of Severn, the approval visceral, instinctive, the shift of color the one thing she could not easily control.

Elluvian felt a pang of envy, of resentment, which would merely show blue, dark blue—a color that many considered to be solid and fixed in Barrani.

"You will think me a terrible hostess," she said to Severn, ignoring Elluvian entirely—as if Elluvian, not Severn, was servant or attendant here.

"I have had little experience with Barrani hospitality," Severn admitted. An'Tellarus lowered her knife; Severn lowered his daggers. Neither sheathed them.

"How did you know I was here?"

"I could hear your breathing."

"You could not see me?"

He said nothing.

"Very well. I offer you a boon, young man. A sign of my genuine contrition."

His face remained impassive.

"I had to be certain." She turned, then, to Elluvian. "You have destroyed a collective century's worth of work." Her eyes were no longer brown. "The enchantments—"

"Enough, An'Tellarus. I anticipate a difficult near future, and the morning could hardly be called relaxing."

"Surely at your age you do not require relaxation."

"This," Elluvian said, risking her wrath as he spoke to Severn, "is why I do not maintain quarters within the High Halls. Everything is a game to the High Court's Lords."

"You are Lord," An'Tellarus said, her tone chillier.

"Indeed. But the games played by our people generally bore me." His tone, however, was colder.

"Oh?"

"The outcome is never in doubt."

"I see I have angered you," she replied, smiling the sweetest of her smiles. "Come. I did not invite you here simply for the joy of provoking a reaction."

"No, of course not. You will, however, gain whatever advantage you deem possible if the opportunity presents itself." To Severn, he said, "We are done here for the day."

The doors that had remained closed now rolled open, as if to deny the words. "You are still hotheaded, I perceive."

An'Tellarus used the Elantran word. "If you wish to leave, leave, but I would have a few words with the boy before you do."

Severn, however, said nothing. He had not taken his eyes off her once, and did not sheathe his own weapons until the one in her hand faded—literally—from sight. Even then, the boy was wary; it had just been incontrovertibly proved that what he could not see could still kill him.

Elluvian had half turned from the opening doors to An'Tellarus when he stopped. What awaited him was not the finery and wealth of a powerful Barrani Lord—not a Lord of the High Halls. The room—a single room—was sparsely furnished, but it was not empty; shelves of differing heights and make covered the wall to his right. A plate that contained the remnants of food sat, chipped at the rim, on a table that had seen better days; he could see scratches in the wood that implied it was soft.

The room itself was empty; there were no servants here, or no Barrani servants. The very powerful did not consider them safe. Neither had Elluvian in his tenure in the High Halls. Power attracted those who desired it, as if power itself was a drug. No Barrani born desired only and solely to serve.

Regardless, the state of this room—there was visible dust and crumbs—would have humiliated even the most insignificant of servants. The ceilings were low and squared at the corners; one plant, half-dead through lack of either water or sunlight, huddled in the corner. At its base was a pile of books that looked as if they had fallen many times, and were like to continue this activity.

Corvallan had called Elluvian the Emperor's Dog, which lacked subtlety. An'Tellarus's room lacked subtlety, but the insult was deeper and far more personal. This dwelling could have housed mortals of no import; it was a human room.

Her insults, however, had never been subtle. While she had not descended to Corvallan's words at any time in their long history, she had not quibbled to make clear, in exceptionally blunt words, her disappointment, her disapproval. He did not, therefore, think, after the first blush of anger, that she had done this for him.

This room was not a room he had ever seen before. He closed his eyes, summoning the control required to examine the contents magically.

"Spare yourself the effort," An'Tellarus said, voice both amused and sharp as blade's edge.

There was no magic here. The room was as it appeared. He felt, at the door, the barest hint of sorcery. "This is not the room upon which your doors normally open."

"Of course not," was her dismissive reply.

Elluvian exhaled slowly.

"Will you join me?" she asked—of Severn.

Severn looked to Elluvian for permission. It was the first time he had looked away from the woman who had, moments earlier, attempted to injure him. Elluvian labored under no misapprehension. If An'Tellarus wanted the boy dead, he would be dead. He would be dead at the hands of Barrani, and the laws of exemption would not apply to the crime.

He had not been entirely truthful with Corvallan, but Cassandre at least expected that. What was true, however, was that An'Tellarus could, with some impunity, murder a mortal Wolf without the consequences likely to apply to lesser lords, lesser Barrani.

Or perhaps she did not believe that Elluvian would demand a full Imperial intervention. Perhaps she did not believe that he was willing to shoulder the consequences of that demand. He himself was not completely certain.

She had always understood his lack of certainty. She had always, in spite of his best efforts, seen through him. Even now, in the game she played, she had not put one foot wrong. Were it Corvallan she entertained, she would never have dared to either harm his guards or offer him the hospitality of what would not pass muster as a hovel to the Barrani.

"You have my word, young man, that tests of survival are over for the day. If you accept my offer of hospitality, you will be completely safe within the confines of this room, or any other room that exists at my personal disposal. I will treat you as an honored guest from this point on."

"This is not the Barrani version of honor," Elluvian added. "This room would be considered a dire insult by any of our kin."

An'Tellarus was not looking at Elluvian at all. Severn was; Elluvian's face remained impassive, short of any expression but deep irritation. He realized the cub was waiting for his response and considered spiting An'Tellarus. He shook himself mentally—the desire, if acted upon, would have consequences, and the problem with those consequences was reflected in An'Tellarus; they would be unpredictable in both timing and activity, or lack of activity.

It had been a long time since he had had to struggle to do the intelligent thing; the desire to lash out was so strong. He attempted to consider the situation dispassionately, coldly. Cold anger was better than hot. At length, he nodded to Severn, granting the permission it was his to withhold.

An'Tellarus marked it, of course.

She did not comment. Instead, she stepped aside and allowed Severn to enter the room. Severn did not ask Elluvian in any way if her word, her promise, had weight or meaning. His own did, but he could not have survived to be this age had he assumed that all oaths offered by others carried as much significance.

But his daggers were no longer in his hands. He asked no questions, or none that could be heard; An'Tellarus had always provoked confusion among her own kin, her mode of thought was so peculiar. Had she not also been deadly when crossed, she might have perished long ago; she had never been someone who conformed to the Barrani norm.

And yet, she had always been someone who demanded that others do so.

Of course, her voice came, at a remove of centuries. *You cannot break rules if you do not completely understand them. They are mechanisms, akin to arcane arts; one shift of word, one shift of thought, can spell disaster. Mastery—of oneself, at the very least—is vitally important.*

The memory surprised him, returning as it did without conscious effort on his part. Yes, he thought, there had been a time when she had been willing to instruct him. That time had long passed; he was yet another of her failures.

Did he resent Severn, then? Did he resent the way the boy now entered a room Elluvian had never seen, more comfortable here than he had been in any other part of the High Halls? An'Tellarus had tried, twice, to injure him. Caution was the correct response; caution and distance. He could not now tell if Severn understood this—but he must, he must.

"That was unnecessary," Elluvian said, his voice low.

"Necessity is bred by context," An'Tellarus replied. She did not turn toward Elluvian, but spoke to him; her eyes were on Severn's back.

"And this room?"

"Not all contexts are understood. Nor can they be. I have taught you not to trust. You have learned that lesson poorly."

"You have taught me," he countered, "not to trust you."

"Ah, clumsy of me. I meant to teach you not to trust at all. How is the Emperor?"

"He is well."

"A pity." She lifted a hand to forestall further comment. Severn had stopped at one of the shelves in the center of the room, an older edifice that looked as if it needed either repair or replacement. "Yes," she said, before Elluvian could ask. "There are few things in this room that the boy cannot read."

"He was raised in the fief of Nightshade," was Elluvian's sharp response. "Reading was not a skill highly prized there."

"By whom? You have spent much of your life's blood on mortals. Can you understand them so poorly after all this time? Now, hush. You will distract me."

Severn continued as if he had not heard or could not hear their conversation. He seemed to peruse the spines of these shelved books, lifting a hand to retrieve one from the shelf; the shelf itself was packed so tightly it took effort.

Elluvian now watched An'Tellarus; her attention was once again solely focused on Severn, her eyes shading from the normal blue to a shade of purple. It was not as rare as brown, but rare nonetheless. Had he not been aware of Severn's early life, Elluvian might have believed that she knew the boy far more personally than he.

But no, no alchemy of thought led to that as fact, rather than absurd fancy. An'Tellarus, however, cultivated absurd fancy; it was one of her many weapons.

Severn had a slender book in his hands; the covers, or at least the corners, were worn. Elluvian could not see the book itself, but could see, as Severn opened it, some of its contents; there were pictures on either page, with text written by a scribe of some competence.

An'Tellarus left Elluvian's side and came to Severn's, standing far enough to the right that she would invoke no reflexive defensive response. "Why that book?" she asked, her voice as soft as Elluvian had heard it for centuries.

"I recognize it," Severn replied, eyes still absorbed in pages, the hint of a smile touching his lips. "I've seen it before."

"Where, if I might ask?"

Severn shook his head. "I don't remember where, I'm sorry. I just…remember these pages, this story."

"And the other books?"

"I don't know—I haven't looked at the others."

"Then look," she said. "I will go and return with lunch, if you are hungry."

His smile—and it was genuine, to Elluvian's eye—was rueful. "I'm always hungry," he told her.

When she had left, Severn continued to look at the book and the images it contained. Elluvian stepped into the place that An'Tellarus had vacated. He read one page, perhaps one sentence—the pages themselves did not contain many words. All of the words, however, were in Barrani.

"Where," he asked, "did you learn to read this?"

"I don't know," he repeated.

"From whom?"

This time, Severn shook his head. Odd that An'Tellarus had not asked that question. It was as if she knew it would not be answered. Refusal to answer her questions had always been costly. Had she thought to spare the boy the price for the crime of withholding information?

It made no sense to Elluvian. "May I see the book when you are finished with it?"

"It's not mine."

"She will not mind; if it was likely to annoy her, we would not be in this room. I have not seen it before," he added. "You were a child when you read this?"

He nodded.

Too many questions filled the silence in Elluvian's mind. He did not ask any of them. The only question he wished answered was not one that most people of any race could clearly articulate. *Who are you, boy?*

Severn handed the book to Elluvian and returned to the shelving, a frown folding his brows. He continued to peruse the rest of the books, although he touched none of them. He did, however, put the single book he'd touched back in its place on the shelf when Elluvian was done.

"You recognize these," Elluvian said.

Severn nodded. "Not all of them, but I'm not Barrani. I think these are the same books as the ones I once read. Not copies, not similar books—but the same."

"Why?"

The young man shrugged. For perhaps the first time, he seemed to be struggling with embarrassment. "I spilled food on one of the pages. I was younger," he added, as if to explain himself. "The mark is still there."

"Who owned these books before An'Tellarus?"

Severn was silent. After a long pause, he said, "I'm certain he wasn't a criminal. He's not in the files the Wolves keep."

The boy had checked even that.

"This person taught you to read?"

"He read to me," Severn said, which was a compromise. In a far lower voice, he added, "I thought these were lost."

"Your teacher died?"

Silence again. This silence would not be broken until An'Tellarus returned; it was a silence of memory. It did not imply secrecy, as it would have in most other men; it implied, instead, a respect for someone else's privacy, a desire to protect that privacy.

An'Tellarus, however, did return. She carried a large tray,

balanced on one arm and hand, as if she were accustomed to serving others. Once, in the distant past, she must have been. No Barrani started at the top. Elluvian, however, had never asked.

She carried this tray to the abused table in the center of the room and set it there. None of the foods required any sophistication to consume; they could be eaten by hand, should one choose to eat at all. Severn looked at the tray, and then lifted his gaze to meet hers.

She nodded, as wordless as Severn. As if to prove that the food itself was harmless, she picked up a small sandwich and bit into it. This proved nothing, of course. She had prepared the food and she had carried it in; it would be trivial for her to know which parts of this spread were safe to consume.

Severn, no doubt, understood this. It therefore came as a surprise to Elluvian when the young man sat cross-legged on the floor across from An'Tellarus's position on the single long couch before the table. He lifted a sandwich, just as she had done, examining it.

One quick glance at An'Tellarus made clear that she took no offense at the examination. She watched Severn, yes, but what she saw, or what she inferred, from his examination was not what Elluvian would, or had.

A long moment passed before Severn ate, and even then he ate slowly, as if waiting for the effect of each bite, each swallow. As if time, once he had committed to taking the risk of eating, would somehow save him. But no, Elluvian thought, puzzled. It was not suspicion.

He had seen this infrequently in the expressions of the mortal Wolves he had collected and trained, but seldom in circumstances such as this. He was remembering. And committing, to memory, the experience of being in this room, with this woman.

He asked no questions of her.

She asked no further questions of him. They seemed content, the ruler and the probationary Wolf, to eat in a silence that implied not walls but familiarity, companionship.

"I doubt you will take me up on my offer," she said quietly, when he had finished. "But should you desire it, you may return to my quarters at any time; this room will be open to you while we both live. It would not be entirely wise to attempt to enter the High Halls on your own; you are mortal, and it is, as you suspect, unwise for even my own kin to enter the High Halls without escort. Not even I do it, unless I wish to make a statement.

"Elluvian will attend you."

"I have attended far less respectable people in my time," Elluvian said. "I am sure this would be no burden to me." An'Tellarus's eyes narrowed, as he intended. If this was the game she desired to play, he had mastered most of its elements since the last time they had engaged.

He knew Severn would not ask.

He also accepted, wearily, that should Severn not ask, An'Tellarus was certain to demand Elluvian's attendance. She needed no pretext. But her assumption that Severn was his to command in the foreseeable future had flaws. If An'Tellarus understood the Barrani—and she did—she did not understand the Emperor or his Wolves.

But that was fair; Elluvian found them mystifying on many occasions, and he had worked with both for over a century.

They left the High Halls; no further command performance interrupted Elluvian's day. Severn did not speak until the grounds on which the High Halls stood were no longer beneath their feet.

Elluvian had expected Severn to ask about An'Tellarus. The boy surprised him. "I would like to visit the Tha'alani quarter."

"Permission is required." Surprise, on the other hand, was—like any other weakness—best not revealed.

Severn nodded. "Would I seek that permission, or would you?"

"In general, you would. If you ask it of Helmat, he will want to know why. But you are on probation; I am not certain he will grant it without justification. Why do you wish to visit? This is not the usual reaction to an encounter with the Tha'alani."

The ghost of a smile played across the boy's lips. "Ybelline isn't the usual interrogator sent by the Imperial Service, either."

CHAPTER TWELVE

HELMAT WAS, IF NOT HAPPY TO SEE SEVERN, NOT annoyed, either. He had questions to ask, and while Elluvian could answer many of them, it was not Elluvian's answers Helmat desired. Severn was not gregarious; he was not, in the way Darrell had been, charismatic or charming. His silence, however, was not a silence of reticence or fear. It simply was.

"Rosen says that you have requested permission to visit the Tha'alani quarters."

Severn nodded.

"Why?"

"I wish to speak with Ybelline."

"To what end?"

Silence again, but this was the silence of thought. Severn knew why he wanted to go; he wished to express this in the clearest way possible.

"Twenty years ago, ten of the Tha'alani were murdered. They were killed by a crowd of humans."

Helmat nodded grimly.

"It has only recently come to light that at the back of the crowd, keeping his hands clean, was a Barrani man."

The Wolflord nodded again.

Severn exhaled. "The Tha'alani memories are part of the group mind. The deaths would have been recorded in the Tha'alaan."

"Not those deaths," the Wolflord said. "The Tha'alanari have the ability to keep such memories separate from most of their kind."

"But the Tha'alanari will know."

Helmat nodded.

"Had the victims witnessed the Barrani man, he would be part of those memories. He has never been mentioned in any of our legal Records."

Helmat was almost surprised. "You've accessed Records?"

"With Elluvian's permission. And," he added, before Helmat could draw breath, "with Rosen's. It was her mirror." This last was said almost apologetically. "It was only the awareness of one of the perpetrators that brought the Barrani connection to light."

Helmat nodded again, folding his hands atop his desk as he stared intently at Severn's face, at his expression. "Go on."

"The Barrani man must have stood well away from the crowd—and well away from the victim—for his presence to remain undetected." When Helmat did not interrupt, Severn continued. "This implies that the Barrani man in question understood the limits of the Tha'alani perception." Now he hesitated.

"Most of my recruits want nothing to do with the Tha'alani again. They are considered a necessary evil, a condition of employ. Why are you different?"

"Ybelline," he replied, the single word unadorned, it was so neutral. Seeing that this was not quite enough of an answer, he fell silent for three beats. "She has seen the worst that I have done. The worst I've ever been. And she accepted that completely. How could I be afraid that she would somehow ferret out other secrets?"

"I'm sure you've been told this before," Helmat said. "But you are a strange young man."

His brief smile illuminated the lines of his face, the warmth of his eyes.

"What do you hope Ybelline can tell you?"

The warmth ebbed away, replaced by intent, focus, the folding of a brow too youthful to retain those lines, as Helmat's brow now did. "All of the murders happened within a small period of mortal time. Our time, or the Tha'alani's. The deaths caused extreme difficulty for the Tha'alani—because the memories of the murder, the hatred, the fear and the pain of the dying, are imprinted within all the rest of the memories."

"Yes."

"The Emperor wasn't able to protect the Tha'alani from this scar."

"That is perceptive."

"I would want to," Severn replied. "If I were the Emperor. And the guilt would—" He swallowed. He had some experience with the scars guilt left. "Sorry. The murders happened around the same time period. A Barrani man likely orchestrated the deaths. Most of us fear the Tha'alani, and it's easy to manipulate people who fear.

"But the Barrani don't interact with the Tha'alani. If someone Barrani was behind this, there must be a reason for it."

"And what do you now suspect?"

"That somewhere around the same time—twenty years ago, maybe twenty-one—someone Barrani did interact with the Tha'alani."

"The Tha'alani would not willingly touch an Immortal.

While it is not strictly speaking illegal for such contact to be made, no member of the Tha'alanari would condone it."

"So Records say. It would require Imperial permission—if the Tha'alani in question were a member of the Tha'alanari, the organization that serves the Emperor directly. The laws of exemption, in the case of the Tha'alani, make clear that—"

Helmat, who knew this quite well, held up a staying hand, and Severn fell silent. It was a pity that such a gesture didn't have the same effect on Elluvian.

"You have the makings of an excellent Hawk," Helmat told Severn. "Which is a pity—for them. You believe that somewhere, in the Tha'alaan, there are the memories of someone Barrani?"

"I think it a high possibility. And I think the murders themselves were meant to overwhelm the Tha'alaan so completely, any notice of that would be submerged by horror and fear. But I don't understand entirely how the Tha'alaan works. I don't understand how the Tha'alanari work. I believe Ybelline could explain both."

"Do you feel it's necessary? You went to the High Halls with Elluvian yesterday. Elluvian feels he has the case in hand. Do you not believe him?"

"I'm not certain that the Emperor's Laws are enacted by feelings."

Helmat's laugh was an explosive bark. "You haven't discussed this with Elluvian."

"No. I told him only that I wished to visit the Tha'alani quarter, and he said I would require permission."

"I might be moved to grant that permission if you detail your day as Elluvian's escort."

"He hasn't reported?"

"He has. The report was absent details."

"No one attempted to injure—or kill him. We met with

Lord Corvallan and Lord Cassandre." Severn paused. Helmat recognized the names, although technically the Wolves did not involve themselves with the Barrani except at Imperial command. "He told them that the Barrani man seen at the edge of the crowd during one of these murders was also a Lord of the High Court."

"Absent *many* details. This is not good news."

Severn said nothing.

Helmat, however, was not Barrani. There were subtleties Elluvian missed that Helmat did not. The Wolflord's eyes narrowed. "You don't believe Elluvian was telling them the truth." *How will you deal with this, Severn?*

"I believe," Severn said, without hesitation, "that Elluvian believes the Lord in question—"

"Which lord?"

"An'Sennarin."

Helmat cursed. "Continue."

"Elluvian believes An'Sennarin is responsible for the deaths, or rather, for commanding that they take place. I don't believe that An'Sennarin was personally present and implicated by mortal memories, but he allowed the two Lords to believe that he was."

"Did they believe it?"

Severn shrugged. "They were upset—or unsettled—enough that it was hard for me to tell."

Fair enough. "I think I will partner Elluvian with you for future visits to the High Halls. You at least returned alive." Helmat turned to the mirror on his desk. "Imperial Service," he said. "You will not have Elluvian's company for your visit to the Tha'alani quarter."

Severn didn't point out that the permission hadn't yet been granted. Nor did he seem at all uncomfortable with the lack of Elluvian.

"Before you leave I have one piece of advice."

Severn, who had not yet turned toward the office door, nodded.

"Do not get personally involved in crimes. Your job—our job—is to follow the Emperor's command. Each crime, and each criminal, has been examined by Imperial judicial process. Do not place any of your own ego in the outcome."

Elluvian's clothing was far more suitable for visiting the Tha'alani quarters than the clothing Severn otherwise owned. As he hadn't been required to pay for any of it, Severn hesitated; the hesitation was brief. He understood Mellianne's instinctive distrust and resentment of what the clothing itself might signify, but Mellianne wasn't with him. No other Wolf was.

Rosen was annoyed on his behalf. If the Wolflord had advised Severn to treat each job as impersonally as possible, he hadn't ordered Severn to treat the men and women who were part of the Wolf pack beneath his command in the same way. And even if he had, he hadn't told Rosen.

"I can't believe Helmat is sending you to the Tha'alani quarter. It's been less than a *week* since you were examined."

"He isn't sending me against my will," Severn began.

"No, of course not. You're young and you want to make a good impression. But this is beyond the pale. He should send Jaren if he wants information."

Any attempt to tell Rosen that the information desired was desired by Severn himself was going to end in dismal failure. Severn did try. Although he knew very little about Helmat Marlin, he instinctively almost trusted him. He didn't want to cause trouble for the Wolflord.

That trouble, however, was not his to mitigate. Rosen was annoyed. Severn accepted what he couldn't change, as he always had.

He discovered that the Tha'alani quarter, unlike the Leontine quarter, was heavily walled and guarded. Both mortal Imperial guards and Tha'alani guards blocked the only visible entrance Severn could see. He hadn't fully scouted the entirety of that wall; he didn't want his progress to be noted as suspicious activity. He'd do it later if he felt it necessary.

And on some level he did. But maybe, twenty years ago, security had been more lax; people were viscerally afraid of the Tha'alani, and were unlikely to seek them out. Those who sought them had murdered them. It seemed, to Severn, that the Tha'alani had more, much more, to fear than the mortals who resented their racial abilities.

Everyone had secrets. The darker the secret, the greater desire that no light ever be shone on them. And the Tha'alani, mythically, could unearth them all with a simple touch.

The thought that the unearthing would be costly to the Tha'alani never occurred to anyone who feared them. And why would it? Secrets—the secrets of others—were a tool the powerful could use. Or the weak could use as a lever to gain power. When one didn't have power, the weakness of others looked a lot like strength.

Not to the Tha'alani.

Severn spoke first with an Imperial guard, who had been informed of his visit. The guard was brisk, efficient, and slightly bored; he passed Severn off to the Tha'alani guards. Unlike their human counterparts, they didn't look bored; they looked alarmed and slightly angry.

He treated them the same way he had treated the human guards. He answered their questions clearly and waited with patience. He had always been good at waiting; it was a lesson he'd been taught early. Waiting here was necessary. The Tha'alani guard wanted to turn him away. Although he didn't speak, and did not send a messenger into the closed quarter itself, Severn was certain he was nonetheless communicating with his superiors.

If Severn was to be allowed entry at all, he would not enter unescorted.

His hope that Ybelline would be sent to meet him was dashed when the gates were finally opened; a man of an age with the Wolflord stood in the open arch.

Age appeared to be the only thing the two men had in common, at least at first glance. The Tha'alani man wore robes, not the fitted jacket and pants that Severn now wore. His hair was darker than the Wolflord's, but glints of silver brightened it. He paused a moment by the gate guard, stepped in; their antennae tangled briefly before the gate guard squared his shoulders, nodded, and returned to his position.

"You are Severn," the man from the inside said. "I am called Scoros by my kin. Come, you are expected." He couldn't have been delighted to see Severn, but no hint of displeasure or worry colored his expression. "You were not expected, and I should perhaps warn you that your visit has caused some agitation." He spoke gently, his smile rueful. It was impossible to take accusation from the words. "I admit that I am surprised. You were visited by the Imperial Service less than a week ago, by our count."

"By mine as well. The Wolflord was at least as surprised."

"And far more blunt?" The smile deepened.

"…and more blunt, yes." Severn smiled in return.

"Tell me, how do you find him?"

"Find him?"

"Ah, forgive my Elantran. What do you think of him?"

This wasn't the question Severn expected. He punted. "What do you think of him?"

This deepened Scoros's smile. "I believe—and this is not a universally held opinion—that he is an honorable and honest man, in as much as he can be."

Severn was silent.

"You do not agree."

"No, I believe you. I just don't understand something."

"And that?"

"The Tha'alaan."

"Ah. You believe that because we can hear and understand each other's thoughts, we must have the same thoughts and the same beliefs? It is idyllic to consider, but no. We are mortal, as you are. We are gifted with the ability to make ourselves completely understood—but our experiences are nonetheless individual, and our understanding shaded, as it is with all living beings, by those experiences.

"We are therefore not all of one thought, one mind. We merely have the ability to understand fully those whose thoughts do not agree with our own. We argue, of course. The bulk of those arguments do not have the same teeth, the same claws, that your arguments do; you are left only with your own context, your own experience, and the shading of that hardens your stance.

"Does this answer the question you have not quite asked?"

"Yes."

"And will you answer my question?"

He nodded as Scoros began to walk down a road unlike the roads in the rest of the city. In construction it was similar; the Tha'alani must eat and trade, and roads were considered necessary to support the wagons that would deliver goods— if those wagons were allowed entry.

But to the side of the road were grassy mounds, with doors and windows built into their sides. The day was warm, the sky clear, and Tha'alani children, antennae weaving frenetically through empty air, were staring at him, wide-eyed and curious.

Nor did their guardians tell them to stop. Or not most of the guardians. One or two lifted the children from the ground and stared at Severn as if he were a rabid dog. Only one or two. The fact that he walked beside one of their kin was probably the only thing that stopped them from running through a door and bolting it behind them.

That, and the wonder of the children.

"If they have access to all of the same memories, why are some of your people not afraid?"

"That is a question I have already answered, even if you don't understand it. Some will be afraid, because they have tasted the results of human fear, and it is scarring. It is," he added softly, "the thing we most fear, and the reason, in the end, the Tha'alanari was created at all. Not every Tha'alani can serve as the Tha'alanari do; those who might are vetted very early, and observed.

"It can drive a man mad to witness—to *participate* in—the fears of your kin. The hatreds. The desires. The pain. The terrible isolation. Some, however, do not lose themselves to it, and will not lose themselves to it. We understand what the cost of that would be. These children," he said, without glancing back, "stare at you in open wonder and curiosity. One has just asked his grandmother if you are, I'm sorry, crippled or defective." This did not remove the smile from Scoros's face.

Nor did it remove the smile from Severn's.

"They were chided for the question. They are now asking why your eyes don't change color. Humans, for the very young, are almost mythical creatures."

"So are the Tha'alani, to my kind."

"Yes—but we are terrifying and demonic in your myths."

"And humans?"

"Just people."

As they reached a bend in the road—a curve rather than an intersection—Severn could see children, older children, ahead. The Tha'alani had clearly heard about his visit. They could look at him through the eyes of others, or at least this was what was believed, yet they still desired their own individual experience.

One or two of the faces seemed normal, to him. He realized that they seemed normal because they were shadowed; they hadn't come to witness his passage because they were curious, but rather, because they were afraid. They were facing that fear by standing in the road.

He wondered if they had been urged to face their fears by the voices of an entire quarter—and wondered, as well, if those voices were gentle, chiding, or demanding. He didn't know. He couldn't hear them. What must it be like to grow up with a constant chorus of critics on the inside of one's head? What must it be like to have no privacy, ever?

Would one expect privacy? Would one desire it?

But the presence of the children who seemed to be standing in the shadow of fear made clear to him the truth of Scoros's words. The Tha'alani were individuals. They were not of one mind or one singular belief. They had the freedom to think, and feel, their individual thoughts and emotions.

Which made Ybelline not an extension of her people, but simply Ybelline. When he spoke to her, he didn't speak to every living Tha'alani. Every living Tha'alani might hear, but they might not. Ybelline was of the Tha'alanari—the subset of Tha'alani that could, and did, keep their thoughts and experiences to themselves, not from a desire for privacy or secrecy, but from a desire to protect the children in these streets from the weight of, the knowledge of, the worst possible fringes of society.

Protect them, and they will grow in ignorance.

Who had said that? He shook his head; the words remained in memory, but the context was far enough in the past that he could not see the speaker. The Barrani forgot nothing. The Tha'alani deposited the whole of their lived experience into the Tha'alaan. They had ways of remembering that Severn didn't.

Ybelline's investigation of his past had forced him to relive it. The memories that had not had a chance to fade or lessen were now as visceral as if the events had occurred yesterday. He'd made no attempt to forget. He'd made no excuses, had no way of justifying his actions to himself, of lessening the brutality of the choice he had made.

Do not judge the entirety of a life by its ending.

He didn't want to forget. Jade and Steffi had been of no use to anyone when they had been plucked from the streets of the fiefs. If he didn't remember them, no one would. No one but Elianne.

He shied away from that thought, inhaling sharply enough that Scoros turned to look at him with obvious concern. He didn't ask Severn any questions, which saved Severn the effort of lying.

Ybelline was waiting for them in the open doors of a large, almost rectangular building. Compared to the houses they had passed on the way, this building looked almost normal. It would have been at home in any of the better streets of Elantra.

Ybelline, however, would not. Although she didn't wear the robes that most of the Tha'alani citizens had made themselves visible in, she would always be possessed of the antennae that marked her race.

She offered Severn a very Elantran bow, but made the short burst of motion look graceful and natural. Her eyes were hazel, a blend of brown and subtle green. It was the Tha'alani equivalent of Barrani blue. Oddly, in the Tha'alani, green was the dangerous shade.

Severn returned the bow with less grace but more power. Her eyes had shaded toward gold by the time he rose.

"I did not expect to see you again so soon—and certainly not here. This is not normally where I receive guests. Helmat conveyed your request for permission to visit our quarter."

He'd requested permission to speak with Ybelline, not the quarter—but in most cases, the quarter would be implied. Given the nature of his unspoken questions, he very much doubted the rest of the Tha'alani would become aware of his reasons for visiting.

Her eyes were now completely gold. "Your request for permission caused some difficulty on our end."

"Ybelline," Scoros said, in a tone that could best be described as long-suffering. "You were exhausted when you returned, and the Tha'alanari are very, very short-staffed at the moment."

Her eyes lost some of their light. Severn was sad to see it dim. "I will not leave you standing at the door," she said, ignoring Scoros's spoken words, which had no doubt been uttered for Severn's benefit. "Do you drink?"

He shook his head. He had never fully understood the lure of spirits, perhaps because they were expensive and unpleasant to taste. Had they been a delight to taste, the expense would have prevented it, regardless. He had nothing against necessary theft—if offered a choice between starvation and theft, theft was, and had always been, his choice.

But drink? No.

"I feel that perhaps I will require one. Come," she said again, extending a hand. The hand froze in midair, and then returned more woodenly to her side. "Apologies," she said. "I forget that our modes of polite interaction are not yours."

"It would be impossible for your manners to offend me,"

he said, smiling. "I grew up as an orphan in the streets of the fief of Nightshade."

"Yes," she said. "I know. You speak so formally when you speak, it's easy to forget."

"Not for me," was his grave reply. He now offered her his hand, in the same way she had offered hers before she'd returned it to her side, and after a pause, she took it, eyes once again gold. He wanted, for that moment, for her eyes to remain that color forever.

They entered normal doors and walked through normal halls. Although the ceilings weren't tall, this hall wouldn't have been out of place in the Halls of Law. Doors, however, didn't exist as demarcations for rooms; arches did. Beyond those arches, he could see desks of wood, with trays stacked to hold papers. Offices, he thought.

"You are wondering why this building looks as it does."

Severn nodded.

"It is a reminder for those who are Tha'alanari that the work they do here is Imperial work; it is not life. It is not our life."

He nodded again.

Scoros continued to walk by his side, which meant Ybelline led; the halls weren't wide enough to comfortably fit three adults walking abreast. But the older man's brows were a knit of creases, many deeper than they had been when he had greeted Severn at the gates that kept the citizens of this quarter safe from the citizens of the rest of the city.

The hall turned left; Severn followed Ybelline to a closed door, which stood out because, aside from the front door, it was the only actual door he'd yet seen.

"We do have rooms that are designed to baffle sound," Ybelline told him. "While we are accustomed to constant background interruption, visitors to the Tha'alanari often find it taxing. Closed doors," she added, smiling, "stop almost nothing among my kin."

"Tell that to the parents of tired, screaming children," Scoros said, his tone both wry and affectionate.

"It is possible I will soon have much in common with them," Ybelline replied. "Another reason a closed door is useful."

Alcohol, a golden honey color a similar shade to her eyes, was already in the room on the table. Severn found the multitude of different glasses in which alcohol could—or should—be served mystifying. There seemed to be an underlying set of rules. For himself, there was water and a sweeter, pink liquid that in other circumstances he wouldn't have touched.

Scoros joined Ybelline in her choice of beverage. The older man's eyes were decidedly hazel, but the flecks of green were stronger.

Severn, seated, suddenly found he didn't know where to start. The drinking, the eye color, the slight tension across Ybelline's lower jaw and shoulders, made it clear—or clearer—that they expected this session to be horrifying.

He hesitated as they watched him. The urge to apologize was powerful—but an apology, in his mind, meant he should never have come at all. There were questions he wanted answered, because he *wanted* to catch the person responsible for those deaths twenty years ago—the repercussions of which would always be with the Tha'alani.

It was the first new thing he had wanted in months. Years, maybe.

He considered polite questions, pretty words, and in the end discarded them all. He would ask them to do what he wanted them to do. Leaving was not an option.

"I want you to look through the Tha'alaan," he said.

"The Tha'alaan is not like your Records—" Scoros began.

Ybelline lifted a hand. She was not—yet—the castelord of her people, but clearly as heir she was accustomed to command.

"To what end, little Wolf?"

"The murders that, even now, destroy your people, occurred within the span of a little over a year two decades ago. I wasn't born. You were a child."

She nodded evenly.

"If Barrani were involved, they were involved for a reason."

She was silent, utterly still, her eyes open. They were green.

"Barrani were involved," Scoros said. His eyes had also shaded to green.

Severn nodded. "The Barrani are, at heart, a political people. Ruthless but pragmatic. There have been exceptions; they've been dealt with by the Barrani. I'm not sure the Emperor intends to let this one be resolved in the same way. Had the victims been Barrani, he would—by his own laws—have no choice. They weren't. They were Tha'alani."

"Go on," Scoros said.

"I assume that there was a reason for the killings. And the killings imply heavily that the Barrani in question—or a Barrani—understood how the Tha'alaan functions. They chose these deaths because they wanted to flood the Tha'alaan with memories so dire your people might refuse to look at them at all."

She nodded.

"Buried among those memories, at around the same time—or just before—I think it possible that there was some connection between a Tha'alani citizen and one of the Barrani."

"You think that a Barrani citizen touched the Tha'alaan?" Scoros said, outrage increasing his volume.

"Yes."

"It is forbidden, by law, to make such a contact."

"Yes. Imperial Law. The Tha'alani don't touch the Immortals."

Ybelline's eyes almost defined the color green. But her expression as she studied Severn's face was neutral, remote. Scoros's was anything but. She didn't speak, and Scoros didn't speak in a way Severn could hear—but he'd no doubt the Tha'alanari were now discussing his request among themselves. Given Scoros's reaction, he was certain that the Tha'alanari were now counseling rejection of Severn's request.

He wasn't surprised when Scoros rose, vacating his chair; his glass was empty. Severn thought he intended to refill it, but no—he opened the closed door and walked out of the room, his steps heavy with what appeared to be anger. The door slammed behind him, reinforcing that appearance.

CHAPTER THIRTEEN

"YES," YBELLINE SAID, WHEN THE SILENCE RE-turned in the wake of that closing door. "You have been in-formed that I am the future castelord. You can be forgiven if your understanding of that is minimal—the Emperor does not wish his people to fully understand the Tha'alani. Given the crimes committed two decades ago, it is not hard to fault his protectiveness, but I believe ignorance is a breeding ground for fear.

"Most of the older members of the Tha'alanari agree with the Emperor's stance."

"You don't."

"I understand it. The one thing the Tha'alaan gives us is the ability to understand the views and contexts of people who are not us. But it cannot force us to agree with them. Some of my kin are deeply religious. Some do not believe in gods. They exist side by side, and the belief in gods has not caused war or strife. But it is made possible because the Tha'alaan exists. They can understand the reason for different choices and different beliefs; they cannot use their lack of empathy to make accusations. Or worse.

"I understand it, but I believe the Emperor is wrong. Regardless, Scoros has now removed himself to appeal to the castelord. In no other circumstance would he seek to undermine me in this fashion. But they believe I am too young, or too inexperienced."

It was Severn's turn to frown.

Ybelline waited.

"You can, if you desire it, live the lives that any of your people have lived since the creation of the Tha'alaan."

"Yes. As a child, I was not allowed entrance to the memories of the Tha'alanari; they are withheld from the greater populace, for reasons you now understand. But even so, without the extremes of torture and murder, all people know grief and suffering. All people know fear. It is only in our case that those fears become part of our general knowledge; we have the fear, we understand that we are not alone in feeling it, and we can help to calm it by reaching out to those who have done so themselves in the past. There is very little that reinforces the fear, causing it to plant roots that cannot be removed." She shook herself.

"Will the castelord decide against my request?"

"That is Scoros's hope."

"You don't know?"

"He has not chosen to answer the Tha'alanari, no."

"Has he answered you?"

"I haven't asked." Her smile was a brief tremble of lips. "He understands that he is not my keeper. I understand that I cannot seek to avoid the responsibility of making and standing by my own choices by disguising my desire that he decide as asking for advice. He will leave the decision in my hands."

"But he's the castelord."

"Yes."

"Technically the decision *is* in his hands."

"That is the hope of most of the Tha'alanari. He did not, however, stop me from attending you in the Halls of Law. He feels that I am perhaps not exposed enough to mortals outside of the quarter; I see only those who are maddened beyond endurance. He knows that Helmat—the Wolflord," she added, correcting herself, "feels protective of me, in as much as his duties make that possible.

"We are not a people who are accustomed to any command from above save the Emperor's. The only time a single adult has complete control of our lives, we are in leading strings. They think of me as one who is barely out of leading strings. They love me as they can, they value me. And as all people who love can, they desire to protect me because they think I lack information and experience; that if my experiences more closely mirrored their own, I would believe what they believe."

Severn shook his head.

"You don't agree."

"No."

"Why?"

"You've seen far more than they want you to see already."

She nodded, her eyes shifting from green to hazel.

"Have I asked for too much?"

"No. Perhaps they are right in one way. I want to protect my people. I hope never to be in the position you found yourself in, but I think it possible that I would make the decision you made. I hope never to find out."

Scoros did not return. Ybelline, however, made clear that he would not. "He was not pleased with the answer he received," she told him, a slight smile changing the contours of her mouth. "The decision is mine. The Tha'alanari cannot prevent me from entering the Tha'alaan; they might, with more success, prevent me from breathing.

"What will happen to the criminal behind these killings, if he is apprehended?"

"He will be executed. There are Wolves, and a few of those Wolves are Shadow Wolves. We're called either assassins, if you despise us, or executioners. The Wolflord calls us executioners."

"You don't see a difference."

"I do. But the word is just a word."

"Words have power."

Severn nodded. "I'm not a Shadow Wolf. I'm only barely a Wolf."

"If you are here, Helmat has every intention of keeping you in his fold. This is not a request made lightly, and it will have possible consequences for the Halls of Law in the future. He must believe as you believe."

"You do."

"I am less certain—but from what I have learned, both of your kind and of the Barrani, it seems the most logical explanation. It is a good thing that I am capable of containing my thoughts," although she spoke softly, her eyes were green. "My people would be dismayed or horrified by the thoughts I have just had."

"You want him dead."

"I want to kill him with my own hands," she replied serenely. "A sign, among our kin, of dangerous instability."

"And the other Tha'alanari?"

"This work can destroy us if we are not careful," she replied. "It is the reason Garadin was so emphatic—even if he should know by now it has the opposite of the intended effect on Helmat. What I do know, however, is that the desire is a dark dream, a terrible undercurrent of anger. I will never be allowed to set eyes on the perpetrator. I will never be allowed to kill him."

He understood the men and women who wanted to protect Ybelline. He understood Helmat's visceral refusal. But he thought, listening to her, watching her breathe, that they were wrong.

"Let me tell you why we are not allowed to interact with the Immortals. If mortals have guilty secrets and the fear of those secrets being revealed, they have accumulated only a single life's worth of such. Their lives, as ours, are not endless.

"The Barrani have far more time, and therefore more secrets. They do not appear to feel guilt as we understand it; secrets cover weaknesses. They fear to be weak—it is seen as death. It is why I believe you might be correct. But I think it impossible that a connection to the Tha'alaan would be made without being heavily noted."

"One of the Tha'alanari, perhaps?"

Her nod was almost invisible. "Or one who might well become Tha'alanari. There is a childish pleasure in knowing that you *can* keep secrets, if you have that capability—that the thoughts and notions you have can be hidden."

"You think a child might have made this contact?"

"Not a child, but not—quite—an adult." Her eyes remained closed. "I am searching now, but Scoros was correct: this is not Records. If I wished to ask the people in the Tha'alaan about a specific event, those closer to the memory might offer me figurative directions. I cannot, for obvious reasons, ask. But the easiest memories to find are those bound to other, similar memories—it's like following a city street or road."

"And this is like trying to find a footpath in a forest?"

"Similar, yes, but in this case we're not completely certain the footpath exists."

Severn fell silent. Minutes passed as he watched expressions flicker across her face. "If the person who made contact with the Barrani were to keep this information entirely from the Tha'alaan, would this memory be lost with them if they died?"

"Yes."

He rose. "I can't help you search."

She shook her head.

"Will you send a message to the Halls of Law—or the Wolflord—when you have an answer?"

"I might not find the answer you seek."

"Which is also an answer."

She opened her eyes; they were hazel now. "Yes. If I can find nothing, I will send that message. If I can find something, I will visit in person."

Severn returned to an office that, over the course of less than a week, had become familiar. It wasn't home, but home had never been a physical location to him, he'd been forced to move so often. He didn't have an office, as the Wolflord did, but neither did Mellianne. Rosen had an office that never saw use. Since her injury had made it difficult to run—or to fight well—she'd taken up residence behind the desk that faced the doors through which any visitor, high or low, arrived.

Rosen looked up as the doors opened, her brows dipping when she saw Severn. "You're a popular young man today," she said curtly. "There are messages for you, which you'll see after you've attended his highness." At Severn's expression, she exhaled. "Helmat."

"You call him 'his highness'?"

"Depends on how much of a pain he's been—but today, he's earned it. He's waiting for you in his office."

He could wait a few more minutes. "I have a favor to ask."

Both of her brows rose. "Go on."

"When the murders of the Tha'alani occurred, they must have been investigated."

She nodded.

"I want to see the records of those investigations."

Her nose wrinkled, as if at a viscerally unpleasant odor. "That's not a favor. You've been given a job. The Halls of Law contains that information in Records."

He waited. It was clear to her that he didn't understand the full import of what she was saying.

"Come back to me after Helmat's finished with you." Her tone implied, clearly, *if you survive*.

Severn nodded and headed beyond her desk—and Mellianne's, and the desk he would eventually call his own—toward the hall that led to the Wolflord's office.

When he opened the door—after knocking and being granted muffled permission to enter—he saw that the office wasn't empty. Elluvian was there. And a Tha'alanari man he recognized as Garadin. In person.

"Private," the Wolflord said, his eyes hooded by the line of a single brow.

Severn bowed.

"Enough. This is Garadin. He is in the employ of both the Tha'alanari and the Imperial Service. Garadin has come to our office with a request."

Garadin was bristling; his eyes were green. Elluvian's were blue, but shaded with the green that meant the opposite of the Tha'alani green.

Severn understood Garadin's presence. Without pause, he turned toward the Tha'alani man. "It is not me of whom you must make that request. It is Ybelline herself." He spoke quietly, the tone weighted with genuine respect.

When Garadin failed to reply, Severn continued. "I'm new

to the Wolves, so I may misunderstand the situation." He was certain he hadn't. "But Ybelline made her decision. It's not for us—not even the Wolflord—to give her orders."

"I am not here to ask you to command her," Garadin snapped. "And you are under Helmat's oversight. He *can* command you."

Helmat nodded almost regally. Severn, thinking of Rosen, wanted to smile. The smile, however, didn't reach his lips.

"Do you understand her role among our people?"

"Not completely. She told me that she is the next castelord."

"She will be—and we would like a castelord who is sane. The Tha'alanari has been damaged by the recent investigation; we do not have the numbers to keep abreast of the Imperial Service's demands. Had we, she would never have come here over the trivial matter of recruiting a Wolf."

But she had. Severn said nothing.

"As castelord, she will be required to make decisions and choices that can't be countermanded," Helmat said, rescuing Severn from his own silence.

"She is not castelord yet."

"No. But there is no question that she will be. Garadin." The Tha'alani man reluctantly turned to face the Wolflord. "I understand how you feel. I tried to order her out of the office the day she arrived."

"She is not yours to command."

"Clearly. She is of the Tha'alanari. She has been among you for what, a decade? More? If this is too much for her, she will never be able to guide and lead the Tha'alani. Your role involves outsiders. It involves—how was it put?—the criminally insane. Us.

"I've no doubt you fussed at her or over her when she returned from her interview with the private. But fussing will not change facts. She has decided. If every decision is to be undermined by those who wish to protect her from reality, you will succeed in crippling her reign."

"She is young, and she is not yet castelord."

"She is young," Helmat agreed. "But she has access to literally centuries' worth of experience and wisdom. She needs to be able to make decisions of her own."

"Says a man whose purpose she serves."

"We all serve the Emperor."

Elluvian had not spoken a word. He was leaning against the wall, his arms folded, his chin tilted slightly toward the floor.

Severn's gaze slid between Garadin and the Wolflord, assessing. He then glanced at Elluvian and found the Barrani gaze almost welded to his own. He had been taught to observe, but that had always come naturally to him. He had always chosen to survey the lay of the land before acting, had always listened to the conversation between people to judge how to join it—or how to avoid it.

He observed now.

Garadin was pale with fear. It was a fear Severn understood; he held it in no contempt. He desired to protect Ybelline, but not, in Severn's opinion, because she was hierarchically important to the Tha'alani; that was an excuse he expected would hold water with the Wolflord, and he had grasped it in desperation and wielded it badly. Helmat Marlin was never going to be a man with whom *she's too important to work* would be a good lever.

As if in agreement with Severn's thought, the Wolflord said, "She cannot rule and guide your people if she does not understand what they suffer. But Garadin, she knows this.

"If all of the Tha'alanari were like Ybelline, the fractures between our peoples would occur far less often. She came to interview Severn."

"Interview? Is that what you now call it?" the Tha'alani man said in some disgust.

Ignoring this, the Wolflord continued. "I am aware of the effect of such interviews on our applicants. The majority do not consent to serve the Wolves or the Halls of Law in the wake of their meeting with the Tha'alani. The private not only agreed to serve but sought Ybelline out in the Tha'alani quarter a scant week after their interaction.

"Ybelline agreed to speak with him. I am certain that the Tha'alanari advised against such a meeting."

Garadin's silence was confirmation.

"She chose to meet with him anyway. They spoke."

"What did they speak of?" Garadin demanded.

"The private has only barely returned; he has not had the time to tender a report, which I'm certain will be forthcoming. You are Tha'alanari—you have direct access to Ybelline in a way the private never will. Did you not ask her?"

Of course he had. She had, probably politely, refused to discuss it. She had refused Scoros; she had rejected the entreaties of the Tha'alanari as a whole. Severn had not been privy to those pleas. But she had informed him that Scoros had gone in search of the castelord, and she had not been forced to vacate either the room or her search for the information Severn felt necessary in the wake of Scoros's errand.

To his surprise, Severn spoke. "What you want for her," he said, "she wants for all of her people. She desires their safety; she wants to protect them. She's done this by serving the Tha'alanari, and she'll do more when she becomes castelord. But…she believes that she can't know how to protect her people, how to *be* the castelord she wants to be, if she doesn't understand all of the dangers they face."

"No single person understands—"

"No human, no. I don't know her as well as you do—I

can't. But do you honestly believe she hasn't examined the full information the Tha'alanari carry with them, as a burden, so that most of the Tha'alani won't have to? She has to know what you're facing to change anything."

Garadin was arrested; his glare had removed itself from the Wolflord's face, and now rested firmly on Severn's. His eyes, however, were no longer green. They weren't gold, but the hazel implied a much calmer anger.

"How long did her…interview…with you last?"

Severn frowned. The question implied that Ybelline hadn't shared the whole of that interview with the Tha'alanari.

"I don't know. Judging the passage of time wasn't my first priority."

"What was?"

Severn shrugged. "What you feel about Ybelline, she feels about the entirety of the Tha'alani quarter. What I asked her to do is relevant to that. She wanted to do it, for the same reason that drove me to the quarter in the first place. I'm human. She's Tha'alani. But the bridge between us is the need to catch the criminal."

"Catching him will not change the past. It will not magically extirpate the horror of those experiences."

Severn nodded, unmoved. "It will prevent the same crime from ever happening again. That's what she wants. It's what I want. But neither is relevant. It's what the Emperor wants."

"And if she had refused you, boy? If she had declined your request? Would you have then gone straight to the Emperor?"

Severn's brows folded for a moment at the outrageous suggestion. "How would I speak to the Emperor?" he asked in honest confusion.

The Wolflord cleared his throat. "I am not, of course, the Emperor we *all* serve, but I am the voice of the Emperor in the

Halls of Law; the Hawklord, the Swordlord, and the Wolflord are empowered to give commands in his name."

"And would you have come to Helmat, to force her to do the work?"

Severn met, and held, Garadin's eyes. "No."

"It was Helmat who acquired the requisite permission for you to come to plead your case at all."

Severn nodded. "But it was not the Wolflord's request. It was mine. I asked permission to visit Ybelline because I think we need answers."

"Do you even understand the question?"

"I understand the reason I asked."

Garadin snorted. His eyes were a lighter hazel now, his skin no longer leeched of color. "You are young, as she is young. I cannot imagine you will make a good Wolf." He turned to Helmat, his shoulders slowly relaxing. "Empathy is the bane of our existence."

"It is what makes you more than human," Helmat replied, his eyes almost hooded. "But I understand that the Tha'alanari fear to lose her, as they themselves are almost lost. She is warm in a way that very few people—of any race—are."

"She has always kept us sane," was Garadin's quiet reply. It was a surrender. "She has always noted which of us were closer to the edge of madness than we thought, and she has called us back and away before we fall. Yes, we fear to lose her. But Severn," he added, "you were not yet born when the murders occurred. Ybelline was—and she remembers them all. She does not need to enter the Tha'alaan to touch those memories; she lived them. At that age, she understood that she was powerless.

"And perhaps at our age, the powerlessness was far more scarring." He bowed—to Severn, not to the Wolflord.

"I want to protect her, too," Severn blurted out.

"Yes. I can see that. She trusts you. I cannot think why, given her experiences."

"You don't."

"No, of course not. You are not only a servant of the Emperor, you are a Wolf."

When Garadin left the office—without slamming the door—Helmat turned to Severn. He was surprised at the boy's conversation and observations, which was why he'd made no attempt to take back the reins of the conversation, if it could be called that.

"The Tha'alanari, as you may have guessed, are not pleased with your request."

"No. But they were never going to be pleased with it."

"If we haven't called the Emperor in as mediator, I can assure you that some of them have. They are of vital import to the Imperial Service."

"And we," Elluvian said, almost grinning, "are not."

"The Imperial Service does not move at the whim of the Tha'alanari, except at need. The loss of several Tha'alani agents has made them far more careful than they otherwise condescend to be."

"How does it work?" Severn asked.

"Pardon?" It was not the question Helmat had expected; in truth, he'd expected no questions at all.

"The Tha'alanari and the Imperial Service. What rights of refusal do the Tha'alani have?"

"None. They have the right to choose which agents attend the Service's demands, when choice is possible. They have the right to withdraw an agent if the interview is considered harmful—but they must offer a substitute." Helmat exhaled. "It is a sword dance. The Tha'alani are necessary. The Emperor is cognizant of the effects of interrogation on the Tha'alaan. He does not desire to wield a tool until it snaps or breaks—not when it is so singularly important.

"While the Tha'alanari are, as loyal citizens, beholden to the Emperor, he will often accept their evaluation of the state of the Tha'alanari. His laws do not require such consideration; he attempts to be pragmatic. He is well aware that the Tha'alani would, if offered a true choice, never approach the Imperial Service at all.

"What did you discuss with Ybelline?"

"I asked her to find a Barrani memory within the Tha'alaan." The boy's glance flickered over Elluvian's face, and returned to Helmat's.

"Why?" He knew. He wanted to know how Severn would handle the question.

"Because the deaths don't make sense otherwise."

"You think a Barrani of note allowed himself to meld with a Tha'alani?"

"It's the only thing that would explain the risk taken. The Barrani involved humans. The victims were Tha'alani. The laws of exemption don't—can't—cover the murders. Elluvian says—"

"I have already spoken with Elluvian."

"—that the laws of exemption are very seldom broken by the Barrani, or by the significant members of the Barrani people. When crimes that would fall outside the exemption occur at the hands of Barrani, their bodies are often deposited on the steps of the Halls of Law. They are dead. Their deaths, at the hands of their own people, are not illegal."

"They are, technically," Elluvian said.

"En."

"We do have laws."

"*En.*"

"Do you expect to find that information? Or rather, do you expect Ybelline to find it?"

Severn hesitated for three solid beats. "I'm not certain. I hope she will, but she considered it highly unlikely; if the memories existed in the Tha'alaan, they would be heavily examined, heavily visited, by the curious. She didn't think they would be hard to find, in that case."

"But you believe they exist."

His hesitation this time was different. "She believes they exist," he finally said. "And Garadin's presence here today implies that she's right."

Helmat allowed himself a wintry smile; he wanted to shout with something perilously close to joy. "Very good. I have not rescinded permission to continue with this aspect of the investigation, nor will I.

"You will not, however, be waiting in the office for Ybelline's response. I believe Elluvian is about to continue his own investigations." Helmat glanced at the mirror as it flashed twice. Rosen had sent a mirror message.

"In the Halls of Law there is a Tha'alani who is on staff in a more permanent fashion; he is an adjunct Hawk. I wish you to speak with him. He is Tha'alanari, and he is also something of an artist. He works in Missing Persons.

"Rosen has found the Records you desire. You may invoke them with the use of her name."

At the boy's expression, Helmat paused and considered his own youthful experience with mirrors. "Have you used a mirror before?"

"Rosen's. She activated the mirror."

"Very well. Rosen will teach you how to invoke Records while within the Halls of Law. Such invocations will not be effective if you attempt to do so from a personal mirror."

Which, clearly, the boy did not possess. "The Emperor will be pleased if this hunt is successfully concluded."

Severn's expression didn't change. Helmat might as well have said, *if it does not rain today.* Had it been so long since Helmat himself had been such a youth? Helmat's youth had been defined by unnecessary skirmishes in the warrens. Or perhaps by surviving them.

There, trust had a different meaning. Did he trust the members of his gang? Yes, in a fashion. He couldn't trust them not to steal any money or items briefly in his possession; he couldn't trust them to leave food at what passed for a table in the open streets. But he could trust them at his back, and when the knives came out, they were never pointed at Helmat. Or almost never.

He had called this office home for well over a decade, and the desk that now housed Severn for another decade—perhaps closer to two. He had risen through the subtle hierarchy of the Wolves, and had at last come to command them all; the lessons of his early childhood, replete with men of power and their abuse, had, in the end, served a useful purpose. He met with the Emperor. He met with the people in charge of the Imperial Service. He could, without difficulty, name all of the lords of the various caste courts, with the single exception of the Leontines, who were otherwise absent from the power plays that riddled courts, high and low, of any other race. Politics as it existed among the Leontines was brutal and ended in death. He didn't have to struggle to understand the games they played: he knew them intimately and viscerally.

And he liked them the better for it.

Once, however, he had been a young man to whom the Emperor was almost mythical. A Dragon, yes—every child over the age of three knew that—but one so far above him that he was rendered irrelevant, as if he were the god of a religion Helmat did not follow.

And his opinion, like that of irrelevant gods, had meant nothing to Helmat, either.

He turned to his mirror. "Rosen."

"Here, lord and master," came her sarcastic response. She didn't put the mirror into its visual mode; he couldn't see her expression. He knew what it was, nonetheless.

"Private Handred has not yet had any experience with active mirrors or our Records. Show him how it's done, or your research will have been wasted."

Severn headed toward the door.

"Not you, En. I'm not finished with you."

Elluvian did not offer sarcasm, as Rosen had done. That should have been a warning flag.

CHAPTER FOURTEEN

ROSEN WAS WAITING AT HER DESK, LOOKING harried. Her companions were large piles of paper, from which she clearly expected the opposite of fun.

Her gaze, when it met Severn's, was as friendly as a thrown stone. He weathered it. The words that she spoke, however, changed the context of that ill temper. "None of us," she said, "had much experience with mirrors when Elluvian brought us in. I should have remembered, but it feels like a lifetime ago. Or several."

"You did remember the scarcity of food."

"Which you considered more important." Rosen had a dimple Severn hadn't seen before. "So did I. But you'll need to know how to use the mirrors. We send messages through the mirror network, and we access Records that way as well. Some of the Records won't appear until you've finished your probation. These ones will, because they're part of the job you've been assigned."

"Or because it was you doing the search?"

She smiled again. "Or because I'm a Wolf and have been for too many years, yes. Records."

The mirror, which had reflected her face with all of its expressions, seemed to almost shatter at the word, although none of the silvered glass left the frame.

She caught his involuntary movement, and her smile deepened the dimple that framed it. "I've been injured," she said, "but I still have my reflexes. Far worse has been thrown at me in my time than a few shards of random glass." The smile dimmed. "I appreciate the thought but I don't need protection. I don't need to be saved."

It was Severn's turn to flush. "My only family in the fiefs was a child five years younger than me. We weren't used to being around adults."

"You'll get used to it. We're all a bit prickly in our own ways—except Mellianne. She's a *lot* prickly. You're her opposite, but you're on your best behavior because you're on probation. I'd love to see what your normal behavior is like. Records, Severn Handred. Access."

"Access is limited for candidate Handred," the mirror replied. The thing that made that reply disturbing was the lack of any facial features, like lips, to utter the words.

"Rosen."

"You have one saved query. Lord Marlin has approved its release to candidate Handred."

The mirror's murky coal gray began to swirl, to spin, and as it did, colors joined it in a messy blend that ended with an image.

He was looking at a Tha'alani man. The eyes were closed, and the stalks across his forehead broken or crushed, along with some part of his face.

"We have no images of the living man," Rosen said, her voice softer and shorn of amusement. "No living images of any of the dead. What we have captured here are morgue Records. This man's name was Layan. He was, at the time of his death, twenty-one Imperial years of age. His was the first death. It occurred on the nineteenth day of the fourth month. Elluvian took you to some of the later murder sites—why, I don't know. Many crimes have occurred since this one at the same site, admittedly none as brutal."

"Murders?"

"Two, but neither seems to be deliberate—both were drunken fights that ended in drawn knives and blood. Records, location of discovery of the corpse."

Nothing changed. "You try."

"Records, were there witnesses to the killing of Layan?"

The image of the dead Tha'alani man was shuffled to the side, as if it were a card. In its place came smaller pictures, four in all.

"Witness testimony," Severn said.

When the mirror failed to move, he frowned. "Testimony from the first pictured witness."

The picture in the top left corner expanded to fill the mirror's frame. "This is like magic," he murmured.

"It's not like magic. It *is* magic. And no, I have no idea how the magic works. There'll be testing—sorry—if you survive your probation period."

"Testing?"

"For magical aptitude." At his expression, she laughed. "I know, right? None of us have shown any aptitude, but historically, a handful of Wolves have. Elluvian doesn't count."

"He can use magic." It was only half a question.

"Yes, and a damn sight better than the Imperial Mages."

"Why is he here?"

"The Emperor's personal orders," Rosen replied, shrugging. "He's always been here. I think he'll always be here. And we want one Barrani on the roster. Mortals don't do well when they're hunting Barrani at the Emperor's command."

"According to Mellianne—"

Rosen's hand snapped out and flattened. "Don't go there. Your job in this hunt is to keep Elluvian in check. You're not a pawn; you're a necessary sheath to his sword. You're a necessary presence because if you get entangled in Barrani political conflict, killing you has consequences that killing Elluvian won't."

"If Elluvian kills?"

"He'll argue self-defense, and the Emperor will accept that—as long as the person killed is Barrani." The Wolflord's voice barked over the beginning of witness testimony, and Records froze. "Rosen. My office."

"I'll leave you with Records," she said, grimacing as she rose. She reached for her cane. "You'll get used to Helmat's tone. This one is too controlled; it means *drop everything else.*"

"Trouble?"

"You work for the Halls of Law," she replied. "There's always trouble. Most of it won't concern your investigation."

"There is a faster way to do that."

Severn glanced to the side. Elluvian had come to stand beside Rosen's unoccupied chair. Severn was surprised, but not enough to jump or draw defensive weapons. Given Elluvian's race, this said something. Elluvian smiled briefly. "Instincts," he said, "are important. You were aware of my presence."

Severn shrugged.

"You shouldn't have been. I was making every attempt to remain unnoticed. I have observed that human men seem to be less guarded around human females. I accept that this is true in many cases. Having met An'Tellarus, you will understand why that is not the norm for my kin."

"And Cassandre."

Elluvian inclined his head. "What are you looking for?"

"Anything," was the instant reply. "Anything that these cases might have in common. Witnesses. Location. The Tha'alani quarter wasn't as heavily guarded back then?"

"Not in the same way, no. But even now it is not impossible for the intrepid to leave the quarter should they desire to do so."

"Would a death that didn't appear to be murder also exist in Records?"

"If one of the Tha'alani were to drop dead in the streets, it's likely that witnesses who cared enough to comment would call for the Swords. But no, not all such cases would be contained in Records."

"Not the Records of the Halls of Law."

Elluvian watched the boy. "You would, as I said, make an outstanding Hawk."

Severn said nothing.

"It is where the young woman is."

"If she's happy there, she won't want to see me."

"She is not officially a Hawk. She is too young. You are, if you have not lied about your age, considered adult by Imperial Law. Tell me, do you know anything about the marks she bears?"

Severn stiffened, and the silence he offered was a wall—a windowless, doorless wall.

"It is not from your interview that I have come across this information. The marks are known."

Severn's silence became less a wall and more a blade.

Elluvian smiled. "Very well. If you wish to access Records to find commonality, you can choose the person in question—the witness you are currently viewing, for example. You can then bring up any other cases in which the witness was in-volved—either as witness or criminal."

Severn tried this. The witness he had chosen had been in-volved in two petty crimes—pickpocketing—and had served as witness in three other cases.

"The crime didn't take place in the warrens," Severn noted. "None of the crimes did."

"No." Elluvian was well aware of the location at which bodies had been discovered. "Not given witness testimony."

Severn, however, was no longer listening. The mir-ror moved constantly between flickering images. Tha'alani corpses. Street locations. Witnesses. Lists of injuries taken.

Severn shook his head, as if the information was not quite what he was searching for. He expanded the search, or at-tempted to expand it. The mirror resisted him until Elluvian, far more annoyed by this than Severn seemed to be, took over the search. There was nothing in Records to which Elluvian did not have access.

Severn, who hadn't heard Elluvian approach, definitely heard Rosen. It wasn't the cane—although it made her walk distinctive—it was the heaviness of her steps.

"If you have time to peruse Records," she snapped, "do so in your own office. Unless you want to supervise Severn while dealing with paperwork, in which case, do so with my gratitude and my blessing."

"You did not care for— Ah, no. That wasn't you. The last person who made a similar offer disliked intensely the way I dealt with paperwork. It is an honest day's work, yes, but I'm Barrani. I have a reputation to uphold."

Rosen didn't tell Severn why the Wolflord had called her away, which was fair. Severn hadn't asked. Nor, given her expression, would he. These magical Records were exactly what he wanted, and he didn't wish to lose that access by annoying her further.

Rosen wasn't Elluvian's concern. Nor was the paperwork which Severn had already learned was considered a waste of time by most of the people stuck dealing with it.

"Records, pause," Elluvian said to Rosen's mirror. "Resume in my office."

Elluvian's office had a bank of windows on the far wall, which surprised Severn; the Wolflord's office let in very little light. The windows, such as they were, were small and high, beginning at the ceiling and extending perhaps two feet toward the floor. They were barred. Even if they hadn't been, it would be difficult for anyone to break in through them, unless they were very young or very flexible.

Elluvian was not concerned with possible attacks.

He walked over to a desk that seemed to be coated with a fine layer of dust. "You don't drink?"

"Not when I'm on duty," Severn replied. It was true. It wasn't the whole of the truth.

"You will not be outraged if I indulge?"

But Severn was now seated in front of Elluvian's mirror, which was actually much larger than the one on Rosen's desk. Elluvian's mirror did not have to share space with trays of paper, unopened correspondence, and books meant to schedule appointments to speak with the elusive Lord Marlin.

"How much information can Records contain?"

"I am not aware that there is a limit," Elluvian said.

"Why does all the paperwork exist, then?"

"You understand the necessity for paperwork?"

"Rosen explained it."

Elluvian laughed. "I'm surprised your ears are still attached to your head."

"She'd probably be happier if all of it was contained in Records."

"No doubt. So would every person who has handled this particular desk since the inception of the Wolves."

"Why isn't it done?"

"It *is* done. But the paperwork allows for signatures and seals in a way that Records doesn't. And the mechanism by which Records works is not well understood by many. Most of those who could claim that understanding are members of the Arcanum."

"Arcanum? Imperial Mages?"

Elluvian chuckled. "Never, ever ask that where either Arcanists or Imperial Mages can hear you. No. The Arcanum is an ancient institute; it predates the Empire. It is where the best and brightest go to study magic, if they have displayed the aptitude for it. Imperial Mages work directly for the Emperor, and by extension, the Halls of Law. There are no Barrani Imperial Mages. No Barrani palace guards. No Barrani in Imperial Service."

"But there are Barrani Wolves. And Hawks."

"Say, rather, Barrani Wolf." If he expected Severn to ask him to elucidate, those expectations were to be disappointed. Severn was now scanning Records, sifting them for any information he might find that they had missed.

"I want to speak with the Tha'alanari."

"Again?" Elluvian smiled. "When you say Tha'alanari, do you refer to Ybelline?"

There was no answering smile. "It doesn't matter who. It could be Garadin."

"Will you venture into the Tha'alani quarter again?"

Severn shook his head. "I don't think it's helpful to be there. The only people who will speak to me are Tha'alanari—the people who serve the Emperor."

THE EMPEROR'S WOLVES

243

"In which case, they might as well come here?"

"Lord Marlin said there was one man seconded to the Hawks we might speak to."

"I am certain that was not his exact phrasing. Use the mirror," Elluvian said.

Severn blinked.

"Use it like this: Ybelline, Tha'alanari."

The mirror's many disparate images faded. When color returned, Severn was now staring at the face of the future castelord.

"You wish to know about any Tha'alani death that occurred during the serial killings?"

"Yes. Not murders—or not obvious, detectable murders—but deaths. Any age group. Any location."

"If the deaths were suspicious, would it not be more germane to look for unremarkable deaths outside of the quarter itself?"

"I don't think any death that occurred outside of the quarter would be considered unremarkable," Severn replied. "But if there are such deaths, they would be relevant."

"You've searched Records in the Halls of Law?"

Severn nodded.

"And you've not found the information you seek."

"I haven't put all the information together—but no, I don't think so. The deaths that occurred, that were listed as natural, happened too much before or too much after. And there are only two."

"You believe that someone entered the Tha'alani quarter to kill one of my kin without alerting either the victim or the guards?"

"I think there are ways to kill that would be near instant and that would not cause alarm in the victim before his or her untimely, immediate death. Whoever was responsible for this death would understand the Tha'alaan as well as anyone who isn't a part of it. The murders of your kin were brutal."

"You think this was done entirely to harm the Tha'alaan."

"I think it might have been done around the same time to possibly stop any of the Tha'alani from touching those memories or any memories surrounding the deaths, yes. I don't think the person involved hated the Tha'alani." He shook his head. "No, I think he must have hated or feared them—but I don't think he bore ill will to the people he indirectly murdered.

"They were tools."

"Your kin has long feared mine, and fear causes insanity."

"Yes. But… I think he must have understood some part of that as well. If the Tha'alaan was injured enough, things might be buried that would otherwise draw attention."

She was silent. Her eyes were green. In a human face, it would have been a lovely color. "Very well." She closed her eyes. Opened them again. "This is not an avenue of investigation we pursued at the time—we know and fear the fear of your kind. We accept that it exists, but we do not always understand the complexities and the layers."

"You think we're all insane."

"Isolation would drive any of my kin to madness. We do not understand how your kin have survived without destroying themselves utterly—but we understand that they have. So, too, the Barrani."

"We don't trust."

"No. And perhaps that is safest. But I think many of you desire to be able to trust—to find the person or people that you can. And I believe, if you had always had those people in your lives, you would not—or your criminals would not—become what they become. It is hard to feel isolated, to feel unloved, unsupported, unheard."

Severn nodded.

"I will search. For this request, the Tha'alanari have not united against me, and I doubt they will."

"Your cub," Helmat said, as he viewed Records in his office, "is surprising."

"He is hardly mine."

"We were all, at one time or another, yours. None of us were given the mission he's been given."

Elluvian nodded. "He believes his status as an outsider allows him to look at things differently."

"And you?"

"I think he's wrong."

"Ybelline is taken with him."

Elluvian shook his head. "Ybelline is taken with the fact that he doesn't fear her. He knows that she knows what he did, but he doesn't react with guilt in her presence. He doesn't assume that her knowledge now gives her the unavoidable right to judge him. His fears don't warp her behavior in his mind. And the Tha'alani consider mortal—and Immortal—fear to be poison. He is, in my estimation, a gift to her. She does not fear to touch his thoughts or his memories.

"He does not fear to expose them to her. She will be castelord," Elluvian continued, looking at the Records that Helmat had called up. "And her view of Severn will color all their views, both of the boy and of the Wolves."

"Garadin is never going to like me."

"No. But that has never been your concern."

Helmat's grin was a wolf's grin. "The Imperial Service doesn't like the request Severn made. At all."

"You might consider being less gleeful. Will they block it?"

"They made one attempt."

Elluvian looked at the mirror. "Ybelline will be a remarkable castelord, in my opinion." She had overruled the Imperial Service refusal by claiming laws of exemption with regards to the information Severn sought. "I think this is the first time I've ever seen you amused by the invocation of laws of exemption."

"It's the first time they've been used in our favor," the Wolflord replied, grinning broadly.

"You said the Hawks are the investigative branch of the Halls?" Severn asked Elluvian the next morning.

Elluvian nodded.

"Would they investigate these people if we requested it?"

"They investigate crimes after they have been discovered. If you could tie these people to current crimes, yes, absolutely. If you want a meandering investigation about theoretical crimes, it's unlikely. Although the Hawks, like the Wolves, serve the Emperor, our functions are different, and there is some rivalry. Why are these people significant?"

"They were witnesses in eight of the mob-fueled killings."

"The same ones?"

"No, but there's some overlap."

"They are mortal."

"Yes." Severn hesitated and then said, "One is dead. He was knifed on his way home, and left to bleed out his life in the street. Records: morgue report." Severn had been allowed to access Records using Elluvian's permissions.

Elluvian listened to the dry report. The man had been killed quickly and efficiently. The killing blow had been struck first; the half-dozen other wounds had been made afterward, while the man was still alive, but dying. All of the wounds had occurred, in the morgue's opinion, from the same weapon.

No assailant had been caught.

"This occurred six days ago," Severn said, although Elluvian could see the same information Severn could. "Very shortly after Timorri made the connection between one crime and another."

"Timorri has not returned to active duty."

Severn nodded.

"This is not good. Yes, the Hawks will investigate. Don't expect gratitude from Hawks."

Severn shook his head. "I don't want to be on Record as the Wolf making the request. I'm on probation. Even if I wanted the credit, I'm not technically allowed."

"You don't want the girl to know that you're here."

Severn didn't prevaricate. "I don't want her to know I'm here. She's got a home here. She's mostly happy. She's safe."

"You think she'll flee?"

"Or try to kill me, yes." Something in his face implied that death at her hands would almost be a relief.

"I will deal with the request."

"You'll make it?"

"Absolutely not. But I will have Helmat pass the information on as part of a joint investigation."

"What does that mean?"

"They will have access to our files in the investigation—which will not affect you at all. We, however, will then have access to theirs, which might."

In the morning, Helmat's grimmest expression had taken up what appeared to be permanent residence on his face. Severn had barely stepped into the office when Rosen waved him over.

"I'm not sure what you did," she whispered, "but Helmat is in a mood. He's demanded to see you, first thing."

"Is it the Tha'alanari or the Hawks?"

Rosen's mouth opened, but no words fell out. "When Helmat is in this mood, no one asks questions that aren't directly relevant to their mission. Even then, it can be touch and go. You'd better head to his office. He's probably observing us through our mirror connections as we speak."

Severn wasn't surprised to see Elluvian in the Wolflord's office. This time, however, Garadin wasn't present. Elluvian's eyes were blue. Helmat's were the same brown they'd always been, but his brow was furrowed in a way that suggested rage.

"Both of your requests have caused disturbances," the Wolflord said.

"You found the possibility amusing yesterday," Elluvian pointed out. Severn wouldn't have dared. "Which of the difficulties is currently enraging you?"

"We have another body in the morgue."

Elluvian's amusement was discarded instantly. "The Hawks found the corpse."

Helmat nodded.

"Manner of death?"

"Not yet determined. There were no obvious wounds, no obvious broken bones. The person in question appeared to have died at home. It's likely his body would have been discovered in the next few days, as he lived alone, but the Hawks were sent to speak with him."

"On what grounds?"

"Do I look like the Hawklord?"

Both the Wolflord and Elluvian now turned to Severn, as if waiting for his input.

"They know we're investigating," Severn said. "Or they know we will be."

"Give the boy a cookie," Helmat said to Elluvian.

Severn turned to Elluvian. "The High Halls?"

Elluvian nodded grimly. "There is a possibility that the informant works for the Imperial Service, but Helmat thinks it unlikely, when the High Halls are already in play."

The Wolflord's eyes widened before they narrowed to slits. "Dismissed," he said, clearly to Severn, as he turned to face Elluvian.

"Does he often shout like that?" Severn asked Rosen.

"Not normally, no. The last time it happened, someone had just blown the hinges off his doors. The explosion was meant for Helmat," she added. "Helmat survived. The would-be assassin didn't. On the bright side, you can be certain he's not pissed off at you—he threw you out before he started. The new door has a few magical enhancements."

"To protect it?"

"To protect the rest of us from hearing most of his ire." Rosen shook her head. "It's Elluvian again." She glanced at Severn. "Do I want to know?"

"I wouldn't if he was that angry."

She chuckled. "Do you know?"

"Not exactly. Does Records have information about the Barrani High Court?"

The good humor drained from Rosen's face, leaving an expression that was much closer to what the Wolflord's had been before Severn was ejected from the office.

"No. There are no members of the Barrani High Court who have ever been arrested and brought to trial. There are no Barrani informants. Severn, you're young enough that you probably don't listen to advice when it's offered. I've been you. But I'm going to offer advice anyway."

Severn waited.

"Do not involve yourself in Barrani politics. Not now. Not ever."

"Laws of exemption—"

"Laws are at best estimates of decent behavior. If they were set in stone, if they were immutable, the entirety of the Halls of Law would cease to exist. Murder is against the law. People still murder. The laws of exemption—as far as I can tell, from years of experience—are a game to the Barrani. They understand that to lose is to enrage the Emperor, which is why they play this particular game more carefully than most of their games."

"I've been assigned to partner Elluvian. Because of the laws of exemption."

"Which is why Mellianne's been in a mood." A volley of poorly enunciated syllables shook the Wolflord's office door, almost literally. "You keep your head down if you're following in his footsteps. Understand?"

Severn nodded. "The Wolflord obviously has some knowledge of the Barrani High Court."

"Did you hear a single thing I just said, or was I wasting my breath?"

"I heard you. Practically speaking, though, there's no way I can avoid the Barrani. They're the only reason I was assigned to Elluvian. I'm not going to jump into any fight Elluvian starts. I'm not suicidal."

"Don't jump into any fights the other Barrani start with Elluvian either. He's likely to survive. You're not."

"This is about Darrell, isn't it?"

Rosen nodded. Exhaled. "You're not Darrell," she said. "But you're asking too many questions where the High Court is concerned." The brief, grim set of her jaw slowly relaxed "…and apparently where the Tha'alani are concerned, as well. The Hawklord has queued up a session with the Wolflord, which I assume is also the result of your current investigation. If it weren't for the Barrani problem, I'd say you're doing fine."

At his expression, she laughed.

"You're not a random shit-disturber. Helmat thinks you have good reasons for the trouble you've caused him, and he's willing to shoulder it."

After a moment, Severn said, "And he thinks Elluvian has bad reasons?"

"Exactly. The query you sent to the Tha'alani was surprising and unexpected—but it was smart. The examination of the Records—Halls and Hawks—was both, as well. Keep that part up. I think Helmat would rescind his command with regard to Elluvian if he could, but at the moment the only other available partner is Mellianne."

"He's the Wolflord."

"Elluvian is a special case. He found us all. He trained most of us. But he's Barrani. None of us are certain what his role is, in the Emperor's eyes. He's not officially in the pay of the Halls of Law. It's never been safe to partner with him, but it almost never happens. If I had to guess, the Barrani he feels is suspicious is someone highly placed in the court."

Severn nodded.

"Unless the Emperor *really* loses his temper, this entire case has to be approached extremely carefully. Tell me, does Elluvian strike you as careful?"

"I don't know."

"Oh?"

"I don't know enough about the Barrani High Court."

"The short version is: if he suspects that this tangle of a case has the approval of a Lord of the High Court, it's bad."

Severn nodded again. "Where would I find the information I lack? Without it, I won't be able to assess the danger I'm facing."

"Barrani bad," she said. "For us, it doesn't really matter what titles they use among themselves."

"If they have titles, they've got access to a lot more under-lings than we do."

"Yes. Barrani underlings. They have money, which gener-ally also means human underlings. And given the nature of the Hawklord's request, they've got human underlings. Try not to get killed, hmmm?" She turned, once again, to the paper-work that was theoretically occupying her attention.

"I'll do my best." He cleared his throat. "The information?"

"The Imperial Service will have it," she said without look-ing up. "But they're incredibly difficult to deal with."

"Are the Tha'alanari part of the Imperial Service?"

"Yes."

"Thanks, Rosen."

"You owe me."

"I do."

"Pay me back by surviving." She turned to face him again. "I think we'll lose Mellianne if we lose you. And it won't be as clean a loss, either."

CHAPTER FIFTEEN

WHEN ELLUVIAN FINALLY LEFT HELMAT'S OFFICE, he was not in a good mood. This was fair; while Helmat had stopped shouting, Elluvian suspected this was more due to exhaustion than depletion of anger.

"Severn is not Darrell," Elluvian had said, in response to most of Helmat's hurled invective.

He understood Helmat's concerns. He'd recruited all of the Wolves as they were currently constituted, and believed he understood their weaknesses. And their strengths. The two were tightly entwined. He understood what Severn's death would mean to morale.

Severn himself might not understand why; he was an outsider, on probation, not fully Wolf. The loss of an outsider, given his prior life, might strike him as irrelevant. Or perhaps not. There was something about Severn that implied a flexibility that Darrell—or Mellianne—had never possessed. If Mellianne survived, she would learn. Darrell would not.

Elluvian would have considered Helmat's concerns trivial had it not been for An'Tellarus. Even at a remove of centuries, she still knew where to point the knife and how to drive it in. Not, of course, to kill him, because then her games would be over.

What surprised him was her interest in Severn. It was a surprise weighted by unease. He had avoided An'Tellarus for so long, were he human he might have forgotten her existence entirely. Or perhaps not. Barrani memory was reliable, and, as was the case with any living being, the events that caused scars became the memories closest to the surface—no matter how long ago those injuries had taken place.

Elluvian, still musing, headed toward Rosen's desk. It pained him to see her stuck behind it; it pained her as well. But she had come to accept that this desk served a necessary function for the Wolves. He wondered if her injuries could be healed with sufficient magical power. It was not an entirely idle thought. He now knew the location of a healer.

She glared at him as he approached her desk.

He chose to ignore the glare. "The Hawks will take the two surviving witnesses into protective custody," he told her.

She didn't ask for any context whatsoever. Her nod was grim, her eyes narrow. She, like Helmat, was not best pleased with him.

"I wish to make certain that the Hawks sent to secure that protection are Barrani."

Some of the tension left her face, her jaw. "Severn is worried."

"He is not, despite his age, a fool."

"He thinks that his investigation caused the deaths of two of the four witnesses."

"As I said, he's not a fool. On the other hand, it's unlikely the murderers were Barrani."

"Then why send Barrani Hawks?"

"Because I might be wrong."

Her eyes rounded.

"How big is this?" she demanded, although she took a moment to activate her mirror. "How big is it going to be?"

"If not for Severn's early intervention?"

The mirror chimed three times—a wind chime sound that Rosen had chosen because she found it calming.

A familiar face filled the frame of Rosen's mirror. Garadin, eyes emerald. "Ybelline will attend the Halls of Law in three hours."

Elluvian frowned. When Garadin failed to add more words, he said, "I will meet her at the gates, and I will escort her here personally."

"And home?"

"And home."

The emerald of the Tha'alani's eyes barely shifted.

"It would make more sense to send Severn back," Elluvian then offered.

"It would, yes." Garadin's words were clipped. Ah. "Be at our gates in one hour."

The mirror chimed again. This time, Helmat's craggy face occupied the space. "If you're to serve as her escort, take Severn with you."

"Of course."

"What exactly did you do this time?" Elluvian asked as they exited the Halls of Law.

"The Records of the Halls of Law didn't have the information I needed."

"And you asked Ybelline for it? You've already stirred the pot by asking for information that Tha'alani wouldn't otherwise cede to outsiders."

Severn nodded.

"Her visit today is not about that information."

"Probably not." He hesitated and then added, "Although she'll probably have that information as well."

"You don't wish to tell me what you asked of her."

"No."

A short bark of laughter surprised Elluvian, as it was his. "My permission, as you must be aware, is not required. Rosen?"

Severn nodded. "She didn't entirely approve."

"She doesn't entirely approve of anything."

"She trusts the Wolflord."

"Trust and approval are not the same, at least among my kin."

"Your kin doesn't trust anyone." Severn's voice held no accusation; it was neutral, observational.

"True. We have some cause."

The cub nodded. "Do you think the Hawks will arrive in time?"

"I think they might be able to save one of the remaining two witnesses. I asked that the Hawks sent to provide protective custody be Barrani."

"You trust them?"

"What did I just say? No. But unless they arrive to a cooling corpse, they have the best chance of offering substantive protection."

"And if they fail?"

"That will give us information as well. Helmat is not pleased. The Hawklord is not pleased. In less than two days you've ruffled feathers—and in the case of the Hawklord, that description is literal. There is some chance the Barrani Hawks will have their pride on the line. Avoid bruising Barrani pride where you can."

Severn nodded. He was, in silence, scanning the streets, his gaze flitting across the heights of buildings. Elluvian did not tell him that this caution was wasted. Caution, unless it devolved into fear, was never wasted.

★ ★ ★

Ybelline met them at the gate with a group of four Tha'alani guards as escort. She did not wear the flowing robes that were at home in the Tha'alani quarter; she wore, instead, the darker suits occupied by the Imperial Service. That, and the visible antennae, made her look far more intimidating to the mortals in the regular streets.

Elluvian tendered her a perfect bow. He nudged Severn, and Severn did the same, but it had not been his automatic response. Neither man held their bows; she was worthy of respect, not obeisance.

The four Tha'alani guards were green-eyed to a man. Or woman. They said nothing, but their antennae wove frantically in the empty air.

"No," Ybelline said, her voice gracious, the word unadorned. She spoke it out loud; she meant it to be heard by those who had no access to the Tha'alaan. "I am certain I will be escorted back to the quarter when my work is done."

The Tha'alani did not condescend to break the surface of their own silence. Common courtesy was not their priority at the moment.

"I am uncertain how long I will be absent," she replied. "I will inform Scoros when I am done."

She stepped away from the guards. For one moment, Elluvian wondered if those guards would obey her inaudible commands. They did, but their eyes never lost their deep green.

Elluvian was accustomed to being given a wider berth when he walked Elantran city streets. With Ybelline as companion, however, the streets were all but emptied; people literally pushed themselves up against nearby walls or windows to avoid even touching her shadow.

If he had thought Severn cautious on their walk to the Tha'alani quarter, he reassessed now. The cub was tense and focused. He did not miss an open window—or a closed one, for that matter. Ybelline's eyes, unlike those of her guards, were hazel. If she did not want to be here, she was not upset about the necessity.

Still, they proceeded in silence toward the Halls of Law, and did not break the silence until they had passed the guards at the door and made their way to the Wolves' offices.

There, Severn did one quick scan of the interior before he relaxed. He turned to Ybelline and offered her a bow that was suitable for High Lords, if one was a servant. He held that bow until she touched his shoulder.

"You are certain you wish to do this?" she asked, her voice softer, the doubt in it clearer than it had been when she had stood outside of the quarter she would one day rule.

He nodded. His pallor was off, but a rueful grin eased the effect of his color. "I'm sorry," he said.

"Never say that," Ybelline replied. "You do what you feel must be done. As do I. A simple apology changes neither fact." She exhaled. "I have some information to offer from your first request. I have information from your second. The Emperor, however, had to grant his personal permission in the latter case, and the Imperial Service will not be best pleased with Helmat." She closed her eyes briefly. "I was granted permission, but the Imperial Service bureaucracy is not without spite."

"You can't just give me Records access."

"No. If you wish the information, I must give it to you as if you were a criminal."

Severn said, "I probably am—I've just been lucky enough not to be caught." He didn't even look surprised.

"Is there an office we can use for the duration of the interview?"

Elluvian said, "You may use mine. It is seldom used; I dislike the enclosed space."

★ ★ ★

Ybelline entered Elluvian's office first; Severn followed her.

"Wait one minute," a familiar—and annoyed—voice said. Severn considered closing the door anyway, but the voice was the Wolflord's. He therefore held it open as Lord Marlin stopped in its frame.

"What are you doing here?" he demanded. The question was aimed in its entirety at Ybelline.

It was Severn who answered. "She has come as a member of the—"

"I can *see* what she's wearing, and I didn't ask you. I'm having more than enough difficulty with an ornery Garadin; I don't need further complications."

"The Emperor," Ybelline said, her voice almost serene, "has given his personal permission for this interview."

"His personal permission."

"Yes. It was required. Saidh considered the request unusual."

Helmat snorted.

"He is very efficient at what he does, and he's one of the few men the Emperor trusts completely."

"One could say the same of a corpse."

"Corpses are not efficient, Helmat."

"They're efficient at being dead. Mankev resembles them."

Ybelline said nothing. Severn thought, from both her words and this silence, that she liked Mankev. But it was Ybelline who finally broke that silence. "Saidh cannot be bribed. He cannot be threatened. He does his job completely without flexibility."

"He can't be bribed because he doesn't have normal, human desires," Helmat snapped. "And if he called in the Emperor—"

"He did, of course. I explained the need. He agreed that it was possibly necessary, but he didn't feel he had the authority to step outside of the bounds of the Service. Or perhaps he didn't feel I had the requisite authority to do so."

"What, exactly, did the private request?"

"Information."

"Ybelline, I have had an extremely trying day."

"If you wish to know, you will have to ask Saidh for that information. I am empowered only to speak to Severn, and only in the manner of my kin." Her eyes were now almost gold.

"You realize the private is on probation?"

Her smile deepened. "I do. But the Wolves serve the Emperor. Even those on probation. What the Emperor commands, your private will have to obey—just as you would in a similar situation."

"What information is he allowed to share?"

"At the moment, none."

This surprised Severn.

"We'll see about that." Helmat stepped out of the doorway.

"He's going to mirror the Imperial Service," Severn said, voice low.

"I know."

"You like the Wolflord."

"I do. But I also like Saidh. Everything I've said is true: he is trusted. He cannot be bribed—I'm not sure the purpose of a bribe even makes sense to him. He is rock solid, and he is much easier for me to deal with than his predecessor." Here, her eyes shaded toward hazel.

"Is his predecessor still alive?"

"No. Except in memory, I will never have to deal with him again. And," she added, "that was something that Saidh would never say, and I should not have. I believe it is considered poor manners to speak ill of the dead."

"It isn't for the Tha'alani?"

"No, but it wouldn't be. The dead are still alive in some

fashion within the Tha'alaan. We can see the whole of their lives." She sat in one of the two chairs that fronted Elluvian's mostly unused service desk. "Mirror, off."

"Authority?" the mirror said, although no image broke its reflective surface.

"Ybelline Rabon."

The mirror made no further inquiries or reply.

Severn then knelt in front of her chair, straightening his upper body. "Will this be easier for you?" he asked. Her eyes lost hazel, adopted gold.

"You are unlike your kin," she said. "Yes. It will make things easier. I did not lie to Elluvian or my kin. I do not know how long this will take. I have found relevant Tha'alani deaths within the time frame you specified. I have found no contact with Barrani, no hint of their presence within the Tha'alaan. But I am not a Hawk; I am an investigator in title only. I am not entirely certain what you would consider suspicious circumstances."

"If you have the memories of the men and women who died—"

She shook her head, reached out, and brushed strands of dark hair from his forehead. "I will show you what I've found. You will see it, briefly, as I see it, but it will become your experience and viewpoint. I am not certain I have the information you requested, but I've done my best on my own. I require your help."

Severn nodded. He didn't apologize again, nor did he ask if she would be all right. She had made clear that this was the choice she had made, and if it was the best choice among a host of bad choices, it was still hers.

For her part, she was afraid only of traumatizing him. He felt that fear the moment she placed her slender antennae against his forehead.

The fear was for, not of, and it felt a lot like warmth.

Can you get confused? he asked, almost without intent.

Between who I am and who you are?

Yes.

No. If we could, the Tha'alaan would be far more of a dangerous place for us. Did you feel, the first time, that you were somehow me?

He shook his head, and felt her amusement. *Don't move your head so much—I'll lose contact.*

Sorry.

This will be a little bit like your Records.

Is that what it was like for you? The Tha'alaan.

No—but the Tha'alaan can be frightening for your kin. I will hold information, and I will answer your questions. It won't be exact—but this was the best option I could choose in the time allotted. You must understand that this is new for me, as well; it is not my usual function as part of the Imperial Service.

From the Wolflord's reaction, you don't generally function as part of the Imperial Service.

Not generally, no. There was a thickness in the thought, a hesitance, as if it came from a great distance. *But that is not my role in the Tha'alanari in general. Only in emergencies am I free to act, to pick up the burden that my companions face daily.*

I'm grateful that it was you.

Yes. But Severn, you are unusual. If my kin weren't so burdened with those whose lives they have viewed at Imperial command, I do not think contact with you would have injured them. They disagree, of course. Experience scars and shapes us all. It's hard to focus on a single task when you're here like this.

Why? He didn't ask the question. It was a thought, like any other thought, something he tucked away for consideration, should more information come to light. She could hear it. She could hear it all.

Yes. That's why we're hated and feared by your kind. What they don't understand is that we hear it all, all the time; to us it's natural. The reason it's difficult for me is that I have a task. I have to operate in the confines of that given task, with all of the necessary security precautions. It's much easier to separate our own thoughts from the Tha'alaan than it is to separate our thoughts from someone we're in contact with.

Severn stilled.

What are you doing?

He didn't answer. He could feel a curiosity tainted by fear, but it was distant now.

After a silent pause, Ybelline began.

She was much like Records, but better; he didn't have to remember the exact commands in order to shift the scene or the flow of information. When he focused—and he couldn't help but focus here, there were no other distractions—the images that she showed him brightened, darkened, or faded away without any conscious effort to remember new commands on his part.

She didn't show him faces; didn't caption any of the memories she had brought forth with names, verbal or printed; she didn't bring him clear, sharp vignettes. He was deposited *into* the life of the Tha'alani whose memories she thought might offer some hint, some way forward into the grimmest of the memories the Tha'alaan held.

In one way, the filtered recall was more difficult than Records, and that was the collation of information; he couldn't simply freeze and hold a single image, adding it to a magical stack that could be recalled with a few words. That work, Ybelline had to do on her own, separating strands of lived lives into flattened sections.

Severn focused not on the deaths—the unsuspicious, natural deaths—of the men and women brought forward for his perusal, but on the lives they had lived near those deaths. Had they left the Tha'alani quarter? Yes? No? Had they ever left the quarter?

Those for whom the answer could safely be said to be *no*, he discarded—but there were precious few of those; Ybelline, understanding on some level what he'd been looking for when he made this request, had already filtered out most of them.

Even filtered, there were a surprisingly large number of people, or people's memories, in the samples she'd chosen.

We were not as afraid of the city streets. We learned.

It's not that—it's just the number. It's the number of people. It seems high.

For a moment he felt a piercing grief and an abiding anger. No, not anger, rage. It startled him enough that he moved, his hands falling to his weapons reflexively, his eyes opening.

She stood, her eyes hazel—not the green the emotions suggested—watching him; she hadn't moved at all. "Did you believe," she asked verbally, "that I am without anger?"

He nodded. He saw no point in lying to a woman who would once again return him to the state of communion in which all truths were laid bare.

Her smile was odd, more sorrowful than any smile had the right to be. "We are all people," she said, her voice, like her smile, soft. "We know anger, fear, pain. The difference between us is that the anger, fear, and pain do not become the focus of our existence, influencing and coloring all of the choices we make from the point it takes hold."

He swallowed. His hands remained free of weapons; the tension ebbed slowly from the line of his shoulders, his jaw. He met, and held, her gaze. "There were three," he finally said.

She knew which three.

"They were young in the memories you showed me; young

when they died. I want to see the memories they shared with each other."

"We all share—"

"No, *share* is the wrong word. Sorry. They shared more than just memories; they shared events. One of them once led the others through the hills and around the walls."

Her eyes widened slightly. "I don't believe—"

"He thought of it. It embarrassed and amused him. There were three—a girl, two boys. Can you find those memories?"

"Of course. I didn't—" She exhaled. "Of course." She leaned forward, but Severn, prepared, leaned toward her as well.

He had no words for the childhood of these three. And that was for the best. He'd long since accepted that the life he'd led in the fiefs was his life, for better or worse; that others—across the Ablayne—led safer, happier lives; that Ferals didn't hunt there. That parents didn't disappear.

But the sting of an envy he thought long dead touched him anyway. He let the envy be; he didn't try to suppress it. There was no point. Ybelline would see it, know it. It would become just another guilty secret.

Or not; when he reacted, she'd already begun to show him other memories, other lives, small glimpses of similar envies, similar sadnesses, all from the viewpoints of children. She didn't tell him he wasn't alone, because she didn't need to tell him that. She let him feel it, know it, experience it.

And he took, from those experiences, dropped so casually into his thoughts, what she'd intended—or perhaps what her own young kin took, time and again: that it was natural to feel envy, that it didn't make him somehow a terrible person. It was just one of many feelings in a stream of feelings, some better than others.

He had always desired privacy. Had always kept his thoughts

to himself when sharing them served no greater purpose. In the Tha'alaan, there was no privacy, ever. He wondered again what it might be like to grow up with no privacy. Where there was no privacy, it seemed that there was no judgment.

He righted himself with her silent help, and she once again returned to the three children. They weren't fearless, but the giddy daring that characterized the young and secure brought them a measure of joy and pride; they looked over their shoulders as they walked away from the Tha'alani quarter, muting their thoughts, highlighting their emotions.

Everyone who belongs to the Tha'alaan has access to every other person. We know we can keep no secrets, she told him. *But we, too, must turn our thoughts towards those secrets. We must pay attention. It is different from the way you guard your children, but not so different.*

It was very different.

Secrecy for our young involves the ability to whisper, not to shout. These children, these three, were clever—they focused on each other, and on their delight in the escapade. They did not focus on their fear of getting caught. Those who minded them—and they were not so young that a minder was required—would not be alerted if their attention was elsewhere. Not in time, she added ruefully. *I am certain harsher words were spoken when it was too late to stop them.*

He saw the city streets as they had seen them thirty years ago. Forty, perhaps. The shape of the streets hadn't changed, nor had the cobbled stones, the buildings that stood on either side of open road. There were wagons; he could smell the passage of horses. But if Elantra was his home, it hadn't always been his home. He had to make the effort to orient himself to understand where they were.

Their first surprise—more fear here than instant delight—was the Leontine quarter. That quarter, unlike their own, was not walled in any way; the open streets led to it, and eventually through it. But there were *people* in those streets with golden fur, and the livid eyes of Dragonkind. Taller, wider, with fangs that suggested their origins, they had looked at the Tha'alani children, growling their questions.

Do not touch any who are not of the people. All three thought it. All three understood the unspoken law. Only one wanted to break it—curiosity drove them like a whip. But the Leontines were so visibly different from the people, even that girl couldn't find the courage to do more than mumble a response.

"You are lost," a Leontine man said. He was gray around the muzzle, his ears irregular in a way that spoke of physical combat decades past.

If the girl wasn't brave enough to touch the white-tinged fur, she was brave enough to speak, and in the end, staring at her, he had given her directions. "If you do not have an appointment, you will not be allowed entry—and I very much doubt an appointment has been made on your behalf."

I'm certain very harsh words were spoken. They made it all the way to Elani.

They hadn't stopped there. They had a location in mind—a mythical location, a place where magic happened. They had been startled by the Leontines, although they had, of course, heard of Leontines; the boy continually looked up at the sky, hoping against hope for a sight of the Aerians; the skies remained disappointingly empty of all save sun and scant clouds.

They had the good sense to understand that Elani didn't house what they sought, but their trek kept them clear of the warrens; it must have. They had survived this outing.

They survived hunger, as well; the city was much larger outside than they'd expected. Yes, they'd drawn upon the memories of the few intrepid Tha'alani who made their way beyond the far less guarded gates, but…so many of the memories were lost to them, walled away behind the sacrificial Tha'alanari.

Sacrificial was exactly the sense of the word they didn't know to use; Severn could almost taste it; there was both curiosity and a kind of pity. The pity would have killed him, had he been Tha'alanari. It didn't bother Ybelline at all. Without the memories of the Tha'alanari to guide them, they were left with a patchwork of impressions, and they had had to search for those, taking care not to be noted. They had, of course, been noted, but their curiosity was natural, and as it hadn't been tinged with dread, no adult swept in to offer context.

We let our children dream, Ybelline said.

How can they dream? Everything they might want to do has already been done. They don't have to leave home to experience any of it.

No? Perhaps not. Perhaps our dreams are the desire to bring, to the Tha'alaan, something new, something different. Or perhaps we understand that our own experiences have more weight, more personal meaning, than the experiences we share only through the Tha'alaan. I do not understand how other people dream. I have touched some of those dreams, and they are... She did not find words to describe the experience.

These memories, however, were not those. He concentrated on these, watching the children from within their thoughts, and evaluating them from his own.

He was surprised when their trek led them, at last, to the place of their dreams; he recognized the building only because his own curiosity had moved him to look at maps of Elantra, and notable buildings, in the Records of the Halls of Law. They walked toward the Oracular Halls. They had come, as some did, to see some fleeting glimpse of the future.

The future, then, was as much a land of magic and promise for the Tha'alani children as it was for any child, even a child of the fiefs who dreamed and longed for a happy, safe life across the bridge over the Ablayne.

As they grasped hands and walked three abreast up the

road, he looked at the building through their eyes; their eyes were better, here, than Records, which was dry and lifeless.

Any dreams they brought with them colored the picture, and the three saw the building differently; Ybelline had stitched all of their impressions together in a way that made the sight almost, but not quite, overwhelming.

He knew that this visit must end in disappointment; the children didn't have an appointment, and they were never likely to be granted one. It took them hours—subjective time—to reach the very closed doors, and the doors *were* guarded. These children were not the only people in Elantra who dreamed of a glimpse of the future, with all its promise and all the happiness it might contain.

They had had happy lives. One broken arm—a fall from a tree—one broken leg, one bruised eye, both, like the arm, the result of accidents because they had been so busy paying attention to the Tha'alaan they had lost track of their surroundings. This wasn't, from their reaction, uncommon. The happy lives, however, had not changed their hopes, their desire for better.

You would have been content with their lives, Ybelline said, *because you had already lived your own—you could compare what you had with what they had. Had you been one of the people—our people—you would not have seen it the same way.*

No one appreciates what they have?

Not in my experience, no. They must learn to fully understand what other people have—or have not had—first. Gratitude is a lesson we learn as we mature.

The guards at the door were not as stiff and formal as guards Severn had encountered at Elluvian's side in other locations; they stared down at the children with mutual expressions of shock. Had they encountered three adult Tha'alani, that shock might be tinged with fear—but the sight of three children holding hands as they made their approach could not quite be translated into a dangerous threat.

The older of the two, a woman, spoke first. "Are you lost?"

"We were almost lost," one of the boys replied. "But a giant cat told us how to get here. And a man on Elani street."

"You passed through the Leontine quarter?"

"I guess?"

"Do you realize where you are?"

It was the girl who took over the conversation. "We've come to the Oracular Halls." Her voice was grave, or at least that was the intent.

"Yes. Yes, you have. Do you have an appointment?"

The three conferred in silence, skirting the edge of Tha'alaan. Two adult voices had been raised in the background, both aimed at the absent children. They didn't have much time.

"Can we make one now?" the girl asked.

With what appeared—to Severn's eye—to be infinite patience, the older woman said, "That is not, unfortunately, the way appointments work. You don't ask us—we're guards. We're meant to keep the Oracles safe. You have to ask the Emperor."

Silence, then. The word *Emperor* put an instant damper on dreams, and increased the sense of danger. They had thought nothing of coming to the Oracular Halls—they would probably never leave the quarter again if they thought they'd be forced to encounter the Dragon. The Emperor and his wrath were *feared* in the Tha'alaan. The Emperor was the reason the Tha'alanari, and its sacrificial members, existed at all.

None of the three dreamed of becoming Tha'alanari, although given the way they'd gone about escaping the grasp of their minders, Severn thought at least one of them would be a good candidate. At least from the outside, with his limited understanding of the Tha'alanari.

He wondered, then, how the guards saw them when they reacted to this news. The Tha'alani would have been perfect marks. It didn't occur to them to hide their feelings or the expressions that made them clear to outsiders, because their feelings were always clear to their kin; they hadn't yet learned the value or importance of secrecy, and the Tha'alaan was not the place to start.

But the guards were not interested in hiding their reactions, either. Clearly, the children looked crushed. The older woman turned toward her partner; she spoke words that were inaudible to the children, and the younger guard, casting a glance at the three, shook her head before she turned, opened a side door, and entered the building.

The boy who had engineered and planned this escapade craned sideways in an attempt to get a glimpse of the interior before that door was closed.

"Wait here," the remaining guard said.

CHAPTER SIXTEEN

THE YOUNGER GUARD RETURNED. SHE SHRUGGED at the older, but offered no words in the children's hearing. The doors, however, rolled open. This surprised Severn, but he'd never come close to the drive that led to the Oracles, never mind the front doors. The Oracles didn't feature prominently in any of the cases the Wolves had faced that had seemed relevant when he studied them in Records.

A man stood between the opening double doors. He was taller than either of the guards at the doors, but not obviously armed; he wore flowing robes much like the robes Ybelline wore, albeit in a different color. The children were wearing similar robes that better suited their heights.

Even had the man not been standing at the height of the stairs, they would have had to look up to meet his gaze. They looked up as one. Nothing about his gaze was friendly; they were all intimidated. But they believed him to be either an Oracle, or *the* Oracle, and they were hushed with awe and a giddy fear.

"You walked all the way from the Tha'alani quarter to the

Oracular Halls?" he asked, his voice conveying a hint of surprise.

They clearly expected him to know all this—to know everything on sight. Severn realized, with a flash of insight, that they somehow expected the Oracles to be like the entirety of the Tha'alaan, but with the ability to see the future. The Tha'alaan existed as a weave of the present and the past; the future remained closed.

Expectations or no, they answered. "Yes."

"You perhaps were not aware that an appointment is required."

Again, they nodded.

"You have not made that appointment, and I cannot, therefore, take your request to the Oracles."

Something pushed against the robed midsection of the man who now spoke. "I am not an Oracle," he continued, as if he expected this not to become an interruption.

A younger face—much younger than the man in the robes—now peered around his waist. Bright-eyed, even if the eyes were a brown that was almost black, stood a child of a similar age. "I'm Random."

"I'm Tessa," the Tha'alani girl said. It was the first time Severn had heard her name. "This is Jerrin, and this is Tobi."

"You're Tha'alani," Random said—if that was really her name. They nodded.

"I'm not!" She looked up at the man who had opened the doors. "Master Sabrai, can they come in? It's almost time for tea."

As if in response, Jerrin's stomach made a loud rumble.

"Random," Master Sabrai began, his expression forbidding.

Random then ran out from behind his back, leaped down the stairs in one jump, and came to stand before Tessa, who happened to be the middle person in the grouping of three. "You want food? Today, *I* want food!" She caught Jerrin's hand—he had one free—and tugged at it; as the Tha'alani hadn't let go of each other's hands, they were dragged up the stairs.

"Can they?" Random asked again.

"They have not been given leave to visit an Oracle," Master Sabrai said, in the same forbidding tone.

"They haven't been given permission to *have* an Oracle talk about the future," she said. "But—we're not in jail, right? We haven't done anything wrong?"

Clearly Random understood Master Sabrai better than three children who had never before encountered him.

"And I'm *hungry*," Random continued. "I haven't eaten in two days. I promise I'll eat if you'll let them visit with me." She hadn't let go of Jerrin's hand. "They didn't bring money and they didn't eat lunch, either. So they're hungry. Please?" Even adding that word, she had already begun to drag the three down the hall and away from the man who probably should have said no.

If the room into which they were led was a disappointment, the children didn't seem to feel it the way some children would have. They had stories of what Oracles *did*, not about how they did it, where they lived, or what they were like. They had expected Oracles to be like the man Random had called Master Sabrai, but accepted his word that he wasn't one of them.

It was Tobi who asked Random if she knew who the Oracle was.

Random stared at him in some confusion. "The Oracle?"

"Well, there's supposed to be a person here who can see the future."

Random nodded, still confused. After a moment, in which her expression much more closely matched Master Sabrai's, she said, "There's more than just one." And then, expression more guarded, she said, "I'm an Oracle."

There was instant excitement, but muted. Interacting with legends was not part of their training, and regardless, Random was obviously a child, as they were, and probably excluded from the lives of adults in just the same way.

"How does it work?" Tessa asked.

Random hushed them loudly, and not ten seconds later, food was brought into the room. There was a lot of bread, some cheese, apples, grapes, and something pink none of the Tha'alani recognized. Milk, however, was milk anywhere.

"Have you really not eaten for two days?" Jerrin, whose stomach had intermittently been complaining, asked.

"Jerrin can't go without food for two hours," Tobi added.

"I wasn't hungry," Random said. "Sometimes that happens. Food tastes wrong, or bad, or I can't keep it down." Her smile was conspiratorial as she leaned across her plate. "Or maybe I knew that you'd come and I had to starve so that Master Sabrai would say you could come in. We're not allowed to leave," she added. "Not without guards." Before they could comment, she added, "Imperial guards. I don't like 'em. I like ours better."

"Imperial guards guard the Emperor?" Tobi asked. He couldn't believe that a *Dragon* required guards—but maybe they were all Dragon guards, in which case, he wouldn't like them any better.

"Well, I guess so. I've never seen the Emperor, not in person. There's a really big painting on one of our walls that kind of looks like what he'd look like if he were to turn into a Dragon—and Master Sabrai says it's accurate. I can take you there, if you want."

Tobi definitely wanted. It was Tessa who said, "We don't want to get you in trouble." The rallying cry of considerate children everywhere.

"You won't," Random replied cheerfully.

★ ★ ★

"Master Sabrai says that Oracles are like artists. We don't just look into the future. It's not like opening a book and reading it."

"What's it like?"

Random shrugged. "It's different for all of us—that's why he says it's like art." This appeared to make as much sense to Random as it did to any of the Tha'alani. "But sometimes we get these feelings, or these images, or these words—except for most of us it's not actual words, 'cause that would be too easy." Her frown, like her smile, was mercurial.

"Do you get to choose?"

"What to think about? No, not really. Sometimes we get visitors. I mean, not like you guys—you're fun. Mostly the visitors aren't. They're kind of mean, or they're frightened, and they want answers Right Now. Answers that make sense to them, I mean."

"Do they make sense to you?" It was Jerrin, whose stomach had finally shut up, who asked.

"Not really? I mean, I knew I shouldn't eat any solid food for two days, but I didn't know why—not until I heard the door." Her grin was infectious. "Sometimes some of us forget to eat. If we're having oracles, all we see, or hear, are the oracles themselves, not the people. We don't notice food, and we often don't eat it unless someone spoons it into our mouth."

"So…he thought you were…busy?"

She shrugged. "Who knows? I don't. I mean, it would be *great* if I were like you guys—then we'd all understand each other." She hesitated. "That *is* the way it works, right?"

They all agreed that it was.

Random wasn't afraid of them. She wasn't afraid of her own secrets, if she had any she felt needed guarding. She wasn't afraid of the demands they would, or could, make. She also wasn't really afraid of breaking the rules; Severn wondered if there were any, beyond the rule that kept her safely in the house.

"Why aren't you allowed to leave?" Jerrin asked.

"People have really weird ideas about how Oracles work," Random replied. She no longer had to grab Jerrin by the hand, but had done so anyway. "They think that they can just ask us questions about the future, and we'll answer clearly in a way they can understand.

"They think that if they know the future, they can do things that people who don't can't. Or plan things. Or kill people." She shrugged at the last one. "I don't understand why we can't explain it to everyone—but Master Sabrai thinks no one would believe us anyway." Her expression grew shadowed. "Sometimes people really don't like it when they hear the future. They don't like the future, and instead of figuring out how to avoid it, they blame us—they say we're cursing them."

The Tha'alani didn't need to look at each other to share what would, in humans, require a glance.

"So it's not really safe, because people are like that. And we don't know which people will be like that. It's *exhausting* to always be afraid of people." She turned toward them. "But I guess you kind of know what it's like."

"What do you mean?" Tessa asked.

"Well, you can read minds, right? You can know what we're thinking. You can know everything about us. We can't have secrets. We can't lie."

"We can't just do that without touching you, though."

Random nodded.

"And you don't care?"

"Well, ummm, not really, no. Should I?"

Oracles, Severn realized, were strange. Random seemed to be open and truthful; he couldn't confirm that the way he could with the three Tha'alani children, because he wasn't privy to her thoughts. Without Ybelline, he wouldn't have had access to the Tha'alani children, either. But he thought Random meant what she said, and regardless, he was carried along with the Tha'alani children until they had climbed a wide flight of stairs and had entered a hall that was full of light.

The light itself didn't appear to emanate from windows—there was simply too much of it—but shone on paintings that adorned the side of the hall that had no doors to break it. At the end of that hall was a painting that was taller than any of the children present, and wider as well. It was above the ground by a good three feet, but that didn't matter.

Severn stood staring at a painting that was almost preternaturally alive. The Dragon's eyes were red; the scales that covered every inch the painting had captured were a dark shade of blue, with hints of purple sheen.

"The Emperor," Random grinned. "Isn't he amazing?"

That wasn't the word any of the Tha'alani used. In fact, they were surprised enough they didn't resort to words at all; their communication was a tide of different emotions, which had no need of words.

"Do you have one where you can see his wings?"

"Not him, but I think there's another Dragon. It's not in the hall, though."

"Why?"

"The paint's not dry yet?" She shrugged. "I'm not sure. It's not like this one, though."

"Well, not if you can see wings. Mostly you see eyes and teeth in this one."

"Yeah. It's not even life-size, you know?" Random's shrug deepened. "But I can't show you the other one. We're not allowed to go into the workrooms."

"Workrooms?"

"Some of us have rooms. To work in," she added, in case it wasn't obvious. Her brow was puckered in thought, as if she were speaking a second language but laboriously translating between that and her mother tongue.

"Do you?"

She nodded.

"Do you paint?"

"Sometimes. I'm not as good at it as he is, though." She gestured at the painting she'd brought them to see. "Sometimes I sketch. Sometimes I make things—like sculptures."

"Is it ever just words?" Jerrin again.

"Not for me. Stuart's are almost always just words but... sometimes he speaks them in a language none of us understand."

"Can anyone?"

"Yeah. But we have to have a bunch of outsiders here when he does it on purpose—and Master Sabrai is *sooooooo* grouchy when that happens." As she spoke she looked over her shoulder, in search of a glimpse of that master. Then she leaned in. "Do you want to see my room?"

There was no way that the Tha'alani would say no, although Tobi had the uneasy feeling, given the conversation that preceded the invitation, that *no* was the right answer. "We don't want to get you in trouble," he told her, lowering his voice to a whisper. Whispers, on the other hand, were hard for Tha'alani children. They had, of course, learned to speak out loud in their version of schooling, but they didn't see the point in the activity on most days.

It was like trying to communicate poorly on purpose. It was a frustrating activity. This was the first time that any of the three had seen the use for, the practical necessity of, those lessons. But even so, they knew there was a better way to communicate with Random.

Years of admonitions prevented the attempt.

Severn felt uneasy and realized that it was Ybelline's response, mirroring his own.

This happened at least two decades ago. Closer to three, I think. There's nothing here that can harm you. And nothing here that can harm them now.

He felt her agreement. He had stated facts plainly, facts she knew better than he. The blend of discomfort and fact still remained. He thought he knew why. But he followed the three children who were only a memory as they followed Random. She stayed on the second floor, but moved away from the paintings and the open hall, into a narrower hallway, one that had doors on either side of the wall.

The rooms weren't numbered; no nameplates distinguished their owners, if they had owners at all. Random put her palm in the center of one door. Her hand glowed a pale blue as light flared beneath it.

Names weren't necessary. The door was warded.

None of the fief buildings that Severn had sought temporary shelter in had had door wards. He was grateful for the lack; he had a suspicion that even if these halls were abandoned, the wards would continue to prevent entry for as long as the doors remained standing.

He'd have to remember to ask what happened to door wards if someone used brute physical force to open the doors they were placed on.

It depends on the ward, Ybelline replied.

As both adults reviewing these memories—living on the inside of them—suspected, Random was at her most furtive, her most obviously worried, once the door was unlocked. She spun her head up and down the length of the hall so quickly she should have been motion sick, and then proceeded to shove them through the open door. She entered in a rush and shut the door firmly.

The Tha'alani weren't even afraid. They understood her actions: she was trying to prevent being caught doing something she shouldn't be doing. Since they didn't see themselves as dangerous, and their activities thus far couldn't be considered criminal, they assumed she was breaking normal adult rules—the ones that mostly made no sense to apply to someone who wasn't adult yet.

They were only almost adult in their own minds, but Random was, or appeared to be, of an age with them. And Random was an Oracle, both anointed by fate and simultaneously as human as they.

They forgot even these thoughts as she spoke two words and the room was bathed in light. This was magic. It wasn't as mythical as an oracle—they'd all seen light when no sunlight shone and no lamps had been lit—but it was not a magic they themselves had invoked.

Was she a mage as well as an Oracle? Tessa thought it unfair.

"You can do it too," Random said. "It's just words, right? You can say *darken* or *brighten*."

They weren't words that the Tha'alani children understood. They understood the rest of her spoken words, but these were unfamiliar. She repeated them, inviting the Tha'alani to do the same.

"What do they mean? Are they magic words?"

No, Severn thought, although he understood their reaction. They were Barrani words, both. He'd heard and understood them instantly.

Barrani is the language of the laws, Ybelline said. *It is not much taught to our children. The merchant tongue, however, is. It is what most people will speak outside of our quarter.*

Do you have *a spoken native tongue?*

Once. She offered no further answer; he felt a tide of information rising like a wave—a tidal wave. She suppressed it. It wasn't why she'd come here. But…showing Severn this visit to the Oracular Halls wasn't why she'd come, either.

He understood every word, every thought, the Tha'alani children had had. Language didn't appear to make a difference.

No. Not when we are like this.

Random chattered endlessly in the confines of this room; it was her happy place. No, he thought, that wasn't it. It was the place in which she felt most confident. The Tha'alani had come to see an Oracle. She knew that Oracles were misunderstood by people who weren't Oracles. But she still hoped. She wanted, he realized, to impress the Tha'alani.

She took out sketches from a portfolio leaning against the wall opposite the door; she showed them various sculptures that rested on shelves; there didn't seem to be any organization to their placement; they'd been put wherever they would fit.

She told them what the sketches meant—or what others realized they meant after the fact. That was the problem with oracles. The Oracles were driven to express the knowledge that filled the inside of their heads, but that knowledge wasn't based on facts. It wasn't based on the lives the Oracles had led. It came to them like a compulsion, and they could only get rid of it one way.

There were three items in this room that told no stories, or invoked no stories. Random didn't know what they meant, or who they were meant to guide—if oracles were meant to guide anyone at all. Two were sketches, and one was a carefully sculpted piece of rock. Or at least that's how the Tha'alani perceived it.

She spoke in a hurried whisper; he realized then that she wasn't supposed to be speaking of these things. So did the Tha'alani. But it was a companionable secrecy; she was sharing *with* them, and they understood the necessity of sharing better than anyone.

But they, too, had been warned. One of the biggest warnings was: do not wander out of the quarter. It is the only place you are guaranteed to be safe. They, too, had been told about Bad People who wanted to kidnap them and use them.

They were all outsiders, but the Tha'alani was a huge extended family of outsiders. Random was isolated. They understood the cost of that, the price Random paid.

He knew what was going to happen.

So, too, did Ybelline; he could feel her draw a single sharp breath. If she could have reached into the past with both hands, she would have grabbed the children and hauled them out of the Halls, possibly by the ears.

These memories, however, were just that: memories. More than two decades had passed since these events had occurred. She could no more change that past than any other living being awash in regret. Severn had learned this lesson the harshest way possible.

It was Jerrin of the loud stomach who caught Random's hand. Jerrin who thanked her for sharing, and who asked her if she would like to see how friends among the Tha'alani shared information.

"Will you get in trouble?" Random asked.

"No." Which was a lie. The Tha'alani were not good at lying.

"Maybe," Tobi said. "But it's not like they can do anything to prevent it. Once we talk to you, it's done." He spoke with bravado. With confidence. Severn could feel the ache of both sympathy and curiosity.

A silent argument broke out among the three Tha'alani, and

in the end, Tessa won. It was Tessa who sat Random down; Tessa who bent over her; Tessa who touched Random's forehead with her antennae. Both girls were trembling.

The memories stopped there.

All of them.

Severn had no idea what Tessa had seen; no idea what Jerrin or Tobi saw, secondhand, either. He had been those children; those children were gone, as if suddenly obliterated. Had Ybelline not maintained her contact with him, he would have assumed that she had broken the connection.

No. She was still here, still with him.

What happened?

The memories end here, she replied.

They died?

No. Not then. You asked me to examine our memories for deaths that occurred before the murders that almost shattered the Tha'alaan started. Their deaths were among those deaths.

All three?

All three.

How did they die?

Tobi convinced them to join him in another escapade, for old time's sake. They went. They went out to the port, and they did not return; the boat they were in capsized.

Boating.

She nodded.

Was there anything unusual about that?

Not for Tobi, no. Tessa had become much more reticent in her early adult years—but Tessa's life goal became the Tha'alanari. She showed aptitude for it. I did not examine the memories that we have just shared; I was looking for events that might be related to the current investigation.

You didn't notice they'd left the quarter?

It was not the first time they left; it was not the last. If you wish, I will show you the others that might fit the profile you are building.

There are more?

There are more.

Severn didn't ask. Instinct told him that somehow, these three held keys to part of this crime—or the reason for it. And he thought Random might also hold keys, if she survived.

How old were they when they died?

Almost twenty in Imperial years.

And this occurred over two decades ago. To his surprise, Ybelline was amused.

You intend to ask for permission to visit the Oracular Halls? Helmat will be greatly tempted to show you the door, possibly with more force than necessary.

Only if Random is still alive, still living there. And yes, I'll obviously need permission. He exhaled. *You know why the memories stopped.*

Not with certainty—but with near certainty, yes. I, too, will have feathers to ruffle. Shall I give you the information about the Barrani High Court now?

Severn shook his head. *We need to see the circumstances surrounding their deaths. If this was labeled accidental, we need to examine that accident.*

Ybelline nodded, all amusement gone.

Severn once again stepped into the living memories of people who were no longer intrepid children. He was surprised at the difference in tone, in feel—he had expected more continuity, somehow. On certain days, he felt he was still the child he had once been—just better able to hide it. He wondered if his own internal thoughts would differ so greatly.

Yes. You are not the child you were. No more are they.

He had liked the children they were.

And you dislike the adults they became?

No.

You had nothing to fear from children; you had something to fear from adults; adult lives are more complex and their decisions more deliberate. It is always easier to deal with simple things.

Severn didn't know how to move through these memories.

No. You touch the Tha'alaan through me, but you are not part of it. I'm sorry.

What did you say about apologies? They change nothing? Don't regret it, he told her. *I don't.*

He felt a wry smile that wasn't his, and then she once again opened up the lives of the three.

The first change he noted was that they were not together—not in the way they had been on the day they had undertaken their pilgrimage. Tessa was, as Ybelline had said, at school; much of that schoolwork involved the ability to mute her experiences; to detach herself from the Tha'alaan. It was truly the hardest thing Tessa felt she had ever done—but she'd shown some promise at hiding her thoughts early. It wasn't so much hiding, as binding them to other memories, other places that had stronger meaning to the Tha'alani as a whole. Adding a thread here, a thread there—something that could, with effort, be followed if one had both knowledge and will.

Ybelline did.

The memories that had stopped so abruptly had not been deliberately hidden by the former children. Tessa was the only one of the three who might have been able to hide her own life, her own traces; the other two couldn't.

Tobi contacted Tessa when she left the Tha'alanari compound. She had failed to acknowledge him until she was surrounded by the walls of her home. It was not a home she shared with her family.

Tobi, of the three, had changed the least. He had, to Severn's surprise, the same desire that Tessa did—he just didn't have the talent. Tobi was furtive in some ways—had he not been, they would never have been able to visit the Oracles—but he was slightly larger than life. Hiding his own light wasn't possible, except on the inside of his dreams.

He, too, had been affected by Random. He'd liked her. He felt, in some way, that she had much in common with the Tha'alani—much more than most humans. She hadn't been afraid. He hadn't been afraid, then. As he grew older, he shouldered the burden of fear. It sat very poorly on his shoulders.

It's not fear, Tessa told him. *It's caution.*

Caution is boring. If we were cautious, we'd never have met Random. We'd never have met Oracles. We'd never have met Ollarin.

Both Ybelline and Severn stiffened.

That's not his name.

An image formed in Tobi's mind, then. Ollarin. The faint hope that he was a human, a mortal, was crushed.

It's what he wanted to be called.

Barrani names aren't like our names. Or like mortal names at all. They're like—Dragon names.

The painting Random had briefly shown them took up the whole of their thoughts.

You wanted to do this, he said. *You wanted to find answers to the things that she had no explanation for.*

It was true. She wanted that because it had been so important to Random. The value of, the usefulness of, the gift that had destroyed her early life completely was the single thing that Random held on to: it proved she had value. A lot of value. She wasn't a curse. She wasn't a witch.

Tessa had not known that word, before Random. She understood it now. She also understood that people considered the Tha'alani to be far worse than simple witches.

Severn found that he could only see Tessa's memories now; could only feel what she felt. The conversation with Tobi existed because Tessa was part of it.

Tobi's part—and possibly Jerrin's, who had not yet appeared—was mute.

It is gone, Ybelline said. *Both are gone. Just as the initial memories are no longer present.*

But Tessa remembered.

Yes—but she remembered the events just as you might remember events of your childhood. She could not return to it—as we did—as an adult. She couldn't view her past self from the perspective of her present self. It is probably why she became so careful at navigating the Tha'alaan. She understood that things would otherwise be...lost. It is very difficult to find—to put together—some parts of these events.

Is that why the deaths were considered accidents?

Ybelline, grim now, didn't answer. But he felt the heat of anger wash over her. It was the last thing he felt; she broke contact. He opened his eyes as she pulled away; her eyes were green—the green of perfect emeralds; hard, cold, glittering.

Ah. She was almost crying. He reached out, but let his hand fall away before he could touch her.

"I will return," she told him. "I have yet to give you the information that you requested from the Imperial Service." Her voice was low, trembling.

"Wait. We said we would be your guards on the way back to the quarter. You can't leave here like this."

She wanted to say no. She didn't.

CHAPTER SEVENTEEN

HELMAT WAS WAITING FOR ELLUVIAN AND Severn; his office door was open and he sat behind his desk, glaring at himself in a mirror that was inactive. Reminding himself, as he did, that he had reasons for wanting Severn as part of the Wolves.

Ybelline's abrupt—and utterly silent—departure had left questions, of course. She had made an excuse; Severn's request required her to return to the Imperial Service offices to access their Records.

The Tha'alani weren't natural liars. Ybelline had learned, but learned slowly—and while it was a necessary skill, Helmat did not appreciate it. Then again, he had never appreciated being the recipient of lies. No one did. She had lied. Nor had he had time to grill Severn—a subordinate, unlike Ybelline, who would otherwise be forced to answer his questions—before they departed to escort her.

Severn and Elluvian did return. They entered the open office, Elluvian in the lead.

Helmat folded his arms, leaned back in his chair, and glared.

It was his resting expression. He waited for someone to break the silence that glare enforced.

It was the private who did. "I request permission," he said, "to visit the Oracular Halls."

Helmat could take a body blow without flinching. His expression, carefully schooled, did not shift at all. Had he been another man, his jaw might now be resting on his desktop.

"For what purpose?"

"I wish to interview a person of relevance to our investigation."

Helmat's gaze flicked up to meet Elluvian's.

Elluvian shrugged, a fluid, graceful gesture. "Don't look to me for answers; this is the first I've heard of it."

"You have, in your short time *on probation*, annoyed the Tha'alanari. You have apparently also annoyed the Imperial Security Service. Both of these will have consequences for the Wolves—or for the person in charge of them. And you now want to add the Oracular Halls to that list?"

Severn nodded.

"This had better be good. It had better be *stellar*."

Severn then explained.

Elluvian was amused. Amused and slightly chagrined.

"Helmat dislikes bureaucracy, which is unfortunate in a man who serves as Wolflord. He is adept at dealing with the politics that arise from time to time—but he takes little pride in it. I am certain, however, that Rosen would be delighted if you shared this latest request with her."

"She'll see it even if I don't."

"The Oracular Halls are very, very seldom visited. When they are—at least by officers of the Halls of Law—it is at the request of the Oracular Halls. It seldom goes in the other direction. Master Sabrai is competent. Under his guidance, the

Oracles have flourished for almost three decades. He is not, however, the most accommodating or politic of men."

"Rosen isn't the only one who is—or will be—delighted." Elluvian chuckled. "Tell me, Private, to whom do you think Ybelline will go?"

Severn shrugged. After a pause which Elluvian interpreted as a refusal to answer the question, he said, "The Tha'alanari. They're the only ones who could do what was done."

"It is not nearly that simple."

Severn waited. He asked no questions. Elluvian could not decide if he found this irritating or admirable. It was not Severn's interactions with the Tha'alanari, the Imperial Security Service, and now the Oracular Halls that discomfited Elluvian; it was the High Court. More specifically, An'Tellarus. It had been two days. Not enough time for Corvallan to act—unless the action involved the mortal witnesses Severn had grouped together, two of whom had died in as many days.

An'Tellarus had summoned Elluvian to court. He was not yet of a mind to attend her; he had no business at court until and unless Corvallan had information to impart.

This would be the tricky part. Tricky for Elluvian—Corvallan was not his equal on his own, but Corvallan was not without support, and Cassandre was far deadlier. For Severn? If the situation was as the events now implied, it was death.

Too much was happening, too quickly. But the Barrani were now wed to the mortal clock, and time was always of the essence for mortals. Still, Elluvian was engaged. He felt more alive than he had in decades, trapped in the confines of these dingy offices, these petty mortal politics.

There were stakes here that were larger. He almost felt the investigation had only barely touched the periphery of the matter. Were it not for An'Tellarus, he would have found it almost entertaining, not that he would have used those words when speaking to any of the Wolves.

"You may return to your study of Records," he finally said. "If we are granted permission to visit the Oracular Halls, it will not be today."

Severn had perhaps half an hour in which to continue to make connections between a multitude of different interconnected cases when Elluvian's mirror dimmed the images displayed in his most recent Records search.

Helmat's face, larger than life, filled the mirror display. "Tell Severn he's expected at the Oracular Halls."

Both of Elluvian's brows rose. "When?"

"Apparently, thirty minutes from now."

"We have an actual appointment?"

"Yes. It was, according to Sabrai's secretary, made three months ago."

"Three months ago? Under whose name?"

"Severn Handred and one other."

"Me?"

"No, actually. I've already made my apologies to the secretary, and he has agreed—with alacrity and surprising good humor—to extend the appointment."

"The other participant? Not you?"

Helmat, framed perfectly by the mirror's glass, looked at the newest of his Wolves. "Who do you feel is meant to be your companion in this endeavor?"

Severn bowed his head in thought. A handful of seconds later, he lifted his chin. "Ybelline."

"Indeed. Ybelline. Apparently, one of the Oracles asked Master Sabrai to arrange the appointment. Would you care to hazard a guess as to which Oracle?"

"Random."

"That is not her official name, according to the secretary. It is, however, how she sometimes introduces herself when she is permitted visitors."

"Or when she requests them?"

"Or when she requests them. I have taken the liberty of passing the message on to Ybelline; she has not yet responded."

"It may take a while," Severn replied.

"It may. You are to meet her, as you did the first time, at the gates to the Tha'alani quarter."

"The Oracular Halls is not the Imperial Service," Elluvian said. "They do not have right of command over Ybelline Rabon. They certainly don't have right of command over the Wolves."

"Apparently the Imperial Service disagrees."

"This is petty on their part. We are Wolves, not errand runners or Imperial guards."

"If this is the full extent of the pettiness we face in response to Severn's request, we will be grateful."

"Saidh is not generally petty."

The Wolflord ignored this. "She'll be safer with you—and Severn—than she will with Imperial guards. Saidh knows this. You know it. Ybelline Rabon will, when she is ready to travel, meet you both at the gates. You have a window of four hours."

"I am impressed, I confess," Elluvian said as they walked streets they had already crossed twice. "Helmat is annoyed."

Severn nodded. "How important is his annoyance in comparison to the conclusion of the hunt?"

"Negligible, as you have already observed. Most would find Helmat the most intimidating element—he is your commander."

A shrug. "Can you find out if the Hawks had any success?"

"You are authorized to make that inquiry." Silence. "You

wish to remain anonymous." More silence. "You do not wish the girl to know that you are involved with the Halls of Law."

"No."

"Has it occurred to you that this might be difficult?"

"No."

Elluvian chuckled. "The optimism of youth."

Severn said nothing, and Elluvian reconsidered. Not optimism, he thought. Determination. The Wolves were not required to enter the Halls using the same doors the Hawks or the Swords did; unlike the Hawks or Swords, no part of the Wolves' offices was open to the public.

Ybelline appeared—in the robes of her people, not the garb of the Imperial Service—an hour after the two Wolves reached the gates. The guards were no more welcoming or friendly than they had been the first time, but no argumentative discussion seemed to be occurring between Ybelline and the guards; they seemed slightly relieved to see her.

It was the uniform, of course. She was not wearing the garb of the Imperial Service. She was wearing a turquoise robe with gold trim and white borders; turquoise beads gleamed from the combs in her hair. Her eyes, however, were hazel with flecks of green. She approached the two Wolves, and Elluvian was surprised to see that green recede as she met Severn's gaze.

The cub asked her no questions; he simply waited until she reached him.

He then tucked his chin slightly, holding both hands palm up between them. She hesitated for less than three seconds before placing her hands, palm down, across his. And then, before Elluvian could speak a word, she touched Severn's forehead with her antennae. Severn closed his eyes as Ybelline closed hers.

Elluvian looked toward the Tha'alani guards; their eyes

were no longer the green of anger or fear. He did not, and possibly would never, understand the Tha'alani. Ybelline's greeting of Severn, or possibly Severn's greeting of her, accepted by her, had set them all at ease. Given their paranoid view of human thoughts and fears, the opposite reaction was the one he would have predicted.

It wasn't just a greeting. They stood in the street, bounded by wall, guard and Wolf, for ten minutes. Fifteen. Severn's hands tightened around hers, no desperation in the grip; Elluvian thought the boy meant to offer comfort.

She lifted her antennae, and then, after another pause, opened her eyes and lifted her hands. She stepped back. As she did, Severn bowed. He held that bow until she bade him rise.

"A carriage," Elluvian said, "will take us to the Oracular Halls."

"An Imperial carriage?"

"Helmat insisted."

Helmat had not, of course, insisted, but the window of time granted them was closing, and the carriage would be faster at this time of day than the longer walk. It would also make protecting the Tha'alani agent almost trivial. People would see the Imperial crest, not the passengers—and if they did see the passengers, the one they were likely to note was Elluvian. Ybelline had drawn a hood up and across her face. A second look would, of course, make clear that the shape of the hood's fall was wrong.

The guards at the Oracles' gates did not stop the carriage at all.

The guards at the doors looked both annoyed and relieved; they allowed all three to enter the front doors. Master Sabrai was standing impatiently, all but glaring at an ornate clock;

he transferred that glare to the visitors. He did not, however, accuse them of being late.

"This way," he said, speaking to Severn and Ybelline. "Not you," he added, in the vicinity of Elluvian. "You were not mentioned and the appointment does not cover Barrani visitors."

"Severn Handred is a Wolf," Elluvian began.

"I have cleared the lack of a partner with Lord Marlin. You are to remain either in the waiting room or in the carriage, with his blessing."

"Am I to receive refreshments of any kind while I wait?"

"That, certainly, can be arranged; I am in need of a drink myself and would be delighted to keep you company."

"You are not part of the interview?"

"No. My absence has been requested by the Oracle."

"And you accepted this?"

"She is not one of the children," Master Sabrai replied. "And does not require my intervention in the same way. The Oracle believed that Severn and Ybelline would know both the rules of the Halls and the location of the meeting—and it appears that she was correct."

It was strange to climb these stairs on his own feet, behind his own viewpoint. The first time he had climbed them, he had had three sets of eyes, and they each noted slightly different things. The stairs and the halls hadn't changed much in the intervening years.

Random, however, had.

He didn't recognize her; felt almost embarrassed that he had expected to. He, Severn, had never *met her*. But the meeting between the Tha'alani children and Random in her youth had felt so real to him he felt dislocated, momentarily uncertain of who he was.

She didn't seem to suffer from the same dislocation, but she was older. Older than either Severn Handred or Ybelline Rabon. He thought her forty; he'd thought her thirteen when she'd dragged the three Tha'alani up the stairs to see the amazing Dragon and her private room.

He couldn't imagine this woman dragging those children up those stairs. Time changed everything.

"They died," the woman who had been the child called Random said. "They died. I could not prevent it. I did try, when I understood. But it was late by then. Late."

"You called us here," Severn said.

Ybelline touched his arm gently. He nodded. "You knew that we would learn what had happened that day."

Random inclined her head. She was dressed in much the same fashion as Ybelline. She held out her hands, the same way Severn had done at the gates of the Tha'alani quarter, but her eyes were glimmering. Ybelline walked to where she sat, and carefully took both hands in her own.

"I knew you would remember," Random said, the glimmer becoming tears. "I knew you would both remember."

"When did you know this?" Severn asked, softening his voice.

Random didn't seem to understand the question. Or perhaps Ybelline had asked the question in a different way, because Ybelline was now touching Random's forehead with her antennae—just as, years or decades ago, Tessa had done.

Random didn't speak. Not in a way Severn could hear. Nor did Ybelline. Severn turned his back upon them as they sat in the chairs Random had decorated for today's appointment. There was a chair with his name painted across the back, but he didn't take it.

He turned to the door, and he watched it. There was no other way to enter this room.

He wasn't certain how long the two conferred. No clock marked the passage of time, and he had no idea what Random wanted to convey to Ybelline. The Oracle didn't fear the Tha'alani; she had invited Ybelline in.

He had come here seeking information. He had come to ask her if she remembered the Tha'alani visitors—but that question had already been answered by the style of her greeting. What else had he wanted to know? What they had asked. What she had answered. What they had talked about.

And she had made the appointment to speak with Severn and Ybelline before either had thought to ask to interview her. She had had a vision of her own that had led to this day. They hadn't come here to ask her for an oracle. They weren't here to ask her for a glimpse of their future.

Severn watched the door and focused on the questions he'd intended to ask when he'd made the request to visit these halls. He'd lost ground, lost focus, when he'd found out that Random's appointment had already existed for weeks, and he recovered it in the silence.

He accepted that part of the reason he'd wanted to speak with Random was to avoid speaking with Ybelline. Not that he feared her—but he feared for her, now. The answers she'd left the Halls of Law to seek had caused a kind of grim terror in her. Outsiders like Severn—or the criminals she was sent to "interview"—were sources of dangerous instability, dangerous insanity. But outsiders could not do what had been done to the memories of the three children.

Severn was surprised that the early memories existed at all; had he somehow wanted to bury information about them, he would have destroyed them.

But that, he thought, would be difficult. Tha'alani lives

were so intricately entwined in the Tha'alaan, he wasn't certain what would happen to those who'd already experienced the events, or who had been part of the lives of the three children. He didn't understand what three children had discovered on that day—without being aware of the discovery—that led to the truncation of their memories.

He wasn't even certain how it could be done. Ybelline had had suspicions; she had kept them to herself, but she hadn't hidden the growing dread those suspicions caused. She had gone to the Tha'alanari.

No, he thought, knowing this was wrong. She had gone to the castelord.

Random's tears were silent tears; they fell only when she blinked. Her expression, however, implied that if there was sorrow in those tears, there was also a tremulous peace. Ybelline did not cry.

Severn almost wanted to be part of their communion. He had wasted very little of his life or life's thoughts on envy, but allowed a hint of it to color his thoughts now. What must it be like to be Ybelline Rabon? What must it be like to be able to offer comfort and peace to a stranger?

And if you could offer those things to a stranger, what might you offer someone you loved?

He shook his head to clear it. The thoughts were unwelcome; they led nowhere useful.

He heard the movement of a chair, felt the touch of a hand on his shoulder. Wasn't certain until he turned whose hand it had been. Ybelline's. "Random wishes to speak to you now."

"She must know you could answer my questions."

"I don't know. I had different questions than you had, and perhaps my questions required different answers. I cannot fully describe at least two of the answers."

"Did you understand them?"

"Only because I was with…with… Random. Random feels that the information may be important. She believes that you might be better able to find words to express it more clearly."

"Why me?"

"The Tha'alani rely too much on our native ability; we have never been forced to rely on language to deliver difficult concepts. You have had the advantage of words as communication."

"Is that why she wanted me?"

Ybelline shook her head.

Ybelline moved the chair with her name on it out of the way, and replaced it carefully with Severn's chair. Random nodded, her eyes still reddened, her nose running slightly. He had no handkerchief to offer, but she didn't appear to need one. She had long sleeves, after all.

To Severn's surprise, Ybelline now fetched a small card table; she placed it in front of Random, made sure all four of its legs were firmly on the ground, and then went to the shelves that contained the various products of Random's attempt to capture what she could see.

She returned to the table with three of these items and placed them in front of Random. Random no longer appeared to see Ybelline. She didn't appear to be aware of Severn, either. She was looking at the items on the table. Her frown was mercurial, her brows drawing in and rising, her lips twitching without landing on any specific expression.

"She asked for these," Ybelline said, when Severn glanced at her.

"She seems to think one is missing."

Ybelline nodded. "Now, be careful. You can speak—she won't hear you—but touch nothing on this table until she speaks. I mean, speaks sentences that you can understand.

She said she babbles when she works. Sometimes she sings. Sometimes she screeches or makes animal noises, apparently on purpose. If she screams—" Ybelline swallowed.

"If she screams, I can touch her?"

Ybelline shook her head. "No. But if she screams, she believes that *I* can touch her."

"You mean with your antennae."

"Yes. She doesn't think it's a good idea…"

"Neither do I!"

"…but she thinks it might be necessary. Apparently she's been having visions that have grown increasingly dangerous."

"Dangerous?"

"She doesn't come out of them until she collapses. She has almost died of dehydration twice in the past year. Master Sabrai brings no supplicants to her; he asks no questions of her."

"But he let us come."

"Yes, because Random had a vision. In the drawer in that desk, the middle drawer where the large sketches are, you can see the sketches she did recently."

"You've seen them?"

Ybelline nodded.

"And she's okay with me touching them?"

Ybelline nodded again. Severn left his chair and headed toward the desk. He opened the flat, but long, middle drawer. The first sketch on what appeared to be a stack of sketches was of Ybelline. Ybelline was wearing the dress that she'd chosen to leave the Tha'alani quarter in. Even without the coloring, it was clearly the one she was now wearing.

Severn in the sketches was not wearing the clothing that he had chosen—the clothing Elluvian had decided was appropriate for a high-class servant in the High Halls. He was wearing something darker and less fussy. He appeared to be wearing a belt made of a single row of chain links—which was fanciful and ridiculous—and wielding what looked like two oddly shaped swords.

He lifted that sketch, set it aside, and looked at the rest. "Are all of these relevant?"

"She felt they were. There are no sketches in that drawer that she doesn't feel have a tenuous connection to our visit, or the reasons for our visit."

"This is Elluvian."

"Yes. Oddly dressed, but yes. He looks grim," Ybelline added. "Helmat looks angry."

Severn lifted a sketch of an older Tha'alani man with a slight beard and a stoop to the shoulders.

"The castelord," was her quiet reply. "Mine, not yours."

"And this?"

"Barrani. From his clothing, either a lord or one with the desire to be perceived as lord. Note his servants."

"This one isn't so much a sketch—it has color."

She nodded. "It's possible the colors are necessary. But she made two stone sculptures as well; they're on the table."

"When will it be safe to sit down?"

Ybelline exhaled. "I don't know."

"Should we collect things she might need if she's having a vision?"

Silence. A beat. A longer beat. "...No."

Severn froze. He had lifted the colored sketch. Beneath it was a picture of a young woman. Not a child, not anymore. Her arms were exposed, and her back, and she wore a revealing green dress that she certainly didn't own now; he could see familiar marks across the skin of arms and back. She was looking over her shoulder, her eyes wide with desperation, and behind her he could see trees and a stone tower.

His sudden stillness drew Tha'alani attention.

Ybelline recognized her as well—but she would, wouldn't

she? It was his memory of Elianne, and the terrible lengths he had gone to to save her, that were at the heart of the answers the Wolves had sought.

"She's—" he swallowed.

"She is still alive. I think she is twenty, maybe a bit older—or younger—in this picture."

"She is looking at Severn," Random said. They both turned toward her.

"Does she want to kill me?" he couldn't help asking.

"Yes? No? I don't know. But she was looking at you, because I was standing beside you in my vision. Things are difficult in that then—you'll see. That's not now."

He set the sketches aside and took his seat. He almost abandoned it, but Ybelline had come to stand beside him, and she placed a gentle hand firmly on his shoulder.

Random was creating. She wasn't taking the base materials out of which these various figures and sketches and paintings had been worked and using them to chisel or paint or sketch: she was *creating* the item out of...thin air.

"Is this how it normally works?" he asked.

"No. Normally the Oracles are given the materials they demand or need by those who oversee them."

"And why isn't Random given them?"

"I don't know."

"Is this why she's almost starved?"

"Dehydrated, but yes."

"Do they *all* do this?"

"No, or Random doesn't believe so. I think she believes they *can* if they're desperate enough, or if the vision's imperative is too strong."

"Why is she doing it now? There's no desperate need—"

"It's—it's not the need of outsiders, it's not the need of those who have never been handed the future—that defines desperate or need. If a puppy was going to be hit by a wagon, and it could somehow be prevented, the strength of the oracle itself defines what's produced.

"The puppy might not be relevant to those who want a glimpse of the future. The Hawks. The Wolves. Think of the lives that might be saved, the murders that might be prevented, yes? Nor is the puppy relevant to the Emperor. But the concerns of rulers do not define the oracles. The concerns of the Oracles don't, either—although as they get older, and if they survive, they can sometimes direct the visions. Sometimes, but never reliably."

"And this?"

"What do you think?"

"I think she wanted to know what had happened to her friends. I don't imagine they were allowed to visit again."

"Allowed? No."

"They did visit."

"Not all of them, and yes. I believe she is finished now."

"Finished?"

"She is ready to talk."

Severn moved his chair toward Random; the table stood between them. Ybelline had skirted the edge of the table, but Ybelline, being Tha'alani, required proximity if she was to speak to Random as if she were Tha'alani. Or a criminal. The best, or the worst.

He had spent all afternoon in the grip of Ybelline and the Tha'alani; it was oddly silent, oddly isolated, to sit at a normal distance from Random and Ybelline. He accepted it. He could both understand why the Tha'alani were feared, and resent it. The resentment, however, changed nothing, and he let it slide. There was no profit in holding on to it.

Random had not been afraid of Ybelline. She'd had no fear

of the Tha'alani method of communicating. She'd willingly, possibly eagerly, allowed the child Tessa had been to touch her and draw her into the Tha'alaan, or the children's version of it.

He knew this, but had no idea what had been communicated. He wasn't certain if Ybelline had known before she set foot in the Oracular Halls, but was certain she knew now. Her eyes were emerald as she withdrew her antennae.

"She knows," Random said, although Severn hadn't spoken the words aloud. Her eyes, like Severn's, didn't change color; they weren't an indicator of strong emotion. He was surprised when Random laid both hands, palm up, on the table. He responded to those hands the same way he'd responded to Ybelline's; he immediately placed both of his hands, palm down, across hers. Her skin was calloused, weathered, although it was pale with lack of sun.

"These," Random continued, "are the things I have made. I didn't realize the first one was for you until after I knew you would visit. It's the Barrani."

Severn nodded, looking at the sculpted figure she'd indicated. To most mortal eyes, the Barrani looked the same. They had hair of the same color, and eyes of the same color, the latter a sign that they were never comfortable when in the presence of others. Their skin was pale, flawless; he knew they could be scarred, but Elluvian had none, and Elluvian was the Barrani with whom Severn had the most experience. They were almost always the same height, as well.

The figure, however, was not Elluvian to Severn's eye.

"No. He is called Ollarin."

"Is he still alive?"

"He is alive. They are not." These last words were spoken in trembling syllables, as if words were too meager a container for the emotion that lay behind them. "Ollarin is what Tessa called him. It is what he told her to call him. It is not what he is called by his own kind.

"Take it with you. I think your companion will understand more when he sees it."

"Do you?"

Random frowned.

"Do you understand what you think he'll understand?"

She shook her head. Stray and graying curls had escaped the wild nest of her hair. "But I don't care what he understands. You might. It is up to you to decide. I made it for you." Her gaze then moved to the second statue. "Ybelline knows this man."

This man, as Random called him, was Tha'alani. Random's gaze did not linger on the figure; whatever questions the creation had given her, Severn was almost certain Ybelline had already answered.

"But this one," Random said, "is for you." It was what she had created, from nothing, before his eyes.

It was more tableau than single statue. There were three figures sculpted in the stone she'd pulled out of nowhere, and they shone as if lit from within.

He recognized none of them at first glance; they were all Barrani. But their mode of dress was different from the clothing worn by the Lords of the High Court that he'd met in the line of duty. One of the Barrani was, on second glance, An'Tellarus. He leaned in to get a better view, and found the single advantage to magical stone: the closer he got, the more detail he could see. The stone itself implied color when seen inches away.

"Do you know them?" Random asked.

"I think I recognize one of the three. But she's holding something I've never seen before."

Random nodded. "You came to the Wolves," she said. "And the Wolves will keep you. That's what Helmat said."

"You've spoken with Lord Marlin?"

Ybelline shook her head. "The sketch," she added, voice low.

"The sketch spoke to you?" Severn asked Random.

"That one did."

"And...the one of me in the ridiculous belt?"

Random nodded again. "You spoke to me as well." Her smile was fey, too young for her face. "You remember them."

She was speaking of Tessa, Jerrin, and Tobi.

"I don't think Tessa would mind," she added. "The Tha'alani don't keep secrets."

"Tessa did," Ybelline said.

"Yes." The word was sadder. "But that was only later." She looked at Ybelline and added, "And you will. I'm sorry."

"So am I," Ybelline said, although she smiled at Random.

Severn was looking at the other two Barrani; they were dressed oddly, as well. "Did any of these statues speak to you when you made them?"

"Ollarin did. And the castelord. The three haven't, yet, but Barrani don't like to talk much, so it might take a while." As if the figures were alive and reticent, not things of stone.

"I don't think Master Sabrai will allow you to give these to us," Ybelline said.

"Why not?"

The Tha'alani and the Wolf shared a glance, but didn't fill it with words.

"There are too many secrets," Random continued, brooding. "I think it would be better for all of us if we had none. Like you."

"I have secrets."

"Not because you're afraid the truth will be known."

"But Random, I am."

"It's not the same fear as his," Random replied, a frown

creasing most of her expression. *His*, Severn thought, was Ollarin, Elluvian, or the two Barrani he did not recognize.

"It's still fear."

"I like your fear better."

Ybelline's smile deepened, and for a moment her eyes were the color of pale honey.

Severn inhaled, exhaled, and began.

CHAPTER EIGHTEEN

THE QUESTION HE HAD COME TO ASK HAD BEEN answered before his arrival: Random remembered the pilgrimage of the high-spirited Tha'alani children. She remembered them clearly.

"When Tessa, Jerrin, and Tobi came to visit you, you were expecting them."

"I was expecting *something*. I wasn't expecting them. No one here could have expected that."

"But you refused to eat for two days so Master Sabrai would allow them entry."

Her smile was an echo of her younger self's gleeful pride. She nodded.

"Did they ask you any questions?"

"They didn't have permission to ask questions."

"No. They didn't understand the rules that govern the Oracular Halls. They didn't understand how Oracles work."

"Not when they first arrived."

"And when they left?"

Her glance slid away from his face. "They understood."

She looked down at their joined hands; hers were trembling. When she lifted her face, it was to Ybelline she looked.

"You were not responsible for their deaths," the future castelord said, no doubt at all in her tone.

"I couldn't save them."

"You were trapped in these halls. We weren't—they were *our kin* and we didn't save them either."

"You didn't know."

Ybelline said nothing for one long beat. "The blame, if blame must be assigned, is ours. Not yours. You gave them something humans seldom give the Tha'alani. You weren't afraid. You were never afraid of them. You were curious, you were as excited as they were, and you accepted...everything."

"But—"

"There is no but, Random. I know what they felt. I've seen it. I will remember it for as long as I live. I imagine Severn will do the same."

Severn looked, with care, at the statue of Ollarin. As he'd done with the odd tableau, he leaned forward until his eyes were less than two inches from the figurine. Proximity made the details clearer.

This Ollarin was not the man Ybelline had glimpsed at the back of a crowd of mortal murderers.

"You can touch that one," Random said.

"This one? But not the others?"

"I wouldn't touch the new one yet. It hasn't stabilized."

He didn't ask her what her use of the word *stabilized* signified. Instead, he retrieved one of his hands—the left—and lifted the figure of this Ollarin.

"When Tessa touched you," he said, "you were given an oracle."

Random nodded.

"Did you tell Master Sabrai?"

She shook her head. "…He would have been angry."

"This," Ybelline said, "is why we have secrets, or keep them. Tessa, Jerrin, and Tobi didn't tell anyone they were going to come here, either—because their parents would have been angry. And they would have said no. But we're not good at keeping secrets like this for very long; they just had to keep it hidden for long enough that they couldn't be easily stopped."

"What was the oracle you offered them?" Severn continued.

"She knows."

Severn met Ybelline's gaze. "Will you tell me?"

Ybelline was silent. After a long pause, she said, "Ollarin was some part of the vision."

"And the rest?"

She shook her head. To Random, she said, "I cannot answer all of Severn's questions. If you can, you must answer them."

"You want him to know."

"I want him to know."

"Tessa wanted to meet him."

"Ollarin?"

"Yes. Tessa saw him, and she wanted to meet him."

"Why?"

"I don't know. I knew that she would want to meet him. After they visited. I knew she would want to come back."

"And she did."

Random nodded. "We were older. She was your age. Jerrin didn't come. Tobi came with her, but Jerrin didn't. Jerrin was scared."

"Did she make an appointment for her second visit?"

"No." Random looked at Ybelline.

Ybelline said, "She knocked on the door. Her understanding of the workings of the Oracular Halls remained incomplete."

"But you met her the same way you did the first time?"

Random nodded. "I knew. I knew she would come. I had made things for her. I had to warn her."

"You were afraid for her."

"I— Yes. But she was afraid, too."

"Why?"

"Because she'd met Ollarin."

Ybelline nodded. "Yes. Yes, she had."

"Random, the first oracle—the one you hadn't expected— did it contain any warning for them? Any hint of the future?"

"No!" Random's hand clutched the one that Severn had not moved; her knuckles whitened, and Severn's hand tingled almost painfully as her grip cut off blood flow. "No! It wasn't! There was no warning! She wanted to meet him because he...he wanted to..." She swallowed. "He wasn't afraid of the Tha'alani, either. He wasn't afraid of the Tha'alaan."

"Did Ollarin come here, Random?"

Random's eyes widened, revealing whites. She didn't answer. It was Ybelline who said, "Yes."

Random was no longer the child she had once been, but Random wasn't exactly adult, either. Severn wondered what she might have become had she had more experience of the outside world. He didn't ask her if she could leave. He didn't ask her if she had ever tried.

But she answered the question he didn't ask. "I can't leave. I could never leave. I didn't grow up here."

Severn nodded.

"I grew up outside of the city. That way." She lifted an arm, as if pointing to her left would mean to Severn what it meant to her. "Master Sabrai found me. He rescued me. We almost died. He said if I left the Halls, I *would* die."

"You believed him."

"He's an Oracle, too. Not a powerful one, which is why *he*

can leave. He talks to people like the Emperor. And people like you. Sorry. He doesn't...have visions the way we do. Some of the Oracles he searches for he finds too late. We don't want to die," she added. "Not if there's no reason.

"I wasn't afraid of Ollarin. I wasn't afraid for Tessa—not then. I knew Ollarin would like her. I knew she would like him. She wanted to find people who weren't afraid. He wasn't going to be afraid of her."

Ybelline said nothing.

"But if the oracle hadn't arrived then, if she hadn't seen what *I saw*, she wouldn't be dead."

Ybelline said, voice low, "No. But that is not your fault. Tessa made a choice. She was young, naive. She was hopeful."

"She was like you."

Ybelline's eyes were hazel now.

"I don't want you to die." Random turned to Severn. "I don't want Ybelline to die."

"Is that why you made the appointment for us?"

Random nodded. "I made it because I knew you would come. Like I knew Tessa would come back."

"Why did Ollarin come to visit?"

"He knew."

"He knew that Tessa had come before?"

Random nodded. "I think you can take those with you, now. I think they'll hold their form and shape." She extricated her hand from Severn's, rose, and turned toward Ybelline. Ybelline had already opened both of her arms, and Random walked into them, walked into her, as if she hoped to meld there permanently.

She was crying.

"I need to borrow something to carry them in," Severn began.

"There's a bag under the bench. One of my friends made it

for me. He gave it to me two days ago. It's for you. You don't have to bring it back."

Ybelline's arms were around Random, as words were dissolved by tears. Severn took the figurines, the small tableau, and the sketches. He packed them as carefully as he could, given lack of preparation, and when he was done, he looked at Random's back. He couldn't see Ybelline's face; she had, once again, drawn Random into the Tha'alaan.

Severn almost wished he could join them, and that was a new and disturbing thought.

Master Sabrai might have given Random free rein within the confines of her workshop, but he was clearly concerned. The drink he had offered Elluvian had not kept him from standing outside Random's door with two of the guards. Elluvian was not with him.

The much older Sabrai glared balefully at the pack Severn had shouldered.

"Random thought it was important that I take these things with me," he said.

"Random is not the Master of the Oracular Halls. I am."

Severn nodded and waited.

Master Sabrai's glare didn't change. "What did Random give you?"

"Three carved figurines," Severn replied. He noted that Master Sabrai winced.

"Three?"

"Yes. If you want to inspect the contents, you can. There are also sketches. She seemed to think I would need or want everything she made."

"Who *are* you?"

"Severn Handred of the Halls of Law."

"Which branch?"

He already knew. Severn was certain of it. But he understood that words weren't always meant to communicate actual information. "The Wolves. I believe you've spoken with
Lord Marlin."

"What did she tell you?"

Severn shook his head.

"Why is the Tha'alani still in the workshop?"

"Random had more she wanted to say." Severn exhaled.
"And I have a few questions, as well."

"I am not necessarily at liberty to answer them."

Lack of answers was still a form of information.

"How much longer will the Tha'alani be with Random?"

"I imagine for as long as Random wants."

The guards looked as concerned as their master, but the
master now turned. "Fine. Come to my office."

"All appointments made to visit the Oracles are made
through you," Severn said when they had returned to the office meant for official visitors. Elluvian was seated on a long
chair, a glass in his hand, when they entered. He nodded at
Severn, frowned at the new burden attached to his shoulder,
and otherwise said nothing.

"Yes. Your case is unusual—but the Oracular Halls are
nothing if not unusual."

"The three Tha'alani children who came to visit decades
ago had made no official appointment."

Master Sabrai's expression tightened. He did not ask which
three. "Of course not."

"You allowed them to speak with Random."

"She'd clearly been expecting them." Master Sabrai poured
himself a drink; one of the two guards frowned, but said nothing. Severn was almost certain that if Master Sabrai had been
alone, she would have.

"Do the Oracles normally expect their visitors?"

"No."

"Random is a special case?"

"Random is special, yes. She is also highly stubborn. The effects of refusing to grant those children entry would have lasted years. The children were not harmful in the way many visitors might otherwise be."

"And today's appointment?"

"The appointment for which you were late?"

Severn nodded.

"She requested it weeks ago."

"You scheduled it."

"Yes."

"Had another Oracle made the same request, would you also have accepted it?"

"It would depend entirely on the Oracle in question. Random's visitors seldom threaten to kill her." *Seldom*, Severn thought.

"Does Random often receive visitors?"

"I am not at liberty to discuss either visitors or the reasons for their visits."

Severn nodded again. "How often do Barrani receive the requisite permission to visit the Halls?"

"As you can probably imagine, almost never."

"But not never."

Master Sabrai's glare fell upon Elluvian. "Clearly."

"I am here as a Wolf, not a supplicant. And I was not allowed to wander the Halls at will."

Severn glanced at Elluvian. When he raised a brow at Severn, Severn resumed his questions. "Do you keep complete records of the requests made, even if those requests are rejected?"

A pause before an answer. "Yes."

"We are interested in requests made in the past. Twenty-seven years ago or less."

"We are also," Elluvian added, setting his glass on the table, "interested in requests made in the very recent past."

Master Sabrai's jaw twitched on the left side. "You have not requested that information officially."

"No. And any answer we receive will be unofficial. It will provide some possible context, some possible direction for further investigation. That is all."

Master Sabrai walked over to a desk tucked against the wall. "Very well. On the understanding that our records are not up to the standards of the Imperial Service, or even the Halls of Law, I will attempt to answer your questions." He opened a drawer. From it, he withdrew two large, long books. The covers had dates.

He had already prepared the information he thought the Wolves would ask for. Had Severn not asked, he would not have offered.

"These are the relevant logs." Severn rose and retrieved them. Elluvian was both watchful and silent. He almost reached for the logs himself, but appeared to think better of it.

"Lord Marlin doesn't want the Wolves to become entangled in strictly Barrani affairs."

"And I don't want rain when I'm forced to leave the Oracular Halls."

Severn opened the book while the two older men stared at each other. The dating system was much the same as the dating system used for Records in the Halls of Law. The Oracular Halls weren't as busy as he might have expected, given the information the Oracles could offer. There were requests, yes. But few of those requests appeared to have been granted, and some had been refused outright, with no explanation.

Nor did he think an explanation would be forthcoming if

he asked for one. It didn't matter. The Barrani didn't often ask for permission to interact with the Oracles.

"Do you recall," Severn said, as he turned pages, "a Barrani by the name of Ollarin?"

"Not offhand."

"I ask you to consider it now, because a Barrani man *did* visit Random. The visit occurred after the Tha'alani children visited. Do you have a record of their visit?"

"No. They were not here to receive an oracle."

"Did the Barrani man who was granted permission to visit also peruse your logs?"

"No. He didn't have the threat of the Imperial Service hanging over my head."

"Was the visit by the Tha'alani—the second visit—logged?"

Master Sabrai didn't answer.

Severn had found the entry, the first entry, of relevance. He didn't recognize the name, only the styling. Elluvian held out a hand, and Severn passed the book to him. He watched Elluvian's face, or rather, the color of his eyes; Elluvian's expression gave nothing away.

The name was familiar to Severn; he'd heard it on his first visit to the High Halls. It was the name Elluvian had given Corvallan and Cassandre: Sennarin.

Sennarin was a family name; it was not An'Sennarin. The Barrani man, however, had given no other.

Elluvian closed the book. He then set it on the table beside his empty glass. Severn had moved on to the most recent book. "How did Sennarin receive permission to visit Random? Did he ask specifically for Random?"

Silence.

"I was under the impression," Severn continued, "that the request is made of the Oracular Halls. The choice of Oracle is not in the hands of the person who makes the request; it is your decision."

Master Sabrai nodded.

"Did Random tell you that Ollarin—or rather, that a Barrani man—would come to speak with her? Did she make the same request she made when setting up our appointment?"

"Yes."

"Did the Barrani man arrive after Tessa's second visit?"

"Yes."

"He has never returned."

"No. Nor will he."

"But he did make the request through the usual channels."

Master Sabrai nodded.

"Do you know what he came to ask?"

"I know what his official request claimed he would ask, yes. I am not at liberty to discuss it."

"Liberty is a quaint notion," Elluvian said. It was a threat.

Master Sabrai shrugged. If it was a threat, Sabrai considered it to be toothless.

"Did Random tell you what he actually asked?"

"If Random did not tell you, I am not at liberty to discuss it."

"In theory, neither is she."

"You don't understand these Halls," Master Sabrai said. "Whatever he did ask was damaging to Random. It has continued to be damaging to her."

"It was not just damaging to Random," Severn said, his tone far less hostile than Elluvian's had been.

"No—of course not." The older man's shoulders lost some of their tension. "That is never the way of the future, is it? She was aware of the errors in judgment hope produced, both in her and in the Tha'alani. There was a boating accident," he continued. "Random could see it coming—or rather, could see the deaths she had no idea how to prevent.

"She is not political. We are not, as a whole, political creatures. But information is a tool, like any other. And fear of the future has oft been a bitter master of men."

"Did she know about the murders of Tha'alani that took place in the city streets two decades ago?"

"You did not ask her?"

Severn hesitated and then shook his head.

A gleam of something that might be very grudging approval changed the shape of Master Sabrai's eyes. "Yes. She was not the only Oracle who was, but it affected her in a way it affected none of the others." He fell silent, as if considering all possible words and discarding most of them. "It has never left her. I am certain that she believes that your visit—and the visit of the Tha'alani woman who accompanied you—will bring a measure of peace or justice for the murdered.

"That *is* why you've come?"

Severn nodded. "It's why Ybelline Rabon is here as well. It's no easier for Ybelline than it has been for Random. And it will be harder, I think, for Ybelline in the end."

"You are not afraid of Ybelline."

"No."

"And you are not afraid of Random."

"No. I understand, on some level, what they both want. Anger might be a terrible bridge—but it is a bridge for the two of them."

"It won't bring the dead back."

"No. But nothing will. The most we can hope for—and work for—is that there will be no new deaths."

"An'Sennarin recently requested permission to visit the Oracular Halls."

"How recently?"

"Two days ago. He was refused outright."

"He did not make the request in person?"

"No. He took the unusual step of writing a letter."

"It's not unusual if the permission granted must be granted by the Emperor." Elluvian's gaze sharpened. "Did you keep the letter?"

"I am not a fool," was the frosty reply. "The letter was destroyed outright. It did not leave this room once it had arrived here."

"How long did it take you to review the request?"

"Two days—which is our norm. The letter was not handled with more care, or less care, than any other unwelcome missive. If you fear for Random, it is unnecessary. The harm she does herself, we accept. We cannot change or prevent it.

"Harm done by outsiders, however, we can."

"Was the request for Random?"

"It was a general request. I believe the point was to gain entry."

Severn frowned.

"The boy who made the pack you now carry," Master Sabrai said, "had an oracle. No Barrani will be allowed across the threshold in the foreseeable future—and the reasons for that have been made clear to the Emperor and his Imperial Service. I do not believe Barrani—present company excepted—could approach the front gates without setting off appropriate alarms."

Severn continued to study the logs.

"This one?" he asked, pointing at another logged request.

"You noticed that one? He is part of the human caste court. This would not be the first time he has made a request of the Halls."

"The timing—"

"And the urgency, yes."

"Could you allow the mortal to visit," Elluvian asked, "and find out what his actual intentions are when he's here?"

Master Sabrai was instantly angry. "No."

"Very well. Severn?"

Severn, however, went back to the first book. "Master Sabrai, have there ever been Tha'alani visitors outside of the three children?"

"They were the first. As Random has informed you, two of the three did return."

"And no other Tha'alani?"

Silence.

Into that silence, Ybelline now walked. Master Sabrai turned to her immediately.

"There was," Ybelline said quietly, "one other Tha'alani visitor." There was no question in the statement, but she held Master Sabrai's gaze.

He nodded.

"Did he come to receive an oracle?" Severn asked.

"Ybelline Rabon seems to know what was discussed," Master Sabrai replied. "I will leave the answers in her hands. It is a caste court matter. The Tha'alani Caste Court." He looked at Ybelline. "Random?"

"She is resting now. She is exhausted, but I think she will be at peace."

"She needed to meet you, I think. The Oracles and the Tha'alani have very similar experiences in the populace at large. It is easier to hide a child like Random than it would be to hide the three who came to meet her—but not when she receives an oracle. Oracles are feared, as you are, and some die just as the Tha'alani did."

Ybelline nodded. "We have much in common, Master Sabrai." And very little of it happy. "Random asked me to tell you that she is resting now. She thinks there might be one more visitor."

"And?"

"Unless the visitor is the Emperor himself, Random should be considered unavailable. She said she would avoid the visitor if possible, but she's afraid that if she does, the visitor might affect the whole of the Halls. She's very concerned about the children."

Master Sabrai's voice was stiff. "Random is a single Oracle in a hall that contains many. We are aware of the possibility of a visit."

"But not the identity of the visitor?"

"That, too, is becoming clearer. The Oracular Halls are not your concern. Do not shoulder burdens that are not yours— the burdens you do carry will be heavy enough."

Ybelline remained where she was standing.

"I was nervous when the Tha'alani children appeared," Master Sabrai said, his voice rough around the edges. "Random was not. I think very, very few of her visitors have ever brought her joy. What happened because of that visit—"

"It wasn't her fault." Ybelline's voice was low, and as rough as Master Sabrai's.

"No. Nor was it the fault of children with more curiosity than caution. I believe the initial visit, surprising as it was, was good for Random." He exhaled. "I believe it would have been good for any of the children in my care. We are all taught to fear."

"There are things it is not safe to know."

Master Sabrai nodded. "But the knowledge did not harm any of our children. The fear that the knowledge *might* exist did. As I said: the Oracles are my concern. They are not yours."

Severn cleared his throat, and they both turned to look at

him. "Have any assassinations against an Oracle succeeded in the past?"

Master Sabrai shook his head. "Not when they are in residence. I'm sure Random has attempted to explain how oracles work?"

Severn nodded.

"And I'm sure it made almost no sense to you. It is like trying to describe color to someone who has never been able to see. The oracles received without instruction or interference are clearest when the Oracles themselves are in some future danger."

"You expect some difficulty."

"I am certain some difficulty, as you call it, has been planned, yes. I do not know this because the person who would cause the difficulty has trumpeted their plans across the city—but in this particular case, they might just as well have. Random will be safe. If she is not, it will be because she has chosen to act in a way that does not, and cannot, guarantee safety.

"Her insistence on making your appointment was one of those choices. My apologies," he said, bowing to Ybelline. "What I cannot guarantee is your safety or your survival. While I would welcome you as a guest or a resident, I do not believe your people would agree."

Both of the guards were staring at Master Sabrai in open surprise.

"Random has never let go of the almost crippling certainty that the deaths that happened after the first meeting were her fault. I have hopes that she will, at last, be at peace."

"She thinks you are angry with her."

"I have oft found her frustrating; she is the least tractable of the Oracles. But no, I am not angry with her. And I understand her guilt; I could have refused to allow those children to cross this threshold. I did not. The responsibility lies with me.

"I will see you out."

The carriage did not return immediately to the Tha'alani quarter. Ybelline instructed the driver to take them to the Halls of Law. She was not wearing the Imperial Service uniform that the Tha'alanari wore when involved in their Imperial duties, but they seemed all but irrelevant to her. Her eyes were almost green—when Severn could see them.

For much of the less than comfortable carriage ride, her eyes were closed.

Severn didn't ask her what she and Random had discussed. He didn't ask her who the Tha'alani visitor—the official visitor—had been. He was almost certain he knew the answer; confirmation was not required.

What he wanted to know now, was what information justified the murders of the three and the brutal deaths that had followed in their wake. And he had a feeling that the answer was in the hands of the Barrani; it was not a question that would make sense to the Tha'alani. To the Tha'alanari, possibly.

What had Random shown Ybelline? Random had been unwilling to discuss it with Severn; she had left that in Ybelline's hands, which left the decision of whether or not to share in Ybelline's hands as well.

Elluvian wanted to see the contents of Severn's newly acquired pack. Severn glanced at Ybelline, but the Tha'alani's eyes were still closed. The decision, regardless, was his: Severn was a Wolf. Elluvian was The Wolf. Being Barrani, he was unlikely to share his conclusions, even if he agreed to do so.

But Elluvian's understanding of the difficulties of this case were greater by far than Severn's. Or rather, his understanding of the Barrani elements. Severn undid the strings that closed the top of the bag. He then withdrew each of Random's gifts, one at a time, starting with the sculptures.

The first was that of the man called, by Tessa, Ollarin, and logged in the request book as Sennarin. Severn handed it to Elluvian without comment. Without expression. He watched the Barrani Wolf, noting in particular the shift in eye color.

The eyes were indigo, not the gold that, in Barrani, denoted surprise or shock. Elluvian had expected to see this sculpture.

"This man identified himself as Ollarin."

Elluvian's eyes met Severn's before returning to the statue.

"Ollarin visited the Oracular Halls."

"Not under that name."

"Not many of my kin would take the risk of lying in the Oracular Halls."

"Why not?"

"Lies have a way of being discovered—and not in a way that one can easily recover from. The discovery, the means of discovery, are not predictable."

"You recognize him. Is he An'Sennarin?"

"He was not An'Sennarin at the time of the visit. His ascension to the title is new."

Severn looked at Ybelline; her eyes remained closed.

"This man visited Random?"

Severn nodded.

"Why?"

"I don't know. She was willing to discuss it with Ybelline; she expected Ybelline to answer any questions it was safe to answer."

"If Ybelline were Barrani—"

"I am not," Ybelline said.

"—she would answer no questions."

"She's not Barrani."

"She will be castelord."

Ybelline nodded. "I will answer questions," she told El-luvian. "But I will answer them in private. I have still not given Private Handred the information I was instructed to give him."

"You believe that information to be relevant now?"

"Yes. I have not been given permission to share that information beyond Private Handred. If Helmat wants to question the private, Severn is a Wolf. Helmat will not, however, question me."

"And I won't, either."

"Not and receive answers, no. I would prefer to have the rest of the interview tomorrow, if possible."

"Then why are you coming to the Halls of Law?"

"I, too, wish to examine what Random gifted to Severn."

Severn wasn't certain that she did. It wasn't his choice to make.

CHAPTER NINETEEN

"YBELLINE," HELMAT SAID WHEN THEY ENTERED the Wolves' office. He was standing, arms folded, beside Rosen's desk—or rather, by her mirror. Rosen, seated, looked past Ybelline to Severn and Elluvian.

Ybelline's eyes narrowed; she stopped in the doorway as she met Helmat's gaze.

"A message has arrived for you."

"Is it from Saidh?"

"No."

"Unless it is from the Emperor himself, all messages are to be put on hold."

"No one informed our mirrors of this prohibition." Helmat unfolded his arms and stood. "The mirrors in the Halls of Law are not under your jurisdiction."

"Apologies, Helmat," she said in a distinctly unapologetic tone. "You are free to accept any messages you desire. I am free to refuse to engage with them. I will not answer any of the messages being routed through you; I have already made that clear to the Tha'alanari." Her eyes were martial green.

"En?"

Elluvian shrugged. "They'll be angry at you, not her. It's your decision."

"They will not be angry at Helmat."

Helmat concurred. Ybelline had never, in their interactions, attempted to give any commands—not to Helmat. The color of her eyes made clear she was upset. "What did you learn in the Oracular Halls?" Helmat's forehead creased further as his eyes alighted on Severn. "What are you carrying?"

Severn spoke as if he hadn't heard the interchange between Helmat and Ybelline; the boy's expression gave almost nothing away. Years from now, Helmat thought, Severn would be controlled enough that he might meet with the castelords and even the Emperor—and in Helmat's estimation the number of years would be few. "One of the Oracles—the one who requested an appointment be made for us—drew sketches and made small sculptures for us."

"For you," Ybelline said, voice softer, eyes still flecked with green. "I do not require them to remember what she showed me."

Helmat's brows rose. "You touched an Oracle?"

"At her request."

"You *touched* an Oracle."

Severn cleared his throat. "Ybelline has an assignment from the Imperial Service she wishes to complete; she was interrupted before she could finish."

"Interrupted by what?"

"Caste court business," Ybelline said.

Helmat stared at Ybelline in consternation. "I have never heard you use those words before—not unless speaking of the humans or the Barrani."

"I wish I had no cause to use them now." She turned to

Elluvian. "With your permission, Severn and I will return to your office."

"While I remain outside of it, I assume."

Ybelline nodded.

"I wish to examine the items the private brought out of the Oracular Halls."

"You will have ample time to do that later. With Severn's permission, you might do so now. I would, however, make one request should Severn grant that permission."

"Oh?"

"I wish Helmat to be with you when you examine the contents of this bag, and I wish the entirety of those contents to be entered into Records."

Interesting. Elluvian had Ybelline's full attention.

Helmat turned toward the Barrani Wolf, who made no reply to Ybelline's demands. What he saw there convinced him that her demands, ridiculous on the surface, might just be necessary.

"I will wait until Severn is available," Elluvian said. "How long do you think this will take?"

Ybelline shook her head. "I don't know how many questions Severn will ask."

"Severn?"

"I don't know yet either."

Severn looked at Rosen, seated behind the desk that served as a choke point for the Wolves. He'd become accustomed to her guidance in the office. Her eyes were gray-brown, but in the muted light, the gray seemed stronger. Expression of any kind had fallen away from her face, banished until she caught Severn looking at her, as if seeking her guidance.

Her lips pursed; she shook her head without shifting her gaze, the movement so minimal he'd have missed it had she not been looking right at him. Her eyes darted, once, to the side; she didn't speak a word otherwise.

He understood.

Severn was on probation. Helmat was the Wolflord, Elluvian the only Barrani to serve the Wolves, and Ybelline was the future castelord of the Tha'alani. No one was paying Rosen enough to interfere with things that were none of her business.

Her pointed, silent direction—to Elluvian's currently unoccupied office—made clear that no one was paying Severn enough, either.

Severn understood. But Ybelline was almost at the end of whatever patience had kept her on her feet so far, and she wouldn't be here—at all—were it not for Imperial demands made of the Tha'alani. He wasn't concerned for Elluvian, nor was he worried for the Wolves or their lord.

He met Rosen's gaze, grimaced slightly, and nodded. He then turned to the three people who might stand for a while in front of Rosen's desk at an impasse, and shifted the straps on his shoulder just enough to catch their attention.

Elluvian's eyes were blue, Ybelline's green. Helmat's expression was grim. Severn bowed his head for a brief moment, and then walked past them all to Elluvian's office. He hadn't yet decided how much of Random's work he wanted to share. Not the sketch of Elianne.

She was looking at you.

Elluvian didn't join them in the office that was theoretically his, but it had become clear to Severn that the Barrani Wolf was seldom there. Severn sat; Ybelline pulled the second chair the office contained toward his, facing him, her knees pressed against his. He set the pack on the floor to one side of the chair and held out his hands—just as he had done earlier—both palms up and open.

She lowered her chin, her hands pressed so tightly into her lap they were edged in white, her eyes closed.

He waited. He wanted to withdraw his hands, to let her leave. But the information would leave with her. The Wolves needed that information.

She knew. She lifted her hands and placed them across Severn's; her fingers were tense, almost viselike. He waited. He was willing to wait the hours necessary for Ybelline to gather her thoughts, to armor herself. He even understood why that armor was necessary.

"Thank you," she said, and he realized that she had touched his forehead so gently he had barely been aware of it given the tightness of her grip. *There is too much of this that is—that must be—only for the caste court.*

Mortals and Barrani were involved in the murders of your people. There's no caste court exemption in such deaths.

No. But there is much that is not death—not murder, that is. This will not be the same style of interview that you have experienced with me before. Ask your questions. I will answer them. But I will answer them as if it were only with voices that we speak.

Could she even do that?

Yes. The answer was hesitant, uncertain. *Yes, because I have to be able to do this. I have to be able to both touch your thoughts, your mind, and shelter my own almost completely. I have managed something similar with my own kin.*

And it was killing her, he thought. The Tha'alani were not a people who had many secrets; they lived in a state where secrets weren't necessary. But she was Tha'alanari, and the Tha'alanari were chosen because they *could.* What it did to them, what it made of them, they accepted.

Severn hated it. And accepted it. And waited.

Your questions?

He nodded. *Sennarin.*

Sennarin—An'Sennarin—has ruled his court for only a few decades. Those decades occurred after the murders or before?

Silence. Severn waited.

During, she finally said, as if she had been reviewing the information she held to derive an answer.

Is he Ollarin? Or was he?

It is not a name by which the Imperial Service knew him.

Did they know him by a different name before he became An'Sennarin?

Is it relevant?

We don't know what's relevant, Severn replied.

She nodded without moving at all; it was a strange sensation. *Before his ascension, he was Ollarin, I believe. He was not the direct heir at the time of the previous lord's death; he was a cousin.*

And the direct heir?

Is dead.

How?

The cause of death of both the lord and his heir is unknown to the Imperial Service.

They have no suspicions?

Of course there are suspicions—but it's a Barrani Caste Court matter. The Barrani are not required to tender information about those deaths. Regardless, An'Sennarin is now his line's ruler. She frowned. *Elluvian implicated him in the murders?*

...Sorry. I'm not as good at this as you have to be. Yes. But I think he was fishing. He wanted to see what Corvallan and Cassandre said or did in response. What does the Imperial Service know about either Corvallan or Cassandre?

Cassandre is of Casarre. Corvallan is of the Mellarionne line. Here, the tone and texture of her words darkened considerably, and the weight of the silence between them grew almost oppressively heavy. He couldn't tell which of the two names had caused this.

We went to speak to Corvallan—it was the reason we were at the High Halls. Corvallan's wife met us at the doors.

What was your impression? The question was controlled.

Severn considered the answer, and then surrendered. *You have to guard your thoughts and your reactions,* he told her. *There's no reason I have to guard mine.*

He felt her surprise.

You don't want to do this, he said. *Neither do I. But you have better reasons—or they seem better to me. I won't apologize—you already told me how unwelcome pointless apologies are. But I won't fight you. You've seen and experienced the worst of my life already, and you've accepted it.*

After more silence, Ybelline said, *Anger and fear are easier to understand in some ways than this.* She wasn't lying, but she wasn't telling the truth; she was speaking almost entirely to herself. And he knew she would never choose anger and fear where any other choice was possible.

He let her watch the entire meeting between Corvallan and Cassandre.

You think Cassandre is the more dangerous of the two.

I did. You don't?

Corvallan is afraid. She seemed almost apologetic. *For my people, it is that fear that breeds insanity.*

It's not just fear that's a threat to the rest of us, Severn replied. *I highly doubt the Barrani who orchestrated all these deaths was afraid. The person who hired him or commanded him, yes—but he was willing to do it all without the same driving fear.*

Corvallan is known to the Imperial Service—most of the active Mellarionne relations are.

Mellarionne is dangerous.

Yes, although Saidh says Mellarionne is ambitious, not afraid. Corvallan is a distant cousin of An'Mellarionne, and if he's at court, he's beholden to the head of his line. There is little love lost between them, but the damage they have done to each other in the past is apparently forgivable to Barrani.

Cassandre?

Casarre. Casarre, however, is less obviously active. It is not considered a family of much power within the High Court, but there is prestige in it: the line is old.

Does the Service have any idea what either—Corvallan or Cassandre—could gain from an alliance with Mellarionne?

It is not Mellarionne that is the danger here, given their reactions; it is Sennarin. They are connected, but the connection is not a full alliance; they are, in some fashion, beholden to their families. Their position within the High Halls depends on those families and the favor shown them.

Before Severn could speak, Ybelline continued. *Corvallan has some connections with a man known as Teremaine.*

You think the Barrani that reopened this investigation is Teremaine?

We think it very likely, yes. He is not a lord of the court. His name has appeared multiple times in Imperial Service Records; he has never—until now—fallen afoul of caste court exemptions. His value to any of the lords with whom he has connections depends on his ability to remain within those laws of exemption.

He hasn't.

No—but that was not known until very recently.

Is it known now?

You are afraid there is someone who informs the High Court, or members of it.

Yes. I think, given the deaths of the witnesses we wanted to interview, there's a leak in the Halls of Law.

The Halls of Law and the Imperial Service are not the same; there is some overlap, but that overlap exists at the Emperor's discretion.

Ybelline exhaled. *The Halls of Law exists as an entity almost separate from the Emperor. The oaths you take are to uphold the Emperor's Laws. The Imperial Service does not take the same oaths you take.*

They serve the Emperor directly.

They serve the Emperor directly. It is why there is conflict between the Halls of Law and the Service. It is therefore entirely possible—even probable—that the leak in question exists only in the Halls of Law.

The Barrani Hawks?

That is the most probable, but no. Money, favors, extortion will affect anyone who works in the Halls. The Halls of Law are examining all Records and all Records access even as we speak. The leak itself will be found.

Severn nodded, although he wasn't as certain. *Did the man Tessa called Ollarin come to visit Random?*

Yes.

After Tessa's second visit?

Yes.

Severn exhaled. *What oracle did Random give to Tessa when they first met?*

A warning, was the bitter reply. *A warning I understand only now, and Tessa did not understand fully until it was far too late for her.*

Ybelline.

I know. But you understand far better than I the weight of, the pressure of, guilt. Give me a few minutes to attempt to set it aside.

You understand what happened.

I understand what I think happened. I am not certain—I cannot be yet.

Random's oracle?

It was—Ybelline was silent now. Severn allowed it. Her first comment when she once again engaged seemed to have nothing to do with the question Severn had asked.

You are aware that the entirety of the Empire is comprised of different races.

Severn nodded.

And there are obvious differences between them. The Tha'alanari have the distinguishing antennae; the Leontines have fur and fangs; the Aerians have wings.

Yes.

We are all mortal.

Severn nodded, waiting.

The Immortals are different again. Pardon me for belaboring the obvious. It is not widely understood why they can, if they live peaceful lives, exist forever, but there are theories. At the heart of those theories—accepted by academics and the Immortals themselves—are their names. Not the names by which we know them; not the names by which they are identified. True Names.

True Names?

They believe there are words at their core. The words are like souls in mortal religions; they are the source of both strength and life. The words endure.

Severn said nothing, absorbing the information. Ybelline waited. *Are these beliefs religious, or are they grounded in provable fact?*

The latter. The names are never shared. To share the name is to invite control, or perhaps loss of control. In theory, if one knows the True Name of even the Emperor, one might, with force of will, command the Emperor—and be obeyed. She fell silent again.

I don't understand.

Ybelline bowed her head, her antennae slightly flattened against Severn's forehead. *I didn't, either. Did you know that if you know the True Name, you can speak to the person who possesses it? You can speak as you and I are speaking now?*

He hadn't known. Although he'd heard whispers and children's stories, he'd had no factual knowledge of what True Names meant. *The communication is like that shared by the Tha'alanari?*

...Yes.

You're certain?

Yes. Now I am certain.

But you can't control people with the Tha'alaan.

No.

The children—Tessa in particular—learned that they could bespeak the Barrani as if the Barrani were part of the Tha'alaan? As if they were Tha'alanari?

...Yes.

Severn's hands clenched in fists around Ybelline's.

You understand, she said, her voice devoid of light.

Random told her someone's True Name. Gods. And then, as the information sank roots, he said, *That name—that experience—existed in the Tha'alaan.*

It is not there now.

Ybelline—

Do you understand? Do you understand why this is a caste court matter? Why it must remain unknown?

He did. He also understood why the matter did not immediately fall under the laws of exemption.

She didn't know, Ybelline continued. *She knew that she could meet, could speak with, this Ollarin. She knew that death lay in the future, and she was young enough to believe she could communicate with this single Barrani man, and those deaths might be avoided.*

He understood Random's guilt, then. He understood the castelord's decision. He understood why oracles were considered unreliable. All the information had been there, but none of it made sense until long after the fact. There was nothing useful that could be done with it.

It would have been far better for everyone concerned if the Tha'alani children, in their daydreaming, hopeful optimism, had never visited Random, or the Oracular Halls, at all.

Severn said nothing for a long, long moment. *Tell me,*

he said, *about Teremaine. Tell me everything—everything—in Records about Corvallan, Cassandre, and the line Mellarionne. Tell me about Sennarin.*

She nodded, understanding that he had chosen these questions to return the interview to what might pass for neutral ground.

And then, because she was there, he added one more name. *And An'Tellarus.*

When Ybelline left both Elluvian's office and the offices that contained Wolves who were not on mission, the office was almost empty. Rosen was gone. Mellianne was gone.

The Wolflord and Elluvian, however, remained. The Wolflord's office door was open, an invitation or a command. Severn had shouldered Random's creations, and he made his way down the hall. He had no office of his own, and no place to put anything he didn't wish to expose to the Wolves; he accepted this.

It was odd, though. He had had no regrets, felt no hesitation, about Ybelline's perusal of things he did not wish to expose; he felt no hesitation about the fact that she knew what Random's works contained. Helmat and Elluvian, however, gave him far more pause.

Why? He had no answer, and in any case, it wasn't the question that was relevant now.

Helmat's mirror was reflective. He spoke a soft word, but the reflective surface remained in place.

"Private."

Severn nodded. Helmat's desk was remarkably empty if one discounted the mirror; the surface was clear. Severn set about opening the pack and began to remove its contents.

The first thing he placed in front of Helmat was a small figurine; it was perhaps three inches in height. Barrani.

"En?"

"An'Sennarin."

"Not a name I've heard you mention often."

"No. You might hear it a touch more in the next few weeks, but it is not considered dangerously significant at court."

Severn then took out the second figurine.

Helmat's eyes narrowed. "Random gave you this?"

"Yes."

"And Master Sabrai allowed you to take it?"

"Yes. I don't recognize the man."

"No. He's Tha'alani." Helmat did not offer a name.

Severn then removed the most complicated of the sculptures—the tableau of three. As he did, he turned toward Elluvian.

Elluvian's eyes were gold. He slid his hands behind his back and lowered his chin as he studied the tableau. His eyes lost the gold of surprise, shading swiftly into an odd shade of blue that appeared to have some purple in it. "When," he finally said, "did the Oracle create this?"

"While we were there."

"Not before?"

"No. The other two figures were carved before our arrival. This one...wasn't."

"She meant this for you."

"She clearly meant them all for him, En. Why is this one significant?"

"Do not waste time asking questions you know I will not answer," the Barrani Wolf snapped. He approached the sculpture of the three figures. "May I?" At Severn's nod, Elluvian lifted the tableau, examining each of the three in turn. "Do you recognize any of them?" he asked.

The question had not been asked of Helmat, to Helmat's surprise.

"An'Tellarus," Severn said.

"Ah, yes. Yes, that is An'Tellarus. Do you recognize either of the others?"

"No."

"One is the Lord of the West March."

"You think the Lord of the West March is involved in this?" Helmat demanded.

"No." It was Severn who answered. The answer should have meant nothing to Helmat. "I don't think this one has much to do with my current—our current—mission."

"You think it's specifically about you? How much did you ruffle feathers during your visit to the High Halls?"

Severn ignored this, his attention on the Barrani in the room. "And the other?"

Elluvian shook his head. "I do not believe it is relevant."

"Let us judge that," Helmat replied.

As if to forestall what was certain to become a more heated discussion, Severn began to pull sketches from the pack. Helmat's face, wearing an expression that implied he was not pleased with life, now stared up at the Wolflord, an artistic mirror.

The second sketch was the one of Ybelline. She wore the robes she had worn to the Oracular Halls, but Elluvian's frown indicated that he had noted some difference. Her expression, unlike Helmat's, was shorn of anger or irritation. Her eyes, in black and white, had no color that could lend emotion to her face.

The third sketch was of Elluvian; unlike the first two, it was the entire upper body, not just the head and upper shoulders.

"En?"

Elluvian said nothing for a long beat. "They are ceremonial robes, of a type not donned in the High Halls."

"Where would they be worn?"

Elluvian shook his head.

"Wedding?"

Both of Elluvian's dark brows crested the line of his hair. "Absolutely not."

Elluvian was discomfited by the things Severn had placed, one at a time, on Helmat's desk. Which was, itself, unsettling. "The Oracle did not say when this might occur?"

Severn shook his head. "I don't think she gets the choice. She tries to capture what she's seen. But some of this is no doubt decades old."

"And some is not."

Severn nodded. "She doesn't know. She believes it's all relevant—but she doesn't know how. I don't think any of the Oracles within the Hall do when they're driven to create."

"So we've been told," Elluvian replied.

Severn's pack was not yet empty. He now drew another sketch from its folds, and laid it on top of the others.

It was Severn. Helmat studied the sketch; Severn's face, the pale scar present, the brows folded in urgent concentration. This image hadn't, in his opinion been taken from the past.

It was not, however, to Severn that Helmat looked; Elluvian had the whole of his attention now.

He had the whole of Severn's as well. His eyes were a gold that seemed haloed in indigo; he was surprised and alarmed. He walked to the desk, lifted the sketch, stared at it, and then turned to Severn.

"Did she give you *any* other information? Anything of relevance to our mission?"

Severn shook his head.

"You are certain?"

One picture remained, just one. Helmat could see its curled edges; he could also see that Severn didn't wish to share it. And that he would. His hands were not entirely steady as he drew the last sketch from the pack; this one was colored.

Severn laid the sketch on the desk; Elluvian had not surrendered the sketch of the boy.

Helmat frowned. "These tattoos—Records."

The mirror's reflective surface swirled as if going down an invisible drain. What was left in the center were marks like those in the sketch, on a canvas that was distinctly flesh colored. The mirror didn't speak. Helmat, however, had turned from the mirror to the sketch. "She's older," he said. "Five years, maybe ten years—she's older. En?"

There was far less gold in Elluvian's eyes now, but it remained; he was surprised. "Were it not for those marks, I think there is no chance at all that she would be wearing that dress." When Helmat failed to comment, Elluvian frowned.

"The style is unusual," Helmat said, "but I fail to see how the marks dictate the clothing."

"The style is singular," Elluvian replied. "As is the fabric. It is not a dress in the sense that your mortal lords wear dresses. Nor is it a dress in the fashion our lords at court do. It is a… ceremonial dress, and it is worn in only one place."

"The West March," Helmat said.

"You were always perceptive," the Barrani Wolf replied. "But it is caste business, Helmat. I would ask that these images remain outside of Records. It is clear that there is an informant or spy within the Halls of Law, and were either of the last two sketches to come to light, the consequences for at least our private would be fatal."

"And for the girl?"

"She is not a Hawk. She is no official part of the Halls of Law."

But Severn had already abandoned his neutrality. He grabbed the picture of the girl—of one Kaylin Neya, who had been installed within the ranks of the Hawks as a...mascot. His own—and therefore his own future—seemed almost irrelevant to him.

"Private?"

"She has nothing to do with this."

"The Oracle does not agree."

Severn said nothing.

"It's possible that this is a warning offered to you for her sake. Are you willing to take the risk of hiding it?"

Severn continued in silence, but he put the drawing back into the pack.

"If she is in danger now," Elluvian said, "she will die."

Severn's hands were white where they gripped the strings of the pack's top.

"She is under the care of An'Teela. An'Teela is old enough to be a power at court."

"She's a Hawk."

"Yes. And An'Teela is powerful enough to *be* a Hawk against all objections of either her kin or the lords of the court. If she cannot keep one fledgling mortal safe, no interference on our part can." Although he spoke to Helmat, the words were meant, in part, for Severn. "I agree, however, with Severn's contention."

"How so?"

"Her age. I have studied mortals for far too long; she is older here than she is in our current reality. Severn is almost the same age in the sketch the Oracle made of him. If the West March figures prominently in Severn's future—and therefore in mine—it does not figure prominently in hers for some time.

"And perhaps this image only exists in order to encourage us to consider the West March and its environs."

"Yet you don't believe the West March or its court is involved in the Tha'alani murders."

"No. It's possible that Kaylin—as she is called by the Hawks—will travel to the West March, but that travel is in a future more distant than Severn's visit."

"Severn's visit?"

"I do not expect to have any reason to take Severn to the West March; the West March is not part of the Empire." Elluvian exhaled. "Oracles are notoriously inexact, their meanings opaque—at best.

"But this sketch involves the West March in some fashion. If I cannot see a reason for a pilgrimage to the West March, that is lack of foresight on my part. In Elantra, Severn's existence renders laws of exemption meaningless. There will be no such protection for him in the West March; it is not Imperial Law that rules there.

"Regardless, I do not believe the West March is relevant to Ollarin and the Tha'alani murders. I believe the oracle is relevant to Severn, and the various physical creations offered him overlap because the investigation, the ground hunt, is also relevant to Severn."

"You're certain?" Severn's voice was quiet.

"I am certain."

"He has no difficulty lying," Helmat pointed out.

"He knows that. But if every word uttered is to be treated as a lie, he will not get far as a Wolf." He was now looking at Severn.

Severn said, "What makes An'Teela different?"

"She is old. She fought in the Draco-Barrani wars. She fought well enough that she earned the right to bear one of The Three—the Dragonslayers created by our greatest smiths in times past. She has spent time in the Arcanum. She unseated the former lord of the line she now rules—and repudiated even his name when she took the seat. If she has decided to take Kaylin under her wing, Kaylin is as safe as it is possible to be.

"Even if there are those who desire Kaylin's death among my kin, very, very few would be foolish enough to attempt to cause it now; the cost would be far too high for one mortal life, and An'Teela's grudge is a long, dangerous thing if one becomes her target. She would have to pose a threat far greater than the threat the Tha'alani posed to the person who did orchestrate the murders decades ago."

Severn kept the sketch.

Helmat growled, wordless, but snapped a command at Records. "I want to know what these tattoos mean."

Elluvian nodded, which meant nothing.

Severn said, "Have you heard back from the Hawks?"

"About the witnesses? Yes."

"Did any of them survive?"

"Yes—one, and only barely." He hesitated and then said, "I believe there may have been some intervention on the part of their mascot; regardless it was the Barrani patrol, with Kaylin Neya in tow, that managed to return one living witness to the Halls of Law. There are no Barrani guards on duty in the cells. There *are* guards, and the cells are being watched very, very closely."

CHAPTER TWENTY

SEVERN WAS ACCUSTOMED TO BROKEN SLEEP during the evening hours, although months living in Elantra—with its utter absence of hunting Ferals—had dulled his instinctive response to evening sounds. The city itself was never completely silent.

It wasn't fear of Ferals that had jarred him from what passed for sleep. Nor was it the constant waking from nightmares; nightmares were old, familiar friends. He assumed they would haunt him for the rest of his life, and accepted that.

He also accepted, as he rose and dressed, that the work he'd been offered, the duty he'd undertaken, was unlikely to lead to peaceful, dreamless sleep. If someone were to ask him why he'd taken the Wolflord's offer, he would have had a hard time answering truthfully. He no longer knew.

Had he accepted the Wolflord's offer, and before it, Elluvian's, only because of Elianne? Because he would be part of the Halls of Law she now orbited? He would have said yes. Yes, that was the reason.

If she is in danger now, she will die.

An'Teela. Teela. Barrani and a Hawk. She had what Severn lacked: legitimacy and power. She had been granted—because of valor in war—one of three weapons created to slay Dragons. She had taken an interest in Elianne, and had taken Elianne under her figurative wing.

She was doing, in the end, what Severn himself had done—and she would keep the person she knew as Kaylin Neya far safer than Severn could. Elianne no longer needed him. She had, once, but she was no longer five. He was no longer ten.

Between then and now lay two dead children.

He accepted what Elluvian said as truth. With An'Teela's marked interest, Elianne was safe. Safer than she'd ever been with Severn. She would be far happier with An'Teela. She would be free to grow as Kaylin.

He had promised Tara that he would protect her daughter. That he would watch over her. But neither his protection nor his watchfulness had mattered. Not in a way that would not haunt her nightmares for the rest of her life.

He was on probation. He could walk away from the Wolves. He knew enough now to know that Elianne—*Kaylin*—would be fine without him.

And yet he found he had no intention of walking away. He hadn't joined because he wanted to be a hero. Hadn't joined them, in the end, to atone.

Atonement implied the possibility of some future forgiveness.

As he made his way through the morning streets of Elantra, he planned his day. He wanted the information the Hawks could provide; he didn't want to be noticed by those Hawks. He had the use of Elluvian's mirror. It had seemed miraculous when Rosen had first demonstrated its use. In a handful of days, it had become a tool, like a knife or a fork.

He didn't know if Elluvian's mirror would log requests made of Records as if they'd been made by Elluvian, and would have to ask. If Severn's name was attached to the request, there was a chance that whatever peace Elianne had made or found would be shattered.

He considered this as he walked. He knew that the requests he made of Ybelline would cause her nothing but pain; he made them anyway. And she expected that he would put the responsibility of the duties he had accepted before her personal pain.

He couldn't easily separate Elianne from those duties, because the very first duty, the driving force of his rapid ascent from childhood to the world of adults, had been Elianne. He had destroyed everything he had built for her in one evening, but he had saved her in the doing.

She didn't know why he'd done what he'd done. He was determined never to tell her. He knew it would make no difference, because the choice Severn had made on that terrible day was a choice that Elianne *could not* make. Not for herself. Not for anyone. And if, somehow, he could convince her, if she came to believe what Severn himself had believed, the guilt would destroy her.

He understood the weight of that guilt.

Rosen was at her desk looking distinctly unpleased with life. This was more or less her resting state. Her expression changed when Severn came into her field of view, her lips quirking up in what was almost—for Rosen—a smile.

"Kid," she said, "you're making the rest of us look lazy and useless."

Severn stopped in front of her desk, glancing over his shoulder toward Mellianne's. Mellianne was not yet at it. "Appearances can be deceiving."

Her smile deepened. "You've been listening to Elluvian."

"The Wolflord," Severn replied, matching her smile. "Has the Tha'alani castelord ever entered the Halls of Law?"

"You're going to give me whiplash if you change subjects that quickly. I highly doubt it. You want to check?"

He nodded.

"Helmat's done the basic groundwork to get you your own mirror."

"I have Elluvian's."

"Funny, that's what I told Helmat. It's not like Elluvian uses it often."

"He doesn't?"

"He does use it—but he uses it far less often than any of the rest of us. Barrani have perfect total recall when they want to do the work."

Severn frowned. "Total recall of anything they've experienced or seen themselves, yes. Most of Records seems to be outside of either category."

Rosen shrugged. "He doesn't really like Records or mirrors."

"Why?"

"Ask him. I didn't get much useful out of my early attempts."

"What did he say?"

"He doesn't trust them."

"Them?"

"Mirrors."

"Did he say why?"

"I think he actually tried—none of it made any sense to me, and frankly, I didn't want to get a longer, fuller explanation because it was all theoretical magic stuff. Way above my pay grade." She grinned, then. "Which leads me neatly to the first point of the morning. You probably didn't have much experience with magic while you were growing up. Even mirrors were strange and new to you.

"Helmat wants this to change."

Severn nodded.

"So...classes. There are two. The first—and the most important—is practical magic."

"I'm to learn...magic?"

"No. I said *practical*. The teachers will be long-winded, boring, and slightly self-important, but they'll tell you things you need to know if you don't want someone who can use magic to turn you into ash, dust, or sludge."

"And the second?"

"Theoretical magic. It's a bullshit course. People who don't know what they're talking about trying to teach it anyway." At Severn's expression, she grimaced. "I attempted to get you out of that one, but no dice. Luckily, it's short. Most of us," she continued, "also had to deal with spoken Barrani. I've been told you can speak Barrani."

Severn nodded.

"Can you read it and write it?"

He nodded again, but this nod was more hesitant.

"Fine—there's a test for reading comprehension; there's a test for writing composition. If you pass one of them, you don't have to take the other. There is also a series of combat classes."

"Weapon?"

"Yes. Basic weapons and unarmed. I figured you'd find those useful."

"Is there a test?"

"It's not called that, but yes."

Severn was silent for one long beat. "How many hours a week are these classes expected to take?"

"Elluvian nixed the combat classes."

"Oh?"

"He told Helmat he'll train you personally."

"I think I'd prefer the classes."

Rosen's brows rose. "You're really not as young as you look, are you?" The words were soft, and far more serious in tone. "Why would you prefer the classes? Most of the younger Wolves would have considered Elluvian's personal interest a bit of an honor."

"You don't."

She chuckled. "I'm not young anymore."

Severn shrugged. "I'd prefer the classes because most of the younger Wolves will consider Elluvian's interest an honor."

"You're worried about Mellianne."

"Mellianne is a Wolf, yes."

"If that's your concern, you're going to have to talk to Helmat. He trusts Elluvian. It's almost safe for him to do so." The implication that it wasn't safe for Severn was so clear, extra words would have been superfluous.

"I'm not sure I have the time for classes."

"No, you probably don't. Your current mission isn't a job for new recruits. Mellianne and Darrell weren't sent on active hunts until they'd passed all of the classes they were forced to take. If Jaren were here, he'd be shadowing Elluvian, not you. Jaren's not here. I can't do it," she added, looking briefly at her leg and the hand that was missing fingers. "Doesn't matter if you have the time or not. We have to arrange them anyway."

"Even if I'm forced to miss them?"

"Yeah. You'll be forced to log missed lessons and to provide written reasons—"

"In Barrani?"

"Barrani is the preferred language for most of our so-called academics, yes. It's not necessary, but it's what the hierarchy expects."

Severn nodded. He glanced, once again, at the mirror on

her desk, which was inactive. "If I make a query, will I be logged?"

"Yes."

"Will anyone who is not a Wolf see that log?"

"Not unless Helmat gives that permission. Hawks and Swords are always logged. Any query that comes through either branch is noted. Wolves have slightly different imperatives."

"Why?"

"Because we're Wolves. Some of the work the Wolves do is more secretive in nature. We're not the Imperial Service, but we're not Hawks either."

"If I wanted to query some of the Hawks' recent work, I have access to that information?"

Rosen exhaled. "Yes. Elluvian's mirror has the relevant reports." At Severn's expression, she added, "You want to know about the remaining witness."

He nodded.

"The information about that witness, and the three who didn't survive to become part of your investigation, are waiting for you. Don't look at me like that—Helmat's been closeted in meetings for the past few days and he *hates* meetings. We know what some of those meetings are about.

"I'd love to know why you think the Tha'alani castelord is relevant, though."

The witness, Dogan Sapson, was in jail. The cells served two purposes, the first being the expected one. They kept the criminals in. Given the nature of some of the criminals and some of their crimes, the cells had been constructed with protections against various forms of magic. Those protections were also useful when attempting to preserve the life of someone who had been targeted by the powerful.

Severn looked at the three morgue reports the Hawks had also filed. He knew what had killed the first two witnesses; the third had drowned. The drowning, however, had not occurred in any of the expected places—which is to say, near any body of water, large or small. If the first two deaths could be passed off as the natural outcomes of criminal activities gone wrong, the third could not.

Practical magic, Severn thought grimly. Of all of the lessons he'd been offered—or threatened with—that was the one he didn't want to miss. He knew of magic, of course—any street child did. He'd never had the means to separate the stories of the street from reality. If a man could die from drowning without being near or in actual water, that was an application of magic he wanted to understand.

The Barrani Hawks had been sent to secure both of the two witnesses who had been alive when Severn's sessions with Ybelline had begun in earnest. The first group had had the witness in custody; he had drowned in the middle of a city street, with no obvious visible intervention. The Hawks in question had failed to find the source of the attack before the man had ceased to breathe.

The other witness had been picked up by Teela and Tain. That witness had survived; there was no morgue report filed under his name. There was no report, he noted, of the event at all; Dogan Sapson was in the holding cells.

"Rosen—"

"The Hawks are famously bad at logging reports," Rosen said, her voice raised to carry through Elluvian's open door. "Their duty sergeant *hates* reports. Even when the Hawks file them, half of them end up shredded."

"Shredded?"

"He's a Leontine."

Leontine. Leontine. Severn grimaced and accepted his ignorance; he then attempted to alleviate it. An image of a golden-furred, long-fanged bipedal creature in what might have been a uniform filled the screen. Sergeant Marcus Kassan. "Do we have a lot of Leontines in the Halls of Law?"

"Nope. They have a problem with territoriality, or so we've been told. We have exactly one. I personally think they'd make excellent Wolves, but no one's asked me. And no," she added, "I've no records of the Tha'alani castelord in the Halls of Law, ever. Not the current castelord, at any rate. We don't get a lot of Tha'alani here when we don't log an official request.

"The Hawks have one at a permanent desk—Missing Persons. Other than that, we get visits. And castelords don't do random visits at the convenience of the Wolves. The Hawks also have Aerians; the Hawklord is Aerian.

"Leontine, Barrani, Tha'alani, Aerians, humans. The only thing they're missing is a Dragon."

"The Swords?"

"There are Aerian swords, but the Swords tend to be human. Humans don't tend to cause panic in the city streets, and quelling panic is the theoretical reason the Swords exist."

That wouldn't have worked in the fiefs. "Can we arrange to speak with the witness in protective custody?"

"If by 'we,' you mean you, the answer is no."

"Elluvian?"

"The answer is probably *hell no*, given the nature of the case and the reason for the custody."

"If Elluvian was working for outside interests, and he wanted to destroy the Halls of Law, he could."

Rosen did not disagree. "We know that. They won't. The kind of magic used to kill witness number three wasn't magic humans can normally use without effort and risk. There's not a lot of crossover between the Wolves and the other two branches of the Halls. They'll know Elluvian is Barrani; his length of tenure here won't make a difference. They won't know that all of our recruitment is done, initially, by Elluvian. If they knew, it would cement their refusal."

"Because Elluvian already has too much power in the Halls of Law?"

"Exactly."

"Will the Tha'alani be allowed to examine the surviving witness?"

"Probably, if it looks like the information is necessary. But he hasn't been charged with any crime, and lying on the witness stand isn't generally considered good enough cause to call in the mindreaders. Your best chance—unless you can somehow manipulate the Tha'alani—is to draw up a list of questions you want the witness to answer. The Hawks will probably take charge of asking those questions, but the answers will be contained in Records."

Severn nodded, and then, catching himself, said, "Thanks." Rosen couldn't see the nod.

When Elluvian entered his office through the open door, Severn was instantly aware of him. He paused Records and turned slightly to face the Barrani Wolf. Elluvian's eyes were blue, which was normal; they were a very, very dark blue, which was not.

He rose as Elluvian reached the desk and dumped what appeared to be a pile of cloth on its otherwise pristine surface. "Wear this."

Severn looked down at the pile. After a moment he lifted it. It wasn't a shirt, pants, or a jacket.

"It's a tabard. It's an official tabard worn by men and women who serve the Halls of Law."

"Where are we going?" Severn asked. He noted that Elluvian wasn't wearing a tabard.

"We are returning to the High Halls," was the curt reply. Elluvian glanced at the mirror, which reflected nothing in the room. "Records," he said, "Dogan Sapson."

The Records replay stuttered.

"Elluvian Danarre."

The mirror failed to return the information Elluvian had asked for. The two words were either not enough of a description or Elluvian didn't have the permissions required. That was Severn's understanding of how Records worked, as explained by Rosen.

Elluvian's lips thinned.

"Morgue. Jenson."

This, unlike the living witness, was apparently not forbidden Elluvian. The morgue report, Severn had already read. He therefore watched Elluvian. No hint of surprise marred his expression, but his eyes remained a blue that could be mistaken for black in different light.

"Rosen mentioned practical magic instructions?"

Severn nodded.

"I am not your teacher. I will, however, begin to apprise you of the facts you would otherwise have were it not for the current situation. You are aware that this man drowned."

"Yes."

"His lungs were apparently full of water. He was in the middle of the street, with a Barrani escort. Even the tabards of the Halls of Law do not diminish the fear in which some Barrani are held. Fear," he added, "is a useful tool to my kin. There were no people within weapon range. Magic, however, does not always require exact proximity.

"In this case, water was used as the murder weapon. Fire could be used in a similar fashion, but it would be obvious the minute it started. Fire is not invisible."

Severn didn't point out that water wasn't either. "Could you do this?"

Elluvian didn't blink. "I could kill, yes—but using magic to do the job of a simple dagger is wasteful."

"Could you drown him while he was walking down the street?"

"Yes."

"Would the guards have noticed?"

"Absolutely. Nothing I do would be invisible."

"How would you have done it, if you wanted to drown him?"

"I would have pushed him into the Ablayne and kept him underwater. But that is not the question you are asking, and he was not near the Ablayne at the time. How much have you heard about elementals?"

Severn said nothing.

"Very well. You have heard, almost certainly, stories about sorcerers and mages who command the use of fire?"

"Yes."

"That fire, in reality, has a voice and will of its own in most cases."

"Most?"

Elluvian grimaced. "Some cases. If a mage has burned a city to the ground, it is almost certainly by commanding an elemental—a fire elemental—that he has summoned for that purpose. Ah, no. It is almost certainly because he attempted to summon a fire he could not control. The fire itself contains the power of fire; the mage's power is bent on control."

Severn nodded.

"Water, air, and earth can also be summoned. They are less malleable than fire. Were I to drown a man in the middle of the street, there would be no question of how it was done;

there would be a water elemental surrounding the victim until the victim was dead."

During this explanation, Severn had donned the tabard. He looked down at it.

"We can continue this; we will be walking to the High Halls."

"No carriage?"

"No. Walking will take longer."

If Severn wondered why he had been asked to wear the tabard, he chose not to question Elluvian's decision. Rosen, however, did. Her initial comment when Severn emerged from Elluvian's office was derisive. The derision was discarded entirely when Severn said they were going to the Barrani High Halls.

"You are taking Private Handred to the High Halls wearing *that*?"

"I am."

"Have you cleared this with Helmat?"

"I would, but alas, he is in a meeting with Lord Grammayre and cannot be interrupted."

"Records," Rosen snapped.

Elluvian's eyes lightened slightly. They were still blue, and his expression suited the color. "Rosen."

As the mirror flared to life, she faced him, rising from her chair. She was angry; her hands, braced across the top of her desk and stray bits of paper, were trembling. "Why? You might as well paint a target—"

"If it will comfort you, I will don the tabard myself."

This silenced Rosen.

"But I have been *summoned* to the High Halls, and I wish the summoner to understand that Severn Handred is a Wolf. He is not a servant; he cannot be bartered for or traded; he cannot be commanded by those who have the authority to command *me*.

"If not for Helmat's orders, I would not have brought him to the High Halls the first time. It did not work out well for Darrell. As a Wolf, Severn is clearly a statement: no harm done to him will be dismissed or hidden by the laws of exemption. His very duties demand the opposite.

"I do not think it will damage him to be presented thus. It might damage me, but only peripherally; anyone of import understands quite well what I do." There was a tinge of bitterness in the words. "I am called the Emperor's Dog by people who believe they will suffer no consequences. To take a mortal to the High Halls is, for most, proof of that assertion."

"Helmat won't like it," Rosen said. Her hands, however, had relaxed. "And Mellianne will attempt to kill you if you lose another Wolf—another new Wolf—to Barrani." She spoke without humor. Without anger. The flat words, unadorned by either, were a statement of fact.

Severn believed them.

"Private Handred is not Darrell."

Rosen sat down. "No. Get out of here before I change my mind."

The walk to the High Halls started in a silence underscored by the noise of the city streets. It was broken by Elluvian.

"The death was a drowning death. This could be achieved by elemental, but the summoning would have to be absolutely precise to escape the notice of the Barrani Hawks."

"Would the killer have to see his victim?"

"Yes. Not only would he have to see his victim, but he would have to summon the elemental at a safe distance, and the elemental would be summoned within the victim, not outside of him."

"A small elemental couldn't achieve this from the outside?"

"Not without being instantly noticed, no. An elemental of that size takes a negligible amount of power to summon, and a negligible amount of power to control. To summon one inside of a man's lungs takes knowledge of anatomy and a precision that would require decades to achieve. It is not commonly done."

"Are you aware of cases where it has been?"

"No. None. There is far, far too much that could go wrong. It was a bold, calculated risk."

"Were either Teela or Tain injured in their attempt to protect the witness?"

"I have not seen their report. Mascot injuries, however, were avoided entirely."

Severn said nothing. Ybelline, he thought, would never take the knowledge she had seen on the inside of his head and use it against him in any way. She wouldn't know, and wouldn't want to know, any more about Elianne than Severn himself knew.

Elluvian was not Ybelline. He was Barrani. Trust, in as much as Severn felt any, was a matter of power: Severn had none. Trust was irrelevant. Trusting, not trusting, were his risks to take. But he did not want Elluvian to know any more about Elianne than he already did.

The information was welcome, regardless. Severn, however much he wanted to ask questions, had the answer to the most important one: she was unhurt. He now changed the subject. "How long has Mellianne been a Wolf?"

"Just under two years."

"Has she been this angry for all of them?"

"No, as you must suspect. I am not, however, the person to ask. If you wish to know why Mellianne is angry, Mellianne herself is the most relevant source. She will answer your questions. She will not paint me in the most flattering of lights, however."

"And this isn't a concern for you."

Elluvian was silent for half a city block. "It is a concern for the Wolves. If by concern you mean, am I worried for my personal safety, then no, as you suspect, it is not a concern. It is very, very seldom that a Wolf has been foolish enough to attack me."

"But not Helmat."

"It has happened infrequently with Helmat, but yes. The Wolves are, in some fashion, permitted to—groomed to—kill. The killings are not legally considered murders, as I'm sure Helmat made adequately clear."

Severn nodded.

"When people's lives and livelihood depend on their ability to kill, killing becomes part of the fabric of their daily life. Death becomes a tool—a necessary tool—but a tool, nonetheless. I am not part of the hierarchy of the Wolves, although I am considered a Wolf. I have been considered a Wolf since the Wolves were founded."

"Why you?"

"I have asked that question a hundred times—enough, certainly, to become bored with it."

"You found Mellianne."

"Yes. As I found you."

"You found Darrell."

"Yes. Darrell would have been a Wolf for almost the same length of time as Mellianne, had he survived."

"How did he die?"

"He died in the High Halls."

"And the laws of exemption?"

"The decision was not mine."

This surprised Severn. "Not yours? Would you have invoked the Emperor's Law in the High Halls?"

"I think I would have found it amusing, had I survived the attempt—that was not guaranteed. My death, however, was not guaranteed either. The decision was the Emperor's to make: the Wolves are his."

"How did he die?"

"He allowed himself to be goaded into discourteous action by a Lord of the High Court. There was not enough of him left to bury decently."

This, Severn had not heard. "Magic?"

Elluvian nodded. His eyes had been dark blue all morning, and their color didn't change. "Had Mellianne been the attendant Wolf, she would have survived."

"She'd survive magic?"

"She would not have been goaded into suicide. Darrell was talented. He was, on the surface, far more talented than Mellianne. More than Rosen or even Jaren. Helmat was his equal in the early years of his training. This talent at mastering basic lessons quickly seems to impress your kind; it does not impress ours as readily."

"Why?"

"Because it is not the speed of absorption that defines success for my kin. If one cannot survive, talent and promise are utterly irrelevant. He was good, yes—but far too impressed with his own talent. I did not see that clearly when I brought him in. The Wolves were not as impressed with his talent as he was, but it was close."

"But they blame you."

"He was my attendant at the time—as you will be today. For no other reason would he be allowed into the High Halls. His death was seen as my failure."

Severn's face did not take up the frown it might have had he been with Ybelline. "Was it seen as a failure by you?"

"You are perceptive, Private. It was my failure—but not in

the way Mellianne believes it was. I am Barrani. I am, to her eyes, old. She understands some larger measure of my power than you do, and while she has access to Records, she has spent little time with the Barrani."

"She thinks you could have saved him."

"Yes."

"The Wolflord doesn't."

"No. But Helmat is decades older; he has seen far more. In as much as he is willing to trust anyone, he trusts me—but it is a trust born of necessity. He was not happy, of course. But he did not fault me in the way Mellianne does."

"You wanted to leave the office before he arrived."

"Yes."

"Because you didn't want him to see the tabard."

"Indeed."

"The tabard," Severn continued, after a pause in which he gathered words. "It's not for Corvallan or Cassandre or any of the Barrani we might meet in the gallery. It's for An'Tellarus."

Elluvian's eyes lightened slightly as he glanced at Severn. "An'Tellarus is not part of our investigation, and Cassandre has agreed to entertain us. It is the reason we now return to the High Halls."

"It was the reason we went there the first time, as well. You seemed more concerned with An'Tellarus than with the two Lords who could well help us find the person responsible for the Tha'alani murders." When Elluvian failed to reply, Severn said, "It's An'Tellarus you're worried about. It's An'Tellarus to whom you wish to make a point."

Elluvian surrendered, then. "It is indeed. We will need to walk very, very carefully in the presence of An'Tellarus. The oracle made that clear."

CHAPTER TWENTY-ONE

ELLUVIAN HAD LIED. THIS BECAME OBVIOUS when Severn entered the High Halls and made his way to the rooms that Lords Corvallan and Cassandre occupied. The long row of burnished guards were not in the final hallway; the guards that were there numbered four, and they wore far less ostentatious armor. To a man, their eyes darkened until they matched the shade of Elluvian's. None, however, left their post.

This probably meant that guards or pages—he thought the latter word applied, but wasn't certain—were not the sole source of information about possible intruders to either lord. Severn had little doubt that Cassandre at least was aware of their approach.

He said nothing. The tabard he wore drew the eye, but not in a way that implied attention was a prelude to death; that attention was fixed firmly upon Elluvian.

Only when they reached the doors did the guards closest to them raise weapons; the gesture was clearly ceremonial. "You have no appointment and no permission to enter the chambers of our lord."

Lord, not lords.

Elluvian made no reply. He didn't touch the doors or take another step toward them, and Severn walked one step behind. Elluvian simply waited.

The guards were not Rosen; they had done their duty. They had stopped him from touching the doors. But they didn't attempt to remove him or drive him back, nor did they attempt to speak for their lord in any other way.

Severn didn't know how long they waited; time always passed more slowly when one was aware of it. He'd taken the posture of servant, and the tabard seemed to grant him an invisibility that Elluvian's fancier clothing had not. He didn't touch his weapons. He didn't raise his voice. He studied the tops of his boots while he waited. Elluvian would decide when enough time had passed. Elluvian or Lord Cassandre.

It was Lord Cassandre who blinked in this figurative staring contest; the doors rolled open. She stood between them looking every inch the militant her guards had not.

"Elluvian," she said, smiling. "I am gratified to see you again so soon after your last visit." Everything about her expression all but sparkled—except for her eyes, which were indigo. That color didn't lessen when she extended a smile to Severn. "And you have brought your cub."

Honey was decidedly poisonous here. Severn, however, offered her a very low bow. It was almost the equal of Elluvian's.

"I was not expecting you," she said, "and my lord is away. I hope he will return before you must leave. Please, come in."

The guards that had halted Elluvian's passage to the door now stepped back, their movements graceful. Their weapons were once again put aside, although their eye color matched that of their lord.

★ ★ ★

Lord Cassandre led them to a different room—a smaller room that was, to Severn's eye, no less expensively furnished. A desk stood in the corner to the left of the door; shelves, glassed, lined the walls that did not possess windows. The windows, however, were the center point of the room; they had been built to occupy the entirety of the wall that faced the door. Through them, Severn could see a garden, in which a fountain was perfectly framed.

"We have done as you asked." The moment the doors closed, Cassandre's face lost its bright, welcoming smile. Her eyes lost none of their indigo.

Elluvian nodded.

"You will not, I'm afraid, find Teremaine to question. We have been unable to ascertain his whereabouts ourselves."

"As of when?"

"As of your last visit."

Elluvian nodded. "I am aware that Teremaine is neither Casarre nor Mellarionne. He is an associate—perhaps not even that. His location is no longer your concern. The information we hoped we might receive from your lord has been superseded."

Cassandre indicated chairs and took one herself. She then offered Elluvian a nod better suited to a monarch than a host. "I see. You will forgive me for asking the purpose of your visit in that case."

"I would forgive you almost anything you asked," Elluvian replied. These words were less stilted, his posture less perfect; he had leaned slightly toward Cassandre as her expression receded into distance.

"Almost anything?"

"Almost. We are a people to whom contingencies are as necessary—and natural—as breath."

"It was not always thus between us."

"No. I regret the changes that time and circumstance have wrought."

She stared at him as if she couldn't quite make herself believe his words, which was fair; Severn didn't.

"What would you have me say? Your regrets are pretty, but they are the consequence of your choices. As," she added softly, "are mine." She bowed her head, just as Elluvian had done. When she lifted it, her expression was harder and colder. It said much about the Barrani that that harshness seemed to feel more open, more honest.

"Teremaine has served many lords when it was convenient for the lords in question; he has many connections in the mortal world and few of relevance at court."

Elluvian nodded.

"He has been of service to Sennarin in the past—but that service was offered and accepted by the previous An'Sennarin and his heir. To our knowledge, he has never served the current An'Sennarin."

Elluvian frowned.

"An'Sennarin does not seem to care for him; nor does he seem to have much use for Teremaine's various associates." Cassandre's frown hardened. "An'Sennarin came to power a handful of mortal years ago."

"So I've heard."

"It was an astonishing ascent for one so young and so new to court."

"Yes. And you believe he had no help in this from Teremaine or his peers?"

"They were the ruler's associates, not his. One would almost say that his ascent appears miraculous from the outside;

Teremaine was firmly in the pocket of the previous lord and his daughter."

"Both of whom perished."

"As you say."

"Was An'Sennarin ever considered for the Arcanum?"

"We were not part of An'Sennarin's close circle. Certainly the previous heir was; she was part of the Arcanum, with all of the rivalries that implies."

"How did they die?"

Cassandre was silent for a longer stretch, as if considering the danger of offering Elluvian any information. It was, however, information he was likely to find with little effort. Apparently, she thought so too. "Water," she said. "They both drowned."

"A boating accident."

"No. They were found, drowned, in their quarters. The current An'Sennarin was present, as were their guards and a few cousins at An'Sennarin's level of significance." The tone implied that level was next to none.

Severn studied his boots.

"When did these deaths occur?"

"I am uncertain of exact dates; I was not present and the information came only after An'Sennarin was confirmed ruler. Were you not present for that?"

"I was not, as you must be aware. The politics of the court were ever the bane of my existence, and his confirmation as relevant as any other."

Her brows rose, her expression softening slightly. "And my lord?"

"Lord Corvallan was of interest to us only because of his closer association with Teremaine."

"It is not a close association that he has personally cultivated. Teremaine has done work for Mellarionne in the past, and the work has never risen to the attention of the Emperor."

"Until now."

"Until now."

"Where is Lord Corvallan?"

"He speaks with An'Mellarionne," was her cool reply, "having finally received the audience he has waited for far too long."

Cassandre did not care for An'Mellarionne, Severn thought. Then again, it was likely she cared for no Barrani, possibly not even the husband to whom her fate was tied by marriage. "But I suppose we must thank you."

Elluvian stiffened.

"Were it not for your first visit, I doubt that the meeting would have yet taken place." There was no hint of gratitude in her tone.

"We are who we are, Cassandre. We must take advantage of even the most unpleasant of condescensions, where it is possible to do so."

For one moment, her eyes lightened, although their color remained martial. So, too, Elluvian's. "That was ever your skill, your art. Very well. In my considered opinion, Teremaine is unlikely to survive your inquiries."

Elluvian nodded, as if Teremaine were now irrelevant.

"Even were An'Sennarin not to hear about your inquiries, it is highly likely that they would come to nothing. An'Mellarionne has endeavors I'm certain he would wish to protect. Nothing Teremaine says, of course, would implicate An'Mellarionne directly; there is a reason that Teremaine has long been considered a reliable associate.

"But none of our kin can be reliable forever; all it takes is one small slip. Lord Corvallan will, of course, obliquely discuss the difficulty; I am uncertain that the information would reach An'Mellarionne so quickly, otherwise."

"I am not, for reasons that cannot be divulged."

"Why, then, are you here? It has been a very trying few days, and I ask you not to lay further burdens at our feet, perhaps in remembrance of what we once shared in the distant past."

"Corvallan is not implicated in any of this," Elluvian replied. "Nor will he be."

Her gaze fell on Severn and remained there.

"It is a caste court matter," Severn said quietly. "And the caste court is no province of the Wolves; the caste court exemptions are written into the laws we have sworn our lives to uphold."

Her smile was less practiced as she offered it to Severn. Of course it was. Severn was a mortal youth who could not, in her estimation, harm her at all. Only his placement as one of the Emperor's Wolves could cause complications, but those complications were not of grave concern. Elluvian, however, was.

"You must take care to keep yourself both safe and alive while you are here," she said, her tone almost fond. "It is the only way to ensure that the caste court exemptions are irreproachable."

Severn nodded. In spite of himself, he liked her, liked the sound of her voice, liked the cool smile and the color of her eyes. She was, as all Barrani were, beautiful.

Beauty, however, was a tool like any other in the hands of the Barrani. He wondered, briefly, how they saw themselves.

"I have prepared some information," she said. "Which I will deliver to you when you feel it is time to leave." Another smile, this for Elluvian, touched her lips; it was not, in any way, kind or warm. "And I believe that you will be departing soon; you are to meet An'Tellarus in less than an hour."

Elluvian's sigh was theatrical; his smile was warmer than Cassandre's. "You were always the best among us," he said. Severn thought he meant it. "And your ability to charm even the snakes, stopping them a moment in their path, has not diminished in the slightest."

"Ah, but it has, Elluvian. In days past, those snakes that stopped died instantly without causing harm. If it will be of any comfort—and I know it will not, but feel obliged anyway—An'Tellarus does not bear you any ill will."

"At present. Her moods are capricious, and her wrath unpredictable."

"It is why she has always been feared. Even those who are dedicated to our fall are less dangerous because they are focused and predictable. I am curious to know what you have done to merit this much of her attention this time."

"And perhaps she will tell you. She has certainly not scrupled to inform me."

Cassandre's laugh was like a plant blooming in the dead of winter. It was out of place, and more beautiful because of it.

Severn did not speak a word as they once again traversed the publicly accessible galleries that occupied much of the interior of the High Halls. He walked a step behind Elluvian, as if he were still servant. Elluvian allowed this because he had no wish to break the silence himself, but he was chagrined. As a young man in that tabard, he was not subservient; his entire life was not supposed to be about the whims of an entirely theoretical master.

As a servant, as an attendant, his position and posture were acceptable; even among the Barrani, proper forms could not always be elegantly followed or aped in an instant. But the boy was a Wolf. The tabard implied an equality before the law that subservience of this nature subtly belied. When subservience was automatically offered where it was not due, it implied hesitance or fear. Had he not been human, it would mark the boy as a target—or more of a target than his presence at Elluvian's side already did. He made a mental note to speak of this later, when the High Halls no longer enclosed or eavesdropped on any possible conversation.

An'Tellarus's chambers had not, of course, moved, but the objects that now adorned the alcoves that led to her doors had been changed in the scant days between their previous meeting and this one. Severn, having been given oblique permission to consider and study the things she had replaced them with, moved more slowly as he did.

One was an ornate book with a cover of gold and platinum; it looked armored and unapproachable. Severn nevertheless approached it, his brows furrowing in concern or confusion. As well they might: the title of this book was a single word, and it would have been risible to a Barrani youth, even one of Severn's age. *Honor.*

Elluvian was not surprised to see the next book; it was similarly adorned, and possessed, along with an excess of precious metal, an obvious lock, such as one might put on a child's diary, if a child were of a mind to ape mortals. Above that lock was the High Barrani word, *Duty.*

The third book was not adorned in the manner of the first two; it looked drab and well-read in comparison. It, too, possessed a single word at the center of a cover that was worn at the corners.

"Ancestry?" Severn asked, as if this word, of the three, was the only one about which he was uncertain.

"Yes. The letter style is highly antiquated—it's as if the ancients decided that reading was far too simple an activity and wished to add severe challenge by forming the words in incompetent calligraphy."

"It does not look incompetent to me," Severn said, which was a second surprise. "It looks like art."

"Which would be acceptable if it was. It is, however, printed language, the point of which should be to enlighten or educate."

"Pay no mind to him, Severn," a familiar—and disembodied—voice said. "It is, indeed, artistry. Form is not always dictated by function except in the minds of the small."

"An'Tellarus," Elluvian said. He did not bother to bow or otherwise indicate the respect a superior was due; she was not present.

She ignored him. Were it not for her correction, he might have been invisible. "You have seen that book before," she continued.

Severn said, "I'm not certain it's the same."

"Nor should you be. I believe it to be the same, but we have never occupied the same room prior to your first visit. Do you understand why it is there?"

"No. But I don't understand why the other two are there, either."

"You understand their titles."

He nodded.

"Both books are old—older than the one that looks most worn. And as my kin oft do with precious things, they are armored as well as they can be against the passage of time and the fingers of the careless. If you could take only one of the books, which would you choose?"

"I would take none of them. The first two, as you have said, are precious to you. The third, while it may not be precious, is relevant to you. We share no ancestry, and collections of names would mean little to me." He spoke quietly, but without apparent fear.

"Perhaps they would mean much to you in the future."

Severn said nothing this time. When An'Tellarus failed to ask another of her hectoring, testing questions, he once again resumed his approach to her closed doors, Elluvian by his side.

Ah, he thought. Severn walked beside him, not behind.

Books were not the only items on display, although it had been to the books Severn had first been drawn. In the other alcoves were weapons, housed in glass cases, and two statues.

The statues might have been entirely decorative in purpose, like many similar statues the galleries contained, but they had not been present on their last visit, and Severn gave them as much of his attention as the weapons—swords, all. One was a man, and one a woman.

It was not the genders that distinguished them, however. Nor was it the oddly stylized armor the man wore. It was his humanity; he was mortal and human, just as Severn was. The woman was Barrani, her stone expression proud and cold as she gazed across the hall to meet the stone gaze of the man.

Elluvian closed his eyes. He should not have come. He did not know where An'Tellarus had found these statues—into what basement or cellar or dusty room of useless relics she had descended. Nor did he care. He was, he realized, angry.

Severn seemed to be staring at the mortal man rendered in stone. The stone was not in perfect repair; it bore small cracks, and in one or two places along the seams of its cloak, small chips. Artifacts aged, just as mortals did. Or mountains. Or oceans.

"Who was he?" Severn asked.

"He was—"

"*Enough,*" Elluvian snapped.

"These halls are mine, not yours. You have no halls or home of your own that any of our kin would care to claim. When you do, you may issue *commands*, Elluvian, and those commands will not be considered irrelevant. You are, however, a guest and your manners remain, as ever, appalling. Continue, and I will invite Severn in alone while you wait for him in the Halls. Ah, no, boy. Do not touch that—it is extremely delicate."

Elluvian said nothing, but it was difficult. An'Tellarus was one of the few living beings who could cause these lapses in self-control. He almost turned heel and walked away; he was certain that Severn would follow, avoiding the game she seemed to be playing.

But he had seen the results of the oracle.

The doors, untended, rolled open. An'Tellarus was nowhere in sight; nor were any of the many servants who obeyed her commands so deftly. No guards, no servants; the chambers might have been unoccupied were it not for the visible change of decor in the outer hall.

The statue, however, had been so unexpected that Elluvian struggled to regain his balance. Severn had no need to struggle. The High Halls, replete with Barrani craftsmanship and enchantments, were unfamiliar to Severn, and the oddities in An'Tellarus's hall were of a piece with the rest of it. He understood that the statue was significant because of Elluvian's intemperate reaction. Had Elluvian maintained his stony silence, it would be just another adornment.

Or perhaps not. Severn was perceptive, and even Severn might be surprised to see a human of any type given pride of place in such displays. Regardless, he had turned away from it the moment the doors had begun their slow movement, and he joined Elluvian as they opened.

"Please, come in," the disembodied and despised voice said. Elluvian did not cross the threshold. He closed his eyes, concentrated, and opened them again. The weave of enchantment that became visible with modest effort subtly changed the color of the foyer, but no other obvious sign of magical danger leaped out at him. The enchantment that lay across the doors protected them from magical intrusion and possibly fire; the floors themselves, except for a single, marble square, were otherwise as they appeared.

The walls to either side of the door contained windows—but each window opened into an entirely different landscape.

"You are my guests," An'Tellarus said, her voice implying fraying temper. "If I wished to cause you harm, you would not be."

Severn glanced at Elluvian. Elluvian's jaw locked in place; he finished his inspection. Only when it was done did he move forward, deftly avoiding the one square across the floor whose enchantment he could not easily place. Severn followed, noting the placement of Elluvian's feet. He chose, in silence and without instructions, to follow Elluvian's path almost exactly.

Their progress, interrupted by An'Tellarus's mocking—or annoyed—words continued in such a fashion until they at last reached a set of doors that were not as ostentatious as the doors that allowed them entry to her chambers, but were nonetheless clearly doors that fronted rooms appropriate for dealing with dignitaries of note. They were very different from the doors that had led to the crammed, dingy room a mortal might have called home.

Severn glanced at Elluvian; the doors remained closed.

"They are warded," Elluvian said, when the boy failed to move. "I will open them."

"Allow the young man to do his duty," An'Tellarus said.

"His duty, An'Tellarus, is defined by neither you nor me; he is a Wolf, not a page or a footman." Ah, he had done it again. He wanted to turn on heel and march out of the rooms over which An'Tellarus was master. He should never have responded in any way to her summons. But a lack of response often caused interference in any of the other activities that demanded his presence within the High Halls.

It was not Elluvian, in the end, who would pay the price.

Severn waited while Elluvian considered her words and his own.

"Everything she does is a test of one kind or another. You have seen her casual tests. Had you failed you would either be injured or dead. She has had time to prepare something more deliberate and less casual. Caution is not only advised, but necessary."

Severn, however, bowed to the closed doors. "An'Tellarus," he said, as if she were his master. He held that bow.

Elluvian did not raise a hand to touch the doors. Every word he had spoken, he believed. An'Tellarus had no interest in those who failed. The mode of failure, the result of failure, were therefore irrelevant. Elluvian had come to understand that inherent in failure was information, some lesson to prevent that failure in the future. Survival, however, was necessary.

She did not generally play her games with mortals; they were too fragile and they were not Barrani; harm done to them, should they survive, removed all of her playful hostility from beneath the umbrella of the laws of exemption. Her interest in Severn was highly unusual, and it presented a risk she did not normally choose to take.

But it was the room into which she had eventually led Severn on their first visit that disturbed Elluvian; the contents implied—strongly—that she had some prior knowledge of the boy, a child who had grown up anonymously in the fief of Nightshade.

A child, he thought, who had been both friend and protector to the new Chosen. Fate's hand here was not subtle; it was ugly and poorly understood, at least by Elluvian. Woe unto any who chose to enter An'Tellarus's arena in ignorance.

Severn did not rise.

An'Tellarus did not bid him rise.

Minutes passed. Despite his misgivings, Elluvian was almost impressed. He thought Severn would hold that bow, as if it were one half of a staring contest, until An'Tellarus bade him rise. Or until these doors, as the first, rolled open. Elluvian raised a hand. An'Tellarus had time to play these games; Severn did not.

Before he could touch the surface of the door, however, the doors began to roll open. He was almost shocked.

Standing in the center of a large oval room was An'Tellarus herself.

Severn rose when the doors began to move. Not for the first time, Elluvian wished that human eyes shifted color; no part of the boy's expression gave any hint of what he might be thinking or feeling, and absent the shift in eye color that denoted emotional response in any other sentient race, it was difficult to judge his state of mind. If he was afraid of An'Tellarus, it did not show. His posture was perfect, his hands steady, his expression shorn of any ticks that might have implied fear.

Her eyes were blue, but there seemed to be a distinct shade of purple in the mix of colors, and purple was rare for his kin—especially those who had survived to reach her age.

"Come," she said. "This room is unlike the last room in which we met. It is entirely a Barrani room, but it is one not much used in these modern times."

He nodded and walked the length of the room until he reached her. No hesitation marred his approach.

To Elluvian's surprise, she offered him her right hand in a gesture he didn't immediately recognize. Severn, however, didn't have that problem. He took her right hand in his.

It was a human gesture, a mortal greeting, a *handshake*.

Elluvian wondered if all of this was somehow another test of Elluvian; if Severn himself was ancillary. If it was, he had come close to failing in that moment. But he thought it was not; An'Tellarus's focus was entirely absorbed in the newest Imperial Wolf. If she had noticed his tabard at all—and she must have—she paid it no attention. No derision, no suspicion, no mockery, shifted her expression. He might not have been wearing it at all.

"Have you spent time with Imperial Mages?" she asked.

Elluvian frowned.

"No."

"Ah. Well, you will. I wish you to examine a few objects." Severn nodded.

"What are the purpose of these objects?" Elluvian asked.

An'Tellarus did not choose to hear him.

The oval room was large, the center portion recessed. Two long couches faced each other across a table that was the shape of the room itself, shrunk down to accommodate the smaller space. At the midpoint of walls, alcoves were adorned with plants. None of those plants now grew within the confines of the city itself, although they could be found within the environs in which the High Seat was placed. Gardeners tended those, of course.

The only gardener here was An'Tellarus. Elluvian frowned. As Severn moved toward the couches and the table between them, Elluvian looked at the chairs themselves. They appeared to be rooted in the wood of the floor, vines that had entangled themselves to create a place where people might be seated in comfort.

Chairs such as these were never found in the High Halls.

He examined the chairs more carefully.

"Elluvian, is that necessary?"

The examination itself was his response. The chairs were not illusory; they were as they appeared. They were growing, had been grown, in this room. He sat heavily and gracelessly. The chair shifted beneath his weight, and as he closed his eyes, he heard the distant song of the Western reach.

He almost rose, then, to take Severn out of this room, out of this suite, and out of the High Halls. But Severn was unruffled, almost unconcerned. Any warning Elluvian cared to offer would be considered and, in Elluvian's opinion, ignored.

She led Severn to the couch opposite Elluvian's. As Elluvian had, he noticed the unusual construction, but his knowledge of the Barrani did not immediately place the creation of the chairs; he saw nothing political in them. At her nod, he seated himself.

When he did, his brows rose. Surprise, not alarm, and had Elluvian not been watching him so carefully, he would have missed it.

"What do you hear?" An'Tellarus asked, her voice soft.

"Music. It's faint. When I speak, I lose the thread of it."

"Do you recognize the song?"

Silence. Elluvian had spent enough time observing the young Wolf that he knew the answer was *yes*. That was disturbing, but not unexpected given their last visit.

"Where have you heard it before?" she asked, an indication that her observation was, given their time together, more acute. "It is almost an anthem of my people—but not those who call Elantra home."

Silence as well. This silence was less pleasant to An'Tellarus, and therefore more pleasant to Elluvian.

"I don't remember," Severn finally said. "But it's familiar."

The annoyance faded from An'Tellarus's expression. "Very well. There is no harm in it for any of us." She gestured as if pulling back an unseen curtain, and the surface of the table was no longer empty.

Severn's gaze alighted on the objects she had gathered for his perusal. A faint smile changed the contours of his mouth: recognition. Familiarity.

An'Tellarus was still as the stone out of which the two statues had been carved. Severn did not notice. Instead, he reached out and picked up a child's toy—a spinning top that would only be of value to the very young among the Barrani, and at that, only those who were raised outside of the confines of the High Court.

As Elluvian had been.

He said nothing; there was no harm in it, or none that would result in physical injury. But he knew what the toy was meant to test. And he knew that Severn did not see it as a test. Had not seen it as a test when he had first encountered it. Elluvian watched just as closely as An'Tellarus.

The very young could be frustrated by it; their attempts to get the top to spin absorbed the whole of their attention. In some fashion, it absorbed the attention of the adults as well; there were always adults present. The toy itself gave the first early indicators of magic affinity, of magic potential—if it could be properly used.

Severn's smile grew lopsided as he removed himself from the couch, found a patch of gleaming wood, and set the top down. "It took me a while to get the hang of this," he said, the words the first Elantran he'd spoken in An'Tellarus's hearing.

The top itself began to spin.

CHAPTER TWENTY-TWO

ELLUVIAN AND AN'TELLARUS KNEW HOW TO watch its progress. They knew what to look for. They understood the significance of the toy itself.

Whoever had allowed Severn to play with it in a childhood that was mostly beyond the reach of his mortal memories had clearly not chosen to explain its purpose.

"Who taught you how to use it?"

"I did." He replied in Barrani this time, the language in which the question had been asked.

The top continued to spin; what was remarkable to Elluvian was the length it traveled while spinning. It would slow and topple eventually. How eventually offered information to those who sought to test. This was not the only test, however. It was merely the earliest and the simplest.

Elluvian said nothing. Imperial Mages had their own tests, their own ways of ascertaining possible magical potential, but those tests had been designed for mortals. As if those tests could not be used by anyone—just as this "toy." The potential it registered was not dependent on race, although Leontines were an exception; in the experience of academics and arcan-ists, the race almost defied magic, and its future use.

Severn, as a member of the Halls of Law, would be ex-posed to the tests, formal and procedural, invented by Imperial Mages. The information gained by An'Tellarus would soon be gained by those who came to the Halls of Law to teach.

"Do you recognize the other objects on the table?" An'Tellarus's voice was soft, almost gentle.

Severn left the top spinning and returned to the table. "No. If I have touched these, or objects similar, I do not remem-ber doing so."

An'Tellarus nodded. She gestured again, and this time an ordinary quill replaced the objects on the table. "And this?"

Severn frowned. "It's a quill."

"It is perhaps a quill you might once have used. You were taught to read and speak our language—and you speak it well. I am uncertain if you were likewise called upon to write it."

An expression flickered across the boy's face. "It's difficult to learn to read and speak without also learning to write—or so I was told."

An'Tellarus laughed, the sound low and warm. "Many times, from the look on your face. I also believe it to be true."

"Most of the people I met in the fiefs could speak without learning either."

"They could speak Barrani?"

"The important words."

An'Tellarus did not ask what *important* meant; nor did El-luvian.

Severn lifted the quill and frowned. There was no paper, and no ink, to accompany it.

"Ah, I forget myself."

Severn looked up, quill in hand. His skeptical look caused

her to laugh again, as if Severn was in truth a child—and moreover a precocious child that she held in affection.

"Yes," she said, although he had not spoken. "I forget very little. Ink and paper are there."

Severn nodded, although neither appeared. His brows drew together, the neutrality of his expression lost to focused concentration. So, too, An'Tellarus. Elluvian was not happy. Even so, he waited in silence. He could not see what was hidden, and after a few seconds had passed, he looked.

She had lied. Severn could clearly see the ink and paper, but they were illusory; they did not exist.

Severn, quill in hand, began to write. He had no ink, no safe surface on which to do so; his quill skittered across the gleaming tabletop as An'Tellarus leaned forward, elbows lodged against her knees. It was a singularly graceless pose.

Across the surface of the pristine table, words began to appear; they followed the movement of quill. The quill made no sound; no one did, except Severn, who had not apparently forgotten how to breathe.

Elluvian recovered first. "The letter forms are shaky," he said, in a tone that implied poorly formed letters were just short of criminal.

Severn stopped as he examined the product of his effort. He nodded, focusing on the shapes of the very Barrani words he'd been writing.

An'Tellarus looked up, her eyes indigo, her lips a thin line. Elluvian gestured, the movement economical but necessary. "Whatever you desired to ascertain," he said, his voice even, his anger now firmly under control, "you have ascertained. Unless you have information that pertains to our investigation, we do not have the luxury of time."

Her glare lost the intensity that implied death was an immediate concern. Severn, however, had set the quill aside. He stood; he did not return to his chair. It seemed to Elluvian that the effort of writing had tired the boy. But no. He was looking at the words he'd written; he had not finished what he had started.

Nor would he, now.

"Very well. We have some time, but time is short." An'Tellarus rose, her expression shuttered, her eyes blue. "I wish you to resolve your current crisis as quickly as possible."

"That should be possible without irrelevant interruptions," Elluvian replied.

"None of these are irrelevant, except to the narrow-minded and the careless. They are certainly not irrelevant to Severn. Have you some need to question Teremaine?"

"Is he one of yours?"

"Please. I am already vexed with your interruptions; descend to insults and Private Handred will understand why you feel compelled to offer me a semblance of obedience. I have chosen not to take offense at your actions today because he is a Wolf, and he might feel it his duty to come to your aid."

"I am his partner," Severn said quietly. "But mortal Wolves die frequently. It is the loss of Elluvian himself that will cause complications for you; the Emperor favors him."

"I am certain the Emperor himself wonders why from time to time."

"It would then be the Emperor's prerogative to dismiss him. If you have information that might lead us to Teremaine— and lead us to an understanding of the motivations behind the events we investigate—we would be grateful."

She turned from Elluvian to Severn, her brows gathered as if the words themselves were familiar to her, and yet could not be placed.

Elluvian felt no need to explain to Severn that the word

gratitude had a different weight among the Barrani than it did among mortals, in part because he suspected that Severn already understood this.

"Very well. I shall offer you a warning. You believe that An'Sennarin has a use for, or has used, Teremaine in the past. In my considered opinion this is completely, irrevocably untrue. An'Sennarin's power at court is a far cry from the power his predecessor once wielded. Were it not, it is my belief Teremaine would already be beyond your reach.

"Teremaine will be beyond your reach soon. It is known that the Wolves hunt him now."

"It is not Teremaine we hunt," Elluvian said.

"That is unfortunate—for Teremaine. Regardless, Teremaine now has nothing to do with the line Sennarin. Nor will his unfortunate death have much to do with Sennarin; he is much involved with the mortals, their caste court, and the Lords of the High Court. He knows too much. He has been far too careful to use any of that knowledge against those to whom it might be costly. But where the Wolves are involved, where the Emperor is involved, the Tha'alani are also involved."

"They are forbidden, by Imperial Law, to interact with the Barrani in that fashion."

"Exceptions can be made at the discretion of the Emperor."

"The Emperor," Severn said, an edge in his voice that had not been present at any other time within the High Halls, "would make no exception in the case of this particular Barrani. Any information obtained should Teremaine be lawfully detained would be gathered without the Tha'alani. Even if the Imperial Service desired the expertise of the Tha'alani in this specific case, they would require a permission that would never be granted."

"You seem certain."

"I am certain."

"Very well. Elluvian has not disagreed with either of us; I
perceive that even he does not feel as you feel. Regardless, it
is not your opinion, or mine, that will be the deciding factor.
I am willing to accept what you say as truth. You will not
find another Barrani Lord who will do so. Teremaine's survival does not depend on my belief; he is not a man I would
entrust with any task, no matter how trivial.

"It will be dependent on the beliefs of those who have
condescended to purchase his services." She turned to Elluvian. "You have implied that An'Sennarin is at the heart of
this investigation. Consider what you now do with care, Elluvian. He is a Lord of the High Court." She bowed her head
for a moment, and then said, "And he has won my personal
support."

Elluvian said nothing to Severn until they were well quit of
the High Halls. Not just the building itself, but the grounds
upon which that building, and its few outbuildings, sat. He
did not speak a word until they were once again accosted by
the noise, the smell, and the overpopulation of the midday
market streets.

"I do not know what game she is playing," he said, as if the
walk to this point had interrupted nothing. "But it is never
wise to involve oneself in the games An'Tellarus controls."

"Does she control this one?"

Elluvian frowned. He was not certain what he had expected
Severn to say, but it wasn't this. An'Tellarus had the ability to
knock him slightly off balance in the best of circumstances.

"She controls some part of it."

"Do you think she's the hand behind An'Sennarin?"

After a pause to consider things from Severn's point of

view—a much narrower field of experience—Elluvian said, "It is not impossible, but...no. It *is* unusual."

"How?"

"Considering his meteoric rise to power, it is no surprise he has allies; the greater surprise would be that he has none. But it is not An'Tellarus's way to support people who are driven by ambition, or rather, that style of ambition."

"You've said she's powerful."

Elluvian nodded. "But so, too, An'Mellarionne, and she would never support him, although on the surface Mellarionne as a line offers far greater advantage to her than Sennarin. Sennarin is so new, the greater weight of the power of such an alliance would be almost entirely An'Tellarus. He has nothing to offer."

"You are certain?"

"I am. I have done some research, and he *is* of the High Court."

"When did he assume the rulership of his line?"

"I believe you already know the answer."

Severn shook his head. "I know that it was roughly around the time of the Tha'alani murders. Possibly just before—which has been my assumption—and possibly just after."

Elluvian frowned. "What are you suggesting?"

"An'Tellarus supports An'Sennarin. Or do you think she is lying?"

"She is almost certainly lying about something; you will find that common among interactions at court."

Severn nodded.

"Do you think she was telling the truth?"

He nodded again, almost without pause. "But I'm not certain why."

Elluvian's brows rose. "Of course you are not certain. It is difficult with An'Tellarus to be certain of anything. What do you think her reasons might be?"

Severn glanced at him and fell silent, as if considering the question—or perhaps considering the audience. Elluvian was not at all certain he would receive an answer, and his curiosity sharpened.

"She seems," the boy finally said, "to care for you."

"I cannot possibly have recruited anyone who lacks that much perception."

"I did not say that her affection or attention would be comfortable—but I think, in her own way, she does."

"She is interested in *you*," was Elluvian's bitter reply. "I am irrelevant."

Severn shrugged. "She's Barrani," he said in Elantran. "But I'd guess she's also interested in An'Sennarin. She either offered the information to warn us away from him—and an investigation we can't avoid—or to sharpen your interest in him."

"Pardon?"

"I think she was attempting to say—in Barrani fashion—that she actually likes him. She clearly doesn't care for Teremaine."

"Teremaine would, as she said, be irrelevant to her."

Severn nodded. "But he's irrelevant because she doesn't like him."

"Like has very, very little to do with Barrani politics or Barrani power."

"Maybe."

"Private—"

"She's a power. Teremaine isn't. Even if she did like him, there's probably very little he could do to harm her. She couldn't trust him."

"She doesn't trust anyone. That's the entire point." Elluvian had also descended into Elantran.

Severn frowned. "I think she avoids Teremaine *because* she doesn't trust him."

"No one who uses his services trusts him."

"Yes. For An'Tellarus, the lack of trust means she'll never hire him. It's too easy to open herself up to blackmail, among other things."

"You have failed to understand both the Barrani and An'Tellarus."

Severn shrugged. "Probably."

"And you now think, with this imperfect understanding, that An'Tellarus is attempting to warn us off because she's concerned for our safety? If true, that would be almost insulting."

"Or to warn us off because she's worried about his," Severn said.

"And this warning has now changed the shape of this case, for you?"

"I'm not certain. Are all of the Emperor's hunts going to be this tangled?"

"No. I can think of very few in the recent past—which would be the whole of your life should you die of old age—which have been nearly as complicated as this. Were it not for Ybelline, you would not have been the partner assigned to me, either. And the partner assigned to me would not make the mistake you are making."

Severn let this pass without comment. "Given her warning—regardless of the reasons behind it—what do you intend to do? She didn't give us Teremaine's location."

"I doubt she knows it."

Severn, clearly, did not.

"We're not here to execute Teremaine; the interest in his activities—no, *our* interest in his activities—has become his death sentence. It is how things are done. The Emperor very rarely takes an interest in the petty crimes of those Barrani associated with the lords. When he does, it serves one specific function. It rids his city of the petty criminal. It is its own Imperial writ of execution.

"Teremaine was present for at least one of the murders. If he did not lift a hand to cause injuries that led to deaths, he was the driving force behind them. Do you not feel that his death would be justice?"

Severn nodded. After a long pause, he said, "Where I come from, death is death. We were taught not to look for justice in anything but our own behavior, because we had control of that. In theory.

"If Teremaine won't lead to Sennarin, what's the point in pushing for more information from him?"

Elluvian shrugged. "There is always a point," he said in his native tongue. "It is never wise to allow your opponent to understand the whole of your thought or intent; if they do, it will be trivial for them to block you."

"She doesn't believe we care about Teremaine."

"She doesn't believe Teremaine is the true focus of our investigation, no. But she is not a fool. Teremaine is the murder weapon; he is not the murderer. What we want is the man or woman who chose to use him. She knows this. Everyone of note knows this. But Teremaine knows too much about too many."

"The Emperor's prohibition on using the Tha'alani—"

"They cannot believe that the Emperor's prohibition forbids the Emperor from taking advantage of the Tha'alani when it serves his own purpose. The truth, in this case, is irrelevant. As would be any protestation based on Imperial Law. Even if the Barrani who employ Teremaine's services chose to believe no Tha'alani would be involved, it would make little difference. Before the advent of the Tha'alani, information was still retrieved. The people Teremaine has served in the past will lose face. In the worst case, they would lose their lives if they are not powerful enough; Teremaine interacts with the mortal caste court. His crimes are therefore crimes that the Halls of Law would, by mandate, investigate. Teremaine will die if he remains within Elantra; there are few places in which he could now find safety."

"Few, but not none?"

"Indeed. And he is not our concern."

Severn nodded again.

Helmat was unaccustomed to unexpected knocks at his closed door. If the door was open, he was willing to take visitors; if it was closed, he was not. Only two people knocked at his door when it was closed. Or perhaps one. Elluvian generally opened the door unless he knew an actual meeting was ongoing.

The other person was probably Private Handred.

Helmat spoke a single word, and the door rolled open. It was indeed the private, but Elluvian was not far behind. Wearing his best *this had better be good* expression, Helmat stared at them until they entered the room. The door closed behind them.

Helmat did not particularly care for this door. He vastly preferred the old one. But waiting for the preferred replacement would leave his office open at any time of day or night, and he had accepted the practical necessity of a lesser choice. He glared at Elluvian.

En actually smiled in response.

"The private wishes to see the actual orders the Emperor handed down."

"Pardon?"

"He wishes to see the wording of the orders themselves."

"And your reason?" Helmat asked, deciding to abandon the third person.

Severn's hands were behind his back, his chin slightly tucked. He lifted that now. "In a technical sense, the Barrani we've been attempting to find did not commit murder."

"Yes, and?"

"He's considered important because we're to find his master. It's the master who's the target of the execution orders, yes?"

Helmat said nothing.

"Are we empowered—no, are we *commanded*—to find and arrest the person or persons responsible for the murders, or are we instructed to execute him or her?"

Helmat's eyes narrowed.

"And if there is more than one, are we then instructed to either arrest or execute all of them?"

"En."

"It is a fair question, Helmat."

"It's a selective question. Private, you are ordered to assist Elluvian. *You* are not ordered to execute anyone. You are on probation. If you survive probation, you will be a Wolf. You will not be a Shadow Wolf. Any killings that occur in the line of duty had better be for self-defense, or you won't continue to be a Wolf.

"You are required to unearth the individuals responsible for the murders. You are then tasked with arresting them. If, as we suspect, the person responsible is Barrani, you will not succeed. If, as you imply, there is more than one criminal, you are then responsible for apprehending two people. Or three. Or four."

"If the perpetrators weren't Barrani?"

"It is highly likely that they will also perish. Three witnesses didn't survive to grace our jails; none of the three were

Barrani. Regardless, that is not the command the Emperor has given. You are, of course, to preserve your own lives in any conflict that arises. If your attempt to apprehend becomes a fight, survival is your immediate imperative."

Severn nodded again.

"You cannot believe that the human caste court is somehow involved?"

"The humans hate the Tha'alani as much as the Barrani do—maybe more," Severn replied. "We know a Barrani was involved in the killings—but each of the murders was carried out by a human crowd. We assume that the Barrani was responsible for the behavior of the crowd."

"Yes."

"Why?"

"Why else would Barrani be present?"

Severn nodded and moved on. "If, in our opinion, the cost of bringing this case to a conclusion might involve more deaths, and far more conflict, are we free to abandon it?"

Helmat coughed. "Are you Wolflord, boy?"

"No, sir."

"Are you Emperor?"

"No, sir."

"When you are either of these things, you can feel free to make those decisions. Or," he added heavily, "if you are Elluvian. Why have you come here to ask?"

"I believe," the private replied, in his careful Barrani, "this is a case in which solving all elements may cause irreparable damage that was not foreseen when the request was made."

"First, the Emperor does not *request*, he commands. Second, Elluvian has some discretion in that regard—as, of course, does the Emperor. Let Elluvian decide whether or not the cost of your mission is far too high a price to pay for its completion. Let Elluvian make that argument to the Emperor.

"Now, get out. I have an angry Scoros on hold." This was not entirely true, and it would be some minutes before Helmat chose to return the interrupted call. He was now mulling over the question Severn had asked. Elluvian had allowed the private to interrupt Helmat for a clarification the Barrani Wolf was entirely entitled to make.

Regardless, it was not an angry Scoros that caused Helmat's jaw to clench; it was a graciously furious Hawklord.

Severn once again took over Elluvian's desk. He spent the rest of the afternoon struggling with Records; twice he asked Elluvian to intervene, because the information was locked behind a series of words the private didn't know.

Elluvian's research could not be accomplished so easily. Cassandre had offered information of a kind, but no Barrani Lord of any worth relied on information provided by a single source. The value of information was always weighted by context, and the games the lords played provided that context. Most of the games were hidden, and some, hidden well.

Ollarin, as he had chosen to be called, was a context he was attempting to understand. Ollarin was young. Even by Barrani standards, he would have been considered no wiser, stronger, or more powerful than any of the privates of Elluvian's recent acquaintance. He had not been born within Elantra; he was an import from the West March.

He had no obvious connection to An'Tellarus, which was to be expected; he had no hidden connections to An'Tellarus, either, or none that Elluvian had found with careful digging. None of that digging now occurred at court; Elluvian had been forbidden the High Halls without the private as escort, and while he did not care to follow all of Helmat's mandates, he understood that this one was supported in its entirety by the Eternal Emperor.

Many members of the court did not have the resources to live in the High Halls. These would be the most junior members of that court. Those who made Elantra their home without taking the test that granted status as a Lord of the High Court did not dwell in the High Halls either, except as servants or guards.

An'Sennarin had very tentative alliances with other lords. Ollarin had become An'Sennarin, and those families who had chosen to ally themselves with the former lord had not yet abandoned him. His rise to power was so sudden that they could not discount his strength, even if little of it was otherwise displayed. Elluvian privately thought that it was only a matter of time. If Ollarin was responsible for the spate of murders decades past, he would meet the fate desired by the Emperor without the intervention of Wolves.

An'Tellarus, however, complicated matters. She had no close allies in the traditional sense of the word, but the alliances she did have were solid. Once you entered her orbit, for however short a period, you never fully escaped it. And it was never wise to anger her.

It was never, of course, wise to anger any Lord of the High Court, but one might safely dare the anger of An'Sennarin; one did not dare the anger of An'Tellarus. How public was her declaration of support? How well-known was the alliance she had claimed so baldly?

These questions occupied his time for the remainder of the day. They occupied his time for all of the next three, during which Severn studied Records and attempted to glean information from the Hawks. This information required Elluvian's presence, and it was therefore gleaned slowly.

Elluvian did not speak with An'Sennarin at all. If An'Sennarin was not a half-wit, he was now well aware of Elluvian's interest. He was not enough of a power that people were terrified at the mention of his name—but the name of the line did give pause to those like Corvallan. Dread of a particular type took centuries to firmly entrench, and the young An'Sennarin had not had the time required to build that.

The reaction was therefore due the previous title holder, or so he assumed. If An'Sennarin of old had been that terrifying, his death was almost inexplicable. Perhaps, Elluvian mused, that was the focal point of this investigation. The current An'Sennarin had taken the seat only upon the death of the ruler and his chosen heir. There were bound to be other deaths, other examples set, and the history was so recent, they could not be fully hidden.

On the fourth day of Elluvian's intermittent presence in the office, Severn left. He required permission to visit the Tha'alani quarter, and the Wolflord was unamused enough that were Severn a different person, he would have simply failed to acquire that permission. He was, however, on probation, and his furious studies of the Wolves, their various cases, the likelihood of both survival and success, had not yet given him the certainty about the nature of both inquiries and cases.

He relied to a greater extent on Rosen. She was willing to discuss—often at length—previous missions; she preferred to discuss those that had been successful, but given the recent thinning of the Wolves, had been willing to discuss the failures. She had also, less happily, discussed the internal office squabbles that had led to that thinning.

He had some sense of what had caused Darrell's death. He didn't understand Mellianne's rage, but rage—when confronted with things that were immutable and could not be changed—had never been his first reaction. Nor had revenge.

He made no attempt to engage the Barrani—those outside the High Halls—at all, but his foray into the various Records,

and his discussion with Ybelline, had given him some idea of
where those Barrani might be found. The information was
useful if one wanted to avoid interacting with them entirely.

The majority of the cases the Hawks—and Swords—dealt
with involved humans. There were, however, scattered cases
in which the criminal was Aerian or Leontine. The Leontine cases tended toward aggravated assault, sometimes leading to death; the Aerian cases, like the human cases, covered
a range of crimes.

The Barrani didn't make their way into Records either, unless they were the author of the Hawks' reports. There were,
however, cases that had been logged in Records, in which suspects—not criminals—were Barrani. They always appeared
to end in one way: a Barrani corpse was found shortly after
the name had been logged. Sometimes the corpse was found
on the front stairs of the Halls of Law; sometimes it was found
in the Ablayne. Twice the corpses had been discovered in the
warrens.

No Barrani had been arrested; no Barrani had been sent
to trial.

Finding information about Barrani informants—because
such informants did exist—was not more difficult than finding information about human informants, but there was no
easy way to list them. They gave information to the Hawks
investigating various crimes; they were part of the budget the
Hawks were granted. They weren't officially involved with
the Halls of Law in any other way.

This made sense. Severn, in his early days in the streets of
this city, might have made coin by offering information—if
he had had information of worth—but he would never have
wanted to be fingered as the person who had provided it.
There was a layer of politics in any interaction between two
people; even those who barely kept a roof over their own head

or food in their mouths. No one wanted to be sold out, no matter what their activity.

The Tha'alani occupied more and more of his attention. They were never, as far as Severn could determine, criminals. No matter how central the Tha'alaan was in their lives, people were people. Tha'alani criminals must exist.

But Tha'alani Caste Court laws were not inscribed into Records Severn could access. He needed to speak to Ybelline.

The Wolflord very grudgingly made the call to the Tha'alanari. Ybelline was not the person who answered that call, but according to the Wolflord, she never was. No, it was Scoros, looking hazel-eyed and extremely tired. His answers to the Wolflord's questions had been monosyllabic. He didn't ask questions, and he made no argument on behalf of Ybelline.

A lot of nothing was said; the Wolflord's expression, by the end of the very short mirror call, was as dour and grim as Scoros's. "You have permission to visit Ybelline. She will not come here unless you intend to ask questions that require Imperial Service answers."

"I don't."

"I want," the Wolflord continued, "a report on your progress in this case. Preferably before you leave, but given the time, it can wait until after. Immediately after."

Severn nodded.

The guards who greeted Severn at the gates to the Tha'alani quarter were green-eyed to a man, but he now expected this. When they asked his purpose, he said, "I have an appointment with Ybelline Rabon of the Tha'alanari." When they demanded to know the reason for that appointment, he failed to answer. There was no politic way to do so. The investigation was the reason, in the end, for the creation of—and the separation of—the Tha'alanari from the rest of their kin. The guards weren't Tha'alanari.

He knew that he wouldn't gain access to the Tha'alani quarter without an escort. He expected Scoros to be sent. Or possibly Garadin. If he was lucky, Ybelline herself would come—but Severn doubted that she anticipated his arrival with any joy whatsoever.

The gates, however, did open with the intervention of the guards. These gates, unlike the gates that fronted many of the richer mansions, were not a grille; no one standing in front of them could now peer through to catch a glimpse of the people protected by their existence.

This also made sense. Severn waited.

The gates weren't fully open before they halted in their figurative tracks. The guards made haste to offer a very visible obeisance to the man who stood in their partial frame. They then rose and finished what they had started, although it was hardly necessary; the gap in the partially opened gates was more than wide enough for either Severn or his escort to fit through.

Even had the behavior of the guards not been unusual, Severn would have recognized this man, although he hadn't yet put name to him.

He was the Tha'alani castelord.

CHAPTER TWENTY-THREE

SEVERN HAD NOT, IN HIS BRIEF TIME AS A WOLF, had cause to interact with any of the other castelords. He now knew the names of the human and Leontine Caste Court leaders; he knew what the castelord of the Barrani High Court was called by those who were not Barrani. He knew nothing of the Tha'alani Caste Court or its structure.

But he had two things: a sketch and a carved figure, if carved was the right description. This man was older than Ybelline, his hair white; some small hint of iron gray implied that it had not always been so. He wore robes of green and blue, and a carelessly tied sash that implied that he, unlike the Barrani nobles, was responsible for the state of his own clothing.

And he had not let the gate guards know—before the gates opened—that he would serve as Severn's escort.

His entire carriage and bearing spoke of age, of the weight of age; his eyes were darkly circled, his beard slightly wispy and unkempt. His eyes were green.

The man nodded to Severn. Severn offered him a very correct Barrani bow of respect in return. He rose when the man cleared his throat.

"I am called Adellos by those who speak with me in the fashion of outsiders. Adellos Coran'alani."

"I am called Severn Handred," Severn replied. It was superfluous; he was absolutely certain this man knew his name.

"Yes. Come. You have asked to speak with Ybelline; she is momentarily occupied and has sent me as escort in her stead." The old man's smile was benign, his tone apologetic and friendly.

Severn didn't believe a word the castelord had just spoken. For the first time since he had met Ybelline, he felt a growing dread of the Tha'alani. Dread, however, would not become terror. He bowed to the castelord.

"Come. We do not want to keep Ybelline waiting." Adellos turned and began to walk down the street the gate bisected. Severn glanced once at the guards. They had not risen.

He had walked these streets before; the layout hadn't changed. But the number of people, or more specifically, young children playing in them, had. They existed, but they did not leave their lawns or the area in front of their hill-like homes, and they neither approached nor gaped; nor did they lift hands to point.

He wondered what Adellos was saying or had said. And that was unfair. Adellos might not be the speaker. Scoros, however, had not had this effect on the children. Nor had either he or Ybelline had that effect on the gate guards. He felt as if he had wandered into a different Tha'alani quarter.

Because of one man.

Not two blocks passed before Severn stopped walking. His arms were at his sides; he looked as if he had paused to survey the landscape. He had.

Adellos paused half a block ahead, as if he expected Severn to simply follow. He too stopped and turned, but he had eyes for Severn; Severn's were upon the Tha'alani, far fewer in number in the streets.

They had green eyes, or perhaps it was a trick of light and distance—but given the stillness, he didn't think so.

"Does something trouble you?" Adellos asked, in the same benign tone.

"Yes."

The Tha'alani castelord's brow rose.

"There are no children in the street."

Silence.

"There are almost no people in the street. What are you saying to them? What did you tell them?"

"I have said nothing," he replied.

"Nothing?"

The castelord nodded.

"Nothing at all?"

A three-beat silence followed the question before it was broken. "I can see why Ybelline likes you. Yes. I have said nothing at all. They have not heard me—and I have not heard them—since I walked to the gates. I am not, now, in the confines of the Tha'alaan."

They were not afraid of Severn.

They were afraid of, or for, the castelord, one of the few who could sunder himself from the racial mind of his people and survive it.

Every element of the case itself rearranged itself in Severn's untouched thoughts. The oracle. The Oracular Halls. The visitors. The sketch and the figurine. Ybelline's reactions to all of it.

For the first time, he regretted the absence of Elluvian. Elluvian would survive here. Severn Handred might not. One of the two witnesses gathered by the Barrani Hawks had been safely on the way to the Halls of Law in the crowded city streets—and they had died. The Barrani Hawks had been powerless to save them. The only surviving witness had been saved by An'Teela and Elianne, if the gossip was to be believed. Severn did believe.

He considered turning on his heel and leaving the quarter, but the gates were now closed.

"I like Ybelline," he said instead as he stood his ground.

"She should never have gone to bespeak you on behalf of the Imperial Service." Adellos walked to where Severn stood. He couldn't force Severn to walk beside him.

"She had reasons for doing so. Reasons I'm certain you understand."

Adellos's nod was heavy.

"Did you serve the Imperial Service in your time?"

The castelord's face had lost the avuncular, almost affectionate expression that had been pasted across it since the gates had opened. "Yes. In the time before I became castelord. It is one of the requirements."

"And she is your daughter?"

"No. We are related only distantly by blood—as we are to most of our kin. We do not choose castelords by heredity."

"How do you choose them?" Severn asked, partly because he was curious, and partly because he was stalling for time.

"How do you think we choose?"

It was a serious question, not a flippant one. Severn exhaled. He wondered if Ybelline would become Adellos with time and experience; it was a bitter thought. "Castelords would have to be Tha'alanari."

Adellos nodded. "The legal structure of the caste courts was devised by the Emperor. The word *castelord* is not one that is native to our people."

"They would have to be able to keep their thoughts—possibly the whole of their thoughts—from the Tha'alaan."

He nodded again.

Exhaling, Severn said, "They'd have to be able to keep their thoughts entirely to themselves. There are things that they won't share with even the Tha'alanari."

"Yes."

"You think I'm a threat."

"I do not believe you bear us any malice, but in my experience the most dangerous of threats can come from a place of genuine affection. A place of hope."

"If you can keep your thoughts to yourself, is there any record left when you die?"

"There is. And those memories will be given to only one person upon my passage."

Ybelline.

"The memories and experiences I have shared with the rest of my kin will become—have already become—part of the Tha'alaan. No doubt some of the witnesses here search it as we stand in the street and speak."

"Forgive me," Severn replied. "I am—as any other person—reluctant to walk peacefully to my own death."

"You are so certain that that is where we walk?"

Severn said, "No—but I'm certain now that that's your intent. Does Ybelline even know I've arrived?"

Adellos said, "Come. I would not have the rest of this discussion in the open streets."

"I almost prefer the witnesses."

"Do you? I know why you are here. I know why you are a Wolf. I know of your past, just as Ybelline does."

Severn's breath was singular, sharp, the sound similar to the drawing of a dagger.

"I am castelord, boy. Did you think she could protect her experiences from me?"

"I didn't think about it at all," Severn replied, voice even.

"Your expression says the opposite."

"It's nothing."

"No, it is not. It is hope. It is the death of hope. Hope is perilous, Severn Handred. We take risks because we have hope. We extend ourselves. We fail to understand too much because we look only to a bright, shining future, a place different from the one we now occupy."

"What did Random tell you when you visited her?"

The castelord frowned. The frown seemed to be his natural expression, given the way the lines of age fell perfectly into place around it. "Random?"

Severn stilled again. This time he fell silent as he met the castelord's stare. He said nothing else. He knew no thought was safe from the castelord if the castelord touched his face with the racial stalks of his people; he calculated that even with few witnesses in the open street, Adellos would not make the attempt against Severn's will.

He suffered no other illusions. But if hope was deadly or dangerous—and it had been, he couldn't deny it—it was also necessary. Painful or no, it was the dream of a brighter future that allowed some people to crawl out of the perpetual shadows of the present.

Adellos did not immediately know who Random was. Adellos did not know that Ybelline had gone to visit the Oracular Halls—with Severn.

If she had not guarded her thoughts, if she had seen no reason to guard them before, she was doing so now. And she could, or she would not be heir to the castelord.

Severn lifted his chin, swallowed air, and expelled it in three syllables.

"Ybelline!"

"She cannot hear you."

"No, of course not," he replied. "But *they* can. They are not Tha'alanari. They are not castelords or castelords in waiting. If she did not know, she'll know now."

"You are certain of that?"

"I'm not certain that this visit—my visit—will remain within the Tha'alaan, no. But neither do I understand how such memories are excised. I can't imagine that it's done quickly. Apologies, castelord. I cannot die here, not yet."

"Oh, child," he replied, the benign expression once again molding the contours of his expression into something less harsh. "Not even you believe that."

Severn moved; he rolled to the side. He couldn't break line of sight easily, but he made the attempt. Those few witnesses in the street scattered, as if Severn was the threat, not the castelord, who had not moved more than lips.

If he had wondered—if Elluvian had wondered—how the witness had died while guarded by Barrani Hawks and surrounded by civilians, he had his answer: his lungs began to fill with water. He opened his mouth, but those lungs had no room for something as petty as air, and without air, he couldn't form words.

He couldn't shout for help; couldn't ask for mercy; couldn't tell the castelord that this death in this place was as damaging to the Tha'alaan as the other deaths had been, decades past, when fear of humanity, fear of outsiders, had taken permanent root in the Tha'alani.

He thought of Ybelline as the world began to blacken.

And Ybelline heard him. He felt her wordless discomfort sharpen into horror, into visceral fear. He couldn't see her, couldn't hear her, but she was, somehow, briefly present. He struggled to cough up the fluid that deprived him of air and failed—of course he failed.

Light dimmed and guttered.

He woke.

Green eyes were the first thing he saw. The rest of the face followed, and to his surprise, the face was not Ybelline's. Nor was it the castelord's. It was Scoros's, pale as death, his brows rising, his eyes shifting almost immediately from emerald green to amber.

"Severn." His hands were on Severn's shoulders. "Severn, are you there?"

As if the hands that were shaking him—unintentionally, in Severn's admittedly groggy opinion—were lying to their owner.

His first attempt to form words failed, as did his second. His third, however, succeeded. "I'm here." The voice was weaker than he'd intended.

Scoros closed his eyes. "Ybelline will see you now," he said.

"Why are you here?"

"She asked me to stay. She was afraid to leave you alone."

"Are we in the—"

"You are in Ybelline's home."

"Why?"

"It was closer," Scoros replied, running a hand across his brow. He'd been sweating. Relief, however, had broken some essential wall, and his expression dissolved into the type of pain that leaves sorrow in its wake when it has finally become almost bearable.

Severn sat up, the movement sudden enough it made him dizzy. He didn't touch the Tha'alani man, but didn't attempt to evade his touch, either. The absent castelord would cause no further harm while Scoros was present; he was certain of that.

"Where is Ybelline?"

"She is here. Garadin is here as well." He exhaled. "As is Timorri, who should be well away—*well*—from any of these events. He has not fully recovered from the incident, and it is unlikely that he is stable enough to be of useful aid."

"The castelord?"

Scoros's eyes darkened to green. "He is with Ybelline. I would join them, but keeping watch over you was the only thing she asked of me. You are lucky, Private. Even had one of us arrived in time, we could not do what she did."

"What did she do?"

"She saved your life. She's the only one who could." Seeing Severn's expression, Scoros said, "I am getting far, far ahead of myself. Ybelline is coming." He stiffened. "Ybelline is coming with the castelord. You are safe," he added, the three words spoken in a rush. "He cannot harm you here, and he will not make a second attempt. He should never have made the first one."

"Why?"

"We are not murderers," was the simple response. "We have spent our lives scarred by the fears that drive your kind *to* murder, and that is not what we are. Not what we should be." Scoros was afraid.

But Severn had seen his almost golden eyes when he had realized that Severn would survive. He was not, would not be, afraid of Scoros.

There were no doors in this room; there was a hanging curtain composed largely of beads that tinkled pleasantly when they were pushed to the side. Draped by these beads—strands of which fell across her shoulders—was Ybelline. She wore a robe of emerald green, and something across her forehead that might have been a slender tiara, had it been made of metal.

She approached the bed without haste. Her eyes, as Scoros's had been, were momentarily gold. As Scoros's had, they darkened. Behind Ybelline came Adellos Coran'alani, and behind him, Garadin, he of the enlarged, angry face so familiar to the Wolves' Records. There was no sign of Timorri.

Severn had drawn himself into a seated position to calm Scoros; he was grateful that he'd maintained it. He rose steadily, forcing his knees to bear his weight. He offered Ybelline a bow. He didn't offer her his open hands; he didn't think she would take them.

Only when she was certain that he could stand did she nod, allowing him to once again sit. There was a single chair in this room, which Scoros now vacated; there was a round, high window, something that looked like a dresser with every single corner rounded down, a vase with flowers. Nothing else.

Scoros nodded; he and Garadin then left the room. "We will be outside," he said, "if we are necessary."

It took Severn a moment to realize that the words had been spoken for his benefit—but of course they had. None of the Tha'alani required actual speech. The beads tinkled as they departed. Only when the motions of that permeable curtain had faded did Adellos take the chair Scoros had vacated. Ybelline stood, her hands behind her back, her eyes green.

Adellos's eyes were green as well.

"Ybelline feels that I owe you an apology."

"Apologies are considered too trivial for attempted murder, at least among my people," Severn replied. He had chosen to speak High Barrani.

Adellos smiled. His eyes remained green as he offered Severn a small nod. "As they are among almost all of the people of my acquaintance. She feels I owe you an explanation."

"And you don't agree."

"No. Had explanations been a possibility, I would not have made the attempt."

"It seems extreme, but I lack all of the necessary information."

"I do not believe you do." His eyes, green, darkened. "I believe you have far too much information; you are a threat—an unintentional threat—to our people and their sanity."

"Not nearly as much of a threat," Severn replied, "as the castelord committing murder would be." There was accusation and heat in the words; Severn abandoned any attempt to hide them.

"There was no threat in that," Adellos replied. "My memories, as I said, would not touch the Tha'alaan. They would not darken the Tha'alanari. It is only Ybelline who would be forced to bear their burden—and given the memories themselves, the burden would not be heavier."

"I do not believe Scoros or Garadin—or Timorri for that matter—agree."

Adellos said nothing. He started to rise, and then returned, heavily, to the chair.

"You met the Oracle," he then said. "I had not expected that. Had not, in fact, been informed about it at all. Ybelline did not inform the Tha'alanari."

"With cause," Ybelline said.

"Do you now believe that I would kill or harm any of our people?"

"Do I believe it? No. But my beliefs are now just that—they are conjectures, where you are concerned. It is a risk I was not willing to take."

"You were not willing to take that risk before I attempted to harm Severn."

"To kill him," she said.

Severn lifted a hand; he touched Ybelline's elbow and she turned her attention toward him. She was distant now, the warmth that had seemed so essential a part of her nature frozen by her anger, her sense of betrayal.

"Why did you choose to close your thoughts off entirely?

As I said, I had not yet attempted to harm Severn. I had not interceded in the investigation."

"That, also, is not true," she said. "You did not attempt to gainsay the Imperial Service—we both know any such attempt would have ended in failure. But the witnesses Severn wished interrogated? Those deaths are on your hands."

"I did not kill any of them."

"They would not have died had you not passed the information on. You gave the names and locations to the killers. I believe that makes you an accessory to murder. An accomplice."

"Tell me, Ybelline, do you no longer believe in justice? Was justice not served by their deaths? They had quick, painless deaths in comparison to the deaths of our people, and their deaths—unlike the deaths they helped orchestrate—did not scar the Tha'alaan."

She turned to face Severn. "I was the source of the leak."

But Severn had inferred that from the conversation the two Tha'alani were now having—a conversation that he could hear. He had thought that this was done for his benefit. It was the reason the Tha'alanari spoke out loud in his presence.

He understood then that it wasn't the reason Ybelline had chosen verbal communication. She was unwilling to share any part of her thoughts with the castelord. There was no other way of communicating.

"Do you believe that those witnesses died to hide or cover up the crimes that even to this day reverberate in the Tha'alaan?" the castelord continued. "Is that what you now think of me?"

"What I think of you is irrelevant," Ybelline replied, her voice controlled in a way that Severn's had not been.

"It is not irrelevant to the Tha'alanari. It is not irrelevant to *me*."

She closed her eyes. "I want to believe," she said, the harshness of her tone at variance with her expression, "that you would not—that you would *never*—harm us in the way we were harmed by human mobs. I want to believe it because you have been our castelord, the single person responsible for our safety and our sanity.

"And perhaps that is our fault, in the end—we allowed you to carry this burden in isolation for far too long. You should have retired."

"I could not," he replied, his eyes open and entirely focused on Ybelline. "You know why."

"I was not yet born."

"You were, but you were an infant. You were not even under consideration, and Ybelline, there was no one else. You know the Tha'alanari—you are familiar with all of their number. Could they do what I have done?"

"No—but that is to their credit."

"Could they keep what I have done a secret? Could they carry that burden, and the guilt of it, on their own?"

She was silent.

"Do you believe that that knowledge would be of benefit to the Tha'alanari?"

"You are no longer my teacher," she said. "Nor my master. I will not play these games with you again."

Severn looked at them both. To Adellos he was barely in the room. But he thought his presence was more significant to Ybelline. And he understood what had happened, what was happening, even now.

"No, she does not. She does not believe that this would help the Tha'alanari in any way."

Her eyes opened; they met Severn's. He hated the color green in that moment. He thought he might hate it forever. The green of her dress. The green of her eyes.

"You went to the Oracular Halls," Adellos continued, as if

Severn had not spoken. "You spoke with the Oracle. You understand what Tessa was offered. I do not believe the Oracle herself understood it—not at the time."

"But you did."

"I would not have understood it had I seen it myself—not when the children were younger. There are laws for a *reason*, even be they Imperial Laws."

"There were no laws to forbid the interaction of two mortals. Master Sabrai broke no laws in allowing the visit."

"It is his lack of oversight that led, in the end, to everything that happened afterward."

"No." The single word was a study in fury, in rage. "It was fear that led to everything—your fear. Barrani fear."

"Which would not have existed were it not for that visit." This time, when Adellos rose, he was not ordered back to his seat. "They were young—all of them. They understood the world they wished to build, but did not see with any clarity the world in which they lived.

"The justice you desire, and the desire which led you to take part in this unearthing of past atrocities, has already been accomplished. It was accomplished long ago, when I was a younger castelord. I ask you to leave it now. I will offer you everything that I have kept from any of our people."

"You will offer that anyway," she countered. "You will have no choice."

"And will you now turn your experience with the Imperial Service against me? Will you force me to surrender my thoughts and my experiences without agreement? Will you take from me what the Emperor commands we take from his citizens at his whim?"

"Will you force me to do so?"

"Yes, if that is necessary."

Severn closed his eyes. Opened them again. "Ybelline."

She stared at Adellos.

He tightened his hand around her elbow, demanding, in silence, her attention. She struggled to break not his grip but the grip of her own anger.

Severn bent his head; he did not remove his hand. "Ybelline Rabon'alani."

As if the words were a key that could unlock the grip of pain and grief she did not choose to share, she turned to Severn. "He tried to murder you," she finally said. "That act is against the law—of both your kin and mine. He cannot be castelord."

"No one else knows."

"The Tha'alanari know," she said, her voice softening slightly as she met Severn's gaze.

"I won't ask that charges be pressed. I won't mention it at all. Don't be angry on my behalf."

Almost grudgingly, she said, "Someone should be." She spoke Elantran.

"No," he said. "That's where it always starts. Pain. Anger. Neither of which can change the past."

"It's not the past that concerns me. His attempt didn't occur decades ago, but now. And we don't know what he attempted decades ago."

"The boy does not want you to take the mantle," the castelord—the former castelord—said. "He does not want you to bear the burdens I have borne. I understand why you value him, castelord. And it is far too late for me. I have done what I have done. I will not regret it. If it were given to me to change my actions, I would not. I might, perhaps, make those actions more effective."

Severn understood the words; Ybelline was slow to arrive at the same understanding. Her eyes flashed green again.

He was not afraid of Adellos now. And he could never fear Ybelline. "He didn't kill Tessa or her two friends."

Adellos's posture and expression didn't change.

"How can you be so certain?"

Adellos closed his eyes. "Daughter," he said, sinking, once again, into the room's only chair.

"Because he held their memories."

"The Tha'alaan—"

"He can't return the memories to the Tha'alaan. He's right in that. There will be another Tessa, another Jerrin, another Tobi. If you find ways to hamper them—and you will—they'll find ways to sneak out of the house. But the memories he took he can't return."

"What better way to assure that those memories remain hidden than to kill them?"

Severn nodded. "That's probably why they were killed." To the older man, he added, "Those deaths weren't accidental, were they?"

"No."

"And you knew they'd been murdered."

"I did not know it at the time of their deaths. Had she not died, I believe Tessa would have been capable of bearing the mantle of castelord. There were memories that she kept hidden by threading them through the Tha'alaan in strands so fine they were impossible to entirely disentangle. Jerrin and Tobi were not her equals."

"Why did you not hide the early memories?"

"They had living parents, living family. They had friends. They were dead—some token had to be left so that the burden of their loss could be shared. And Tessa was, as I said, adept at hiding."

"Did you know that their deaths weren't accidental when they died?"

"No."

Ybelline's brow rippled.

"Do you know the identity of their killer or killers?"

Silence.

"They weren't Tha'alani."

"No."

Severn exhaled. "You said that justice has already been done."

The old man—and it seemed to Severn that he had gained decades as he occupied this chair—nodded.

"You didn't kill the witnesses that were to be questioned by the Halls of Law."

"No."

"You know who did."

"I did not command them," was the almost testy reply. "I did not order those deaths, if that is what you have understood."

"But you knew of them."

"Grief can cause madness," Adellos said. He spoke to Ybelline—or to himself; his gaze had moved off Severn's face. "It is not the madness of fear, but it can cause as much damage, in the end. Especially ours."

"Then I will start my reign," Ybelline replied, "in madness."

Adellos once again closed his eyes. "Child," he said softly, "I did my best not to hamper you."

"*Hamper* is far too kind a word for what you've done."

"Yes. Perhaps the desire to be kind to those we love is also a type of madness; kindness does not change reality."

Severn said, "We will go to the High Halls."

Adellos's eyes were already too green to darken further in color. "I ask you, castelord, to refuse."

"Then clearly Severn's suggestion is correct."

Severn had not meant to include Ybelline in that nebulous *we*. "It's not safe for you—for any of your kin—in the High Halls."

"And it has been safe for you?" she countered.

"I'm human. I'm beneath notice; I enter the High Halls at Elluvian's side."

"And only then?"

Severn nodded.

"Then Elluvian will have to accompany us."

"Do not do this," Adellos whispered.

"I cannot be castelord in ignorance," was her soft reply. "If you will not give me the information I seek, I will investigate using other avenues that are open to me."

Severn said nothing. The Wolflord wasn't going to be pleased. "I have one request," he said.

"And that?"

"I don't wish the incident that occurred here—"

"The attempted *murder*."

"The attempted murder," he continued, "if you prefer. I don't want it reported."

"And if it were your decision," Ybelline replied, "or his, it would not be."

"Ybelline—"

"It's not about your life or death," she said, relenting. "It's about *us*. Us as a people. It's already dangerous to separate the Tha'alanari from the Tha'alaan at large—but all who serve understand why we must. If this is the end result of separating the leader from their people entirely, it is far too high a price to pay."

"You will not say so," Adellos said, "when you understand the entirety of what occurred."

"You assume that my understanding, or my judgment, would be the same as yours. We are not the same person. Our knowledge of experiences does not immediately render our prior experiences irrelevant. You should *know this*. It is what you have taught us *all*."

"Leave this, Ybelline."

Severn knew, without touching her or being touched by her, what her answer would be.

CHAPTER TWENTY-FOUR

SEVERN WAS NOT PARTICULARLY SURPRISED TO return to an office that sounded like a human version of a thunderstorm. Rosen waved him over to her desk. The mirror on it wasn't reflective; it was a glowing, almost pulsing, gray.

"Why are they shouting?"

"Helmat's shouting. Elluvian doesn't, generally."

"That was definitely Elluvian."

Rosen winced. "I didn't understand half of what he said. I'm taking it from your expression you did. You know what it's about?"

"No."

"But you have your suspicions."

"The Tha'alani and the Barrani High Halls."

"Those two phrases should never be used in conjunction." She studied Severn's expression, cursed genially in a way that would have been extreme had she lived in the fiefs, and said, "No wonder they're shouting."

"Is Ybelline here?"

Rosen's jaw hung open for five seconds. "Gods no. *Please*

tell me you're not expecting her." When he failed to answer, she turned and reached for her cane. "Mellianne is still out fact-finding. I'm shutting the office down and going for a walk. There's no reason—at all—that I need to be here when things get *really* heated."

There had been no ill effects to the lungs full of water. Certainly less than having lungs full of the Ablayne river would have caused. Severn made his way, in the now-empty office, to Elluvian's desk. The Wolflord's voice was raised; it clashed with Elluvian's. Ah—a third voice had joined the discussion, a male voice. Garadin.

Severn didn't understand why the three bothered. It had been clear, from the first time she'd entered these offices, that Ybelline could not be cowed, or begged, into obedience. She didn't raise her voice; she accepted the concern of all those around her, and she continued with what she felt were her duties.

This time would be no different. The risk was higher, yes. But risk wasn't the defining part of the calculation for Ybelline. She would be as cautious as she could while performing her duties. Yelling changed nothing.

The mirror, inactive, responded to his voice. He began to look through Records—in particular, the Records of the Hawks. Murder, attempted murder, was the province of that branch of the Halls of Law. His name was mentioned nowhere.

No complaint of attempted murder had been lodged here.

Severn had no access to the Imperial Service Records—not yet. There would be some overlap if he was sent to—commanded to—kill, but the overlap would be slight. There was no way to assess whether or not Ybelline had taken the accusation to the Imperial Service instead of the Halls of Law.

She had said the decision was hers. Perhaps she had not decided. Or perhaps she had. She had clearly decided to ask for an invitation to the High Halls. That invitation, in Severn's estimation, had probably been granted—which was part of the reason the two, Wolflord and Elluvian, were arguing. Garadin's response was in keeping with all of his prior interactions with the Wolflord where Ybelline's safety was involved.

Garadin didn't want Ybelline anywhere near the High Halls. The Wolflord didn't, either. The odd thing about the argument—the words were entirely muffled by some enchantment laid on the closed door, but the tone and volume breached containment regularly—was that Severn would have bet that all three would be on the same side of it.

Ybelline wasn't present. She might have a mirror connection to the discussion—the timbre of her voice wouldn't breach the closed door, and her anger often caused her voice to become softer, not louder.

"Records," he said. "Interview. Witness protection, Dogan Sapson."

"Interview not yet complete," Records replied. "Stay of interview requested by Lord Montrose."

Records contained very little other information about Lord Montrose. It was a faintly familiar name. Lord Montrose. Lord Montrose. Ah. He was one of nine or eleven—he could not immediately recall the correct number—lords who presided over the human caste court.

"Reason?"

"None given. The request has been relayed to the Hawklord; the Hawklord has not yet handed down his decision."

Of course not. Montrose was wealthy and powerful. Severn wasn't certain that information about the serial mob murders of Tha'alani over two decades ago would change anything.

The information they had been hoping for seemed almost irrelevant now.

They knew that Teremaine had been the instigator; that Teremaine, not a Lord of the High Court, was involved at the behest of someone in the High Halls. It was almost certainly An'Sennarin.

Ollarin.

Records, of course, contained no information about An'Sennarin. The Imperial Service knew only that the current An'Sennarin had occupied the seat for two decades, a period Elluvian thought paltry. If he could hold the seat for a century, Elluvian would consider it truly won.

It was simpler for Severn. The former An'Sennarin was dead. The current An'Sennarin was alive. In fief terms, the current An'Sennarin had won the fight.

But the manner of the deaths of the previous ruler and his heir had complicated that equation. Severn assumed, on some base level, that the An'Sennarin who ruled now had risen through the ranks because of his interaction with the Tha'alani; he had then discarded his allies because of the danger they presented, and he had damaged the Tha'alaan in the most efficient way possible so that people shied away from the terror of those memories and the time period that surrounded them.

This made sense to Severn.

He pulled up the Records of the murders. He looked at the dates. Frowned. He recalled the conversation—the end of the conversation—with An'Tellarus, and his frown deepened. He could make a mirror connection to Ybelline, but if he did, it would be logged and it was highly likely to be overheard.

They had been commanded to find the person responsible

for the deaths of the Tha'alani that had preceded Severn's birth. They had not been commanded to kill—or rather, Severn had not. He was almost certain that Elluvian had been handed a writ of execution. But if his understanding of the application of laws of exemption was correct, Teremaine was a dead man walking, and the Emperor had not commanded them to find Teremaine.

Severn had seen the Barrani man in the crowd. Elluvian, who would not submit, ever, to the touch of the Tha'alani, had not. Severn was to identify the man he'd seen second- and third-hand, and only upon positive identification was Elluvian empowered to act. None of that was relevant. Teremaine was the person spotted in the crowd. Teremaine was not the intended target.

If, indeed, the man in question *was* Teremaine.

Severn frowned. Elluvian had made that assumption. All of the information he had levered out of Corvallan, Cassandre, and An'Tellarus depended on that assumption.

Severn didn't understand the politics of the Emperor, the High Court, or the human caste court. He understood the Tha'alani Caste Court better; he was almost certain that the Tha'alani Caste Court was comprised of members from the Tha'alanari. He'd been assigned to Elluvian because Ybelline had let him glimpse what she herself had seen in Timorri's mind—and Timorri's information had come from a human criminal.

A human criminal that the Imperial Service was questioning.

That criminal was not one of the four witnesses that Severn had discovered by searching Records.

The Tha'alani were not called into the Halls of Law for many cases, relative to the number of legal infractions the Hawks dealt with. The investigations in which they were considered necessary involved crimes that weren't considered petty. They didn't call Tha'alani to pick over the thoughts of pickpockets. The Hawklord, the Wolflord, and the Swordlord had discretion in the calls they made.

Employment in the Wolves—as opposed to Hawks or Swords—required vetting by the Tha'alani. This probably meant that the Wolves were known to the Imperial Service in a way none of the other officers of the Halls were.

"What has captured your attention so thoroughly you fail to hear a visitor?" a familiar voice said.

Severn transferred his gaze from the mirror to the door; he rose slowly, the desk between an extravagantly dressed An'Tellarus and him.

"It is not, that I'm aware, your duty to greet visitors," she said, glancing at the mirror with a mild expression of disgust.

"We don't have unannounced visitors often," Severn replied. "The offices of the Wolves are not open to the general public as a rule."

"I have seldom considered myself a member of your general public," An'Tellarus replied. Her eyes were blue, but a blue green that was as close to green as he had seen them. "I cannot believe Elluvian calls this his office," she added, with obvious disdain. "It is practically a coffin."

"Coffins for mortals," Severn replied, "are generally far less extravagant than their Barrani equivalents must be."

"Clever boy," she said, her eyes darkening slightly. He thought the half smile genuine, but she was Barrani. "I believe the shouting has stopped."

"How long have you been here?"

"Not long, even given mortal time. I dislike the lack of sunlight and the lingering smell of blood."

He abandoned both mirror and desk, and offered her a more correct bow.

"I cannot believe that you have learned your manners from Elluvian; his are dreadful."

The last person Elluvian wanted to set eyes on in the next decade was waiting, like a grim specter, when Elluvian emerged from Helmat's office. The door had not closed quickly enough that Helmat could fail to notice the unannounced visitor. He considered closing the door from the inside, but half suspected that An'Tellarus would open the door one way or another, and if Helmat was forced to replace doors again in such a short period of time, the Imperial Order of Mages was likely to demand his head.

He therefore walked down the hall toward An'Tellarus. He offered her a curt nod, rather than a formal bow; she was not at court, but in offices staffed entirely by humans, not servants.

Severn stood beside her. He would have to do something about the accessibility of his own office and the enchantments on his own doors.

"An'Tellarus. What brings you here?"

"Not you."

"I am certain that makes us both much happier. These are not, however, public offices, and we are not equipped to handle visitors of note."

"No mortals are," she replied. "And yet, welcome is extended regardless. You may rest more easily; I have no interest in you whatsoever."

"I would take considerable comfort from that sentiment if you offered it from your own chambers in the High Halls."

"A pity. It is not your comfort that is my chief concern. Nor is it your safety. I feel that you are old enough and—should you choose to be, which happens lamentably seldom—wise enough to see to your own safety."

"Severn is my concern, not yours."

"So I had assumed. It is not, however, for either you or Severn I have come, and I have come in some haste. I am certain some eyes will be upon me when I leave this building, should we leave it the usual way. I am doubtful that I escaped detection while entering."

"What game do you play now?" The closed door opened at Elluvian's back. Of course it did. An'Tellarus was significant enough that Helmat couldn't remain on the wrong side of his door.

"More than one, of course. I find it marvelously diverting, given the alternatives. What have I told you in the past?"

"Since you are well aware of what you said, and I could easily be as aware should I choose to do so, I fail to see the relevance."

"Perhaps," Helmat said, "You might explain what you do consider relevant, An'Tellarus." He did not offer her even the curt nod Elluvian had offered. He was not amused.

"Very well." Her eyes were the same shade of blue they had been on sighting Elluvian. "I have been asked—as a favor to one who is less experienced and less powerful than I—to serve as escort for a mortal visitor to the High Halls."

The silence that followed seemed to remove all of the air from the office. She knew. Helmat did her the courtesy of acknowledging this. "The visit will be forbidden."

"I do not believe that will be the case," An'Tellarus replied. "Difficult situations require flexibility. The rules that confine the castelords of various races have been given that necessary flexibility.

"You have no say, Lord Marlin. Nor does Elluvian. According to his own laws, your Dragon Emperor cannot intervene in the perfectly *legal* actions of a castelord. Or perhaps I have failed to understand the laws?"

"She is not castelord."

"Is she not?"

"En?"

"Adellos is castelord."

"I believe you will find that that is inaccurate, at least in tense. Adellos *was* castelord. He is not castelord now."

Helmat did not return to his office. He marched, instead, to Rosen's abandoned desk and barked at Rosen's mirror. It flared instantly to life, as if it were terrified of the Wolflord's temper. "Garadin."

The image of Garadin's face—pale and green-eyed—instantly filled the mirror's frame. "Who is the castelord of the Tha'alani?"

"Adellos Coran'alani."

"And is Adellos intent upon leaving the quarter to visit the High Halls?"

"Adellos is currently indisposed. It is highly unlikely that he will visit the High Halls in the near future."

"Good." Helmat waved the mirror to stillness and silence.

Severn had already moved toward the Wolves' outer office doors, as if instinctively drawn there. He opened those doors when he saw a shadow of movement on the far side.

Ybelline was waiting.

Severn offered her both of his hands, rather than stepping out of the way. She stiffened before she closed her eyes and laid her palms across his. Leaning into him, she touched his forehead with her antennae.

The Wolflord is not happy, he told her. *Elluvian is not happy. Rosen is absent.* This amused her, but did not surprise her. *An'Tellarus has been waiting for you.*

Yes.

Severn didn't tell her that the High Halls weren't safe to visit. He did allow her a glimpse of his first encounter with An'Tellarus, and followed it with his second. On both occasions she had attempted to injure—if not kill—him to satisfy her curiosity.

Ybelline didn't approve, but the disapproval was unadorned with words. *From Helmat's expression, he is pleased with neither of his visitors this morning.*

Since this was the truth and Severn had nothing to add that would make it more palatable, he said nothing.

You will accompany us?

With Elluvian. Given his reaction, I wouldn't be surprised to see the Wolflord join us.

This amused, rather than angered, Ybelline. *He will not, but yes, he is almost alarmed.*

He was well past alarmed, in Severn's opinion.

You are not.

I know why you're going. No—I know what you hope to discover. I don't know how you intend to discover it. For the Barrani—almost any Barrani—it would be safer if you were dead.

It would be safer if all of my people were dead. Safer for them. Safer for you.

Severn shook his head, and then stilled; the gesture was only likely to dislodge the delicate connection between them. *That's not safety.*

We can, with a touch, know everything about you that we want to know.

You don't want to know anything.

No. But the knowledge is a powerful tool—and the powerful believe that if it is not a tool in their arsenal, it's best that it not be in anyone's. Apologies, Severn. You know all of this.

You're nervous.

Yes. A faint sense of warmth or amusement accompanied the word.

You asked An'Tellarus to escort you?

No. I was told only that an escort would come for me in the Wolves' office. Her grip tightened briefly. Severn thought *nervous* was the wrong word to describe what she was feeling, but didn't try to find the right one.

Why have you not told them that you're the castelord?

Them? You mean the Wolves and the Imperial Service?

Yes.

Technically, I am heir designate, not castelord. Yes, in any way that matters, I have made my claim—but there are ceremonies that must be observed, and they have not occurred yet.

When will they occur?

It depends on the outcome of this meeting.

Who are you visiting?

As you must suspect, An'Sennarin.

He released her hands, stepped back, and bowed.

The Wolflord had words to say, and given they were in his domain, those words were heard. But hearing the words changed nothing; he was not Ybelline's commander.

He was, however, Severn's. He made clear to Severn in no uncertain terms just how unhappy he would be if Ybelline Rabon came to any injury at all. He didn't attempt to order Severn to remain.

It was thirty minutes before the Wolflord grudgingly allowed them to leave. An'Tellarus appeared to have chosen to find him amusing rather than insulting, and Ybelline was accustomed to him. She made no attempt to stop him from speaking his angry piece.

They didn't leave the Halls of Law through the front doors. A carriage was waiting for them in the coach yard. It wasn't an Imperial carriage; it was too delicate in appearance for that, and lacked the crest of the Eternal Emperor. Elluvian gave the crest that did exist across the narrow doors a look of wary disgust.

In some fashion, Severn thought, the Barrani Wolf trusted An'Tellarus. For no other Barrani Lord would he have exposed such open disdain. Ybelline entered the carriage first, followed by An'Tellarus, who invited Severn to follow before Elluvian had been seated.

Elluvian found this mildly irritating.

Severn, however, held the door for a long beat before Elluvian seated himself. Severn then joined them.

The ride was not silent. An'Tellarus, seated across from Ybelline, began to speak. "I do not believe a Tha'alani of any rank has visited the High Halls before. Very little warning has, of course, been given to the people who dwell within."

Ybelline nodded. "It is why I wished to visit as quickly as possible."

"Very little, of course, is not none. I am watched—we are all watched—by rivals, enemies, and even allies. Perhaps especially allies. Rivals and enemies make no promises and therefore cannot betray you. I do not know what the topic of discussion will or might be—as I said, this is, to my knowledge, unprecedented. It has been some time since I have spent so long in the High Halls, but my information sources are generally good. I would not expect your visit to go unnoticed."

Ybelline nodded again.

"Were the meeting to occur on neutral ground—the High Halls will never be neutral—none of this would be necessary. I would, with your permission, avail myself of the arcane arts and alter your appearance. Alterations of that nature are possible in the High Halls, but they will draw more attention."

"Not more than her race will naturally draw," Elluvian said.

An'Tellarus inclined her head. "I am certain that any panic her presence might cause will be allayed by my presence at her side."

"How were you chosen as her personal guard?"

She smiled indulgently at Severn. "That is a question I will never answer to those outside of my household. Do you consider it a reasonable question?"

Severn met, and held, her gaze. "I consider it a practical question," he finally said.

"How so? In what way is it practical, given your audience? It might be considered dangerous or foolish, but practical? No."

"You will either answer, or you will not. If you do not answer, it means that you consider an answer disadvantageous. Or you consider the person asking beneath you."

"And the offense I might take at the question?"

"The question would be offensive to you if the association was one you wished to remain in shadows. You've already declared your support—your recent support—for An'Sennarin. I am not familiar with the factions at court; I do not know if your connection to An'Sennarin is of value to him. I assume it must be."

"But you are not so clear on the advantage I gain?"

"In that circumstance, I wouldn't be."

Her brows rose. "You can see an advantage for me in the association? It is very, *very* seldom that I am asked to serve as messenger and bodyguard."

"The advantage must be strong indeed," Elluvian added.

"Do not interrupt me," An'Tellarus snapped.

Severn and Ybelline exchanged a weary glance; it was followed by very slight smiles as they realized they had had the same thoughts about squabbling in the carriage.

An'Tellarus, however, said, "Do not relax yet. I have more

information to convey before we reach our destination, and we will not exit my carriage until that information has been delivered."

Severn didn't approach the entrance of the High Halls as a Wolf. As he was already in the presence of An'Tellarus and Ybelline, the subtle warning a tabard provided would be irrelevant. Ybelline would draw all attention. No Barrani who was breathing could possibly consider a Tha'alani's death a crime subject to caste court exemptions. Severn was beneath notice. He fell into step beside Elluvian, aware that their strides now matched. Aware that they were now here as An'Tellarus's servants or aides in the eyes of most of the witnesses.

The halls weren't as empty as they had been either of the times Severn had previously visited. People gathered by alcoves and beneath works of art; they talked in small pockets, their eyes blue as Ybelline walked past them, although he caught hints of a brighter gold in some. She wore no hood, made no attempt to hide her race. Once or twice she turned to speak a few words to An'Tellarus, but none of those words made enough sound that Severn could hear them.

For her part, An'Tellarus wore white and gold to Ybelline's green and gold; the Barrani Lord looked formal, even regal, as she escorted Ybelline, leading her subtly in the direction she wished Ybelline to go. Or so it appeared at first, but as Severn watched the two women in front of him, he revised his opinion; Ybelline chose the direction.

He watched the halls for any sign of movement; unlike city streets—some of which were narrower than the gallery from side to side—there were no second- or third-story windows behind which an assassin might take a shot at the Tha'alani; there were no crowded corners, no passing wagons. There was no way to follow the Tha'alani castelord—or almost castelord—without being seen.

No natural way.

Severn had played games in smaller spaces than this; had learned to listen for breaths, footsteps, when simple vision was otherwise impaired. He had scoffed—he had been very young—at the preposterous idea that people might somehow have, and waste, magic in order to cross a room undetected. He'd learned, a painstaking and even humiliating task, to be aware of that possible waste of magic.

He had had no such magic, and had also learned the importance of pillars, statues, fountains; he had learned to follow, exactly, the movement of wagon wheels or wagons if he wished to pass unseen in the open streets.

Did he expect that those lessons would come in useful in the High Halls? Possibly, but not today. Still, he watched, his hands empty. An'Tellarus's feet made no sound at all across the marble floors; her shadow, unlike Ybelline's, seemed to defy the actual fall of sunlight through the enormous open spaces in the ceilings above.

One glance at Elluvian made clear that if Severn thought attack unlikely, Elluvian didn't. But Elluvian approached the High Halls as if they were a battlefield of old—one that contained stragglers, carrion creatures, and corpses. He didn't walk through Elantran streets that way. Then again, those streets were full of mortals, most of whom were irrelevant to his survival.

The turnoff from the open gallery was at the far end; a T-junction formed between this open, almost majestic space and a hall that was slightly narrower. Ybelline paused and then turned to the right. An'Tellarus had already begun to move to the left; she was forced to correct her trajectory, making it clear that it was indeed Ybelline who led.

Ybelline, for her part, paused to allow An'Tellarus to join her. "You are certain?" An'Tellarus asked, her voice soft. Ybelline nodded.

Elluvian, eyes darkening with every step they took, glanced once at Severn. One glance appeared to be all he was willing to spare for the Wolf, but it was a telling glance, a commanding one. He had been alert while they proceeded through the main gallery; he was actively worried now. He said nothing to either Ybelline or An'Tellarus.

In this second hall, there were far fewer people. Those they did encounter appeared intent on travel; this was not a hall in which to gather, apparently. The ceilings were as high as the main hall's, but the light that fell from it, less; there were statues here that seemed older and more severe, placed between paintings and tapestries, all of which seemed to depict war.

Severn almost wished that this hall was An'Tellarus's hall; he might have asked her to identify which wars, although the answer was semi-obvious: there were Dragons in these paintings. Dragons whose wingspan became almost all of the sky; Dragons who, scales cracked, had taken root in the earth, where they continued to exhale the fire for which they were known, even in the stories meant for very young children.

Three of the paintings were smaller in width and height. They portrayed a central figure each; all three wore armor that resembled burnished silver, and all three wielded great swords. One man wielded a two-handed sword in one hand, a shield in the other, but the other two—one man, one woman—had chosen to forgo shields.

Severn knew, peripherally, that the Dragons and the Barrani had gone to war three times in the distant past. To the Barrani and the Dragons, Immortal both, he wondered if the final war had truly ended. Maybe war never did. But given the choice between a Barrani fieflord and a Dragon Emperor, he would choose the Dragon every time.

Ybelline stopped twice in this hall. The second time, she allowed An'Tellarus to walk ahead. The air around the lord seemed almost viscous for those few steps, although An'Tellarus herself lifted neither hand nor voice to pass through it. Severn could see odd ripples in the air, marked more easily because of its effect on the paintings on either wall. He reached for his dagger, but Elluvian lifted a staying hand. He, too, said nothing.

Severn remained behind Ybelline; Elluvian stepped in to the side An'Tellarus didn't occupy.

Ybelline hadn't spoken a word. In silence, they continued.

When they reached the final set of doors, they had passed through a total of three areas in which both Elluvian and An'Tellarus took the lead. There was no fourth.

The doors appeared to lack guards, but the door itself was warded; it was An'Tellarus who placed her palm against the engraved surface of dark wood. She stood, hand against door, but lowered her hand when the doors themselves began to glow, the light pale but distinct.

"I have never liked these doors," An'Tellarus said. "There is something distinctly messy about the ward."

Ybelline, however, seemed to be almost smiling. She recognized the magic that An'Tellarus disliked.

"Please," a disembodied voice said, "enter and be welcome."

Ybelline spoke in a language Severn did not immediately understand; it surprised him. He had never heard her speak her native tongue before.

"Yes," the voice replied. Ybelline spoke again.

"The choice, I leave to you, Ybelline Rabon'alani. There

are things that must be discussed that may affect you in your new role; among my own kin the fewer witnesses, the better."

Ybelline turned back to Severn, and offered him one hand. He took it with almost no hesitation. She touched his brow, her antennae brushing strands of hair out of their way, and said, *I do not think you will be able to enter if you are not physically anchored.*

What about Elluvian and An'Tellarus?

They are his kin; the risk is his, and therefore the decision.

You don't care if they know?

I believe An'Tellarus already does, but I am not certain what she was told when she was asked to escort a guest through the High Halls.

Elluvian?

He is a Wolf, as you are; he will know what you know, in the end, should he desire that knowledge. Come with me, she added. *You saw the beginning of this story. Come see the end.*

Once they passed through the doors, the external hall vanished—before the doors had closed on it. Severn felt a momentary disorientation; a visual ripple passed through the air, as if everything they now saw was beneath a curtain of falling water. The world reasserted itself quickly, but the floor beneath his feet felt carpeted or padded, although his eyes told him it was composed of unadorned stone.

The foyer itself seemed similar in style to An'Tellarus's interior foyer, but it possessed no paintings; flowers filled the alcoves and spaces meant for display. The foyer opened up; there were no doors to enclose it.

There were no visible servants, no visible attendants, and no guards. Perhaps they now waited with their lord for the arrival of Ybelline.

She had released his hand, and didn't reach for it again; it was not for comfort that she had reached for it the first time.

"Come," she said, as if she knew these rooms, as if they were completely familiar to her.

They followed. Severn now occupied the space to her right. An'Tellarus and Elluvian walked behind, their eyes a martial blue. If Ybelline had relaxed—and she had—her companions had done the opposite, as if fear and its resultant tension were a constant shared among their party.

Stone floor gave way to wood; it was the wood Ybelline now followed, and it led to a large open space that seemed to have no roof. The skies here were a crystal blue that Severn didn't recall from their carriage ride or the climb up the steps that led into the High Halls.

A table occupied space directly ahead of them; around it were tall, narrow chairs. At the head of the table sat a lone man. He rose as they approached, his gaze momentarily arrested by Severn.

He tendered Ybelline the deepest of Barrani bows, and held it. She bade him rise, but even so he did so slowly.

"You are Ollarin," Ybelline said.

"I was," he replied. "I have seen you before. You and your mortal companion. Will you join me?"

An'Tellarus's gaze shifted to Severn; he failed to meet it. This man's eyes were green, a color he had almost never seen Barrani eyes take. He was aware of what that color meant: he was happy. Genuinely happy.

Maybe happiness denied age in the Barrani; Ollarin—no, An'Sennarin—seemed young to Severn. Much younger than either An'Tellarus or Elluvian.

"But I forget myself," Ollarin said. He turned toward An'Tellarus and offered her a bow that was not quite as deep as the bow he extended Ybelline. "I am in your debt, An'Tellarus."

"What have I told you?"

"I trust you enough to acknowledge my obligation."

"That is far, *far* worse."

Elluvian was staring at An'Sennarin. "You must have been barely of age when you took the seat," he finally said.

"Yes. It has been challenging."

"You still hold the title."

"For now, yes."

Ybelline accepted a chair to An'Sennarin's right; she indicated that Severn was to take the chair to his left.

An'Sennarin passed his hand through the air immediately above the table at which they were seated, and something shimmered into view. It was a painting. No, he thought, a sketch. He recognized the artist.

It was one of Random's sketches. Random had drawn a picture of the end of this table—and seated at it were Ybelline, Severn, and An'Sennarin.

CHAPTER TWENTY-FIVE

SEVERN LOOKED AT THE PICTURE. YBELLINE wore an emerald green in Random's sketch; it matched the color of the dress she had chosen. There was no tiara across the sketched Ybelline's forehead. Severn in the sketch wore the clothing Elluvian had purchased for his use what felt like months ago, but was not.

Ollarin, however, was dressed exactly as she had sketched him.

"I am afraid," An'Sennarin said, "I do not know your name."

"I am Severn Handred. Private Severn Handred."

"Yes. You are a Wolf."

Severn nodded.

"Do you see the shadow you cast across the table in this drawing? I believe it reflects your service."

Severn had noticed. He didn't expect anything Random produced to be literal. But he noted that neither Ybelline nor An'Sennarin cast any shadow at all—or not that Random had chosen to capture.

"I have agreed to meet you here," the young lord said, "to ask you to abandon your investigation."

Ybelline said nothing. Her pallor was off.

"That is not a request I can fulfill," Severn replied. "I serve at the command of the Emperor."

An'Sennarin nodded, as if it was the answer he had expected; his eyes darkened, but still contained more green than blue. "As do we all." He turned to Ybelline.

She said nothing, but reached out—almost in spite of herself—to offer An'Sennarin a hand. He took it without hesitation.

Elluvian joined them, taking the seat beside Severn. "An'Sennarin."

Now the Sennarin lord's eyes became Barrani blue. "Lord Elluvian."

"While the private has no direct channel to the Emperor, I do. The Tha'alani were greatly harmed by the crimes committed decades ago. The criminals were brought to justice in a fashion; the presence of a lone Barrani man at the edge of the mob went undetected until very recently.

"It is out of concern for the Tha'alani that this investigation—this hunt—was called. It was assumed, as it must be among our kin, that you took the title and then caused the deaths as a way of overwhelming any information about the Barrani that the Tha'alaan might contain."

"And that is not your assumption now?"

"The dates," he finally said. "The murders began before you took the throne. Had you been older, had you been more significant at court, it is safe to assume that what happened to the Tha'alani was part of your plan of ascension. But you were newly come to the title. I am not certain any of us were aware of your significance until after you inherited."

"You are not perhaps aware of my significance now," An'Sennarin replied.

"Anyone who can rise from your former position to your current position is worthy of note."

Ybelline said, "I was sent here by Adellos."

An'Sennarin shut his eyes briefly. "You have not seen what he has seen."

Her brows rose in some surprise; when they fell, her eyes were narrowed, their color darker. "No."

"He asked you to come in his stead for a reason." An'Sennarin rose, pushing his chair soundlessly back as if to escape its confines. "He has no need to visit in person if he wishes to speak with me."

Silence, then. Utter stillness from both An'Tellarus and Elluvian.

Without thought, Severn reached for Ybelline's hand. He understood what Random had given Tessa. So, too, did she. And it was fear of that oracle, that peculiar gift, that had caused everything that had followed.

As if aware of this, An'Sennarin turned to An'Tellarus. "Yes," Ollarin said, although she hadn't spoken. "Adellos holds my name."

"Speak less," was An'Tellarus's sharp reply. "You are now in the presence of Imperial Wolves."

An'Sennarin nodded. "If he has my name, he can control or destroy me. If he dies, the name will be lost—but he has not died."

"And if the deaths of the Tha'alani were meant to draw him out?"

"They failed. I am not a threat to the Tha'alani." He turned away. "I was never a threat to them." But these words were softer. Thinner.

Ybelline rose. "An'Tellarus, Elluvian," she said, "I must

ask you to withdraw. There are things to be said here that are caste court business."

"Ours or yours?" An'Tellarus asked, in grim amusement.

"Mine."

An'Tellarus raised a brow. "Child," she said, her voice honeyed, "that is not the way you show gratitude."

"No," Ybelline agreed. "And I am grateful for your escort. But the gratitude and obligation will fall upon An'Sennarin's shoulders; you will not seek me or my kin in the immediate future. It was for his sake that you agreed, not mine or my people's. It is for my people's sake that I am here."

"Very well," An'Tellarus replied. She turned and walked out of the sunlight, pausing only once to glance over her shoulder at Elluvian, whose hesitation was marked, and longer. Caught between his duties as a Wolf and An'Tellarus's silent command, he chose to navigate the danger that was immediately in front of him. He followed.

"He is not wrong," An'Sennarin said, when they were gone for some five minutes. "The dates could mean many things. My rise to power."

"The death of the previous lord and his heir," Ybelline said. Her eyes were now hazel, but flecks of green were emerging. It was the manner of the deaths that had struck Severn. Clearly they had struck Ybelline in exactly the same way.

"Did you know Tessa?" the Barrani Lord asked. It was not the question Severn had been expecting; it was one of the possibilities Ybelline had been prepared for, given her lack of visible reaction.

"She was dead before I was six years of age." The words were flat, neutral. Her eyes were fixed to his face, as if vision could give her, momentarily, what she could not retrieve without physical contact. "You knew her."

He nodded and began to fidget. "I was not the heir designate when I came to the High Halls."

"No."

"I was not a Lord of this court before I arrived."

"You arrived, I assume, to take that test?"

He nodded. "I came from the West. The politics of the
High Court are...different."

"More deadly?"

He grimaced. "Differently deadly. I had been summoned
to court by An'Sennarin, from an insignificant branch family in the West March."

"Why?"

An'Sennarin was quiet, but not still; he opened his mouth,
closed it, opened it again, in a sequence that implied he was
searching for words and failing to find the ones he wanted.

Ybelline waited.

"You are perhaps not aware of how Barrani society is struc-
tured."

"No."

"We are not like your kin. From the moment we are born
there are words we must not speak. Words we must not hear."

She nodded.

"The West March is less formal than the High Halls; it
does not exist in the shadow of a Dragon. The Eternal Emperor's reach does not encompass the West March; we are
not part of his hoard. The rigid formality of the High Halls
is necessary—or so I've been told—because we *do* live in
the shadow of a Dragon. We live at the foot of his throne.

"There are tests given us when we are young."

Severn's eyes left Ybelline. He was not afraid that
An'Sennarin would harm her.

"I did well in those tests. Remarkably well, considering
the significance of my parents and siblings. My parents were

proud." The words were laced with bitterness. "My siblings hated it. I survived that displeasure because I was never officially made heir. I was much younger than either my brother or sister. Too young to make the journey to Elantra.

"But not too young to be commanded to make it. You cannot imagine what your city looked like to my eyes. The streets are crowded, smelly, oft hot; there are too few trees and the buildings are made primarily of stone or dead wood. I was considered lucky, even exalted—I was given a room within the High Halls themselves by An'Sennarin.

"He did not otherwise condescend to speak with me; he arranged the time and the hour for the Test of Name. I would not, of course, be of use or value to him because my potential could not be properly exploited were I not a Lord." He spoke bitter words in an entirely pragmatic way.

"I found the High Halls...difficult. Where the High thrones stand there are trees, but they are almost silent, and elsewhere nature is caged and forced to conform."

"And the West March is left to grow wild?"

"Not all of it, no. But much of it. The High Halls were not my home. In truth, I had no desire that they become so. But the test was mandatory; the only way I could escape it would be to flee in the middle of the night. I knew—we all know—that one passes simply by surviving. But great are the number of my kin who do not pass. They enter the Tower, and they never emerge.

"Children are children," he said, his voice lower. "And childhood fears, writ large, make the test a terrifying thing. Thus I was terrified. I was young."

"You are still considered young by your kin."

"An'Tellarus is ancient," he replied. "We are *all* young to her. Young, and foolish with youth."

"How did you meet her?" Severn asked.

"She spent centuries in the West March, and she is known to be unusual in her choice of social companions. She can be. She might befriend the lowest of servants, the most humble of guards, and no one looks askance. Approaching me would have raised no brows at all; I was sponsored by An'Sennarin, and therefore of interest."

"Did the An'Sennarin of the time encourage this?"

"He could not discourage it," An'Sennarin replied, with the hint of a smile. "He could attempt to order her not to interfere with his kin—but he was not a man who gave orders he knew would not be obeyed; it would force him to act if he did not wish to be perceived as weak. It is why An'Tellarus has always felt free to come and go as she pleases.

"She guessed, I suppose, that I was terrified of the Test of Name. I had two weeks of terror to go, and she attempted to distract me. She failed, of course. I was younger. I did not believe that my life had no value if I was not a Lord of this court. If failure did not mean death, I would have gladly failed. But An'Sennarin wished me to join the Arcanum; he wished to train the talent that existed as potential."

"What talent?" Ybelline asked, something strange in her tone.

"Can you not guess, future castelord?"

She closed her eyes. "You are an elementalist."

"Yes. I am a summoner. I am a summoner with a very strong affinity."

"For water," she whispered.

"For water. In the West March, if I touched the water meant as defense and shield, I could hear its voice. If I asked it to become my playmate, it would. It did not ever seek to harm me; it was more home to me than the home into which I was born. As a child, I did not understand that this took power; it took effort, at times, to make myself heard, but I did not consider such effort magic. It took as much effort to make myself clear to the adults that surrounded us. Possibly more.

"But it did take power. And when that power was discovered, I was severed from the West March and brought to court. To this court, with its stone and its poisons and its lack of any familial structures that I could understand. It was an *honor*, you understand. My success here would lend my family prominence."

Ybelline was pale. "You found a way to speak to the water in Elantra."

"There was so much of it, in comparison. The Ablayne. The harbor. There was no living water in the High Halls— not to begin with; there was one fountain that would have worked perfectly, but to approach it without invitation was, and is, death. I reverted to my early childhood ways; I felt trapped and the horror of the test grew and grew until there was no way out from beneath it." His hands were shaking as he spoke, although they lay flat in his lap. "I am sorry," he said, lifting his head. "I am a terrible host when the servants are sent away. Are you hungry at all? Would you drink if drinks were offered?"

"I am not hungry," Ybelline said. She glanced at Severn; he shook his head.

An'Sennarin nodded, as if he expected no less. His hands stilled. Blue-eyed now, he held Ybelline's gaze. "You are caste-lord, now? Or you will be."

"Yes."

"You understand what happened?"

She shook her head. "I have made what the Halls of Law would call educated guesses. They have shifted with this meeting, but no—they are still guesses."

"Then guess, for me—share that vulnerability with me. I will not think less of you if you are wrong."

Severn stood and moved away from the chair he had occupied.

"No," An'Sennarin said, voice soft. "This concerns you. I believe it must. I have held this sketch since my only visit to the Oracular Halls, and I have waited."

"For what?"

"You. You and Ybelline."

"Why?"

"I know why she is here, Severn Handred. I do not yet know why you are. Perhaps I will never know; an oracle, once given, is only truly understood after all events that concern it are out of reach." He turned, again, to Ybelline.

Her eyes were green now. Almost the exact shade An'Sennarin's had been when they had entered his presence.

"I will guess, as you have asked," Ybelline said. She lowered her chin, as if in thought. "But answer a question before I do."

"Any question I can answer, I will truthfully answer."

"This request—this game of guessing—did not originate from you."

He laughed then, his eyes clearing until they had become almost as green as hers. "No. It wasn't my idea. If I'm to tell you—and I will—all that occurred from my perspective, I can't see that having you guess has any use to us."

"It was Adellos who asked you to ask me."

"Yes."

The silence was thick. Severn wished he had been allowed to leave the table, to join Elluvian and An'Tellarus, although the latter guaranteed that the meeting would be dangerous in ways he couldn't yet predict.

"He still wants to know what your guess is," An'Sennarin said, when Ybelline did not speak.

She exhaled. "You sought the water when the burden of fear proved too great."

He nodded.

"You went to the harbor?"

He nodded again.

"And what you touched, when you reached—what your shouts raised—was not the small elementals of your past."

"No. It was—" he shook his head. "It was wild, loud—the difference between summer showers and bitter storm. I heard the voice of the water, and it heard me. And it rose from the ocean like a wall of death."

"That death was not your death."

"No—I think, if I had not somehow caught the whole of its attention, it would have walked all the way to the High Halls. My death, should that happen, was not guaranteed—but the same cannot be said for much of the population of the High Halls."

She nodded. "But the water heard you."

"It did. And when it paused to listen, when it rejoined the ocean from which it had drawn its form, it heard my loneliness and fear. I could not summon an elemental in this place to keep me company—"

"You already had."

"Yes, but—unintentionally. The water itself would have stayed by my side, but to reach the High Halls I would have had to walk from the harbor through the city streets. And the rules that govern use of unsanctioned magic in this city are strictly enforced."

"When it is recognized, yes."

"I did not know how to summon water, not consciously; I had gone, always, to the water when I wished its solace. I had never used water as a weapon—and I believe that was the intent of my admission to the Arcanum."

"That was not what you wanted."

"It's not what I wanted. I know that the water does, at times. To drown. To destroy. But that is not all water wants."

"No."

"Because of you. Because of your people. The water is where the Tha'alaan resides. It *is* the Tha'alaan."

She stared, then. "Adellos told you this?"

His smile robbed his face of grief, of age. "The water told me." He exhaled. "And the water told me where I must go if I wished to find peace away from the High Halls."

She frowned.

"I was exhausted by this point with the effort of convincing the water that an attack on the High Halls—and An'Sennarin—was the exact opposite of what I needed. But the water's voice was a comfort to me, I cannot deny it. And perhaps the knowledge that I *could* ask the water to act on my behalf, and it would do so willingly, was a comfort as well. I followed the water's direction."

"You said the water did not leave the harbor."

"No."

"But you could hear it?"

"Yes—with effort. I cannot raise voice from here—or could not at the time—and be heard."

"No wonder An'Sennarin wanted you. That is a level of power, of connection, almost unheard of."

"Adellos asks—"

"Adellos is attempting to speak with me now; I am not of a mind to allow it, given his absolute silence in the past few days." The words were both frosty and heated.

"He wished to spare you—"

"He is castelord," she replied. "He knows that the castelord is, and can be, spared nothing. He is perhaps afraid of the decision I will make when all becomes known."

An'Sennarin nodded.

"But you are not."

"I think I would almost welcome it."

"Where did the water take you? It did not bring you to the Tha'alani quarter."

"No. But away from the harbor there's a small inlet. The water led me there." He closed his eyes. "Tessa was waiting there. Jerrin was with her, and Tobi. They were waiting for me."

"They had been warned," he said, when he returned from memory to the thread of his story. "They were not to communicate with outsiders. Such communication was feared; it made their kin anathema to every other living race. I was young, but I understood the importance of secrets; had I understood what would occur when my magical affinity was discovered, I would have done everything in my power to hide it.

"They didn't touch me the way you touch your criminals."

"They are not our criminals."

"Ah, apologies. The Emperor's criminals. They spoke—but they spoke slowly, they struggled to find words. I guessed that they weren't used to speaking at all."

"No. Speech is taught, but not well. It is not necessary when we are all part of the Tha'alaan."

"Tessa explained that. But she—" Silence, then. "She said that she'd discovered that we *could* talk the way they spoke in the Tha'alaan."

"And Random had given her the words by which to do so," Ybelline whispered.

"Yes. Years earlier, they had traveled to the Oracular Halls. I would have loved to have joined them. I think I wanted to be part of that, and it was...it was still alive, for them. For Tessa. I could see it, I could feel it, I could live through it as if I had been there.

"She called my name. She called my True Name. I would have heard her had I still been living in the West March."

"You weren't afraid of her."

"I wasn't—how could I be? Tessa was—" he shook his head. "All *my* life I was told that True Names must be hidden. They must be secret. Death—or worse—awaits those who share them."

"The Tha'alaan is not like your name." It was Severn who now spoke. "The Tha'alaan exerts no control; everyone can be aware of everything anyone else is thinking. Anger is tended; fear is tended—neither are allowed to grow unchecked. But no member of the Tha'alaan can force another member to obey; no one can take control of their body, their actions.

"True Names allow this."

An'Sennarin nodded without surprise. "She spoke to me. I heard her."

"She did touch you."

"Not then—but yes. She wanted me to understand that there was no fear in sharing. No fear in being known. She wanted me to see—" He closed his eyes. "And I did see."

Severn, listening, understood. Tessa was not a threat to An'Sennarin. She would never have become a threat—he had seen the thoughts she had never tried to withhold. He had not killed Tessa or her friends. Would never, Severn thought, have tried.

"You were discovered."

"My association with Tessa was discovered, yes. It was forbidden, and I understood, by then, what forbidden meant. I didn't have to see her in person to bespeak her. I could continue the interaction." He swallowed. "Tessa helped me to pass the Test of the Tower. She swallowed my fear; she told me what I was looking at when I could barely see. She…hated the Barrani, for a while, because this test was what they forced on their children or their family." He lifted his head. "Do you understand? I could not *be* An'Sennarin were it not for her.

"But it was passing the Test that caused the attitude of the ruler of Sennarin to change. I was going to be useful now. I was significant. I had, in an attempt to allay his suspicions, stopped leaving the High Halls; I went to the Arcanum and agreed to be tested. I understood what the tests entailed. I could have failed them comfortably, but it seemed prudent to keep An'Sennarin happy."

Ybelline was watching him carefully.

"I was despised by his heir. I was disliked and feared by the woman who stood in the ruler's shadow, waiting her chance to step over his corpse to stand closer to the throne of Sennarin. This was not unknown in the West March among the significant families, but ours was not considered significant enough. My brother and sister—I had both—never cared for me as Tessa's family cared for her, but they would never have considered murder.

"I did try. In the end, I discovered—from Tessa—that I could summon the water in a different way. And I created a small fountain in the Sennarin halls. It was considered a risk, but it was also considered a display of Sennarin's power; it was the first such fountain to be created in centuries. I could hear the water when I was in need of retreat, of peace."

"Tessa told you how to do this?"

He nodded. "She was worried for me, I think. And I grew worried for her, because the interest in the Tha'alani grew." He closed his eyes. "And I should have known. I should have known, then, what that interest would mean.

"I was sitting in a suite of rooms, granted me when I passed the Test. Had I not been seated I would have fallen, I think—but regardless, they knew. They knew that I knew the instant she died."

"Did they ask?"

"No. They knew, but they did not acknowledge it; it would be acknowledging my weakness. It would make me a target, and if I were a target, my power would become a threat, a liability. It was my fault that she died; my fault that her death was considered necessary. My fault, in the end, that the deaths that followed were considered necessary as well."

"They were not your fault," Ybelline said. "They were never your fault. Tessa continued to want what she wanted the day she first met Random: to open up the world in which she lived; to understand the people who could not share in it. If anyone is to blame it is the Tha'alani. We did not keep her safe enough as a child. Had we been then what we are now, she would not have met Random. She would not have learned...what she learned.

"You did not kill her. You did not kill the rest of my kin." Ybelline rose.

An'Sennarin reached out and caught her by the hand. "Adellos asks you to stay."

"Adellos may speak to me in person." Her tone implied that she would not speak to him in any other way.

"He asks that you listen."

"What you say now is not something relevant to the Tha'alani," she replied, the words brusque, her eyes green. "I am satisfied that you had no part to play in the long-ago murders, and I am unwilling to revisit them now if it is not necessary. I am unwilling to force the Tha'alanari to revisit them; one unguarded rediscovery damaged two of them."

"Adellos commands you to listen," he said.

"Adellos cannot command me."

"He is castelord, Ybelline."

"Not in any way that now matters. By our standards—the

standards of our caste court, our people—he is too broken to continue to shepherd us. The Tha'alanari will not follow him."

"Then Adellos *asks*. I did tell him," he added, chagrined, "that asking would be better. But he said he can't ask when there is only one acceptable answer. It's too much like a lie."

Silence. Ybelline's hand—the free hand—bunched into fist before she once again sat at the table.

"I did not know about the Tha'alani murders. I knew, by this point, that the Tha'alani were feared. I did not know that they were being murdered in the city streets. Not until Adellos spoke my name. My True Name."

Ybelline closed her eyes.

"He understood, better than Tessa, why those names must never be shared. I had not given him my name; Random had not given him my name, although he did meet with her in person. But Adellos understood what had happened, and Adellos found the memories and excised them. Tessa had hidden them—"

"She could not hide them from Adellos."

"He says you are almost wrong. She was strong enough; she lacked experience."

"She was desperate."

An'Sennarin bowed his head in acknowledgment. "Tessa discovered that parts of those memories were no longer available in the Tha'alaan. Adellos started this work before she died. Before any of your people were killed. He understood what Random had given Tessa unintentionally. And he understood why that would be feared among *my* kin.

"I'd been open with Tessa. I did not fear her." He closed his eyes, but continued to speak. "We were both too young. We were both naive. When the castelord found our memories, he understood the lengths to which my kin would go, because he was neither young nor naive.

"The first time he used my True Name, he was angry. He demanded to know what part I had to play in Tessa's death. And Ybelline—I had no choice but to answer. He could have killed me on that day. He did consider it."

She was pale now, almost colorless; her eyes were green when she opened them. "He clearly did not act."

"No—because he knew. I could not lie to him." An'Sennarin opened his eyes. They were blue to Ybelline's green.

"He told you about their deaths."

An'Sennarin nodded, his expression grim, his eyes affixed to hers. "He told me about *all* of the deaths. I confronted An'Sennarin—carefully. It was the first time he approved of my demeanor at court. He was—" Words dropped away. The Barrani had a memory that was akin to Records, and he was in the grip of those memories now. "He was almost smug. Condescending. He told me—he told me—"

She caught the hand that held hers with her free hand, sandwiching his between the two. "You do not have to do this."

He shook his head. "I have been waiting for this day for decades. Because I visited Random. I will do this thing, and it will be done.

"An'Sennarin—my predecessor—told me that he had done this deliberately to distract the Tha'alani from the truth he suspected they held; he had done it to be certain that I would be free of their interference. I was *in his debt*. I would have tried to kill him in that moment, but Adellos took control."

CHAPTER TWENTY-SIX

YBELLINE BLANCHED BUT SAID NOTHING.

Severn watched them both.

"Adellos took control of my body, of my hands, of my words. Adellos offered my lord the gratitude that I could not even pretend. Adellos asked if, now that I was safe, the deaths were over, the association with the Tha'alani at an end. Five Tha'alani had died by this time. You must know what the answer was."

There had been more than a dozen deaths. They did know.

"An'Sennarin was angry. Angry and afraid. He didn't know what the Tha'alani knew—only that they knew more than he could confirm. But he understood how to damage them. I think he would not have stopped until he was caught by the Emperor, or until the Tha'alani were broken. Destroyed. He knew that the Tha'alanari were injured, that they had withdrawn from most Imperial duties at the time."

"How?"

"I do not know. Had I asked, he would not have answered."

She frowned, but nodded.

"Adellos released me when I made my way back to my rooms, but he hovered. He thought I was observed, and the observation must return nothing that indicated my displeasure. I suspected An'Sennarin knew it; Adellos agreed. But any reaction that moved this from suspicion to confirmation was certain to be a far greater disaster for his people. For Tessa's people.

"She was never a threat to us."

"Adellos was." Ybelline kept her voice even.

"Adellos did not even attempt to use Tessa's experiences and memories until after the mob-fueled murders began. If he was a threat to us—to me—it was defensive; an act of desperation to save his kin. But he understood what Tessa understood: I had never desired to damage the Tha'alaan. I had never desired to own it, to use it. What I wanted—" He exhaled.

She kept her hands around his.

"We talked. When he found out how I had discovered Tessa the first time we met, he was—shocked? Appalled? But he understood that the elemental water had taken an interest in me. A personal interest. It is the same interest the water has in the Tha'alani. It is the interest the water takes in the castelords of your race."

Ybelline nodded again.

"He thought it likely that even without Random, the water would have brought me into contact with her people—your people. In that case, I wouldn't have been able to speak to Tessa except with words. I would have tried. He thought it likely that An'Sennarin would have murdered Tessa just to be certain."

"But... I wouldn't have known. Not instantly."

Severn cleared his throat, and both Ybelline and the Barrani Lord turned toward him. "If we accept that power is the only legitimate ruler, nothing changes. We are valued only in that we are useful to the powerful."

"That has always been true."

"The Emperor has no need of most humans in that case. What he is trying to build is a place where you and Tessa might meet without the consequences to both of you."

"Perhaps. It is not a risk I will ever take again."

Severn nodded.

"I found a master in the Arcanum. He is known as an elementalist, but his affinity is, and has always been, fire. There were no masters with affinity to water. Few with affinity for earth. I was expected to be slow—a country cousin with little finesse and understanding of the subtle politics of adults. It was not hard to pretend to be what I actually am.

"But I needed to have as much intentional skill as I possibly could. There was only one way this cleansing would end."

"You killed them."

"I killed them."

"Adellos helped."

"Yes. Yes, Adellos helped. What I could do with water, then, I could not do on my own; his was the control, mine, the power. I asked, Ybelline. I think I begged. I wanted the killings to stop. No—I wanted to be the one to stop them. It was the only thing left that I could do for Tessa, and I needed to be the one to do it."

"And the four witnesses?"

He shrugged. "They were, as you must have guessed, complicit in the murders. They were not witnesses; they were actors. They took advantage of the frenzy of the crowd to encourage the deaths that followed. They were not examined by the Tha'alani interrogators; they had come forth voluntarily, after all. And I did not want those crimes to recur. I did not want their study—the study of the witnesses—to once again disrupt the Tha'alaan.

"They deserved to die. Even by Imperial Law, they deserved

it. Had they been taken in, had they been examined by the Tha'alani at the Emperor's discretion, they would have died."

"…But we would have had to go through four sets of memories."

"Again. Adellos did not need to guide my hand by that point."

"He did not attempt to dissuade you."

"It might surprise you to know that he did. He did not, however, attempt to command or control. He had his own ambivalence, and he understood why I wanted them dead. It was not revenge; I had that. It was to protect the Tha'alanari."

"And you knew the effect it would have."

"I have been speaking to Adellos for most of your life; we have been friends, even by your standards. I have heard much about the burden of the castelord, separate even from the Tha'alanari. When it was too much to bear in isolation, he reached out to me—to a Barrani Lord, raised to games in which murder is an acceptable move. Nothing he spoke of could damage *me*. Nothing he spoke of could break me. I knew what the witness testimony, verified by the Tha'alani, would do to the Tha'alaan. I made the decision to kill."

"He provided you the names."

"He could not hold them back," An'Sennarin said with a smile. "That is the thing that is not clear to those who have neither given nor taken a True Name. It is not a one-way exchange. I am far better equipped to hide my thoughts from him now than I was on that long-ago day. And it pains him greatly to attempt to exert control; he suffers even now with the guilt of it.

"If you use my name, as Adellos did, you will discover that weakness as well. I will not fight you," he added, voice softer. "I know that you know it, or can know it, or will know it— you will be castelord. But Adellos has held that name and that knowledge separate from the Tha'alaan. And the water understands; I do not believe she will release it without his permission.

"I would not have become An'Sennarin were it not, in the end, for Tessa and the Tha'alaan. I would give it all back were she to survive. But as An'Sennarin I could end the deaths. As An'Sennarin I could destroy the parts of Sennarin that had allowed the murders to be orchestrated. I could end all threat from my line—and any lesser family—only as ruler.

"The murder of kin, the assassinations of kin, will not trouble the Emperor at all."

"The witnesses were not Barrani."

"No. I will be a Barrani Lord accused of a crime that cannot be dismissed by the laws of exemption. It is my death that will end the investigation, if you carry it through to its logical conclusion.

"And I will not walk to that death now—although there is nothing you can take from my thoughts and my experience that does not already exist somewhere in the Tha'alaan. But it is my kin, not yours, who will perish before I eventually fall, and my kin have done nothing but harm to yours. There will, perhaps, be some poetic justice in my death."

"Is that what you've waited for? Your death?"

"Justice. I am, at heart, a coward."

Severn understood, then, why Elluvian and An'Tellarus had been sent from the room.

"A coward?"

"Death would have been a blessing, but I did not have the strength or courage to end my own life. The lives of others, yes. But not my own."

Ybelline opened her mouth; Severn lifted a hand. She closed her mouth on whatever she had been about to say. It was Severn who spoke. "Why did you visit the Oracular Halls?"

"I wished to meet Random. Tessa spoke of her often."

"Were you the Barrani Lord who attempted to visit her recently?"

An'Sennarin frowned. "No. I visited her but once when I had some hope remaining."

"What did you ask her?"

"I did not ask her anything."

"Oracles—"

"I did not ask her anything because Tessa had asked nothing," he said. He closed his eyes. "I wanted to save them. I was afraid by then. I had told Tessa, clearly, that the only way we could safely meet was through the bond of my name. I thought the suspicion would pass. I had time.

"She didn't. I was allowed to visit Random because Random asked it. She did not know my name; did not know that what she had given Tessa in the privacy of the Tha'alaan *was* my name. I don't think she understands it now, although she is older. You have visited her?"

Severn nodded.

"What did you ask of her?"

"We had no intention of receiving an oracle, either. Random was a person of interest in our investigation. We wanted to ask about Tessa and her friends. No memory of the oracle given Tessa on her first visit remained in the Tha'alaan. It remained with Random, and she wanted, I think, to tell someone. Random had no fear of the Tha'alani. No fear of Ybelline."

"You would have known, eventually," An'Sennarin said.

"The Imperial Service is not willing to wait when other options are available."

"And will you inform the Imperial Service?"

"In this? It is not required. I have been seconded to the Wolves."

He smiled. After a pause, so did Ybelline. "I do not have what Adellos has sequestered from even the Tha'alanari. I have no access to most of what remains of Tessa's life. I have the memories that she so artfully wove in disparate, hard-to-follow strands through the Tha'alaan—but those were later, and they remain if one knows how to look carefully.

"But having seen some of Tessa's life, some of her thought, I cannot believe that what she wanted—even when she began to fear—was your death. She would have believed that she caused it, just as you believe you were responsible for hers."

"But she did die."

"And you did not. Do you think your death will somehow cancel out hers?"

He didn't reply, but the answer was obvious. "Random," he said, returning the drifting conversation to Severn's question, "gave me sketches. This was one—but this was clearest, to me. I knew where it would take place, but not when."

"She didn't explain."

"No, but she couldn't. She understood that this is what she saw, this is what she must capture. I thought perhaps the truth had come to light. I thought," he added, after a brief pause, "that the woman in this sketch—you—must be the new castelord. Adellos explained that the new castelord would know; there was no way for him to completely excise the memory from the Tha'alaan. He did try."

Ybelline's eyes widened.

"I tried as well. But I am not of your kin; I spoke to the water. The water understood what I desired. I could have, at that point, commanded the water. But she asked me if I was willing to destroy the whole of the Tha'alaan in order to achieve my goal—and I was not. I will never be willing to pay that price.

"But it means I will live with an eternity of Tha'alani rulers who know my hidden name, my True Name."

"And we would live," she said, "with the knowledge that you might disturb or harm the Tha'alaan, if what you have just said is true."

"Yes."

Ybelline released his hand. "I am not the Emperor. I am not—yet—castelord, as you have pointed out. It is not I, in the end, who must judge you, if judgment is what you require."

Severn said, "We were tasked with finding the Barrani responsible for the murders. We've completed our mission; that man is dead. He was brought to justice before I was born."

"And the witnesses?"

Severn said nothing. He wasn't certain how those men would be handled now. The Emperor's Law was the Emperor's Law.

That didn't seem to concern An'Sennarin—and perhaps it would, in time. He was, by Barrani reckoning, Severn's age, although he had lived in Severn's estimation at least four times as long.

"Did An'Tellarus see this sketch?"

"Yes."

"And the others?"

An'Sennarin looked away from Ybelline for perhaps the first time in minutes. He smiled; it was almost rueful. "Yes."

"May I see what she saw?"

"It will not have the same meaning for you as it does for us; you have never been to the West March."

"I haven't," Severn replied. The future was foreign territory.

"Let me consider your request. An'Tellarus has not forbidden it, but she is unpredictable, and I do not wish to anger her." He turned back to Ybelline. Met, and held, her gaze.

Ybelline rose. "Tell Adellos that I will speak with him soon."

An'Sennarin nodded. He then held out his hands—both of his hands—palm out before her, turning his body so that

Severn couldn't see his expression. The expression, however, wasn't necessary. The color of his eyes had become, in that gesture, irrelevant.

Ybelline looked at his hands, hers almost stiff by her sides.

But Severn knew what she would do. Both Ybelline and he were caught in some fashion by Tessa's early life, Tessa's early hope. What Tessa wanted was what they wanted. Perhaps that would pass. Perhaps it would not.

Ybelline bent and placed both of her hands across An'Sennarin's. She hesitated briefly, and then the line of her shoulders sank as she leaned forward and placed her antennae gently against An'Sennarin's forehead.

Severn waited, head bowed.

Only when he heard the sound of weeping did he lift his chin. He could see Ybelline's face; it was wet with tears, but her tears were silent. An'Sennarin's, unseen, were not. Severn's hands became fists, reflexive fists. He understood. He could not feel fear of the Tha'alaan, of the Tha'alani, because Ybelline had offered it the first time; there was a warmth, a sense of belonging, a sense of acceptance that he had found almost nowhere else.

An'Sennarin would never have valued Tessa so highly if he had not, in some fashion, wanted that.

Elluvian was waiting. Severn had no difficulty finding either Elluvian or An'Tellarus; they were shouting at each other, and their voices were carried by the acoustics of An'Sennarin's rooms.

He must have grimaced, because Ybelline chuckled. "It is seldom that Barrani are so…demonstrative. There must be some trust between them."

"If this is trust, I'd rather be suspicious of everyone for the rest of my life."

She laughed, as Severn had intended. "What will you do?"

"I doubt the decision will be up to me."

She stopped. "I don't."

"Do you believe that the witnesses we pieced together from the Halls of Laws Records were part of the mob that committed those murders?"

She nodded.

"And you've no desire to confirm it."

"An'Sennarin is not wrong. It will damage us, and we have not yet recovered from Timorri's discovery. We will be better prepared," she added. "The information won't come as a surprise. I would be the one sent to deal with the interview of the remaining survivor."

"If we release him, will he survive?"

She was silent.

"Adellos could stop him."

"He won't. He might argue, but he will not stop him."

"Because he doesn't disagree?"

"Because he doesn't disagree. We are perhaps at our worst when we make decisions on behalf of others. The desire to protect others can drive us to places we would never otherwise dare to walk." She held his gaze.

It was Severn who looked away.

"I could not have done what you did to preserve Elianne's life. Adellos could. And for the same reasons. But—I think I could have done it had Tessa been alive and by doing so I might save her."

He shook his head.

"You don't believe it?"

"I do," he whispered. "But I was Tessa, too, for a while. I think the guilt would have destroyed her had she ever understood the why."

"And Elianne?"

"I don't know."

Ybelline nodded. She then turned a corner and walked into a much more lavishly furnished room. The shouting that had filled the hall before her arrival dropped instantly into a frosty silence. Or perhaps a heated one. Both pairs of Barrani eyes were a marked, dark blue.

"Thank you," Ybelline said, in almost flawless Barrani, "for your escort. I would avail myself of that escort again."

"You are finished here?"

She nodded.

"And you see no reason to return?"

"No. Everything we desired to know, we now know."

An'Tellarus's eyes had lightened, although the predominant color remained blue. Elluvian's, however, darkened. "What will you do with the boy?" Glancing at Severn, she added, "An'Sennarin."

"He is An'Sennarin. The decision is not mine to make."

An'Tellarus smiled almost fondly as she met Ybelline's gaze. "And will you leave the decision in the hands of those who can?"

"Yes."

"In my experience, that is not always the most practical way of getting things done."

Ybelline smiled. "No. But I will never have the breadth and depth of your experience. Nor will that be expected of me. My kin and yours almost never interact."

"And you now understand why."

"I am Tha'alanari," Ybelline replied. "I have always understood why."

They returned to An'Tellarus's carriage, which then returned to the Halls of Law. No words were spoken, but the texture of the silences that crowded this carriage were different. Elluvian was angry. An'Tellarus was content. Ybelline was introspective. Severn observed.

Neither Severn nor Elluvian had killed in pursuit of the Emperor's target; there would be no Tha'alani summoned to review the events. This much, Severn understood.

An'Tellarus did not leave her carriage again. Her silence persisted for the duration of the ride to the Halls of Law's coach yard. Severn and Elluvian exited, Elluvian with more grace but far more speed.

Ybelline began to disembark. An'Tellarus shook her head. "Not you. You shall remain in my carriage until we reach the Tha'alani quarter."

"We're her escort," Severn began. He fell silent at the lift of a dismissive, imperious hand.

"I will take her."

Elluvian was not pleased. He turned to Ybelline. "If the Tha'alanari gives the requisite permissions, we will allow this; if they do not, we will escort you. Without An'Tellarus."

"The requisite permission has been granted by the castelord," she finally replied. "He is willing to entrust An'Tellarus with my safety at the present time." She then turned to the Barrani noble. "It is not necessary, An'Tellarus."

"Perhaps not for you. But I gave my solemn word—and you may ask Elluvian how rare that is—that I would see you to the quarter."

Ybelline turned to face Severn through the open door. Her eyes were hazel, not green, but she looked exhausted. "We will accept any decision you choose to make."

"Decisions," Elluvian almost snapped, "of any relevance are not made by probationary Wolves."

To Severn's surprise, Ybelline smiled at Elluvian. It was perhaps the first time Severn had seen a smile so warm used as a blunt disagreement.

★ ★ ★

Rosen had returned, and now manned her desk. She looked up as they entered. "Helmat is speaking with the Hawklord," she told Elluvian.

"In person?"

"Yes, actually."

"I give you permission," Elluvian said to Severn, "to return to your home. It is late, and the meeting not likely to be brief."

Severn said nothing. The nothing stretched until Elluvian turned toward the hall that led to the Wolflord's office. "You will do me the kindness of remembering that I did make the offer."

When Helmat entered the office, he took one look at Rosen's face and decided a frosty, angry Lord of Hawks was preferable to what was likely to follow.

"They're back, are they?"

Rosen nodded.

"And in one piece?"

"They're entirely uninjured. I guess it is possible for Elluvian to traverse the High Halls without giving offense to the Barrani Lords who inhabit it."

"Are they in my office or En's?"

"Your office."

Helmat cursed. "At this hour of the day?"

"They chose to wait. Elluvian is well aware of how long face-to-face meetings can take; he knows you only ask to meet in person when you're likely to say things you'd prefer not be immediately recorded."

"The private chose to remain as well?"

She nodded. "He's interesting," she said. "Sometimes he's so still you can forget he's there. It's like he has no desire to be seen, or known, at all."

"Unlike Darrell?"

Rosen grimaced. "Unlike Darrell. Darrell's death wasn't your fault."

Helmat exhaled. "They're all my fault," he said tersely. "I'm the Wolflord. I'm the Wolflord, but apparently even I am not immune to charm."

"And Severn lacks charm?"

"Not precisely. He's *earnest*, Rosie. Were it not for the Tha'alani, I believe I would have dismissed him out of hand."

"Funny."

"Oh?"

"I don't."

"You like him."

"He works. He works hard. I've never heard him complain."

"He's on probation. This is the best his behavior is likely to be."

"I'm not sure it will change. Jaren will approve of him, and Jaren never liked Darrell."

"Jaren goes out of his way to avoid liking anyone he thinks isn't likely to survive."

"None of us are likely to survive in this job."

"Probably why Jaren doesn't spend much time here." Helmat shrugged. "Time to chase the two of them out of my office."

"There had better be simple, good news. I've spent most of the afternoon and early evening expending monumental effort not to strangle someone. I have no self-control left."

Elluvian levered himself up from his leaning position against the nearest wall. "Then we will return in the morning, when perhaps your reserve of self-control will be less depleted." En's eyes were blue—not a strange color for a Barrani, but his eyes looked shadowed. One brow rose as Helmat inspected his

face. "I have spent some part of the afternoon in almost exactly the same fashion."

"An'Tellarus?"

"Of course."

"And you?" Helmat asked the private. "Did you also ex-
pend similar effort?"

"It wasn't necessary."

"You were speaking with a Barrani Lord; I find it's always
necessary."

That pulled a wry smile from the young man. "I don't think
you'd find it necessary in his case."

"Helmat is far too suspicious to believe what you believe."

"And you think Lord Marlin is right?"

"I think he is wise."

"Wisdom," Helmat said, "is seldom considered wrong."

"What constitutes wisdom is frequently and heatedly de-
bated," Elluvian replied. He glanced at Severn; it was almost
a glare. "Private Handred wishes to have a few words with
you in private, and I'm of a mind to allow it."

Helmat was surprised. He was tired enough to let it show.

"It is not the first time I have granted Wolves privacy,"
Elluvian said, the words sour with unspent annoyance. To
Severn, he added, "You are certain?"

Severn nodded.

Helmat walked past them to his desk, where he sat heavily,
thumping the desktop with his elbows. "I am hungry and annoyed," he told the private.

En left the room, closing the door behind him.

"Well?" His tone implied that this had better be good.

"The mission given us by the Emperor—or by you—cannot be completed."

"Cannot be or will not be?" Helmat's voice became a wall
of neutrality as he glared at the newest of his Wolves.

"Cannot be. The person responsible for arranging the deaths of the Tha'alani two decades ago is already dead. His death brought an end to further murders."

"And the Barrani man Timorri saw?"

"You wanted—the Emperor wanted—the man responsible for hiring him to orchestrate these deaths. That man has already died."

"How?"

"His death is not contained in the Records of the Halls of Law; he was a Barrani Lord of note and it was considered an internal Barrani affair."

"The Tha'alani are not Barrani."

"No."

"They died."

"Yes."

"Tell me what happened. And drop the Barrani; I've heard nothing but Barrani for the past week, and I'm sick to death of it."

"I am not certain—I mean, I'm not sure—"

Helmat lifted a hand, and abandoned Barrani entirely. "I'm in too foul a mood to handle bullshit. What happened?"

"Barrani were involved in the murders."

"Do not try my patience." He ennunciated each word with force.

"A Barrani man was involved with a Tha'alani woman."

Helmat whistled before he could stop himself. "Was he insane?"

"By Barrani standards, probably. I'd've chosen the Tha'alani friendship over Barrani overtures any day."

And still would, Helmat thought. "And?"

"She died. She was killed, but the death was marked as—and believed to be—accidental."

"And the person responsible for her death was responsible for all the others?"

"Yes. I don't believe the deaths would have stopped if he hadn't died."

"How did he die?"

Severn shrugged. This annoyed Helmat. But something about the boy's expression quelled irritation. What had he said to Rosen? He was earnest. Earnest was often conflated with naivete. That, Helmat thought, the boy lacked.

"You'll have to have better answers than these if you want this mission to be marked as resolved."

Severn nodded.

"And the death of the witnesses?"

"The witnesses weren't witnesses; they were perpetrators."

"And they were murdered in order to hide that fact?"

"No."

"Private—"

"They were killed," not murdered, Helmat noted, "in order to save the Tha'alani from revisiting the memories of those events."

"You believe the Tha'alani were involved in the witness deaths?"

"No. But I believe the desire to protect them motivated the killings. There's a way to determine the truth; one of the four survived." He met, and held, Helmat's glare. "If he's guilty, he would likely face death."

"The Tha'alanari would be called to confirm."

Severn nodded.

"You advise against?"

"The reason the Tha'alani are called in is to confirm beyond a doubt that the condemned is guilty. Without that, we'd have to guess."

"What would you do with the witness?"

"I'd release him."

"Even if he's guilty of murder?"

Severn nodded.

"You don't think he'll survive long on the streets."

"Do you?" Severn countered.

"Don't get emotionally involved with the Tha'alani."

Severn nodded again.

"…I've never been forced to utter those words in this office before."

"You didn't want Ybelline involved in any aspect of this investigation, either. And it would be Ybelline who would conduct the interview. There's no one else she would allow to do it."

"She said that?"

"She didn't need to say it. Timorri might never return to the Imperial Service, and he chanced upon memories of the events and recoiled. She'll be castelord. You said it. Garadin said it. She'll conduct that interview if an interview is demanded."

"You'd rather she didn't."

"I don't see the point. I believe he's guilty. You believe it."

"That is not the way the law works."

Severn bowed his head again. He was silent for long enough, Helmat thought he had surrendered, but there was, in the boy's silence, something almost immovable. "It's not the way the law works for us," he said, when he raised his head again.

"What are you suggesting?"

Silence.

"Do you fully understand what you're asking of me?"

"The Emperor's Laws are the Emperor's. The Emperor decides guilt or innocence. He can't make that call using the Tha'alani to get at the truth—if the criminals were in our custody, there'd be no hunt. He calls the hunts based on information he's given. He can call them off. It's entirely his choice. It's not possible for the Emperor to break the law."

"It is," Helmat said.

"The Emperor *is* the law."

"Did Elluvian put you up to this?"

"Elluvian?" Which answered Helmat's question.

"Tell En," he finally said. "I don't have the Emperor's ear. En does."

"Why do you call him that?"

"Because it annoys him. Tell Elluvian, if you prefer. Elluvian can broach the subject with the Emperor."

"And you'll accept that?"

"I'll accept it. Elluvian might not."

"No."

"Is that why you wanted to speak with me?"

"I thought you'd understand my reasoning."

"And Elluvian won't?"

"Elluvian won't care."

Ah. "Elluvian is a Wolf, but he occupies an unusual position. I cannot command Elluvian to discuss this with the Emperor. I can ask, but I can't control the conversation; I can't control what Elluvian says or requests. If I have no chance, you have—"

"Less than no chance."

Helmat nodded.

Severn surprised him then. "I would like," he said, "to speak with the Emperor."

CHAPTER TWENTY-SEVEN

THE WOLVES HAD A TABARD THAT WAS SELDOM worn; unlike the Hawks or the Swords, the ranks of the Wolves were always thin. Severn was not allowed to enter the presence of the Eternal Emperor without the tabard.

He was also not allowed to enter said presence in any of the clothing he currently owned, and Elluvian's forays into the High Halls had given Severn clothing he would never have owned before because the cost was so high. If he'd thought Elluvian's choice of clothing appropriate for a visit to the High Halls expensive, he repented; he hid both distaste and shock at the cost of the clothing Elluvian considered necessary for a meeting with the Emperor.

Elluvian hid almost nothing. He was appalled at Severn's request—but could, given Severn's relative ignorance, barely accept that it had been made. He was shocked that the Wolflord had passed the request on. Severn was almost certain that the Wolflord had heard an earful of less impeccable Barrani about this very subject.

Lord Marlin had, however, declined Elluvian's "request"

that the request for an appointment be withdrawn. The Wolf-lord had reasonably pointed out that there was no guarantee such an audience would be granted.

He had pointed this out to Severn as well.

No immediate need for the Wolves had been handed down by the Emperor, and Severn was therefore free to take the classes that the Wolves required of their recruits. In theory. Severn, however, was dragged off shopping instead, where he could be confronted with the ridiculous expense of clothing that seemed, to his eye, to be less durable and far less practical, given the general duties he would have as a Wolf.

He was a private, but he was no longer on probation. Rosen had given him the news, but quietly, as if it were a guilty secret. She was of the opinion that cutting off both of her legs with her own daggers was preferable to an audience with the Emperor—and possibly one of her arms as well—but she nonetheless admired either Severn's ignorance or his balls.

The appointment was granted almost two weeks after Severn had made his request.

"You don't seem surprised," Rosen said, because it was Rosen who informed him of the date and the time.

"Should I be?"

"He's the *Emperor*."

"He is. But he commands the Wolves. The cases given to the Wolves come from him. The Swords and the Hawks are different—but without the Emperor's personal oversight, the Wolves wouldn't exist. They wouldn't be part of the Halls of Law."

"You think of him as a step above Helmat."

Severn nodded, because he was. Rosen stared at him. Her stare unearthed more words. "The Emperor's will is law. The Emperor's Laws exist because he desires that they exist—and be obeyed. His laws are commands the rest of us follow and enforce."

Rosen nodded.

"I haven't memorized all of his laws."

"You will."

"Yes. But I've studied enough of his laws—the larger ones, at least—that I can see a connecting thread between them. We're the outliers. We're expected—of course we are—to follow those laws while in pursuit of the criminals the Emperor wishes apprehended. But in some cases, we're commanded to kill on sight.

"That breaks the rest of his laws. His kill on sight command is...it's an exception. It's only legal because the command comes from the Emperor. We're given permission to break laws specifically because his commands supersede his written laws."

Rosen nodded, folding her arms across her desktop.

"The Emperor therefore makes exceptions in his governance." At Rosen's expression, Severn exhaled. "He can do whatever he wants, whenever he wants, and he's not technically a criminal. It's impossible for the Emperor to be a criminal in his own Empire."

"And this leads you to somehow expect that you'll be granted an audience directly with the Emperor?"

"Yes."

"Try a better explanation—the one you made makes no sense."

"What the Emperor wants for his Empire seems clear in his laws. He's not stupid. He understands that laws will be broken, which is why the Halls of Law exist at all. What he wants—from us, and for the Empire—is clear in the laws. He's a Dragon. He's had to create laws that remove friction. It's why the laws of exemption exist."

"You don't like the laws of exemption."

"No one who works in the Halls of Law, in any branch,

likes the exemptions. It allows the castelords to do whatever they want with their own people, free from consequences."

"You don't consider the Emperor's edicts to be the same thing."

"They're not. Except perhaps in the overlap between Wolves and the rest of the Halls. I believe that the laws of exemption exist as a practical measure. Allow caste exemptions based on race, or face another war with the Barrani. Which would kill most of the rest of us. His permanent record of law has already made allowances that would prevent racial war in the Empire, even if justice—such as it exists—isn't served by that compromise. It's practical."

"And you think that whatever you have to say to him somehow falls into that category?"

Severn nodded.

"Why didn't you make Helmat ask?"

"It's Tha'alani Caste Court business."

"You are demonstrably not Tha'alani."

"No. But my work with the Wolves means the Tha'alani will never be entirely free of me."

"You really don't hate them."

"No. Had they any choice, they would sever all such connection without a second thought; they do what they do at the command of the Emperor. As do the Wolves."

She waved a hand. "This is the date. I don't need to tell you not to be late. If appointments run over their allotted time, you'll have to wait—but the Emperor is never to be kept waiting."

Since this was obvious to Severn, he nodded politely and waited while Rosen gave him the date.

The Wolflord didn't elect to accompany Severn to the Imperial palace or his appointment. Elluvian, however, did.

Severn noted that the Barrani Wolf hadn't chosen to escort Severn from the office itself; he met him in the large chamber, with its rows of forward-facing seats, within the palace itself. While waiting, Elluvian was blue-eyed and silent. Any lectures he had were put in abeyance while they occupied the public waiting room, because the room was almost full.

"The Emperor keeps two hours at the end of his day to speak to those who have not been otherwise granted an audience through official channels. These seats will never be empty until the Emperor leaves the throne room in which audiences are held.

"You will never find a Barrani in any of these chairs. No Barrani, no Leontines, no Tha'alani, no Aerians."

"Just humans?"

"There are far more humans in this city than any other race, and far, far fewer Dragons. Most of the humans here will never have seen one—not in the draconic form. To them—to you—the Emperor is almost like a different kind of human, one who lives forever.

"Had he chosen to govern in an aerie, had he chosen to occupy a throne room in full military splendor, these seats would never be filled."

"They would," was Severn's soft reply.

"Oh?"

"Some losses are far worse than the fear of simple death."

"Until one is in the jaws of that death."

"Until then," Severn agreed.

The waiting room was almost full when Severn was at last called forward. Elluvian's name was not mentioned; Severn half expected that Elluvian would be sent back to the waiting room by the guards tasked with ascertaining that the person entering the room was the one expected.

None of the guards, however, seemed to notice Elluvian. They did notice Severn, but as it was Severn's appointment, he was expected. Elluvian might have been a guard, just as they were.

The Emperor's throne felt like it was miles away from the door, and the room, absent the chatter of people both bored and desperate, was silent as a tomb. The ceilings here were high; they reminded Severn of the ceilings in the High Halls. Light fell in almost solid beams from that ceiling, broken only by stray motes of dust.

He felt as if he were one of those motes as he walked the length of a carpet that dampened the sound of all footfalls.

On the dais that was the end of his path sat the Emperor. As Severn approached, the eight guards—four to either side— left the dais at an inaudible command. This left one bearded man by the throne, and no others.

Severn reached the end of carpet, the visual signal that he was to stop and kneel. Elluvian accompanied him, and Elluvian fell to one knee as if indicating wordlessly that this was the stopping point, and this the gesture of respect due the Emperor. Severn had spent hours—literal hours—engaged in nothing but kneeling, until Elluvian felt he had demonstrated the correct blend of abject respect and personal dignity. Severn's attempt to have the word "abject" translated into the human tongue had produced only irritation.

Regardless, Severn knelt, just as Elluvian did, and bowed his head as Elluvian did.

The Emperor showed far more mercy than Elluvian, as a teacher, had.

"Private Handred, rise. You may approach the throne."

Severn rose. Elluvian did not.

"Elluvian of Danarre, rise. Please wait at the end of the hall for the private." The Emperor didn't send the Barrani Wolf from the chamber, as he had his personal guard. Barrani hearing was excellent, but given the size of the room, Severn wasn't certain that the conversation—if it were to be a conversation and not an interrogation—would carry that far.

"You have requested an audience," the Emperor said. "Your concerns were brief to the point of opacity. You are new to the Wolves."

Severn nodded.

"And the Wolves are of personal import to me. They are part of the Halls of Law, the single edifice I consider most important to my Empire; more important than even the palace in which we now meet."

Severn said nothing.

"Your first task with the Wolves involved a series of murders that occurred decades ago."

"Twenty years, two months," the bearded man said, "for the first such murder."

"I have heard no report that your mission was complete."

"The mission," Severn said, "was impossible to complete."

"Oh?"

"The man responsible for commanding those deaths is himself dead."

"Is he?"

"Yes. He died shortly before the last few murders."

"You are certain."

"I am certain."

"If such a death did take place, Private, why were the witnesses recently sought by the Halls of Law killed?"

Severn met eyes that were orange. Red was the Dragon death color; gold the happy color, as it was in Tha'alani eyes. The Emperor's hair, jet-black, was pulled back over his forehead and tied or braided; his unwavering gaze meant Severn couldn't tell.

Severn didn't immediately answer the question. This was a

mistake, judging by the shift of eye color; more orange darkened the Imperial eyes.

"They were killed by a Barrani man who did not wish the
information contained to resurface." No, he thought. That,
too, was wrong. He bowed his head for one long moment,
and accepted that there was nothing he could hide from this
man; nothing he could leave unsaid.

He lifted his head. All of Elluvian's many lessons on proper
posture and proper speech, admittedly less of the latter, Severn
now set aside.

"One witness survived. If it is your desire, the Tha'alanari
can be called to confirm what I now say: he, and the three
who did not survive, were participants in the decades-old
murders. They weren't present as witnesses, but as accesso-
ries. But I would ask, as one of the officers investigating this
case, that the Tha'alanari not be called in. The memory of
one such man was enough to cause possible permanent damage to the Tha'alanari."

"And you believe that the other three were killed in order
to preserve the sanity of the Tha'alanari?"

"I believe that was the intent, yes. The Tha'alani were not
involved in these crimes."

"And the man who was?"

"The man who was is a Lord of the High Court. A ruler
of one of the familial lines of that court. He came to power
twenty years ago. He was not expected to rule; he was, however, expected to be a powerful tool for the line he now rules.

"He took the line itself in order to stop the murders of the
Tha'alani. His lord at the time was responsible for the deaths
that had occurred. Had he not assassinated his predecessor,
the murders would have continued until either the Tha'alanari
were entirely broken, or the Tha'alani themselves were."

"What did the Tha'alani know that made this desirable?"

The silence that followed the question was far too long. Severn drew breath and held it, considering the man—the Dragon—who sat above him. He was the man to whom Severn would swear personal loyalty—a vow that had not yet been demanded, although Rosen had said he was no longer on probation.

Personal loyalty meant many things to many people.

It meant one thing to Severn Handred. He had not fully assessed its meaning when Elluvian had brought him to the Halls of Law on that first day. Nor had he assessed the meaning when he had been offered the job. When he had been accepted. He'd had little time in which to do so.

Little desire to do so. His focus had been the Halls of Law, and some method of legal employment that would allow him to hang desperately to the edges of the only oath he had ever made that mattered to him. He had thought that it would be the only oath that would.

But now he saw clearly. What the oath meant to men such as Elluvian or the Wolflord was not lodged in the spoken words they had offered upon their own inductions. The words themselves were said by every single man or woman who had ever joined the Wolves, but the weight of the oath, the personal meaning, would be different for each.

Would have to be different for each; they were not the same people.

Severn had not, since early childhood, sworn oaths of convenience. He understood, facing the Dragon Emperor, that the oath he swore now—or in the future, when such official ceremonies might take place—could not be an oath of convenience; it was an oath. It was the measure of his value as a person in his own eyes.

He had sworn to protect Elianne.

Could he swear to serve the Emperor if the new oath came

into conflict with the old? And if he could not, could he offer the Emperor assurances that his duties as a Wolf came before all other duties?

It depended, he realized, on the Emperor himself. His first oath, the driving force of his early life, had been offered when he was ten years of age. Ten had seemed profoundly and terrifyingly adult to him at the time. He had not made the vow having judged that Elianne would be worthy of a life of service, had he? She'd been a child of five—a child almost certain not to see six, had she been left to her own devices.

Did he regret that vow now?

No. Nor would he break it. But Elianne was at home in the Halls of Law; she had the protection of the Barrani Hawks, and the tolerant affection of the only Leontine officer. She had a roof over her head, a guarantee of enough food that she wouldn't starve or freeze to death, and there were no Ferals in the streets of Elantra. Only in the fiefs, which they had both escaped.

He couldn't spend the rest of his life tailing Elianne; he didn't believe she required it. His mantle as her protector had been destroyed utterly when he had made the choice he had made. And that choice had somehow proved his fitness—his terrible fitness—to be what the Emperor demanded of his Wolves.

But his desire to be a Wolf was implacably linked to the earliest and most important of his oaths. He accepted that. If he could not be what he had been to Elianne—

He closed his eyes. He had never wasted much time on regret, because regret—or guilt—couldn't change the past. It served no purpose.

Severn made his choice. "The Tha'alani knew the True Name of one of the Barrani Lords."

"You are certain." Although the words could be interpreted as a question, the Emperor's tone made them a statement.

"I am certain."

"And the Tha'alani used the name of this Barrani to assassinate the Barrani Lord responsible for the murders?"

"No. The Tha'alani—the Tha'alanari—provided information that allowed the Barrani whose name they knew to take the seat of his line. The man in question—he was known as Ollarin—wanted to stop the murder of the Tha'alani at any cost; he was willing to risk his own life in the doing. If he could successfully claim the seat of Sennarin, the deaths *would* stop."

"And the Barrani in question did not consider simply killing Ollarin to end the threat the Tha'alani pose? If Ollarin were dead, the Tha'alani knowledge of his name would die with him."

"Apparently not."

The Emperor raised a brow.

"It is what I would have done in his position," Severn said quietly.

"Then we must be grateful that you are an Imperial Wolf and not a Barrani Lord. What do you desire of me? What did you come here to ask?"

"I ask that you mark this case as closed. And that you bury it so deeply even the Imperial Service will not think to touch it in the future."

The Emperor's eyes were orange, but the color brightened until Severn could see flecks of gold. "You know much of the Tha'alani."

"I know only what the future castelord considered wise to impart. But that is enough for me to make this request. I understand the harm we already do to her and her people. I would do everything within my power—and the boundaries of the oath I will swear in the future—to lessen that harm."

"Would you remove the Tha'alani from the Imperial Service, if that was within your power?"

"Yes."

The Emperor's eyes widened at the flat, unadorned word. But his eyes, Severn saw, had continued to shade toward gold. "You understand why that will never happen."

"Yes."

"Very well." The Emperor then rose from the throne he had occupied for the entirety of this audience. "When you speak of future oaths, you speak of the oaths you will swear to me."

"The oath," Severn said quietly. "And yes."

"What do you believe constitutes that oath?"

This was not a question Severn had come prepared to answer.

"Do you expect that the oath, like the laws, is codified and handed down to you? Do you believe that you merely add your name to words that are written and waiting for just that input, no more?"

Severn looked up, met the Emperor's eyes, saw the faintest hint of what might be a smile lurking at the corner of his lips. "Yes," he said. "That's what I expected."

"Ah. Why?"

"You're the Emperor."

"And as Emperor it is my responsibility to decide what oaths you will swear?"

"Yes."

"The oaths are yours to carry. You will live or die by them. Did you believe that you might decide only upon hearing conditions, as if the oaths you swear are a simple—or complicated—matter of bureaucracy?"

The answer to this question seemed to be his answer to the first one. "I am a Wolf, having failed to swear the oath the Wolves are required to swear in the Emperor's presence, in person. I have done the work a Wolf would do had they survived their probationary period and sworn those oaths. No oath was required."

"And if you have done, as you believe, the work of Wolves without such oaths, you assumed the oaths to be entirely ceremonial."

"I did, yes."

"Is your word a simple matter of ceremony?"

"No."

"No, indeed. Tell me, Private, what do you think of my Wolves?"

Severn waited for further clarification. The question itself was vague enough that the Emperor might be asking about his opinion on the Wolves he had met. No clarification followed the question.

"I understand why they're necessary," he finally said.

"Do you?"

"Yes. There are some criminals who cannot simply be arrested and brought to the Halls of Law to eventually face the judiciary. The Hawks are competent, but their responsibilities cover the entire city; they can look for those criminals who've disappeared, but the severity of the crime doesn't change the fact that it's one crime of many.

"The Wolves are not responsible for pickpockets and drug dealers and drunken assault. Nor are the Wolves responsible for the murders that were not premeditated. Gang fights. Family deaths. We are, in fact, responsible only for the murders that you have personally assigned.

"You decide which murders, which murderers, will be too costly for the Hawks."

The Emperor's brow rose.

"I believe we're meant to be more disposable. Losing Hawks is losing the foundation of your law enforcement. Losing Wolves is not."

"Elluvian," the Emperor said, raising his voice and, at the

same time, deepening it, which was a striking combination. "What have you been telling the private?"

Elluvian approached the Emperor no longer seated on his throne. "I have been attempting to make certain that he understands the Barrani High Court," Elluvian replied. His eyes were blue. "It is far too easy for mortals to be lost to the minutiae if they do not understand it—and far too easy for the Barrani to manipulate that ignorance if they desire to take public offense."

"Perhaps the urgency of the mission overwhelmed your customary common sense."

"Perhaps."

The Emperor returned his gaze to Severn. "It is not my oath, Private. It is an oath you swear. It is an oath you offer. I will accept it, or reject it—it is rare, but it has happened—as Emperor, but I offer no oaths to you in return. What would you swear to me, now, if I demanded that you offer that oath?"

Severn said nothing.

"If I accept your opinion that my goals were achieved before you were even born, and I withdraw—and seal—all investigations currently underway, what would you then be willing to swear?"

"Will you?" Severn asked, squaring his shoulders.

The Emperor did smile, then. Severn glanced once at Elluvian, but Elluvian's face was blank, neutral. Only his eyes shifted color, but that shift was brief. And purple. "As you suspected, no doubt, when you were bold enough to ask, I have no desire to further damage the Tha'alani or the Tha'alanari. If past experiences are a guide, they will be some months in recovery.

"I will bury this investigation in its entirety. You will be forbidden to speak of it—but you are forbidden to do so regardless. The Wolves will know. The Wolflord will know.

My decision in this matter is final; it is not dependent on the Imperial Service or the Lord of Wolves.

"In return, Severn Handred, I will hear your oath of service."

Severn nodded. Elluvian moved to stand by Severn's left side, his hands behind his back, his head bowed.

"I will do anything required of me to protect the people of the Empire you rule. Anything that does not force me to break the only other oath I've sworn in my life."

"And what does 'anything' imply?"

"Anything," he replied. "I will kill to protect it, if killing is required. I will kill at your command, trusting that the command itself is built upon a foundation of necessity."

The Emperor's nod was grave.

"I will follow your orders with the understanding that in carrying out any mission you choose to give me, I am to do the least possible damage to your citizens and the laws you have devised." He exhaled. "And when I feel that the commands themselves cannot be obeyed in that spirit, I will ask for an audience to explain my reservations."

"As you have done today."

"Yes."

"And if I chose not to heed your...advice?"

Elluvian stiffened slightly; Severn didn't look away from the Emperor to see the Barrani Wolf's expression.

"I would accept your decision. I would have to accept it."

"Hierarchically, yes."

"No. It's not about hierarchy, or you wouldn't have asked the question."

"Would I not?" Once again, a smile lurked at the corner of the Imperial mouth.

"I would obey you because I've chosen to trust you. Not with my life, of course—but with the things that matter."

"Your life does not matter?"

"It matters—but it's one life."

"And you would trust my decision over your own?"

"You've seen more, done more, fought more, than I ever will; you've lived for centuries. I've lived for almost two decades. But you created an Empire that's meant to preserve not the strongest and most powerful of your citizens, but people like me. Like us. I have to trust that those considerations and the experience I lack are behind the decision to reject my request."

"Have to trust?"

"If I swear my life to your service, yes."

"That is not the case with most young Wolves."

"I can't speak for another person's vows. I can only speak for mine."

The Emperor held Severn's gaze for what felt like minutes. "I accept, Private Handred. I accept what you offer."

It was a dismissal. Severn turned to leave.

"Not you, Elluvian. You and I have words to speak in the wake of this unusual audience."

"You assumed the oaths to be entirely ceremonial," Elluvian said when the door had closed and the private was safely on the other side of it.

The Emperor raised a brow.

"He assumed it because he's not a fool. The oaths *are* entirely ceremonial. They've been written into long, dense, and irretrievably boring phrases."

"Perhaps those oaths have changed in the past few decades—I cannot recall seeing you during those ceremonies for some time now."

"They have not changed."

"No, perhaps not. Ceremony exists for a reason, after all."

"And Severn is to be spared the long, tedious cant?"

"Private Handred has sworn his personal oath to his Emperor, and I have chosen to accept it, yes."

"Why?"

"The pomp and splendor of the Imperial ceremony, coupled with its privacy, elevates the oath, and the import of the oath, in the minds of most young candidates."

"I believe that was the entire point."

"I do not feel it will have the same effect on your private."

"He is not my private."

"Ah, no. I believe Lord Marlin claimed him—first, and most tenaciously. He wants that boy."

Elluvian nodded.

"I begin to see why."

"And the official oaths?"

"I admit that I find them tedious at times. It is tedium I endure because it serves a purpose. Since it will serve no purpose for Severn Handred, I find myself more than willing to avoid them."

"What do you see in that boy?" Elluvian asked, as the silence threatened to become too weighty.

The Emperor's eyes were an orange gold. "I see what you can't. Why do you ask?"

"I am curious. You have long held to traditions, and yet you have chosen to forgo them almost entirely in Severn's case. Helmat did the same."

"You cannot see why?"

"He lacks the charm and charisma of our previous recruit."

"The one who died?"

"Indeed. I perceive you ask because you wish to make a point."

"No. Life has already made the point. Why do you ask? It is unlike you to readily expose ignorance."

"You are not the only person of my acquaintance to show an unexpected interest in the boy."

"Ah. I will not ask a question you will not answer. But I would be displeased should that unexpected interest remove him from the Wolves."

"You would not be the only one. I do not understand the private. He is obedient, silent, studious; he does not seem to be any of these things to curry favor. And it appears to me that he actually holds the Tha'alani in some affection."

"Lord Marlin seems to do so."

"He did not, when he was the private's age. And I would say he does not now—but he understands that they are bound to us by necessity, not desire. His experience has shown him that the Tha'alani use nothing they have gathered in their investigations; that the secrets they unearth remain otherwise buried.

"Regardless, he did not have the private's reaction."

"This worries you?"

"Private Handred came here at his own request; Helmat did not gainsay it. But it appears—to me—that he dared the Dragon in his den, quite literally, because he was worried for the Tha'alani."

The Emperor's eyes lost their orange tint as his gaze met, and held, Elluvian's. "Yes," he said.

"He cannot imagine that he can protect the Tha'alani from you?"

"He can. He is young. But it is the desire to protect that moves him to take risks, to make choices, to dare even the anger of Dragons. And I confess that I am moved by his faith, his trust, in his Emperor."

"Were it not for your demands, the Tha'alani would not require that protection."

"Yes. It is surprising that the boy can have that faith in me, given the circumstances."

"You would have buried this case, regardless."

"Yes. He was not the only person to approach me in regard to this particular investigation."

"He was simply the least significant?"

"Hierarchically, yes, as you must guess. He does not understand the protocols involved with an Imperial audience."

"Granting him this audience is unlikely to teach him anything about correct protocol."

"Do you understand why the audience was granted?"

"Your curiosity."

"That was part of my decision, yes."

Elluvian understood that he was to be frustrated. But this was expected when dealing with Dariandaros. Frustration, and a series of small failures that might extend into the future forever. Still, something in this private, this Severn Handred, was somehow what Dariandaros desired of his Wolves. Perhaps there was something for the lone Barrani Wolf to learn as well.

In the quiet of her rooms in the High Halls, An'Tellarus had chosen to revisit the run-down, almost unsightly room she had built over a decade ago. She looked at the books she'd collected—unenchanted, all—that suited the interior of this place with their bent corners, their fraying covers, their faded pages.

The table, scored and dinged, sat before a couch that had long since ceased to be of use. Nonetheless, she sat, a book in hand. On the table's surface were a top, a quill, and a dagger that was more likely to cause disease than serious injury.

She waited. She was not the most patient of people on a normal day; she had enough personal power that waiting was not generally required. This had not always been the case, and today, while she exercised the patience she had all but outgrown, she considered this with care.

She, too, had been young once. She had survived it.

She doubted that she would have, had she been forced to live those early years in the crushing confines of the High Halls, with its infinitely complex politics. She had not. She had survived her youth because she had been raised in the West March. There, she had divided her time between the family of her birth and the haven of Alsanis.

That Hallionne had fallen silent, had closed his doors to all visitors. Alsanis had turned the whole of his attention inward, to the guests he now harbored against their will. He had become a jail. Even his dreams—the great birds that circled the West March—had become warped, their flight halting, with the passage of centuries.

In the youth of An'Tellarus, the dreams of the young were planted; they flourished in the lee of the wars that defined so many. She remembered the Dragon Flights, and the Barrani companies sent to stand against them. She remembered the burning desire to prove herself worthy to bear one of The Three.

That dream had long since died. An'Teela held one; Calarnenne the other. The third was in the hands of the High Lord's family; she had never seen that sword in the High Lord's hand, and wondered if he could wield it. But she could not. *Kariannos*, the sword that An'Teela now claimed, was the only one of The Three she had touched.

It had not killed her.

It had come close.

That had been a bitter disappointment. It had taken decades to recover from the shock and the sense of permanent loss. But recovery—for those who survived—was the way of her kin. And perhaps it had been for the best. Only one weapon of significance now existed in the West March of her childhood.

She wondered, looking at this detritus, what would become of it. She very much desired that a wielder be found; if one was, Alsanis might at last be freed from his role as jailer, and might once again turn his thought and attention to the rest of his people.

Others desired the weapon, and for different purposes, just as she had desired to wield one of The Three. She did not desire the weapon that waited, nascent, in the West March. Having failed to prove herself worthy of *Kariannos*, she no longer dreamed of wielding a weapon of note. Something in her approach, something in her desire, made her incompatible with the ancient masterworks.

What she could not change, she accepted. This acceptance was almost in its entirety the reason she had lived for as long as she had.

She was not the only person to search for someone who might be able to do what she was now certain she could not. Nor was she the only ruler of a line who had hoped that her own offspring might prove worthy where she had not. She was therefore not the only ruler to be disappointed, time and again.

But she had not done what Verranian had done, and she was certain—almost certain—that she saw his hand in this. These books. This table. These children's toys. And…that boy, with his lovely High Barrani, his exceptional—for a mortal boy—manners, and his gaze, clear-eyed, observant.

It would not have occurred to her—ever—to expand her search in such a fashion. A mortal child of no significance in the fiefs that kept *Ravellon* at bay? No. She could not imagine lowering herself to such mean surroundings, for she was certain that Verranian had chosen to occupy this small, cramped space, with its inherent decay.

She had begun her search for Verranian. Or rather, she had prodded someone beholden to her to begin searching for his own reasons. Elluvian. He was an odd disappointment; someone who had both failed and survived failure; someone to whom the Dragon Emperor condescended in a favorable way.

He had wasted most of his life; he had barely survived that waste. She did not therefore expect that he would recover. But it was in Elluvian's wake that Severn had come.

She was not, of course, convinced that the boy was the answer to her long search; she was merely convinced that he was a possibility. Even a distant possibility was better than none.

She had seen the sketches that An'Sennarin had taken from the Oracular Halls. Oracles were notoriously unreliable, but An'Tellarus had understood what she had seen. She doubted Severn did.

But she did not doubt that Elluvian would.

Elluvian was late.

Elluvian was occupied. The private's audience with the Emperor had not, by all accounts, been the disaster one might have expected, given his lack of familiarity with Imperial hierarchy.

Helmat, however, was feeling somewhat pessimistic. He approved of the private, but he had approved of Darrell as well, and Darrell was dead. Mellianne, far more truculent, was not—but Darrell's death shadowed her; she might never be free of the resentment and suspicion left in its wake.

Severn was not Darrell; that much had been obvious almost immediately. It was not, therefore, any similarity between the two young men that transformed cautious optimism into pessimism. They had age in common, and came from similar economic backgrounds, although the particulars were different.

"Enter," he said when the expected knock on his closed door reached his ears.

Elluvian entered the office. "Well?"

"I see from your cheerful demeanor you've spent some time at the High Halls. You do not seem to be worse for wear this time."

"It is seldom that people attempt to kill me outright."

"Your version of seldom does not match mine."

Elluvian shrugged, and Helmat's gaze narrowed. "Your concerns have nothing to do with the High Halls and its various inhabitants." He might have used the word *rodents* instead, given his tone and expression.

Helmat chuckled. "No. The High Halls, except as a sanctuary, is only of concern to me when I lose Wolves to them."

"Then what? I have had a very trying afternoon, and I am unwilling to play games."

"You are never, in my experience, unwilling to play games."

"I am unwilling to play yours."

"Very well. You are aware that our newest recruit has thrown himself into the classes required of the Wolves."

Elluvian's frown made clear to Helmat that he had been aware of no such thing. "That would make him almost singular."

"In particular, he wishes to be educated in the uses of magic. The illegal uses," Helmat added. "To that end, the Imperial Mages have been sent to their classroom of one."

"He can't be integrated with the Swords and the Hawks?"

"He can take the same classes, yes."

"Ah. The Imperial Mage came to assess him."

"Yes."

Elluvian's shrug was less graceful. "That cannot be avoided. The assessment is done for every student. I assume that Severn's results were considered unusual."

"You assume so without any evident surprise, yes." Helmat folded his hands on the surface of his desk. "Did you know about this?"

"I had some reason to suspect, yes."

"And you chose not to share?"

"Helmat, things have been—as you must be aware—complicated of late. What did the mage say?"

"The mage, as you call him, was Johannes."

Elluvian grimaced. "In general, Johannes feels the aptitude tests are hopelessly optimistic and the results of those tests—when conducted by mages who are not named Johannes—the subject of wishful daydreams. This should be in our favor."

"It should be, yes."

"Johannes feels Severn shows actual promise."

"It's Johannes. But he feels in this particular case—and Severn is not to get his hopes up—that the testing may have unearthed some natural proclivity toward magical arts."

"Arts?"

"I believe that's the word he used; his scrawl is practically code."

"And is he suggesting that Severn should now join the Imperium?"

"He is, if I've decoded his scrawl correctly."

"Has the private been informed of what Johannes clearly considers his incredibly good fortune?"

"I'm sure he has—by Johannes."

"I am far less certain; Johannes dislikes the offensive egotism of youth. He is certain to consider the news itself too much for the young to handle with grace."

Helmat considered this. "You're probably right."

"You disagree."

"Severn is absent any of the obvious edges of youthful 'optimism,' as Johannes calls it. I think it likely that he has told Severn about his great good fortune."

"And you have summoned me, why? Surely this is a topic for discussion with the private."

"I want to know what you know, of course. I want to know why you failed to bring this to my attention."

"It is a test for aptitude, no more."

"You consider it accurate." Helmat kept accusation out of

his tone with years of long practice. His fingers, however, had unclasped themselves and were now drumming the surface of his desk.

"I consider it accurate."

"Why?"

"He has come to the attention of An'Tellarus," Elluvian finally said. "And the tests of the Barrani are, in my opinion, far more accurate."

"They are calibrated for the Barrani."

"They are calibrated for, perhaps, the magical aspects the Barrani might prize."

"And An'Tellarus?"

"I do not know what she hopes for or expects."

"You're lying, En."

Elluvian smiled. "I am. I have every intention of preventing any of An'Tellarus's plans from coming to fruition. The Imperium, however, I consider your problem. You are Lord of Wolves. You may clash with the Imperium on your own time."

"If his magical potential is remarkable—and given your reaction, I assume it is—the clash with the Imperium will become difficult. The Imperium is not the equal, in any way, of the Arcanum, and the Emperor has need of mages whose service he trusts."

"The service, however, must be voluntary."

"If Severn is a Wolf, there is a loophole."

"Indeed. Should the Emperor command him to enter the Imperium, he will be forced to obey. Do you think that command will be forthcoming? Ah, never mind; that was a clumsy question. You do."

"I consider it a distinct possibility. You have been part of the Wolves, and the Emperor's thoughts on their constitution, for all of our existence. What do you believe the Emperor will do?"

"I believe he will leave the decision in Severn's hands."

"You are certain?"

"I am never completely confident when it comes to second-guessing the Emperor—but accepting that, yes, I am certain."

Helmat nodded and relaxed.

"You were worried."

"I was."

"And you are not now."

"If the decision is the private's, no. This might work to our advantage."

"You cannot send him out on any mission of any difficulty while simultaneously forcing him to attend the Imperial Mages."

"No. No," Helmat said, rising, "I can't. But it's been a long time since the Wolves have had a mage—however insignificant he might be—of our own. He can take both our classes and the Imperium's initial classes; I will keep him off the streets unless a situation arises that demands his presence."

"He's a private."

"Exactly."

"He was given this case as a private on probation."

Helmat shrugged.

"You don't believe he will choose the greater power?"

"No."

"Why?"

Helmat met Elluvian's gaze. "Magic is a tool."

"It is a more significant tool than daggers or swords."

"To you, yes. Severn Handred is not you."

"He is not Helmat Marlin, either."

"No—but closer. I will not give him to the Imperium."

Elluvian shook his head. "You will give him the choice."

"Indeed."

EPILOGUE

FOR THE THIRD TIME, SEVERN HANDRED STOOD outside of the closed gates that led to—and protected—the Tha'alani quarter. He had made no request to visit; he understood that his part in the events—past and present—in which the Tha'alani were embroiled was done.

His understanding, however, had clearly been imperfect; he'd received an invitation to visit from the Tha'alani caste-lord. He expected that this time, there would be no attempted murder.

The invitation, delivered by Rosen, had caused minor upset in the office—but not nearly the level of upset his first visit to the High Halls had caused. Rosen looked at him with something close to pity—sympathy was too high a target. She had never asked for permission to visit the Tha'alani quarter, and she had never looked at the post-mission information retrieval with anything other than dread.

Dread and acceptance.

"Helmat isn't worried," Rosen had added.

Neither was Severn. The invitation was from Adellos

Coran'alani. It was written; it was not a message that had been passed from mirror to mirror as if it were official legal documentation. Severn unsealed the invitation—something Rosen had clearly been waiting for—and found that it contained a letter.

It was a letter he had some difficulty reading.

"You can't read it?"

"Not well, no. I think it's the Tha'alani native tongue."

"I didn't realize they even had one."

"I don't think it's much used—they talk to each other in the Tha'alaan, and they speak to us in Barrani or Elantran."

Rosen frowned as Severn passed the letter—a mass of almost unidentified squiggles—to her. "I can't read it at all. You're certain it's an invitation?"

"I was told, by the person who delivered the message, that it was. As the Tha'alanari is not aware of your present schedule, you are to feel free to arrive when you have time to do so; the Tha'alani castelord has no right of command, and would not dream of attempting to give you an order."

"Did the messenger say what was wanted?"

"No. I believe the letter is supposed to give more details."

A letter in a language Severn couldn't read. He returned it to its sealed tube. Elluvian might be able to decipher it, but Severn considered that unwise.

The Tha'alani guards that protected the quarter were waiting for him. When he approached, two guards came out of the gatehouse to join the four on the street.

All six of the guards bowed as he approached.

The gate to the Tha'alani quarter rolled open. Standing in the street just behind the gate, were two people: Ybelline and Adellos. They held hands.

Severn had chosen to wear the clothing in which he'd approached the Emperor; it had seemed a respectful choice. It now felt almost stuffy, far too formal; neither of the Tha'alani wore precise, perfectly tailored, perfectly fit clothing. They wore robes of green.

He wondered at that, given the significance of green in Tha'alani eyes, but couldn't ask. Instead, he offered the two, castelord and heir, the same bow he had been offered by their guards. He then rose and offered his hand—first to Adellos and then to Ybelline—palm up, rather than the sideways of the handshakes with which he was most familiar.

The two exchanged a glance, but they took his hand in turn. Ybelline's hand tightened as she reached out for his forehead with her antennae; he felt the briefest of contacts, a wordless hint of gratitude, before that connection was severed.

They chose to speak out loud as they walked through the streets. This time, the streets remained crowded—or rather, became so as they walked through them. Their walk through these streets wasn't about the destination—but given the direction they were now taking, the destination didn't appear to be the building occupied by the Tha'alanari.

The skies were overcast, but the predominant impression the walk gave him was one of sunshine, of warmth.

"You will visit?" Adellos asked.

Severn blinked.

The older man chuckled. "You are not much given to being social, are you? You are certainly not, what is the word? Garrulous."

"I don't know that word."

"Talkative." It was Ybelline who offered a definition Severn could understand.

"Not very," Severn admitted.

"Were you ever?"

"Not that I remember. Mostly I listened."

Her smile—for she was smiling—deepened. "Perhaps your companions simply desired to be heard."

He nodded, tensing slightly; she didn't ask further questions. But she wouldn't, would she? She knew. And what she knew, the castelord knew. The Tha'alanari knew.

The children in the streets didn't. Their minders probably didn't either. Had they, would he have felt uncomfortable? Judged? Angry to be both?

Probably. There were things that Severn accepted as immutable fact; his past was one of them, because no opportunity to change that past had ever been on offer. What he couldn't change, no matter how bitterly he might have desired it, was simple fact. But some facts, he thought, were not meant to be held up as mirrors. And knowledge, no matter how warped or lacking in context, was exactly that mirror.

Or was it?

What the Tha'alaan knew was never shorn of context. The Tha'alaan—the parts that Ybelline had chosen to share—was almost entirely absent the judgment that swiftly followed in the normal, mortal world.

He couldn't quite imagine knowledge without judgment, although he did try as he walked between the official castelord and his heir, his eyes caught constantly by movements to either side.

He wondered whether the Tha'alanari was actually a good construct; wondered if living in ignorance was ever the preferred way to live. Judging, he thought, almost wryly.

But it was a constant, even in his life: the desire to protect, to nurture happiness or joy, even in places where both were in scant supply. Given the choice—segregation of the Tha'alaan in order to withhold experiences that the young were in no way equipped to handle—he knew he would do as the castelords of the Tha'alani had done for as long as the Emperor's demands had existed.

He wondered, as they continued down streets that were a riot of green, dotted with the colors of skin and cloth and the sounds of laughter, if not words, what love meant to the Tha'alani. What did love of family entail, when the entire Tha'alaan was your family? How did one prioritize importance? How could one make oaths to value one person above all others?

Was it even possible?

He glanced at Ybelline; her gaze was upon the children who had clumped together with nervous excitement at the nearing bend in the road. He understood then why they flanked him; they were his shield. Or rather, they were the barrier beyond which curious, high-spirited children were not meant to pass. The children did not seem to be impressed with either the castelord or the castelord's heir—or if impressed, not intimidated.

But there were things that Severn knew that he could not share—at the will of the castelords themselves, present and future. It was to save the Tha'alaan from such "sharing" that three men had died. And he had accepted their murders, had argued against pursuit of the legal consequences, as if he were standing in the place of the Tha'alanari.

"Did you speak to the Emperor?" he asked softly.

It was Adellos who answered. "Yes. Ah, perhaps this is not the place for such a discussion. The children will not immediately understand it, but they might ask for translations from those who do." His eyes were a placid gold as he spoke. "And yes is incorrect. I petitioned the Eternal Emperor for an audience."

"As castelord?"

"Indeed."

Ybelline caught Severn's hand and held it, as she had held the castelord's earlier. "He has not yet arranged an appointment."

Severn said nothing.

"But I have heard that he did arrange to speak with you."

Severn nodded. "Is that why you're both here?"

"No," she replied, her eyes once again upon the gathered crowd that lined the road, and the few stragglers that were brave enough—or young enough—to cross the invisible barrier that separated that road from the houses and their lots. "But we feel it best to offer a gesture of hope—for the future, which is what hope faces—and so we walk this road with you again."

She didn't speak of the last time Severn had walked by the castelord's side. Severn understood.

"Our people—just as yours—have sharp moments of anger, fear, despair. These emotions are part of all of our existences. We love, and often, the love breeds arguments and outrage—but those arguments don't invalidate the love itself. They don't immediately destroy it."

"And you wish the former events to be classed as an argument between kin?" He kept the incredulity out of his tone with effort.

"Yes." She had reddened. "I know it sounds strange to you—"

"It would sound strange to anyone who wasn't, perhaps, Barrani."

It was Adellos who chuckled. "I thought," he said apologetically, "that you might feel this way. Ybelline, however, felt that you would not."

"I...am surprised. But I don't disagree."

"No." Adellos' expression grew more somber. "She is right," he said. "My time is done."

"What do retired castelords do?"

"They are no longer part of the Tha'alanari. They are free

to rejoin the Tha'alaan in their daily life. I look forward to it. I have spent too long without the steadying voice of the people I have governed and protected."

"But you didn't want her to bear that burden any earlier than she had to."

"No—but that is our way. We believe that we can shoulder a burden we have shouldered for decades for just another day, week, month—just another year. I have regrets and a touch of guilt, but she has made her own will known. She will be our castelord. She will not make the decisions I made; she will make different decisions and possibly different mistakes."

"But she knows the mistakes of the previous castelords?"

"Yes. But ruling is like this walk—we will go to my home, not hers. I believed it was risky and unnecessary. She believed it was risky but necessary. We are both possessed of the same information, and we reach different conclusions based on experience and previous failures. We both have the same desire as rulers. It is the experience and prior failures that shift or change what we feel is best; it is mostly the failures that govern the risks we will take going forward.

"I trust her to do what she feels is best. Always. I do not expect to agree with every decision she makes. We share a racial mind, but we are not bees; we have our own thoughts and beliefs. Different conclusions do not make her evil."

"And yours?"

"As I said, it is time, for me. Were it not for her intervention I would have crossed a line that should never be crossed. It seemed sane to me at the time. Sane, rational, *necessary*. It did not seem sane to her, and in retrospect, she is right."

"Adellos."

The castelord—the man who would not be castelord for much longer—grinned. The grin robbed his face of years, of age; he looked much younger. "It is an advantage we have," he continued, his voice softer. "When we give into our fears, when the fears drive us to act, our people are standing by, ready to grab us, to slap us, to tackle us—to stop us, in the end, from doing things we will regret forever.

"We make mistakes. We demand, often, the right to those mistakes. It is how we learn. Not all choices result in disaster—if they did, the Tha'alaan would have a different weight, a different responsibility. I am grateful that she intervened."

"Do they know?"

"The Tha'alanari?"

Severn nodded.

"No."

"And they will not hear it from this?"

"No. The children watch. They are the predominant witnesses; it is what they see—and what their feelings convey. They hear what we say within the Tha'alaan; they are not adept at uncovering what is simply spoken. Ybelline still considers it unwise."

Severn agreed with Ybelline. He did so silently.

Her hand tightened briefly around his, but she did not release it. He wasn't uncomfortable with silence, not a silence broken by laughter, some of it shrieking, all of it exuberant.

He allowed himself to relax. Allowed himself to watch the children, who were staring at him with open curiosity. Even allowed himself to wink at one or two just to watch their delight or astonishment or confusion.

This, he thought, was what he had gone to the Emperor to protect. This enclave of people who could share thoughts and emotions without words, and who were not afraid to be seen and known as themselves; they knew no other way. These children, so different from the child he had once been, and the child Elianne had become.

He had been accepted as a Wolf. He served the Emperor, and the Halls of Law, directly. What his responsibilities had been on the day he had entered the Wolflord's office had been hazy and unclear; this might have been just another way to earn money, another way to stave off the vagaries of weather and hunger.

What it was, however, was this. The protection of this color, this warmth, this excitement and curiosity. He had helped to buy this moment, had helped to protect it. As he walked between two people who had given significantly more of their lives to do just that, he understood the weight of the oath he had offered the Emperor in an entirely different context.

He could, and did, embrace it.

He tightened his own hand around Ybelline's as they continued to walk toward Adellos's home, and the unknown future.

★ ★ ★ ★ ★

ACKNOWLEDGMENTS

First: thanks to Melissa Pixley, without whose charity bid in the Pixel Project drive this novel would not exist. She also caught a very unfortunate error before anyone else had to see it.

Thanks to Terry Pearson for providing a home-away-from-home and a desperately needed two-week writing retreat on extremely short notice, without which this book would have sailed happily past its actual deadline.

Thanks to my family, who cheerfully sent me off on the aforementioned desperately needed writing retreat. Not because I'm cranky when under the deadline gun. Honest.

My mother and father, as usual, stepped up to do a lot of the running around that keeps the house running.

Thanks to Team Mira for the fabulous cover: Kathleen Oudit, the art director, and Shane Rebenschied, the artist, hit it out of the park.